KATE KARYUS QUINN

The Show Must Go On

www.katekaryusquinn.com

First edition

ISBN: 978-1-7336667-0-1

Cover art by Victoria @VC_BookCovers

This book was professionally typeset on Reedsy.
Find out more at reedsy.com

To my fellow musical theater geeks, nerds, and lovers.
Sing out, Louise!

Contents

Acknowledgement

I have to begin with my incredible agent, Suzie Townsend. Thank you for supporting me in all my writing endeavors!

Thank you also to everyone who beta read including: Jenn Kompos, Demitria Lunetta, Mindy McGinnis, Amanda Cataldi, and Matthew Crehan Higgins.

Dee Romito thank you for all your support and enthusiasm. And thank you, as well, to the Wednesday night (and sometimes Sunday afternoon) writing group: Alyssa Palombo, Adrienne Roeser Carrick, Jenn Kompos (again), Sandi van Everdingen, Claudia Recinos Seldeen, and Shannon Traphagen.

A huge thank you to my husband, Andrew Quinn, for heroically proofreading.

Thank you to my wonderful copy editor Dori Harrell.

And finally, thank you to all the authors who answered my questions on indie publishing. An especially big thank you to Alex Lidell for getting on the phone with me and answering the questions I didn't even know to ask yet.

I've made a Spotify playlist with all the songs from the chapter headings. You can find a link to it on my website http://www.katekaryusquinn.com/the-show-must-go-on

1

"May We Entertain You" –Gypsy

It's second nature to project my voice so that it fills every inch of the theater.

Admittedly, that's a bit tricky in this space—a majestic old movie theater that was closed down and left to rot three decades ago. Now it's an in-progress restoration project. Tarps cover chairs. Scaffolding climbs the walls. And a fine layer of sawdust coats every surface. Luckily, the construction crew gave us the space today, so we don't have to battle the whir and clatter of saws and hammers. But even with those obstacles removed, the combination of soaring domed ceilings and touchy sound system presents a unique challenge.

Still, so long as I control my breath and keep my words crisp, I know that once people are in these empty seats, everyone will hear me just fine.

Being loud has never been a problem for me.

I do, however, occasionally, sporadically interspersed, without quite meaning too, overpower my fellow performers. Sometimes I just can't help it. The joy of the music and the words and the movement all come together and burst out of me—with the same volume intensity as a foghorn.

Today though, that sense of joy eludes me. Or maybe it's being *sucked* out of me by my apathetic castmates. It's funny. We're in the middle of a group number, but the only voice I hear is my own.

"Sing out, Louise!" I hiss from the side of my mouth as I chassé across the stage.

"Who's Louise?" one of the girls asks, her face scrunched up in confusion.

That's all I can take. There are some theater references that everyone should know. "Sing out, Louise!" from *Gypsy* is one of them.

"Cut the music! Cut, please, cut."

After a moment the music stops. Silence fills the room. The cast stares at me in bewilderment. Taking a deep breath, I remind myself they're theater newbies and I need to be gentle with them.

"Ladies, I hate to say this, but that wasn't very good. We're forgetting lines. We're falling behind the music. We're holding our voices in, when we need to be projecting them out to the audience." I fling both arms wide, indicating the correct direction.

The girl playing Molly raises her hand. I can't remember her actual name. Honestly, I can rarely remember anyone's name. But for some reason character names tend to stick with me.

"Yes?" I nod at Molly, thrilled to have this opportunity to share my years of knowledge and experience.

"Does this mean we have to do it again?"

I put a hand over my mouth, hoping they mistake my smothered moan for indigestion. "Y-y-yes. We're gonna take it from the top and this time *really* give it our all. Okay?"

"Ugh."

"No-ohhhh."

"Not againnnnn!"

My castmates, grown adults all of them, were in no way forced to be part of this community theater production of *Annie*. And yet they act like they're doing hard time in a Russian gulag. Sadly, it's the best acting on this stage so far.

"Yes, againnnn. And again and again and again until we all get it right."

This does not go over well. A sea of sullen faces stare back at me.

Well, okay, I probably could've delivered that message in a better way. Tried to relate to them. "Hey, guys, I know it sucks spending your whole afternoon in a stuffy theater. I have other things I'd rather be doing too." That's not true though. The theater is my very most favorite place—even when I'm sharing it with castmates on the verge of mutiny. But maybe great leadership means occasionally lying your face off? I don't know. I have no fucking clue at all. That's the problem here. As co-director, I'm in charge, and my every decision is making everything that's already bad, even worse.

And yet the show must go on.

"Mr. Conductor?" I force myself to look down into the nearly empty orchestra pit. Due to budget constraints, instead of musicians and their instruments packed tightly together, we have a dude in cargo shorts and a stained T-shirt. And his boom box. The last time I peered down there, he was clipping his toenails.

Now he gives me a lazy salute, which seems nice...until I notice his middle finger extended. Clearly he's pissed this rehearsal has run two hours over schedule. No surprise there—*everyone* is pissed. Adding in an extra rehearsal had seemed like a no-brainer, especially considering how underprepared we are for an opening night that's five days away.

Instead it was—cue the minor chord progression—yet another wrong decision.

Turning back to the cast, I clap my hands. "Places, everyone. And let's remember, this is our big opening number. We need to grab the audience or risk losing them entirely. So let's sing out and give it our all. Okay?"

Half-hearted nods and shrugs are all I get in response. After twelve weeks of rehearsal, excitement levels are supposed to be at a fever pitch. The "OMG this is it!" nerves should be spreading like a bad case of the flu. Instead, the prevailing sentiment seems to be a whole lot of meh with a side of the whatevers.

I don't get their attitude. For me theater is more than a hobby. It's more like my baby. I love it beyond reason. I can't imagine life without it. I insist on bringing it up at all times, even when it's unwelcome or inappropriate. Just ask the mechanic at Wally's Auto Lube. Last week I spontaneously serenaded him with "Greased Lightning" while he rotated my tires.

Sure, I understand that non-theater people, like the Wally's Auto Lube mechanic who asked me to "please, knock it off already," may not feel the same way about my baby. But theater people are supposed to get it. We share a secret language. And yeah, this is the first musical for most of them, so I get they're not fluent yet, but every time I translate, they look at me in this sort of dead-eyed way. Which makes it pretty obvious.

They all think my baby is ugly, and they have no idea how to break it to me.

Yet somehow I keep hoping I might win them over.

Holding in a sigh of despair, I glance back down to the pit.

"Okay, Conductor, hit it."

Frozen in our places, we wait out a long moment of silence. Or there should be silence—except someone's phone goes off. Most people would quickly silence it and apologize. Instead I hear a soft, "Hey, I can't really talk right now."

"No phones on stage!" I screech the words like someone just barely holding on to the last shreds of their sanity.

"Wow. Lose it much?" someone whispers to my left. A chorus of giggles follow.

Here's another problem. These people make me feel old. *Old* like my tenth-grade music teacher, Mrs. Phazo, who was only a few years away from retirement and used to constantly mutter, "I don't understand any of you."

Of course I'm not old. Yeah, I turned thirty a few months back. But thirty isn't old. It's not, because I'm not old. Old people have mortgages and children and other things I don't even know enough about to list because of my extreme youthfulness.

But...the cast is *exceptionally* young. Twenty-two is the median age. Our Daddy Warbucks just turned twenty. At the little party we had for him, one of the girls pulled me aside to drunkenly whisper, "Not sure if you know, but he totally has a thing for older women." It didn't even occur to me that *I* was the older women, until she squealed, "He's so into you!"

Damn it. Why is there no music?

"CONDUCTOR!"

Pop. Crackle.

"It's the Hard Knock Life" begins to play.

What happens next is ugly. Like the opening sequence to *Saving Private Ryan*, it's horrifying and disorientating. The choreography seems to have been taken more as a general suggestion of how one might wish to move their body. I have to dodge and weave like a prize fighter just to keep from getting knocked out by one girl's unpredictable twirling broom and another's series of kickboxing moves.

As the last note fades, it's all I can do not to throw my head back and howl. Unclenching my jaw, I force a smile onto my face instead. A smile full of warmth and genuine affection.

It's fake. Of course it's fake.

But it looks real, and that's because I am a professional actress. Well, a professional amateur. As professional as someone who never gets paid can be.

Not many people can claim to have performed in community theater shows in seventeen of the fifty states and in forty-one cities. Okay, *cities* may be generous. Towns. Villages. Once I was Fannie Brice in a production put on by the County Line Theater Company. So I've run the gamut.

Some of those shows were bad. None were as awful as this. Somehow I landed myself in an actual shit show. But when you're sorta the director, you can't say that. So I turn the smile up a few notches instead.

"Great job, everyone. Let's take five."

Retreating backstage, I pull two ibuprofen and my cell phone from the back pocket of my jeans. Almost immediately the phone rumbles. Two more missed calls from my mom since the last time I checked, and one text message delivered in her usual low-key way:

JENNA! CALL ME! IT'S IMPORTANT!! LOVE YOU! MOM!

My mother's idea of important is debatable. As just a recent example: *JENNA! WE GOTTA TALK ASAP ABOUT THIS NEW SEXTING THING THE KIDS ARE DOING. SPOILER ALERT. US OLD PEOPLE CAN DO IT TOO! ;)*

I stash my phone away again. Whatever Mom wants, it can wait.

If only this day was so easily dismissed.

I jerk my wig off and massage my aching scalp, my fingertips searching out the spaces between the bobby pins, trying to convince the headache that started behind my eyes to, if not retreat, then at least slow its advance. I'm tempted to find a corner and grab a three-minute standing nap.

Instead I step off the stage and stride up the aisle, past the empty rows of plush red seats. I glance up at the curving edge of the balcony, struck anew by the size and grandeur of this place. It's not often I get to play a house this big.

Reaching the back, I turn around. There's that classic proscenium arch framing the empty stage, all lit up and waiting for some-one—me—to walk across it, find their mark, and sing.

Even after years and years of doing this, my chest goes tight. The dopamine hit fades quickly though, leaving behind a bone-deep weariness. And with it the question that won't leave me alone.

Is the show shit because of me? Have I lost it? Did I ever even have it?

Trying to shake it off, I push open the double doors that lead to the lobby.

Stella, the producer and other half of our co-directing team, is pacing back and forth on the black-and-white tiled floor, cell phone pressed to her ear as she hollers into it. "I'm gonna call the ACLU. Have you ever heard of freedom of speech? Have you, huh? What about artistic expression? Is that a new one for you too? Well, you better look 'em up, because we're not going down without a fight."

Seeing me, Stella puts her hand over the mouthpiece of the phone. "I got 'em on the ropes here. How's it going on your end?"

"Great!" I lie. What else can I say to the person who considers this show her grand musical theater vision? I can't say, "Why did you ever drag me into this mess?"

Although she did.

Eight months ago I was in Mississippi finishing up a run of *The Sound of Music*, when Stella called.

"Aren't you sick of the same old, same old?" she'd asked. "I mean, how many times now have you done good old *Sound of Music*?"

Seven times playing Maria and singing "Do Re Mi." That's how many. Of course, every production was different. In theory. In reality, some directors played things so straight and by the book that it felt less like art and more like completing a paint-by-numbers set.

Then Stella said the magic words. "*Annie* meets *Fifty Shades of Grey*."

It was so wrong. And ridiculous. I couldn't help but be intrigued. In retrospect, I should've immediately said no. Instead, I heard the word "maybe" come out of my mouth.

Truthfully, my big 3-0 milestone had a part in it. Aging out of my twenties made me want...something. I wasn't sure what.

That "maybe" was all the opening Stella needed. "Oh, Jenna, please say yes. I didn't want to get into this, but things with Brian aren't going great. Also, the theater group is trying to force me out, and well, I could really use an ally. Someone who's on my side one hundred percent." Her voice cracked on that last word.

Due to my nomadic existence, I don't have a lot of close friends...or really any besides Stella. Still, you don't need twenty BFFs to know the rules, the simplest of which is when a friend asks for a favor, you better have a good reason to say no.

"When do you need me there?" I'd asked.

It was only after I'd arrived and unpacked that Stella informed me (in the same tone you might use to tell someone they'd won the lottery) that she'd not only given me the lead part but made me her co-director as well.

I'd never directed anything before. Never wanted to either. But Stella gave me the big boo-boo eyes as she reminded me, "Jenna, I really need you. Puh-puh-please."

I caved.

And now it's tech week, a.k.a. the week before the show opens, when you practice with lights and sound cues and costumes, and all the five hundred things that can go wrong, do go wrong. But instead of five hundred things going wrong, we're closer to five million, and the whole damn production is balancing on the brink of disaster.

"Goddamn it, don't you dare put me on hold again!" Stella returns to her phone conversation, which doesn't seem to be going well.

She's chatting with the fine folks at Musical Theater USA, the company we paid for the rights to put *Annie* on stage. Somehow they got wind of all the shades of gray Stella added to the show, and they are not happy. In fact, they're demanding we close it down. Immediately.

As Stella starts to threaten once more, I decide to get some fresh air. Head pounding more insistently than ever, I step outside, desperate for some sun on my face—and nearly walk right into a sign reading, *SAY NO TO ONSTAGE PORN.*

Ah hell. I'd forgotten about the protestors. They've been coming round ever since an anonymous editorial accusing the show of "sexualizing girlhood" came out in the local paper. The next day a dozen people were out front chanting "Keep Annie clean!" Now as they catch sight of me, several rush over waving bars of soap.

Keeping my head down, I push past them and then, as they refuse to give way, start to run. Luckily, no one follows when I duck into the side alley, and I'm able to lean against the stage door at the back of the building, catch my breath and let my heartbeat slow before finally heading inside.

As the door clunks shut behind me, I take a deep breath in. Slowly exhaling, I try to release all the things going wrong and instead focus on what's going right.

I get to play Annie, a part I'd thought my advanced age made impossible for me to cross off my bucket list. And while the show is a mess, it's definitely not boring. Finally...

I search for a third good thing as I pull my wig back on and return to the stage. Carefully, I step over my castmates littered across the floor until finding center stage, I plant myself there.

This space right here. This is my third thing. My home. My safe space. My own personal center that only needs a spotlight to complete it.

Getting to stand up here is the reward.

But first I have to earn it.

"Hey." I clap my hands to get everyone's attention. A few wan nods and rolled eyes are all the encouragement I get. "Let's work out the curtain call. Once that's solid, everyone can take a break until we meet again tonight for the dress rehearsal."

Actual groans meet this announcement.

"What's the point?" Molly asks. "They wanna shut the show down. I don't care what Stella says about refusing to wave the white flag—whatever that even means. They don't want us to add flags to the show, do they?"

"No, they are not asking for white flags," I patiently explain. "They don't like that Annie and Daddy Warbucks have a sloppy kiss at the end of the show. They also want us to stop stripping during 'You're Never Fully Dressed without a Smile.'"

"Oh, c'mon." The flexible blond girl playing Pepper joins in the discussion. "That is definitely a stripper song. Maybe in a more wink wink sort of way than we do it, but still, it's clearly about getting naked. Am I right or am I right?"

The other girls hoot and holler in agreement. And they'd know. Most of them work at Topaz, the strip club out by the interstate. After we lost half the original cast at the first table read, Stella was desperate for anyone with stage experience. So she went out to Topaz and sold being part of our musical as a mix between a blowout party with top-shelf liquor and a day at Disneyland.

Frankly, I was tempted to drop out too. Once Stella fully articulated her vision, I couldn't help but think it sounded more crass than clever.

"Girls kissing girls kissing boys kissing girls! It's the Great Depression and everyone wants to get laid!"

The words "I quit" were on the tip of my tongue, but remembering I was there to support Stella, I swallowed them down and replaced them with "The show must go on."

Those five words have a near mystical quality to motivate me. I've gone on with bronchitis. Sunburn so bad it left blisters up and down my arms. And even a broken foot. That last was during *My Fair Lady*. With the long dress (mostly) covering the big clunky cast, I didn't just go on, I convinced everyone looking at me that I really could've danced all night.

Now I search for some way to transfer even a bit of that never-say-die feeling to this group of people who are mostly here for fun. As a way to pass the time.

I close my eyes. My head pounds even louder. And then—at last—inspiration strikes.

"Happy hour at the Wishing Well before the next rehearsal! First round of drinks on me!" I announce.

And finally I'm greeted with cheers instead of jeers. Making a mental note to remember my credit card, I circulate around the stage as everyone peels themselves off the floor.

"Great job on that final number."

"Loved your energy in the first act."

"Good recovery after losing your line."

I drop words of encouragement here and there, hoping between that and the promise of free booze we can pull this thing across the line.

As the three stripper poles are moved downstage, I explain how immediately following the final number, everyone needs to gather in the wings. At that point the music for "Tomorrow" will start. I organize the cast in the order they'll come out, in threes, with each swinging round the stripper poles before taking their bow.

"All right, let's do it!"

Everyone stares at me until I clap my hands, and then they scatter into the wings. Again, I point to our conductor. He sighs loudly before pressing Play.

The opening notes to "Tomorrow" begin, and I join the cast backstage. As the lead, my bow is last. Right before me, Mrs. Hannigan and Daddy Warbucks will come out and do their spins round the pole, and then the whole cast will turn upstage and I'll enter stage center.

In theory this should be easy.

But first they forget the order. Then one girl takes too long on the pole, launching into her whole routine from Topaz. The guy playing President Roosevelt stops the whole thing to argue that his character would not use a stripper pole, seeing as how he's in a wheelchair. I explain it's okay to break character for the bows, and he goes off on a ten-minute rant about kids today not respecting history, while I struggle not to roll my eyes because this is already our third Roosevelt and I doubt we'll be able to dig up another. Finally, we compromise. The Boylan sisters will help him out of his wheelchair, and then he'll take a go on the pole.

We run through it six times and not once do we make it to my bow.

As "Tomorrow" starts up again, I can't stand to watch. Hating myself for doing it—especially after my earlier freak-out—I pull out my cell phone.

There are several more texts from my mom, mostly consisting of scared cat emojis and exclamation marks. I can't even begin to guess what they might mean. Below those is a short text from my niece, Maxi. As a teenager she instinctively knows how to compose an attention-grabbing text without resorting to all caps.

Grams really wants to talk with you. I think somebody died or something.

My heart stutters and then stops. *Somebody died or something.*

I peek between the curtains and see Mrs. Hannigan and Daddy Warbucks preparing to step onstage. Mind racing, I watch as Mrs. Hannigan completes her rotation round the stripper pole. Daddy Warbucks follows. It's my turn to step onstage, but instead my thumbs are rapidly typing out a text to my mother.

IS IT DANNY?

I need to move. They finally did the curtain call perfectly, and I'm screwing it up. But I can't go on, and neither can the show—not until I get an answer.

It comes at last.

HOW DID YOU KNOW? CALL ME. OK?

My phone slips from my hand. I don't bother to pick it up as I step onstage, singing along with the rest of the cast, the words coming automatically.

Danny. Dead.

Oh, Danny.

Suddenly my throat is too tight to sing.

I reach the stripper pole and wrap both hands around it. Instinctually I turn my smile up a notch, sending it out to the empty seats as my legs bend, prepping for my turn. There's someone out there at the back of the theater, half in shadow.

I recognize him instantly despite all the years that have gone by.

Danny. It's Danny. Or his ghost.

I am spinning while also twisting awkwardly to look over my shoulder, to see him again. My hands, suddenly clammy, slip. Then I'm flying. And falling. As my head thumps against the hard boards of the stage, I am not thinking about how no one is singing or that we'll have to do the curtain call again or any of the things that have been tying me into knots today.

There's only one thought in my mind. And it's this:

Danny is dead, and it's all my fault.

2

"Mother's Gonna Make Things Fine" –A New Brain

I'm only out for a minute, which frankly is disappointing.

When I open my eyes, Stella's face hovers over mine. She looks tragic. Big tears brim, threatening to overflow. At first, my scrambled brain thinks she's crying about Danny. But then I remember—she doesn't know anything about him.

"Don't cry. I'm fine." I scoot away from her and then carefully touch the bump at the back of my head.

"No, you're not!" Stella counters with a wrenching wail. Tears fall. "You're hurt, and you've worked so hard, and you moved all the way here, and now it doesn't even matter. It's over, Jenna. They're shutting us down."

"Oh." It's an insufficient response, but all I can muster. Honestly, five minutes ago I would've been upset. I would've been wailing right alongside Stella. But none of that matters right now.

Sitting up, I look out into the audience. Of course Danny's not there anymore. If he ever was. What's worse—being haunted by an ex-boyfriend or hallucinating his surprise appearance?

I guess most people have that one ex-boyfriend they can't forget because of how he was in a coma the last time they saw him.

Right? No? Just me? Okay then.

I sat by his bed for a year. Then I bailed. That was over ten years ago. Nearly twelve, to be exact. I can't believe it's been that long. But I'm thirty...so yeah, the math works out.

Persistent vegetative state. That's what they call it. And all this time Danny has been incredibly persistent.

Except it seems he's finally given up the fight.

"Where's my phone?" For the first time in my life, I have an uncontrollable urge to call my mother. Remembering it slipping from my hand, I crawl across the stage on all fours. Finally, I push the curtain aside, and there it is, right where I left it. Standing, I spin back toward Stella, who is in her own world, methodically cursing out all the small-minded, puritanical, overzealous copyright holders who wouldn't know art if it bit them on the arse.

"Hey." I gently break into her diatribe. "I gotta go."

"What? No!" She springs to her feet. "You might have a concussion. And we're all going out for drinks to celebrate a battle well fought."

I shake my head, but Stella slips her arm into mine. "How about this? You go home. Rest. Don't sleep—you might fall into a coma."

At the word "coma," I startle so hard I actually levitate for a moment. Stella frowns. Puts a hand to my forehead. "Maybe I should take you home—"

"No." I step away from her before she can fold me into a hug. I don't need a hug. I need to find out what's going on with Danny. But most of all I need some time alone to process. "You're right. I should rest."

"Fine. I'll give you two hours, but then whoever I convince to be the designated driver is picking you up. Just in time for happy hour, right?" Stella grins in the slightly manic and totally irrepressible way she has. I nod and agree before stumbling out to my truck.

Climbing up into the driver's seat, I turn the engine to get the air conditioning blowing, but I don't go anywhere. Instead, taking a deep breath, I call my mother.

"Ooooooooooooooooohh J-J-J-Jeeeeeennnaa," Mom sobs in greeting.

Immediately I tremble. Mom continues weeping, and I'm surprised to notice wetness on my cheeks, to realize I can still cry for Danny even though, for all intents and purposes, I'd done my mourning a long time ago.

Danny is at peace. After lingering in a coma, hovering indecisively between the living and the dead, he's finally given in and passed away. Which is sad and tragic and all that. I mean, of course it is. *But* it also means that no one will expect me to come home and hold his hand.

"I'll send flowers," I say at last.

Mom's grief abruptly cuts off. "Flowers? But Jenna, *baby*, he asked for you."

"His dad, you mean?" That seems unlikely. But possible, I suppose. Danny's father hadn't exactly liked me, but he didn't hate me the way Danny's mother did. "Look, if they want me to sing at the funeral or something, I'm just...I'm sorry, but I don't feel up to it."

"Funeral?" she says in the exact way she'd said *flowers*. In a way that finally alerts me—

I have the wrong end of the stick here.

She confirms it. "But, baby, Danny's alive. He woke up. And he asked for you."

I stab the little button on my screen that will end the call. Even after the connection is dead, I keep poking it.

Danny isn't dead. I didn't see his ghost.

This is good. This is great.

And yet for some reason, I lay myself across the front seat of my truck and sob.

It's been so long since I've let myself think about Danny. The real Danny. Not the boy silent and still, wasting away in a hospital bed. That Danny haunts me. But the Danny who insisted on rubbing my feet, not minding the calluses or the prickly hair on my ankles from not shaving in three days. I'd forgotten that Danny. Purposely locked him away.

But now he's tickling me, the same way he did then.

I've always hated anyone touching my feet. Too many years spent in tap shoes a size too small because Mom couldn't afford a new pair.

But there was Danny kissing my ugly big toe. When I accused him of having a secret foot fetish, he tickled me until I laughed so hard it hurt. In retaliation, I tickled him behind his ears (he was weirdly sensitive there), and then we were on the ground, all twisted around each other. Exhausted, my head rested against Danny's chest, and I listened to his heart energetically thumping away.

I remember thinking, *This sound is my future.*

It felt terrifying and comforting and inescapable all at once. I was eighteen and pregnant and certain—the kind of certain that only exists when you haven't yet had life smash all your plans to bits—that Danny was my future.

Twenty-four hours later I was sitting in one of those molded plastic chairs they have in hospital waiting rooms. My hands were clasped together in prayer as I begged God for a redo. "Oh, please please please tell me this isn't happening."

I'm tempted to give that prayer another try today. Not that I wish Danny was dead. Or still comatose. No, he's awake, and I'm thrilled for him. Godspeed and good luck to him. The part I object to is him asking for me. I'm the last person he should want to see. The only call I should get is one telling me to stay far, far away.

Speaking of calls, my phone is blowing up. "Don't Rain on My Parade"—my ringtone—plays. Insistently. After blowing my nose, I finally give in and answer.

"Oh, Jenna baby," Mom says.

She does not mention my hanging up on her. I am her baby, and my older sister, Allie, is her angel. In her eyes we can do no wrong. This has, of course, fucked us up in ways both large and small.

"Mom," I say, my voice small and tired.

She *oh babys* me again, and then, "Where are you sweetie?"

"In my truck."

"Oh no. You can't drive all the way home."

"I'm not driving home."

"Oh good. So you're on your way to the airport? Do you need help paying for your ticket?"

"Mom!" Exasperated, I can't stop myself from snapping at her. This is the rhythm of our conversations since the beginning of time. She is nutty but well meaning and desperate to be helpful, until finally, snap. I sigh. "It's tech week." I fail to add the tiny yet somewhat significant detail about how the show has just been cancelled.

"Oh dear. Tech week, huh?" I've been doing theater since I was eight years old, so Mom knows the sacrosanct nature of tech week. "Well, as you theater people say, isn't that a kick in the pants."

"Yeah, Mom, all the theater people say that," I agree, because to do otherwise would lead to a twenty-minute explanation of the many people—well beloved and known within the theater community—who have used that phrase throughout the years. She'd probably wrap it up by quoting Shakespeare's famous line, "To be kicked in thee pants or not to be kicked in thee pants. That is the question."

"And I'm not only the lead. I'm co-directing too," I add. "So I can't just leave. You know?"

Of course she does. "Well, I'll talk to Danny's family," Mom says. "I'm sure they'll understand."

I roll my eyes at this but don't bother to disagree.

"And when your show is over..."

"Mom, let's take it one week at a time. I mean, his family won't even want me there by then. They'll realize I'm nothing more than an old ex-girlfriend."

"Oh, honey, you're not *that* old."

"I meant *old* as in *past tense. Girlfriend* no longer."

"But you said ex-girlfriend, sweetheart, which already means that. So the old—"

I cut her off. "Whatever! I'm not old. The relationship is. Like ancient history."

Mom is quiet for a moment, and then softly, "But you were more than his girlfriend. You were practically married."

"Mo-om." It's half warning, half plea. Please do not go there.

She goes there. Straight toward it as if nothing on earth could keep her away. "You know, after we found out you were pregnant, I took Danny aside and asked him what his intentions were. He looked at me, straight at me with those bright-blue eyes of his. You remember those eyes, the way they sorta glowed. Like an alien almost, but the handsome kind you wouldn't mind being abducted by. And he said to me, so sincere—not sarcastic like you always were at that age—he says, 'I'm gonna marry Jenna. I knew it from the moment I first saw her. This baby moved it up a little, that's all.' Now, I never told you this story before—"

I can't take it anymore. "Mom, you've literally told me this story a thousand times. And that's a conservative estimate."

"Oh fine, I've told it, but you never *hear* it. You roll your eyes or make like the whole thing was a hallucination. I want you to understand the heart of this story. Danny, he wasn't like your father, who ran out and left me with two kids. Or that boy who got Allie knocked up and swore up and down it wasn't his. No, Danny was different. He meant it when he said he was going to marry you and be a father to your child."

I swallow and realize suddenly how dry my mouth is. "But, Mom, there is no baby now."

"But if Danny is awake and he's asking for you—"

Again I interrupt. "Then what, Mom? We pick up where we left off?"

"Well..." She lets that linger, and I think I've gotten through. But no. "Why not? All these years later and you're still single. And *he's* still single."

"Of course he's still single! He's been unconscious. That gets in the way of a person's social life. And now, who knows. He could be brain damaged. Maybe he was trying to ask for more Jell-O and accidentally said my name instead."

The words explode out of me. Ugly. Mean.

This is what family does to me.

The worst part is, Mom doesn't even know she's doing it. She's got no idea that Danny is like a broken bone that never healed right. It doesn't just hurt—it's ugly too. I can't stand having anyone look at it, touch it, or talk about it.

This is why I stay away.

On the other end of the line, Mom is silent, but I can imagine the way she's shaking her head. "Mom, I really gotta get to rehearsal now. I'm running late, and my costume takes forever to get it on just right."

"Oh! But your sister wanted to say hi!"

"No, Mom, no."

It's too late. Angry and loud enough to bruise my eardrum, Allie jumps in. "So you're really not coming home, huh? A guy wakes up from a coma and asks for you specifically by name, and you're gonna be all, 'Nope. Sorry. I gotta stand up on a stage and pretend I'm someone important.'"

I sigh. "Did you just want to bitch at me?"

"Mostly," Allie admits. "But also to say, you know, it wouldn't suck to see your face. Like in person, I mean, if you decided to come home. Nadine and I are talking about getting married, but I've already told her it will have to be a destination wedding because you've got this weird hang-up about coming home."

Nadine is Allie's girlfriend. They've been together for almost five years, which is still difficult to believe. When she first started seeing Nadine, I figured it was a phase. Or that Allie had run through every loser guy in the area and had no choice but to move on to the loser women. But no, Nadine was and still is gainfully employed as a lawyer. As time's gone on, it's become clear—they're the real deal.

"Wow, marriage." And this is the part where I'm supposed to add, "Of course I'd come home for your wedding." But I don't. "Well, a destination wedding *would* be nice. I'll go anywhere you pick. What about New Orleans? Culture, great food, and the beach. You know we all love the beach."

"Yeah, I know. The last time I saw you—what was it, seven years

THE SHOW MUST GO ON

ago now?—we met at Virginia Beach cause you were doing a show nearby."

It was eight years ago, but I don't correct her.

"You coming home could also help Mom and me," Allie continues. "You remember we're trying to get our business off the ground?"

"Oh yeah." I try to recall what exactly this latest scheme is. Mom collects social security, and Allie's been on disability ever since she injured her back a few years ago, but they're always trying to find different ways to make a little extra money. And now that Allie's daughter, Maxine, is sixteen, they've been roping her into their sideshow too. "It's the soap thing, right?"

"Homemade, all-natural bathing blocks," Allie corrects me.

"So...soap."

Allie ignores me again. "There's gonna be a lot of press around Danny. It's not every day someone wakes up after over a decade in a coma. Do you know what kind of free advertising we could get if you put one of our bathing blocks in his hand?"

"You're kidding, right? It's possible he won't even be able to hold something in his hand."

"Jenna, don't be so literal. It could be on his bedside table. Or sitting in his lap. Even poking out a shirt pocket."

"Balance it on top of his head," I interject.

"Hilarious." Allie sneers. "But seriously, Jenna, could you think about someone other than yourself for once? I've been telling you for years, Mom is losing it, so she's not exactly a stable business partner."

"Allie angel, I'm still standing here," Mom chirps in the background.

"Mom, I know. I'm looking right at you," Allie responds in this "you see what I'm talking about" tone. "And if that doesn't bother you, think of Maxi. Your niece, in the basement every day after school, making the blocks. Selling them is pretty much her only hope of being able to afford college."

I close my eyes, exhaustion finding me. Allie often has that effect. "Maybe she should put that time into studying instead."

It's the wrong thing to say. I knew it even as the words came out. Anytime I comment on anything to do with Maxi, Allie takes it as some sort of judgment on her parenting skills.

Of course, she's sensitive about it since she had Maxi when she was fifteen. A few years later when I got knocked up too, Allie was thrilled to have me follow in her footsteps. Like I'd done it on purpose 'cause I'd seen how well teenage motherhood had worked out for her. I miscarried soon after Danny became all distant and comatose. Allie's never forgiven me.

Sure enough Allie drops ten metric tons of sarcasm on me. "Oh wonderful. Here we go. Jenna's parenting tips. Please go on. I'd love to hear more."

Personally, I believe sarcasm should be underplayed. You don't want every word coming out of your mouth like its italicized. But Allie doesn't under anything. Not underplayed, understated, or understanding.

So I apologize. The phone finally gets passed back to Mom so she can tell me to "Break a leg, but not really!" before we all say goodbye, and I promise to let them know if I change my mind.

After getting rid of them, I want to lie down again, but instead I text Maxi.

What's the deal with this whole soap scheme?

No matter what time I text Maxi, she always responds seconds later. I'm pretty sure she has a phone surgically connected to her body.

You mean the bathing blocks?

She adds a winking emoticon to reassure me that she hasn't been completely brainwashed.

Hilarious, I text back. *But seriously WTF?*

Well mom found out I don't always remember to take my birth control. I stare at this incongruous response, and before I can text another *WTF*, Maxi adds, *So she said I couldn't date anymore until I was better about it.*

Okay, I could see where this was going. I may not agree with Allie on most things, but her crusade to make sure teen pregnancy stops being part of our family legacy is one I'm happy to support. Well mostly. Sometimes her methods are batshit insane. She put Maxi on the pill a week after she got her period the first time. She gives the sex talk to every boy Maxi brings home. And one time Maxi called me sobbing, begging me to intervene. She was puking her brains out after a batch of bad grocery store sushi. The whole time she had her head hanging in the toilet, Allie was waving a pregnancy test at her, demanding she pee on the stick right that minute.

And now this.

But she lets Zane come over to help me make soap. Another text pops up followed by an emoticon with a great big shit-eating grin. And then, *So we're making soap.*

OMG. Please tell me you're using protection.

Thumbs-up is her only response.

Okay, I left home because of the whole Danny thing. And I stayed away because of him too.

But if I'd come from a different type of family, the staying away might've been more difficult. Might've felt more like a loss and less like relief.

3

"Out Tonight" -Rent

O nce inside my little apartment, I head straight for the couch, only pausing to kick off my shoes before flopping onto the cushions with my favorite faux-fur blanket. Usually I'm a world-class napper, no sleep aids necessary, thank you very much. You get good at napping when you're bad at sleeping the way people usually do—in long chunks during the darkest hours of the night.

At this moment though, it's not happening. My blanket's bunchy. The pillow's flat. The girl across the hall is practicing her fucking clarinet, and it sounds like a goose being butchered.

And then there's Danny. Not just nibbling at the edges of my consciousness like he usually does. Instead he's set up camp at the center of my brain, infiltrating every thought.

Desperate, I reach for my phone, needing my most soothing tool. I only deploy it when the tension has my shoulders ratcheted up to the tips of my ears.

This definitely qualifies.

No one, not a single person on the planet, knows I do this. It is my secret shame. Secret and shameful because I am watching the 1997 Brendan Fraser movie, *George of the Jungle.* I've seen it so often I have almost every word memorized.

It's not the dialogue or plotting that keeps me coming back. My interest is much more shallow. I am absolutely mesmerized by

Brendan Fraser's abs. From the beginning of the movie to the end, they are amazing and glistening and on full display.

The truth is, I'm a little in love with George. Not, let me be clear, Brendan Fraser, but George. George George George of the Jungle.

And this is why no one must ever know.

For the moment though, it is just me. And George. I can actually feel my blood pressure lowering as I sink into the couch—

Eventually my eyes close and the phone slips out of my hand. I wake to a dark apartment and someone knocking. Groggy, I reach for my phone. It's dead. Remembering Stella's promise to send over a designated driver, I stumble to my feet.

"Hold on a minute," I call as whoever it is knocks again. Pausing by my purse, I dig through it until I find my tin of Altoids. I toss a few in my mouth and quickly crunch them up, not wanting to blast the driver with my nap breath. Then I flip the bolt and open the door.

"Sorry," I say preemptively. "I just woke up. You're gonna have to give me ten minutes to get—"

I stop. This is not the stooge Stella convinced to be the designated driver.

This is Danny.

Not his ghost, but the actual Danny.

His dark hair. His broad shoulders. His—

Holy shit.

Danny.

Danny who is standing at my door, opens his mouth to say something—

I slam the door shut. Bolt it. Then run to the bathroom and lock myself inside.

I crank the water in both the sink and shower, wanting to drown out everything.

All the while I gasp for air. I can't get enough. My heart is hammering away at my chest, beating so hard it hurts. The pounding headache that had finally receded comes back with a vengeance.

This is what dying feels like. I am dying.

No. The voice of reason chimes in, soft and calm as always. This is what a panic attack feels like.

Or at least that's what the emergency room doctor told me a few years ago. That same doctor recommended I find a therapist, maybe start taking some anti-anxiety medication. Instead, I went home and Googled "panic attack."

Now following the good advice of Dr. Google, I sit on the edge of the bathtub and put my head between my knees. Deep breathe in through the nose. Hold it. And out through the mouth. Repeat again and again until the act of breathing no longer feels more complicated than conjugating French verbs.

With the oxygen flowing once more, my brain starts working again. It occurs to me I might have overreacted just a wee bit.

I totter out of the bathroom on shaky legs, feeling all wrung out. I make it all of two steps when there's another knock on the door. Before I can retreat back to the bathroom, I hear Stella's voice interspersed with the knocking.

"Jenna! Wake up! Do not go into the light! C'mon, Jenna! I'm sorry. Damn it. I never should've let you go home alone with a head injury."

I rush to the door, relief flowing through me, and throw it open.

"Thank gawd you're not dead!" Arms opened wide, Stella flings herself at me.

I am not a hugger. Stella is. But until this moment she's respected my stance and has stopped herself from going full boa constrictor on me. But apparently the shackles are off. Both arms wrap around me, and her manic curls tickle my chin.

I'm an average-sized person, but Stella is tiny. She reminds me of an ant. She has the industriousness of one. Always moving about from here to there. Stella is also, like an ant, impressively strong for her small size, so when her arms close around me, it's clear I'm not getting away without a struggle.

"Something's wrong and you need a hug. I can tell." Her hot breath hits my neck in an incredibly unpleasant way.

"Nothing's wrong. Everything is awesome," I lie while holding my body stiff and my arms at my sides in the universal signal of "Please let me go. This is not a hug—it's assault."

Instead of releasing me, Stella squeezes tighter, as if she can extract the truth that way. "Jenna, we're friends. Talk to me. Let me in. Whatever it is can't be that bad."

And even though I hate this, something about her wiry little arms squeezing all the air out of my chest while her head practically rests against my breasts is almost...comforting. Or maybe it's just so weird and awful that it's causing all the feelings to bubble up and out. Either way, I'm cracking.

"It is that bad." I barely get the last word out as my throat tightens.

And those apparently are the magic words, because Stella lets go and takes a step back. The moment I'm free, I peer around Stella, out into the hallway. Across the hall, two garbage bags and a whole army of flies sit outside my neighbor's door. Besides that, though, the hall is empty. No sign of Danny.

I turn to Stella. "Was there someone out here? A guy? Tall. Handsome. Maybe a little sleepy looking, like he just woke up from a long nap?"

Stella tilts her head, examining me carefully. "This isn't about the show, is it? This is something else."

"Stella. Did you see anyone?"

She frowns, and I can see her thinking, realizing this question is important. Finally, she shrugs. "There might've been a guy walking across the parking lot when I pulled in. I didn't get a good look at him."

"Okay." I nod, unsure what to do with this information now that I have it.

"Oh, honey, you're trembling. C'mon. Let's get you inside." Taking charge, Stella steers me toward the couch.

I relax a little bit. The guy, who may or may not have been Danny, was walking away. And Stella is here now. Stella, my friend for over ten years now, ever since we met on the plane that took me away from Danny's bedside. Us being seated side by side in seats 11A and 11B was kismet, as if the universe said, "We've given you a lot of shit recently, so here's one on us."

Stella had been on her way to Miami to meet a guy she'd met on the internet. "Supposedly he's really interested in creating avant-garde art pieces with me, but it's also possible he wants to get into my pants." She'd seemed open to either possibility. We ended up looking for a rental apartment together, and when I auditioned for my first show, she came along just for fun. She was chorus, I was one of the leads, and we had a great time. When it was over, I got itchy and moved on. Stella stayed and got involved with another company whose shows were more experimental.

And that would've been the end of that, but she made the effort to stay in touch and even came to see me and hang out a few times. Stella was one of those people, when after not seeing her for months or even years, we could pick up where we'd left off and have a great time.

In a weird and sorta sad way, she's my best friend. The last time I'd had one of those was way back in high school when my musical theater costar and bestie, Eli Wallace, and I decided to co-write *Mean Girls, the Musical*. Sadly, after one songwriting session, we realized we were no young Sondheims in the making. Still it was so much fun trying.

Now being around Stella, and for the first time in a long time having a friend in my daily life, has made me realize how alone I've been. Not lonely exactly, just adjacent to it.

And it's this that makes me finally say it aloud. "My ex-boyfriend came out of a coma after almost twelve years. It happened today. Or possibly yesterday. I'm actually not sure. But I heard about it today. Sooo..."

That last word trails off. I'm not certain what else to say. This is the first time I've told anyone about my tragic history. Despite hundreds of times trading war stories with other theater friends, the words had always stayed trapped behind my teeth.

Stella stares at me open mouthed. "Wow. That makes so much sense."

"Yes, exactly, that's—" I freeze mid-nod as I realize Stella's shocked expression doesn't match her words. "Wait. What do you mean, *that makes so much sense?*"

"Oh, c'mon, Jenna. Look at your life. You move constantly. You've got your sit-home-in-your-pajamas customer service job, where they keep trying to promote you and you keep refusing."

"It's a lot of responsibility!"

"You've never had a long-term relationship."

"What are you, my mother? And Thomas and I were together for nearly a year."

Stella negates this with a swift shake of her head. "Seven months is not a year."

I throw my hands up. "Okay, I'm a mess of a human being. A failure in all the ways that count. Is that the point you're trying to make?"

"Not quite. You're really not that much of a mess. You're in shows all the time that require a ton of time and dedication. Also even though you move all the time, you do it with amazing precision. When I helped you unpack last time, the way some of those boxes were packed, it was like a work of art. I had tears in my eyes. So no, you're not a mess. It's more like...you're stuck. Take your thirtieth birthday—"

"Oh, c'mon," I interrupt, feeling increasingly betrayed. "*Everyone* hates getting older."

"Yeah, but you didn't seem upset so much as shocked that it was happening. Like you kept expecting a dispensation to arrive in the mail, giving you permission to remain twenty forever."

I cross my arms over my chest and say nothing. But Stella keeps going, oblivious to the "I am displeased" body language.

"So yeah, I've realized for a while now that there must have been something pretty major in your past that totally messed you up. Of course, I always figured you were escaping a polygamist marriage."

"You...what?!"

"Or that you'd gotten thrown out of a convent for sleeping with one of the priests."

"You're insane. Why didn't you just ask me?"

"Ha!" Stella wags a finger at me. "I did. In every possible way, and you stonewalled. Like a secret agent holding on to state secrets. Which was another theory of mine. I had a notebook with at least twenty possibilities, but strangely not one of them was ex-boyfriend in a coma."

"Guess you're not as clever as you thought," I grumble.

Stella's hand settles on my back. "I'm sorry, Jenna. I think ex-boyfriend in a coma is the worst of any of them. It must've been awful for you."

And that, right there, is what I need. Immediately my annoyance evaporates and my throat closes up. "Actually," I say as I lean into Stella, "he was sorta my husband."

"What?" Stella rears back. "You are not fucking married."

"Well, technically no. Or actually, technically yes. We were kids. Barely legal. And we only did it because I was pregnant."

"Knocked up? Holy shit, don't tell me you have a secret baby stashed away somewhere too."

This wrings a laugh out of me. "No, sorry to disappoint. The baby didn't take." The glee fades from Stella's face, and I can see an "oh no, so sorry" coming. I head it off. "It's okay. Teen mom was never part of my plan. Neither was teen wife, but Danny thought it was some magic bullet, like it'd make everything better. Including us."

My heart clenches suddenly as I remember Danny down on one knee. "Marry me, Jenna." He held out the ring he'd gotten at Walmart, the $59.99 price tag still attached. A "just for now ring," he promised, until he could afford something better. I still have that ring. I keep it balled up in a pair of old socks at the back of my underwear drawer. Not so I can look at it or try it on. Mostly I forget it even exists. But

29

whenever I move, I double-check to make sure it's safely packed.

Some things you can't just throw away.

"What are you gonna do?" Stella asks, breaking into my thoughts.

"I'm not going back," I hear myself say. "I can't." And that right there is the truth. My chest goes tight at the very thought of coming face to face with Danny again. "I told my mom I can't go home because of the show opening this weekend."

"You mean the show we're not doing anymore?"

I nod.

"Right." Stella nods too, then she goes quiet. Just as I'm getting worried, her eyes light up. "Okay, I've got it. The perfect solution. Hold on a minute. I need to run out to my car for some stuff. I'll be right back!"

Before I can reply, she's off the couch and out the door. A few minutes later she returns, surrounded by a pack of dogs and with a bucket of margarita mix in her hand.

"Look," she calls, holding the mix above her head. "I brought the party to you! And I just texted the whole cast to get their butts over here. It's time to turn it up! What!"

I plant myself in the doorway, definitely not feeling this plan.

"Stella, how are your nine dogs and tequila the perfect solution?"

"My nine *furbabies*." I make a face, and Stella smiles in her ingratiating way. "The dogs aren't technically part of the solution. They've been missing me, so I couldn't just leave them at home. Anyway, everyone knows dogs are comforting and good for the soul. Like chicken soup but with fur."

"No," I start to say, but Stella talks over me.

"I won't have them here long. I promise. Let me just make you a drink first so you can experience the healing qualities of a good strong margarita."

As it turns out, Stella's bucket of margarita mix, when combined with a good deal of tequila, does indeed become magical anxiety-destroying stuff. I drink one after another as cast members fill my apartment and our toe-clipping conductor shows up to blast his boom box. The dogs bark madly with each new arrival. By the time it becomes clear that Stella will not be taking the dogs home anytime soon, I am way past caring about that, or anything else.

Someone plugs the toilet, and I laugh. The little dog steals food, then barfs it back out, and it seems like a delightful party trick. Stella suggests we move to Florida again, and I agree that it's the best idea ever and we should definitely do it immediately. We pinky swear to have our bags packed by the end of the week. The guy who plays Daddy Warbucks—the one who loves "older women"—tells me his favorite part of the show is kissing me, and I give him one last kiss to remember me by.

One kiss that turns into an epic make-out session with a guy who's barely twenty, works as a DJ at Topaz, and despite having a decent tenor voice, has a lot of trouble staying on pitch.

Of course, this isn't the first time I've hooked up with a fellow cast member. When I first started this itinerant community theater thing, part of the fun was picking someone in the show to get involved with. But after a few years and several relationships, one tenor began to look like another. I got pickier, and my relationships became fewer and farther between.

Sure I could have branched out beyond the theater community and tried my luck on Tinder. But between the day job and night rehearsals, squeezing someone else in would've been difficult. It just didn't seem worth the effort.

Except right now kissing Daddy Warbucks requires no effort at all. He's here. He's warm. He's eager. He's...

Passed out next to me in my bed.

4

"Ya Got Trouble" – The Music Man

While tequila might make some girls' clothes fall off, for me it always had a more soporific effect. Which is why I'm fully dressed and on top of my floral comforter.

Thinking hard, I roll back time.

I kissed Warbucks. He suggested we move it into the bedroom. By then most of the partygoers had cleared out. I didn't really Warbucks to stay. But I also didn't want to be alone. So I answered in the affirmative. Moments later Warbucks tugged his pants off and went bouncing onto the bed.

"Hold on," I'd said, sitting beside him. "I'm feeling a little dizzy." I leaned back, resting my head against my pillow.

"Hey, Jenna." Warbucks wriggled next to me like an overactive toddler. "Are you really going to Florida?"

"Florida," I repeated, rolling the word around in my mouth. And then I fell down a drunken wormhole, straight into my past.

There we were, me and Danny, so comfortable together, our bodies entwined on the couch, watching *The Price Is Right*. It was the showcase at the end, and one of the prizes was a trip to the Florida Keys.

"Wow, that looks amazing," I'd said.

"It does feel amazing," Danny echoed back, or at least echoed what he thought he'd heard. His hand was still up my shirt from the commercial break.

I swatted at his hand and wriggled away. "Danny, pay attention. It's the showcase showdown. You totally missed this amazing Florida vacation."

"Oh c'mon, Florida," Danny groaned. "That's not exciting. Everyone's been to Florida."

I sat up straighter.

This was the type of thing that'd been getting to me more and more lately. Everyone knew how to ski. Everyone knew you went to a fancy restaurant on your birthday. Everyone had a car, or at least a parent's car they could consistently borrow. Everyone except me. But that never seemed to occur to him.

It was annoying. "Well, I haven't been. I've never even seen the ocean, and I've kinda always wanted to."

"What?" Danny looked gobsmacked, as he always did when I explained how not everyone had grown up in his uber-privileged world. "No way, babe. I'm taking you to the ocean. We'll go to Florida." Danny launched himself to his feet, pulling me up with him. "And we'll do the hula." He started to hula, his hands on my hips, making me move with him. "C'mon babe. Hula hula hula for me."

So I did. I rocked my hips and waved my arms and pretended I had big tropical flowers in my hair. Beside me Danny pretended to ride a surfboard. It was the sort of ridiculous fun he excelled at.

A cleared throat brought our silliness to an abrupt end. "You know the hula goes with Hawaii, not Florida, right?"

It was Danny's younger brother, Will, a bowl of cereal in his hands. I went red.

Usually he left the house early. He was taking summer courses at the community college. I'd thought we had the house to ourselves. I never would've let Danny feel me up in the middle of his living room otherwise.

"Whatever, bro." Danny laughed, not showing the slightest hint of embarrassment. "Hawaii's, like, right around the corner from Florida. You just get on a boat."

THE SHOW MUST GO ON

I stared at Danny. This was wrong, I was pretty sure, except he sounded so certain.

"Actually Hawaii is approximately four thousand five hundred miles away," Will corrected.

"Yeah, sure it is." Danny laughed as Will turned and walked back out as quietly as he'd come in.

Later, I looked it up. Damn if Will wasn't right. The distance between Florida and Hawaii, according to Google, was 4,644 miles. Will was almost dead on. I couldn't believe he knew that off the top of his head. After that I kept trying to work Hawaii into the conversation whenever he was in the room. For some reason it was important that he knew that I knew Hawaii was not off the coast of Florida. I'd even looked up and memorized the distance between Buffalo and Hawaii to throw in as extra proof that I wasn't an idiot.

But somehow I never found a natural segue to bring the topic up again.

"Buffalo is four thousand six hundred and twenty-nine miles away from Hawaii," I told Warbucks suddenly.

To his credit, he didn't miss a beat. "Yeah? Wow. That's cool. Are you, like, one of those people who just know, like, number things? Like, do you know how far we are from Florida?"

"Um, yes," I lied, for no reason other than my drunken brain told me to. "Just give me a moment to think about it." I closed my eyes, and that's the last thing I remember.

And now it's—I squint at my alarm clock: 9:00 a.m. I slept all night, and Warbucks appears to have passed out beside me.

As I debate whether to wake Warbucks or let him sleep, his phone beeps with an incoming text message. I glance down out of habit and, okay, curiosity. It's from his mom.

Where are you?

He doesn't even stir. I use his finger to unlock it and type back a quick response, *Drank too much last night.*

Ok. Tell Gina I said hi.

I wonder who Gina is and why Warbucks isn't passed out in the middle of her bed right now.

Since peeing is more urgent than Warbucks and why he was ready to cheat on Gina with me, I head for the bathroom. The toilet is still clogged. Cursing, I try to remember where I put the plunger. I'm pretty sure it's in the front hall closet.

I open the bedroom door, already bracing myself for the ugly party aftermath sure to be waiting. But it's way worse than merely messy. Dogs, dogs, and more dogs fill my small apartment. And one of them already took a good morning dump on the carpet.

"Stella!"

No answer.

I remember something else from last night. Stella and her boyfriend, Brian, had a screaming fight in the middle of the kitchen.

"You were gonna move to Florida without mentioning it to me first?" he'd bellowed.

"Like you'd even notice," she'd replied. "We haven't had sex in four months. What am I staying for?"

There was more, but that was the central argument. I can't remember how it ended, but what I do recall is Stella asking if I'd mind watching the dogs for a bit so she could break Brian's heart without them watching.

Grabbing my cell, I dial Stella.

She answers sounding disgustingly chipper. "Jenna! Are my babies behaving themselves?"

"One of them crapped on my floor, so I'd say no."

"Oh, it was Pippin, I bet. You remember Pippin from when he auditioned for Annie, right? Poor little Pips. Change is hard for him. He has anxiety. I left some doggy Xanax for him in one of the bags. He hates taking it though, so maybe wait till I get back."

"And when will that be?"

"Super-duper fast, I promise. I just need to get the rest of my stuff out of Brian's. It won't take long, and after that I'll help you pack. And then...Florida!"

I open my eyes in time to see the little dog, who I suspect is Pippin, tucking into his own pile of shit like it's even better the second time around. Quickly, I close them again. "Stella, about that..."

"I know. I know. Bringing the dogs is gonna be tough. I was hoping Brian would take custody until I settled somewhere else. But apparently his doggy daddy responsibilities mean nothing to him."

Sensing someone watching me, I wink one eye open to see a sleepy-looking Warbucks standing in the doorway of my bedroom. He waggles his fingers at me. "Stella, I got to go."

"Hey wait," she says before I can hang up. "Did Frankie stay the night with you? Not to sound judgmental, but you do know how old he is?"

Frankie. That's his name. Right. I dart a glance at him. He's wrestling with the dogs and asking all of them, "Who's a good boy? Who's a good boy?"

Turning my back, I say in a low voice. "He's in his twenties."

"I don't think at twenty you can say 'in your twenties.'"

"Fine. He's twenty. I'm sure of it. I was at his birthday party."

"Funny, it wasn't that long ago since I was at his high school graduation party—"

I hang up, not wanting to hear any more about Frankie's high school graduation.

"Hey, morning," Warbucks, er Frankie, says. "I didn't wake you, did I? Sometimes I snore."

"Nope, no snoring. But you were talking in your sleep. Muttering about someone named Gina." I don't even know why I say that. I don't care about Gina or if he's cheating on her with me. I want him out of my apartment. But maybe the Gina thing will take that goofy, anybody-up-for-some-morning-sex look off his face.

"Oooh," he says, his eyes wide. "That's weird. Like really freaky. Man, I'll have to tell her. She'll think it's funny."

"Just leave, okay?" I am feeling less charitable.

"What? But why?" It hits Frankie. "Is it because of the Gina thing? It is, isn't it? But yo, that's my grandma. I crash at her place on show nights 'cause she lives down the street."

I scoff. "Oh come on."

"No really."

"I don't even care, but that's the worst lie ever. Who calls their grandma, Gina?"

"Well, lots of people do. It's her name."

I glare at him, but have to admit he seems sincere. "All right fine. It's your grandma. I really don't care. I just...I'm hungover, and as you can see, there are all these dogs in my apartment and it's a bit much, so would you mind leaving now?"

"I don't think you believe me. Do you want to call her?" He pulls out his phone. "She sounds really old. Like, you can tell. So who else could she be? I mean, I wouldn't have a girlfriend that old." He stops as if aware of a faux pas. He backtracks. "I mean old old. Like Gina. Not old like you."

"What do you mean, 'old like me'?"

He ignores my question. Wisely. "C'mon. Dial the contact. Hey, that's weird. I don't remember texting Mom."

"Just *Mom*? You don't call her Jane?"

He looks at me like I'm insane. "Why would I call her Jane?"

My head pounds.

"Hey," Frankie says. "Would you mind if I grab a shower before I go?"

I consider grabbing one of my steak knives and threatening him with it until he leaves. But they got lost a few moves back, and since then I've been using my pizza wheel to cut meat.

"Only if you unclog the toilet first."

"Yeah, no problem." He grins and gives me a double thumbs-up before disappearing into the bathroom.

Well, okay. Good job, me. I was a gracious hostess and also solved my toilet problem.

With Frankie out of the way, I throw on some clean clothes and then start corralling the empty bottles and cups littering my apartment. It's exhausting, and after five minutes I flop onto my bed and catch sight of Frankie's phone lying on my comforter. Picking it up, I walk to the bathroom and try the knob. Not locked. Of course, he's probably hoping I might join him. Truly a person with unflagging optimism. I open the door a crack and yell in, "What's the code on your phone? Your alarm is going off and driving me crazy."

"Alarm?" Frankie yells back. "I didn't set a—"

"Augh! It won't stop. Give me the digits already or I'm tossing it out the window."

Frankie spits out the code. I snap the door closed and then flick through his contacts until I see Gina. I hesitate a moment, remembering that I don't actually care about Frankie. It's true. I don't. I hit the Dial button anyway.

Almost immediately, a creaky voice answers. "Frankie, where were you last night? I made up the spare bed and had some warm milk ready."

I hang up. Well, that was his grandma. For some reason this is comforting.

It's short lived as I glance down and see Pippin with his leg raised. "Don't you do it, you little pisser!"

The little pisser startles and stumbles into the wall behind him. The other dogs bark in response. Pippin meanwhile pulls his lips back and bares his teeth. It seems aggressive, except for the whine and the slight wag of his tail. I look closer and realize he's giving me a doggie version of a nervous grin. His whole vibe seems to suggest, "Hey, hey, I didn't realize that wasn't cool, but now I do. We're still friends, right?"

He's a homely little guy, like a Chihuahua that someone pumped full of steroids. His soft whine is so pathetic only a monster would withhold forgiveness.

A monster who would like to get her security deposit back.

"I'm not a dog person," I tell him. "It's not that I don't like dogs. I feel the same way about them as I do *The Phantom of the Opera*. I know it's a thing lots of people enjoy, but I don't see the appeal."

Encouraged, he wags his tail even harder, as if he didn't understand a word I said. Which, of course he didn't because I'm talking to a fucking dog.

There's another knock at the door. Praying it's Stella, I slip some UGGs onto my feet so I won't discover anything else squishing between my toes.

I hesitate before opening it. What if it's Danny again? Holding my breath, I bring my eye to the peephole.

Oh no. Not Danny. But nearly as bad. My landlord.

"What are these dogs doing here?" he demands as I open the door.

"They're Stella's," I say, hoping this will make him go away. Stella was the one who got me this apartment.

"I know they're Stella's!" he roars. "Who else has nine crazy dogs? The shelter calls her every time they're ready to put one down. Until Brian finally went down there and straightened 'em out like I told him to."

Oh shit. I remember how Stella knows him. Uncle Frank, she calls him. He's Brian's uncle, though, not hers. And there's no doubting where his loyalties lie now that the two of them are broken up.

"We're leaving in a few days," I tell him in my calmest voice.

Uncle Frank leans in, breathing out menace mixed with his morning cup of coffee. "If you want any part of your security fee back, you'll leave tonight."

"Okay, okay." I need that damn security fee for a down payment on a new apartment wherever I end up next. "I'll be gone tonight."

"Tonight? You're leaving tonight?" From behind me comes Frankie's voice. I turn to find him dripping wet with only a tiny hand towel wrapped around his waist.

"Frankie Junior!" Uncle Frank says.

"Dad!" Frankie says.

"Aw hell," I mutter, realizing why Stella would've been at Frankie's high school graduation party. I've really got to be better about remembering people's names. And how they're connected.

"Frankie Junior, put some clothes on. We're leaving," Uncle Frank says.

This is clearly not the right way to handle Frankie Junior. Apparently, he's one of those types that gets mulish when given a direct order. Now his arms cross over his chest, and the tiny towel strains around his waist. "Jenna invited me here, Dad."

"I did, that's true. But I'd actually be fine with you leaving now."

"You hear that, Frankie Junior? This lady's had her fun and wants you gone so she can get packing for Florida."

Oh come on. He's making me sound like some kind of predatory older woman. I'd tell Uncle Frank where to shove it, except I'm afraid he'll kick me out even quicker. Luckily, Frankie Junior steps in to protect my honor.

"You don't know anything about it, Dad! Jenna's nice and smart and has been places. And she's taking me places too. I mean, I'm going places with her. That is..." He trails off, finally looking a little embarrassed. "Jenna, I didn't want to ask like this. I was gonna make breakfast for you first, but since my dad's here..." He swallows hard and looks at me with big pleading eyes. "Can I come to Florida with you and Stella?"

Uncle Frank laughs. Not in the nice sort of way. "She doesn't want you coming to Florida with her."

And as much as it pains me to agree with Uncle Frank, the alternate is far, far worse.

I look at his pleading eyes and decide to keep this quick and painless. For both of us. "No."

His somewhat scrawny chest collapses, and that little scrap of a towel finally loses its battle and falls to the floor. Frankie does not seem to notice.

"Fer fucks sake," Uncle Frank mutters, and he stomps over to

Frankie, grabs the towel, and then propels them both out the door while Frankie sputters about his clothes.

I collapse onto the couch, wondering if someone drugged me last night and this whole thing has been one terrible dream.

Things are bad when being drugged is your best-case scenario.

I close my eyes and let gravity slowly pull my head toward the soft cushions. It feels so good, until my cheek connects with a damp warm spot.

Holy shit. Did Stella fill 'em up like water balloons before leaving them here?

Springing to my feet, I eye the dogs, who are milling about aimlessly now that there's no one new to bark at.

"Which of you fuckers did it?" I demand. "Who peed on my couch?"

They go crazy barking again. I can almost hear them saying,

"Wasn't me."

"I didn't do it."

"Don't look at me."

Behind me someone clears their throat. And that's when I realize why the dogs are barking. There is a strange man in the doorway of my apartment, holding two cups of coffee.

Except he isn't strange. He's Danny.

"The door was open," Danny says.

With those words, finally, FINALLY, my brain realizes this isn't Danny.

It's his younger brother. Will.

And that, in many ways, is so much worse.

Because the last time I saw Will was also the last time I saw Danny.

5

"Being Alive" -Company

Beige.

In my memory everything was beige. Not like someone put an old-timey Instagram filter over it. That would be interesting, and this was the opposite of that.

The beige covered everything. Including me. *Especially* me.

If depression has a color, it's beige for sure.

So it was another day in Beigeville, I was sitting next to Danny's bed in a chair that looked comfortable, but was not. It was also beige, of course, and covered in a fabric that could easily wipe clean. Though stiff, the seat was generously padded, and the back even reclined. In all fairness the chair was comfortable for the first several days you sat in it, but eventually the act of sitting, of waiting, of being beside Danny's bed, became unbearable no matter how lovingly my bottom was cradled.

We weren't in the hospital anymore. Everyone had acted excited about that, like Danny was moving up. But really they were giving up. He was taking up valuable space at the hospital, where people got better or got dead, and either way ceased to need a bed. The rehabilitation facility was the equivalent of putting Danny into a very nice storage unit.

Already he'd been here for...a month? Two months?

Whatever. Like it even mattered how long. There was a clock on the beige wall, but I never bothered with it. Clocks and their counterpart, the calendar, had been rendered meaningless.

I came to this beige room. I sat in this beige chair. I watched my beige boyfriend (and secret husband, but really, did I even really care about that anymore? Did it even matter?) lay in bed, unmoving. I stayed until Danny's mother drove me home. The last thing she'd said was that she'd pick me up the next day.

Always the next day. All my tomorrows, never a day off. No hope of parole for good behavior.

As long as Danny lay in that bed, I would sit beside him. This was the punishment Mrs. O'Leary had decided upon. It was a good one, and it was slowly killing me.

On that specific day, I was turning the pages of an old *Reader's Digest*. I was not reading it. I had already read it. I'd, in fact, read it many many many times before.

Danny apparently loved the *Reader's Digest* humor section. At least according to his mom. The knock-knock jokes, the quotes, the funny true stories. All of it. She had me read them aloud. Sometimes we read them together, playing different characters.

"Isn't this fun?" she'd say with grim determination.

"So, so fun," I'd agree, nodding my head like it was controlled by a string.

I didn't read aloud when she wasn't there to watch me. At first I tried to talk to Danny. Tell him I was sorry. Ask him if he would wake up. But over time my tongue grew beige and heavy, and every word spoken aloud took an incredible effort.

So when someone knocked at Danny's door. I didn't even look up. It wasn't Mrs. O'Leary. She always said "knock knock" when she was already halfway in. One day I was going to explain to her this wasn't how knocking worked.

Whoever it was knocked again. Usually the nurses knocked as a warning, right before walking in. But this person was waiting, which meant this person was someone different, a surprise.

"It's open," I called out.

The door slowly eased open. Despite myself, I sat up straighter. Any small change in the endless beige routine was exciting.

A young man walked in. Tall, dark hair, rumpled clothing, stubble covering his jaw. Not a bit of beige on him. I was almost certain he'd accidentally wandered into the wrong room.

"Hey." He took another step into the room, and suddenly I realized this wasn't a sexy stranger. It was Will.

The last time I saw him...I dug through the endless soup of beige days and realized it was back when Danny was still at the hospital. Of course, Will was away at college studying to be some sort of super genius who would save the world in amazing ways.

Obviously, he was too important to come home and sit by his comatose brother's bedside. Unlike me and my unimportant life. As if that wasn't enough of a kick in the teeth, while I'd been sitting there growing beige, Will was at college getting hot.

Instead of answering Will's greeting, I slumped in my chair and returned to staring at the wrinkled pages of *Reader's Digest*.

In the background, I could hear Will talking softly to Danny. He had that sort of self-conscious tone to his voice that most people get when having a one-sided conversation.

If Mrs. O'Leary had been there, she would've hustled me out the door the minute Will showed up. She had it in her head that with Danny out of commission, I was going to move on to seducing her other son. But she was getting her hair done that morning, an endless process at the end of which she showed up looking exactly the same. But maybe that was the point.

With her gone, I felt no need to clear the room just because Will had graced us with his presence.

I turned another page of the good old *Reader's Digest*.

Will cleared his throat. "Uh, Jenna?"

Ignoring him, I turned the page once more and—

Suddenly it was ripped from my hands. Will looked down at the magazine like he couldn't imagine why anyone would read such a thing and then flung it toward the trash can.

I smirked. "You missed."

He sighed and rubbed a hand over his stubbled face. "I came here to see you. I wanted to talk while Mom wasn't here."

This was not what I expected him to say. At all. I stood, not liking him hovering over me. "Talk to *me*? About what?"

In response he pulled an envelope out of his back pocket and shoved it toward me. I flicked it open and discovered a pile of hundred-dollar bills.

"What the fuck is this?" I asked.

Uncomfortable, Will shoved his hands into his pockets. "It's for you. To go away or whatever you want."

"Go away. Ha. Funny." I laughed. A beige laugh devoid of actual humor.

"I'm serious." Will stepped closer. He pressed his hands over mine. They felt hot.

My hands were always like blocks of ice from the AC. Even in January, cold air came blowing out the vents.

Deliberately, he folded my fingers around the envelope of cash. "Take it. Buy a plane ticket to wherever you want. Go to Miami. See the ocean. You said you always wanted to see the ocean."

I stared at him, surprised he'd remembered that, the day Danny and I did the hula while watching *The Price Is Right*. It was last summer. No, two summers ago. I kept forgetting we'd already lost one. Two summers ago was another lifetime.

And now, all this time later, after I'd long forgotten all about it, Will brought it back up.

"Go," Will said, returning me to the present. The heat of his hands was transferring into my own. I could actually feel my fingertips again. Somehow, though, it made the rest of me colder. I shivered and thought of the hot Florida sun.

I wanted to go. All I wanted was to walk out of that room and never return. Except, I couldn't. Because Danny was lying there. Will had been there the day of the accident. He knew what had happened. Maybe he'd forgotten or convinced himself it wasn't the way he'd remembered. But I knew the truth. Danny was in that bed because of me.

"I can't," I told him. I pulled my hand away. The envelope full of cash hit the floor. "Keep your money."

I sank into the beige chair, settled into place as if I'd never left. "Can I have my magazine back?"

A pile of papers fell into my lap. I looked up to find Will still standing over me.

"Danny cheated on you," he said. "With Heather. It's all there. Hundreds of emails between them."

I glanced down at the papers, barely seeing them, then up at Will. Heather was Danny's ex-girlfriend, and the two of them were always flirtier than I'd liked. But even if he did cheat on me, I couldn't see what that had to do with anything.

"You don't owe him the rest of your life, Jenna. Or however long he stays like this. Take the money. Get away for a while. And when you come back, reassess."

Will dropped the envelope on top of the printed-out emails. The cash spilled out. I reached for it, meaning to tidy up, but instead my hands clenched tight. Somehow my eyes closed, and I imagined the sun on my face and sand between my toes.

My throat tightened. I wanted it so badly.

I stood abruptly, crushing the papers and money into one big messy ball and then shoving it all into Will's chest. "You think Heather or emails or, or anything changes things? Take this. Just take it and get out. Okay? I'm not leaving."

Will stared at me. The florescent lights made his eyes unnaturally dark and unreadable. I could see him thinking, deciding something in his mind. When he finally nodded, I shivered, nervous.

"I get it," Will said. "That pile of money right here isn't the payday you were hoping for. With the baby you were looking for Danny to marry you and our parents to buy you two a house. Right? Or get you both a job with King's Carpets? Finally put you on TV to kick-start your acting career. But you accidentally broke the piggy bank too soon, and instead of money pouring out, you got this. Maybe you think you can still salvage something, but trust me when I say, it's over. Eventually my mother's going to decide you've been punished enough, and that'll be it. My advice? Count your losses. Take the money. And run."

I slapped him. The crack of it filled the room. Will's head snapped sideways. All the papers between us fluttered to the ground. We stared at each other, my breath ragged as if I'd run a marathon. Slowly the shape of my hand bloomed red across Will's cheek. I tried to apologize, but my lips were numb. Silently, I watched as Will bent down and corralled the money back into its envelope and the papers into a neat little stack. As he straightened, I waited for him to turn and walk out the door.

Hopefully, without saying anything else. Surely it was clear he'd said enough.

And it was, because he didn't say another word. He simply held the money and emails out to me once more.

If it wasn't for that mark on his cheek, I'd have thought I was the one who'd been slapped. I felt as if I'd been spun around. Disconnected from myself.

Later, Will's words would repeat in my head. I'd replay them again and again. Just like I'd read all those emails between Heather and Danny. He was cheating on me almost from the beginning. Though he didn't see it that way. At first he rationalized that things weren't serious between him and me, and anyway he and Heather wouldn't do it again. Then they'd do it again, and he'd say for sure this was the last time. Later he decided that being with Heather didn't count as cheating because they'd already been together. Her vagina was somehow grandfathered in.

But at that moment I wasn't thinking about any of that. I honestly wasn't thinking anything at all. There was a loud buzzing in my head, and I watched, almost as if it were happening to someone else, as my hand reached out and closed around the envelope. I found my ratty backpack where I'd left it beside the beige recliner and shoved the cash inside. Then I took the emails, rolled them into a tube, and jammed them in too. My coat was on a hook near the door. I shoved my arms in, not looking at Danny or Will. Not considering how I'd get home (I ended up walking to a McDonald's down the road and calling my mom) or what I'd do with the money.

I walked out without saying goodbye. It didn't even occur to me.

At that moment I didn't know I was leaving and never returning.

But I was. The very next day I was on an airplane to Florida.

This is the worst part. Almost as bad as putting him into that bed in the first place.

I left Danny there and never looked back.

6

"I Won't Grow Up" –Peter Pan

My whole body is tensed, ready for flight. Or to hide in the bathroom again. But it's too late for that. And now I'm standing here stupidly staring at Will.

"The door was open," he repeats in this oh-so-reasonable tone.

There's something about the way he states this obvious fact—for the second time—not like he thinks I'm hard of hearing, but more as if he wants to make sure I get it.

It's been years, but suddenly it's like no time has passed.

Nice to see Will hasn't lost his talent for making me feel small and lesser than.

Another thing that hasn't changed: I'd rather gnaw off my own knuckles than let him see how much I care.

"Oh, wow, that's right. Thanks so much for pointing that out," I gush in my best faux-chipper voice. "I've always had trouble distinguishing the difference between a closed door and an open one. But I think I got it now, so if you wouldn't mind taking a few steps out into the hallway, I'll go ahead and close it."

Will sighs. No, he doesn't. Sighing is for weaker, less rational people. Will looks like he wants to sigh, but instead he just slowly breathes out through his nose instead.

"Can we both be adults here?"

He puts a slight emphasis on *both*. As if to insinuate that he, of course, is already comfortably ensconced on adult island. It's been his preferred residence since the age of five or so.

So now I smile. It's my stage smile, which ensures people in the back row can see all my teeth. "You know, Will, the door was open just now, but you might recall how yesterday—" As I say it, my brain catches up with my mouth, and I realize, yes, it was Will at the door last night! And it must have been him in the theater too. "Yesterday," I repeat triumphantly, "I closed that same door in your face. It's what I do to all my stalkers."

"Sensible strategy. To be clear though, you slammed it," Will corrects, which is another awful thing about him. He's one of those people who has to be perfectly precise about everything. "The whole building shuddered."

"Fine," I concede. "I slammed it. And did you take that to mean, please come again?"

Will breathes another non-sigh. "It doesn't have to be this way." He's going back to that whole reasonable thing, like he's hoping it's contagious.

"Doesn't it?"

He holds both cups of coffee out to me. "This one has cream and sugar. The other is black. Which would you prefer?"

I stare at the caffeine, knowing it's not a peace offering. It's a chunk of cheese on a mousetrap. And yet I can't help myself. I grab the black coffee. "I'm taking this because I really need coffee, but I still want you to leave."

"I'm sorry, Jenna, but I'm not leaving." Will takes a deliberate step forward so that he's no longer in the doorway but standing on the carpet—officially inside my apartment.

"Hey!" I squawk as he takes another step and then another until he is standing directly in front of me. "I did not invite you in. Get back!" I wave my hands in a shooing motion, which doesn't budge Will an inch but does set the dogs barking again.

"My brother woke up three days ago after being in a coma for twelve years." He raises his voice to be heard over the dogs, and even though he's still trying to sound oh so reasonable, there's an undeniable edge to it now. "Twelve years since I've been able to talk with him and hear him answer back. Twelve years since he's eaten or laughed or pretended snoring because I was boring him."

"Pretend snore. Classic comedy bit," I interject in an attempt to derail this speech because raw emotion makes me super uncomfortable.

A muscle twitches along the side of Will's jaw, but otherwise he continues as if I hadn't spoken. "I want nothing more than to catch up on lost time with my brother. Instead, I'm here in some dusty corner of California, and I am not to return home until I can do so with you by my side."

"Wow," I say, because *wow*. "Look, just because some crazy person—your mom, I'm guessing—tells you to break into my apartment and abduct me, doesn't mean you have to do it."

I can't resist reaching out to give his arm a patronizing little pat. A way to show him that if he's gonna invade my space, I'll go ahead and do the same. It's on the third pat that I realize my fingertips have connected with what seems to be sculpted marble beneath his shirtsleeve. Suddenly, I can't help noticing Will is tall, but not in the spindly way he used to be.

I'm still patting his arm. I can't seem to stop, as I take in its ropey musculature and how it leads up to a set of incredibly broad shoulders.

And we are close. Too close.

I drop my hand and back away. Not wanting to look like I'm running, I veer into the kitchen, where I pour the paper cup of coffee into a mug and then pop it into the microwave for a reheat. I turn around, and Will is right behind me again.

"My brother needs to see you. He asked for you. By name. More than once. That's why I'm here. If he wanted ice from Antarctica, I'd be there. And I did *not* break into your apartment, nor do I have any plans to abduct you. Instead we are going to sit and discuss and perhaps even disagree some, until at last we come to a mutually beneficial agreement."

"Oh fuck," I groan, as the he once again claims the calm and rational high ground. "I'd rather you just abduct me."

This gets a half smile. A begrudging one that's there and then gone. He looks so much like Danny it's making my dizzy, but oddly when he smiles, he only looks like himself. It's like that optical illusion that's a face and a vase. At first all you can see is the face and you're hunting for the vase. Then it switches. The vase is so obviously right there, but you gotta cross your eyes to see the face again.

Will didn't look a thing like Danny all those years ago. Danny was athletic and confident. Will was scrawny, wore glasses, and stood with his shoulders in a near permanent forward slump. Sure if you looked close they had the same sandy-brown hair (Will's heavier on the sand), eyes with dramatic lashes (though Danny's were a dramatic blue, while Will's were boring brown), and matching killer smiles, but otherwise they were nothing alike.

As if we've come to some détente, Will relaxes. His steady gaze relents. It isn't until he looks away that I realize how on edge I felt having those intense eyes fixed on me.

Now I allow myself to take several long, deep breaths while Will looks around my apartment. It's pretty basic, so there's not much to see. Bare walls because I move too much to bother putting up pictures. A small bookshelf with ten books. Five are keepers. The rest I rotate depending on what I like at any given time. Will actually walks over to it, like he's unable to resist the siren call of literature. Obviously, despite losing the glasses, his nerd instincts are still strong. I watch him run a finger over the spines, and can feel my reading choices being judged. I'm about to defend the two romance novels (both battered keepers), but then remember that I explain myself to no one. I live my own life, and also, fuck him.

Luckily, he turns his attention to the rest of the room. The generic dented furniture that came with the apartment. My own beautiful brown leather couch. And my beloved flat-screen TV. Those last two things, along with my bed frame and mattress, I put into the cab of my truck and take with me wherever I go.

Finally, Will contemplates the dogs milling about. They're a motley crew. Stella takes the dogs no one else wants. Old dogs. Sick dogs. Blind dogs. Three-legged dogs. Black dogs (apparently this color of dog is the least adopted). And of course, neurotic dogs incapable of being house-trained.

I relax, running my hand across the head of one of the elderly black labs, when Will's eyes return to me, stealing my composure once more.

"You're not bringing all these dogs home, are you?"

"Home?" I force out a laugh. "*This* is my home."

"Right. For now. But it seems like you're being evicted—"

"Were you standing out in the hallway? Spying on me?"

I sound like a paranoid lunatic. The truth is, I'm already losing. He knows it too. Will has already shown his not-so-secret strength is being reasonable and logical while his eyes burn a hole through my forehead and eventually my brain. Before I know it, he'll be packing my bags—probably even more efficiently than my own method which I spent years perfecting—by using physics or some shit like that.

"After you shut the door in my face last night, I thought you might need time to process the news about Danny. So I gave you the evening and returned this morning with coffee, at which time I unintentionally overheard—"

"Spy!"

"A discussion between you and your landlord."

I close my eyes. Then I hear myself admit, "I thought you were Danny."

Will nods. "I get that a lot. Especially from people who haven't seen us in a long time."

Ah, there it is. First shot fired.

I could defend myself. Explain the real reason for my confusion. Which is that I'd forgotten what healthy Danny looked like. That seems absurd, but for me, sickly Danny is the only Danny. He's a living ghost, turning my nights into long dark stretches of time where I chase sleep, never quite managing to catch it.

But I already know Will won't accept this excuse. Or even understand it. I run because sick Danny haunts me. And sick Danny haunts me because I run.

Saying nothing, I turn and pull my coffee from the microwave. I watch from the corner of my eye as Will wanders toward the scarred kitchen table.

"Mind if I sit?" Before I can answer, he's already unzipped and removed his hoodie, neatly draping it over the back of a chair.

I'm now staring at what was hidden beneath that layer of fleece. A long-sleeved cotton T-shirt all soft and nubby from multiple washings covers his torso. Not stretched tight like he purposely bought a shirt two sizes too small to show off his awesome pecs. Instead it gently hugs him in all the right places, emphasizing wide shoulders, toned chest, and muscled arms.

Look away, I tell myself. But I can't. My eyes won't even blink as my brain attempts to square this *Men's Health* fantasy with the skinny guy in boxy polo shirts his mom used to buy in four different colors that he then rotated through the week.

This is why I mistook him for Danny. It wasn't his face. It was his shoulders.

I feel betrayed.

"What?" Will asks.

"Nothing," I say too quickly and in a weird high voice. It's not like I can say, "How *dare* you become smoking hot."

"Ooooh-kay." Will studies me for a moment and then apparently decides to let it go. "You're not objecting, so I'm going to sit now."

I slouch into the seat across from him. "Fine. Sit. Make yourself comfortable."

"Don't worry. I'm definitely not comfortable." As he settles into his chair, he adds, "Drink your coffee. Then we'll begin the negotiations."

"The only thing we're negotiating is how soon you're leaving." For emphasis I thump my coffee mug against the table.

If it were a theater prop, the moment would be powerful. But it's an actual cup full of molten hot liquid, so of course coffee sloshes all over my hand. I gasp as my skin relays one singular sensation to my brain: HOT.

The dogs erupt in frenzied barking, while I rush to the sink and stick my hand under cold water.

I don't realize Will is beside me until he takes my hand between his own. "No blistering, some slight redness. You should be fine."

When Will wasn't being a pompous asshole, he could actually be nice. But it never lasted. Something would always put us at odds again.

I jerk my hand back. "The coffee wasn't that hot." This is a lie. I'm pretty sure I'd pressed the Magma button on my microwave. Grabbing some paper towels, I scrub up the mess. Will stands at the sink, watching me. I don't know why this makes me feel flustered. But it does.

"Really, I'm more upset about wasting the caffeine." Feeling like an idiot, I flop into my chair.

Will takes the sodden paper towels out of my hand. I hadn't realized I was still holding them. After depositing them in the trash, he pushes his cup of coffee across the table.

"I think you need this more than me," he says gently.

It is the worst thing he could do. Almost immediately tears threaten.

I cannot cry. I will not cry. Will is the enemy. An enemy who is sometimes nice, but still the enemy.

Will—the enemy!—squats in front of me, his jeans stretching tight against what appear to be incredibly powerful thighs, a thing I am only noting because he is the enemy and one must carefully survey the enemy looking for weaknesses. Weaknesses which are clearly not in his thighs. Or shoulders. Or biceps. Or—

I'm abruptly jerked out of my mental inventory as Will takes my hand. His big hands are so much bigger than mine. My stubby fingers could almost pass for delicate as his much longer fingers gently trace the pink angry flesh. "It's a little red. But I think you're right. The coffee wasn't hot enough to burn."

"It's probably just embarrassed at being so clumsy," I mumble, reclaiming my hand.

Will looks like he's going to say something else, but after a moment he simply stands and retreats to his chair. As he goes, I can't help but note that there are also no weaknesses to be found in his backside either.

I take a sip of Will's coffee, which is cold and sweet and milky. Three things I do not like my coffee to be. But at least it's caffeine, and Will was nice enough to give it to me.

After a few more gulps, the sugar enters my bloodstream and the brain fog clears, making it obvious I'm handling this all wrong.

Clearly Will does not have any weaknesses. I, on the other hand, am full of them. It's obvious to anyone who spends more than five minutes with me. Which means all I need to do is sit here and be myself, and eventually he'll realize that he doesn't want me anywhere near his brother and he'll go away.

"So, Will, let's catch up." I lean forward, propping my elbows on the table. "Are you a doctor or something? Did I just get to see your bedside manner in action? Oh wait. You were gonna work for NASA, right? Something..." I squeeze my eyes shut, racking my brain, trying to recall what he'd planned to major in.

"Aeronautical engineering," Will supplies with a slight frown, obviously suspicious of my sudden mood change.

I snap my fingers. "Yes! That's it. Wow, so fancy. So that's what you're doing now?"

"No," he replies, oddly reticent. I'd expected to settle in for a long list of accomplishments. "I actually dropped out of school—"

"You what?" I screech. I can't help it. "Dropped out of school" are not words I would have ever connected with Will. He was *such* a school person. The type who liked doing homework. The only kid who didn't groan when the teacher announced a pop quiz. He wasn't just a nerd though. Will was super smart. Everyone said he was practically a genius. Destined for big things.

"Danny's accident reordered all our lives," Will says stiffly.

Oh. Someone is clearly defensive. Interesting.

I let it go though. I'm in no position to give anyone shit about their accomplishments, or lack thereof. And anyway, I am being a good hostess. Which means that right now I should...um, hmm...

As I chew on that question, silence settles between us.

It makes me jittery, but Will seems calm. His hands rest on top of the table, and he folds his long fingers together, carefully interweaving them. No ring, I notice. He pulls his hands apart and laces them together again. I watch mesmerized, and as I do, the image in front of me shifts.

Will shrinks in size to the boy he'd been in high school. Skinny in that way where his head seemed too heavy for his neck. He tended to hunch his shoulders forward, which didn't help matters either. He was soft, not fully formed yet. The Will here today doesn't look much like that boy. His shoulders are fully squared out, and he holds his head high with a grown man's confidence. And yet, the look in his eyes...Analytical and assessing. Nearly surgical. That's the same. Thinking constantly. That was always Will.

Now as he stares down at his hands, I can almost hear his mind whirring, and I realize the hand folding ritual is a way to gather his thoughts, that he is a person who likes to think before he speaks. It's a quality I wouldn't have recognized or admired back then.

I carefully wrap my hands around Will's coffee, trying to hold myself here even as more and more of the past begins to overlay the present.

I am not going to flashback. I am not going to flashback. I am not—

"I want to make you an offer," Will says. "Don't say no until you hear the whole thing."

Aw, shit.

I flashback.

7

"Back to Before" -Ragtime

These are almost verbatim the words I said to him the first time we spoke.

"I want to make you an offer," I said, dropping into the chair across from Will. "Don't say no until you hear the whole thing."

After several days of searching, I'd hunted Will down in the school library. Now he stared at me like I was stranger than the alien on the cover of the sci-fi novel clutched in his hand.

Dork. That was my first thought when I saw him.

I watched as Will carefully marked his page with a *Teenage Mutant Ninja Turtles* bookmark and tucked it into the backpack at his feet. With that taken care of, he folded his hands, weaving long fingers together. Finally, he looked at me in this way that was weirdly honest and direct.

I grinned at him reflexively.

He swallowed, his Adam's apple bobbing. "All right. I'll wait to say no."

It was a more gracious response than I had any reason to expect, and yet I remember feeling disappointed. After pinning so many hopes on this moment, it was already not going the way I wanted. He was supposed to be intrigued, even a little flattered to have me approaching him, not sitting there like *he* was the one doing me a favor.

Still, the show must go on, and so projecting confidence, I made my pitch.

"I don't really know you. I mean, obviously. We're in the same year, but otherwise have nothing in common and no reason to be friends. But I know *of* you. You're smart. Everyone says you're going to be valedictorian. Which is a big deal and stuff and, yeah, you'll go to some awesome college, but you still have another year and a half of high school to get through before that happens. Fact is, you'd be totally invisible at this school if it wasn't for your brother, and..."

I trailed off, letting Will fill in the blank. But he didn't. Instead he stared at me.

"The commercial," I finally said. "The one where—"

"I know the one," he interrupted, coming in with his line too late. Stepping on mine.

We stare at one another. I look away first.

Will was only a baby when the commercial was made. His dad, playing the king with his crown and scepter and robe, swooped in, picked Will up, and boomed, "Oh no, Prince Will, did you have another accidental wee wee?" Then Will was passed offscreen while his father explained how his carpets came with a special stain guard to protect against puppies or princes unable to hold their wee.

This was long before YouTube existed. Which means no one should have ever found out about it. We were all babies ourselves when it first aired. Unluckily for Will, Jeremy Garner had every Buffalo Bill's game on VHS tape. While rewatching one of those old tapes, Jeremy saw the commercial, recognized his classmate Will, and...well, yeah. Today it would've been uploaded and spread throughout the school within hours, but back then it rolled out slower. The tape was passed around. Played at parties. Even kids who hadn't actually seen the tape could repeat it verbatim. It became legendary. And Will, well, he became Prince Wee Wee to most of the student body.

"Okay, well, the commercial thing sucks," I told Will, picking the script up where I'd left off. "I know how it feels to have the whole school know all about you because of something you have no control over. You know who my sister is, right? Allie Batton? She dropped out of school two years ago. She was about six months pregnant at the time."

Suddenly my throat felt unexpectedly thick as I remembered the way Allie had screamed at my mom. "I'm not going back! I'm not gonna pretend to care about math or biology or any of that shit, while everyone's calling me slut and whale and fucking white trash."

Will nodded, his neutral expression finally changing. But not in a good way, because it kinda looked like pity.

"It's okay. I mean, it's not okay, because everyone thinks we're the same, and so every guy around here assumes I'm easy. Like everyone knows, sluttiness is genetic."

Will blinked at that. "Okay." He sounded wary, as if sensing a trap.

"I'm not a slut, okay? Not that my sister is. Or maybe she is a little, but there's nothing wrong with it. I'd totally be slutty too, except I have plans. Plans that don't include a baby before twenty." I paused and added, even though it wasn't one of my rehearsed bits, "Maybe not after twenty either." The night before I could barely sleep with baby Maxine crying nearly nonstop. Living with a baby in the house had really put me off the entire idea of reproduction.

"Anyway," I said, pulling myself back on track. "My plan is to be an actress. I'm not sure yet if I want to go to LA or New York after graduation. It's really a question of pursuing stage or screen, you know?"

"Yeah."

"So here's the offer. It's a way to turn both our weaknesses into strengths." I paused and smiled at him, even though my pulse was hammering. "Homecoming is in two weeks. We'll go to the dance together. I'll be all over you. Everyone will assume that you're getting lucky afterward. You won't be Prince Wee Wee anymore. You'll be a stud."

Will was already shaking his head. "Even if that worked—"

"Of course it'll work. Sometimes you simply need to change the conversation. Make people look at you a different way." I'd gotten both these phrases from motivational cassette tapes my mom had been playing lately. It was sorta cheesy, but I figured it'd sound smart. "And that's not gonna happen hiding in the farthest corner of the library."

"Right." He stared down at his hands as he pulled them apart and then laced his fingers back together.

As the silence stretched on, I couldn't help myself. "This is where you're supposed to ask, 'So what's in it for you?'"

His eyes, those piercing eyes, found mine. "You're an actress. You do all the school plays and musicals. But you can't decide if you want to go to LA or New York. New York is theater. You already know what that's about. But LA is film. You have no experience there. But I bet you'd like some. So I'm guessing you want to be in one of my father's commercials."

My mouth almost certainly hung open. "How did you—"

"I don't spend my entire life at this table." Will's mouth twisted into a wry smile. "So yes, I have heard that Heather Bennett's been complaining to anyone who will listen that my brother didn't just break her heart—he also killed her film career."

Well damn. Heather had been complaining loudly. I'd overheard her while walking down the hallway. That's when I'd come up with this idea. If Will's father used his son's girlfriends to cast his commercials, well then all I needed was to date Will and I'd be in. But I needed to do it quickly. I didn't know a lot about Will's older brother, Danny, but I did know the two of them were nothing alike.

Danny had graduated the year before. Even though he was two grades above me, I couldn't help but be aware of him. He was Mr. Popularity. Star of the basketball *and* football teams. Prom *and* homecoming king. Like Will, he'd been in some of his dad's commercials, but he was usually tossing a ball or stretched across a white carpet to show how soft it was. His attitude suggested, "Hey, I know this is silly, but isn't it fun anyway?"

My real hope was to convince Mr. O'Leary he needed a jingle. And who better to sing it than me? That way even when my sham relationship with Will ended, I'd still be getting television exposure, and maybe a little extra pocket change, each time the jingle played.

"Look," Will said, busting into my fantasy. He'd picked up his backpack and slung it over his shoulder. And now was frowning down at me. Like he was deciding how to best get rid of me.

Aw shit, he was turning me down.

The bell rang before he could get the words out, and I went for the Hail Mary pass. "Wait."

Grabbing hold of his arm, I dragged him to the front of the library. Near the front doors were a bunch of comfy chairs meant to trick students into believing the library would be a great place to hang out. I shoved Will into one and plopped myself down on his lap.

All I'd ever heard about teenage boys was that they were endless horndogs. Yet there Will sat beneath me like he'd become part of the chair. I wiggled around, hoping basic biology would kick in and I'd get some sort of response out of him. But his backpack was between us, making that a nonstarter.

"Is that your math book, or are you just happy to see me?" I asked in my best vamp voice.

Will went red all the way up to the tips of his ears. But he laughed too. "I'm pretty sure it's my advanced placement world history textbook."

I snorted. And then clapped a hand over my mouth to keep another one from escaping. I hadn't expected Will to be funny. I hadn't expected...

"I like you." They were the first unrehearsed words out of my mouth.

Will's eyebrows lowered and he stared at me, no doubt calculating the truth of that statement. I stared right back. The moment stretched long enough that I made note of the sprinkling of freckles across the tops of his cheekbones and the little flecks of green hidden in the depths of his dark-brown eyes.

The clatter of students pushing through the library doors broke the moment.

"Will." I giggled, springing up from the chair. "You'll make me late to class again." Leaning over I pressed a quick kiss to his cheek, then whispered, "Sleep on it and give me your decision tomorrow. 'Kay?" Before he could respond, I twirled and was gone.

Rumors flew the rest of the day. Several people asked me how long I'd been seeing Will.

It seemed impossible that he might turn me down, and yet the next day that was exactly what happened. He said the whole offer felt too much like the plot of a John Hughes movie. I was crushed and near tears and ready to tell him where to stick his pop culture references, when he asked if I wanted to come over for dinner that night and meet his parents. As friends.

As it turned out, that was the night I first met Danny. And after that, well, after that nothing was ever the same again.

8

"Maybe" -Annie

"Jenna, you still with me?" present-day Will asks.

I blink, bringing him back into focus, once again adjusting between the boy I remember and the man now sitting in my kitchen.

"Yeah, I'm just..." I shake my head.

"Time traveling? To that day in the library?"

"I was ballsy, wasn't I?" I put a positive spin on it. "Hunting you down. Making an offer."

"Sitting on my lap," Will adds.

"Oh, you remember that part, huh?"

"Yes, it was..." He hesitates, crossing his arms over his chest.

It's a good move because it shows off his biceps. My eyes linger there until I remind them we didn't buy tickets to this particular gun show.

Just as my gaze snaps up to his face, Will finishes with, "Childish."

"You're a prude," I shoot back. "You were then and you are now."

"What if the situation was reversed?" Will asked quietly. "A boy pulled you onto his lap without asking first?"

I stare. And then swallow. He's won this one. "Okay. I apologize for my non-consensual lap sitting. It was wrong."

"That's not—"

"Good enough?" I cut Will off. "Of course it's not. Of course *I'm*

64

not. Never was. Never will be. You'd prefer I built a time machine and made sure it never happened at all. Trust me, I would if I could. I'd go back and do it all differently. If I'd stayed away from you, I never would've met Danny. And if Danny and I hadn't been together—"

"But you were."

"Yeah, I get that. I know that's how it didn't happen. I'm just saying, there were all these times when things coulda gone a different way and…" I bite my lip, refusing to cry.

"Jenna," Will says, his voice almost gentle. "I know this is difficult. Revisiting the past. We were kids. But we're not anymore."

He hardens. I can actually see it happening, and I can't help wondering what's in his head causing the change.

"No one in the past twelve years has asked you to stop by. Or to even call. You left. We respected that. But now Danny is awake. And he needs you." He pauses, and I relax a smidge. Then he adds, "Do the right thing."

"Do the right thing?" I repeat, letting the words sting my mouth. I scrub at my eyes with the back of my fist, refusing to cry. The thing is, he's right. But also, he's not. Resentment that's been living inside me for years bubbles up, and it occurs to me that it's past time to finally get this off my chest.

I stand because this is the sort of speech that needs to be delivered while on my feet.

"I wondered when we were gonna get to the guilt trip portion of this visit. So please, Will, tell me about doing the right thing. Like when Danny was in his coma but you still went to graduation. Was that the right thing? I didn't go. Nobody even mentioned it. But then who cares if Jenna graduates anyway. That's what your parents thought. But you had to give your speech. *You* were the valedictorian. Then the summer passed and Danny didn't wake up and off you went to college. Of course, that was the right thing. You were the Ivy League baby. Why should your world stop? Why should one little thing change for you? Meanwhile, my whole life shrunk down to those beige walls

65

and Danny's boop boop boop machines and your mom glaring at me across his bed. She hated me when I was there. She hated me when I left. Needled me endlessly. How it was my fault. And when I lost the baby..."

My throat closes. Oh, it's all returning now. I let one flashback play out, and now the past is threatening to swallow me whole.

There's Danny's mom screaming at me, her face purple with rage. "It wasn't an accident. You did it on purpose. You killed that baby. The only part of my son left. You took that away too."

I was lying in a hospital bed at the time, with my right leg broken in two different places. I was pumped so full of pain meds that her voice seemed to come from a distance. But later it replayed in my mind. Because she was right. Or close to being right.

Danny's room was on the third floor of the hospital. At night, when I left the hospital, I took the stairs instead of the elevator. At first it was to stretch my legs after sitting beside his bed all day. Then at some point I slid down the bannister. The first time sort of slow and cautiously, but each day I took it further and further. Of course, I finally fell. Right into the empty space at the middle of the stairwell. Two stories.

I should've broken my neck. It's what a part of me wanted. What I deserved to make me even with Danny. Instead my leg took the brunt of the fall, splintering with a sickening snap. A wave of pain followed, so strong I passed out. I was in surgery getting metal pins in my leg when I miscarried. By the time I woke up, it was over. I was no longer pregnant.

And yeah, when they told me, I cried. The baby was only nine weeks old. I'd only known about it for three weeks. Since Danny's accident I'd barely thought about it at all. But with it gone, suddenly I remembered Maxi as a newborn, so small and delicate and perfect.

So I sobbed and Mrs. O'Leary screamed.

"You have no idea," I tell Will again, my voice low and shaking. Pushing my chair back, I collapse into it once more. "You weren't there."

"You're right." He studies his hands again, like they hold all the answers. "I wasn't there, and I should've been. Especially when I know my mother can be a little..." His hand folds and unfolds as he searches for the right word.

"She's a bitch." The past suddenly feels too close for me to be diplomatic.

"It's not that easy." He leans forward, meeting my eyes, daring me to look away. "She was trying to do the right thing for Danny."

After a long moment I look away. The truth is, I always wanted Mrs. O'Leary to like me. To approve of me. To say something like, "My son is so lucky to have you."

Nothing even close to that ever came out of her mouth. Not before the accident or after it.

She never made any secret that she'd preferred Heather, Danny's previous girlfriend. Heather belonged to the same country club as them. Heather lived in a big brick house in one of the nicer neighborhoods, only a short drive from the O'Leary's own big brick house. They all went to the same church on Sunday, not because they were super into Jesus, but because that's just what people do.

There was a whole list of things that people just do, and for some reason I'd never gotten a copy of it.

Maybe it was because I'd grown up in a rundown suburban neighborhood on the older side of town. The houses were a mix of post WWII cape cods and duplexes built several decades later. None of it had aged in a way that could be described as charming.

And then there was my mother.

In second grade some neighbor kids asked why there was a mostly naked mermaid painted across the front of our garage door. A mostly naked mermaid who looked a lot like my mom. I knew better than to tell the truth, which was that my mom's dated an artist too broke for a proper canvas or muse. So I lied and said it was my aunt, and we'd put it there as a way to remember her after she'd died in an awful yachting accident.

Of course, I'm not exactly a beacon of grace and good taste myself. Usually I'm okay with who I am, but Will and his whole better-than-thou family have always had a gift for making me feel like a classless idiot.

Except that's not happening again. One hundred percent no.

Which means Will needs to go.

Now.

"Look," I say, at the same moment Will says, "You sounded great yesterday."

The words I'd been about to say dissolve on the tip of my tongue. "*What?*"

"Yesterday. Singing. At your rehearsal."

"'Hard Knock Life'?"

"No, earlier. You were singing 'Maybe.' I think that's what it's called."

"Yeah, 'Maybe,'" I confirm. "It's my favorite song in the whole show."

"I could tell. Or maybe not, but it was just incredibly..." Will pauses and shakes his head, as if searching for the right word. Or as if he knows the right word but feels weird saying it aloud. "Touching."

"Oh." I am discombobulated by this unexpected compliment. Which is not my usual response. Compliments, artistically speaking, are useless. Usually I let them ping off while acknowledging them with a rotating handful of phrases. "Thank you. How nice to hear that. Glad you enjoyed yourself."

But Will heard me singing my favorite song. The same song Stella wanted to cut from day one. Except I put my foot down. If the song went, so did I. Stella was right though. It didn't fit our crass in-your-face version of Annie. I didn't care. I sang that song with the yearning of someone wishing she was in a different life...or a different show.

I put my heart into that song. And it touched Will.

Now that same heart squeezes in a way that feels dangerous and wrong.

Suddenly it's impossible to ignore the dangerous truth that's been sitting here with us the whole time.

Even after Will goes away, nothing that happens from here on out is ever gonna be the same.

9

"Don't Tell Mama" –Cabaret

AH-OOH-GAH. Suddenly an old-fashioned car horn goes off, the sound coming from Will's hip.

"That's my cell." Will stands and digs an iPhone out of his pocket. "Someone thinks it's funny to give me ridiculous ringtones. The louder the better." He glances down at the screen, then back up at me. "If I go out into the hall to take this, are you going to lock the door behind me?"

I sigh. "No."

Will eyes me, probably checking for sincerity. Finally he nods and turns away. The moment the door shuts behind him, it's like I can finally take a deep breath again. I take several, trying to think of a way to get rid of Will without actually telling him to go.

Deciding some food might help me solve this conundrum, I search for sustenance. Sadly, my rainy-day Pop-Tart supply is an empty box with one half-eaten cherry tart left. After eating that in two swift bites, I turn to the freezer, finally locating a smashed box of waffles. I pop two into the toaster and then debate whether to top my waffles with Nutella or peanut butter (and by debating, I mean eating Nutella by the spoonful), when Will returns.

He carries his phone out in front of him straight armed, the same way one would hold a cross while trying to ward off a vampire. "It's your mom."

I recoil and back away, all while frantically waving my hands in the universal signal for "Get that fucking thing away from me."

Why is my mother on Will's phone? They shouldn't be talking or anywhere near each other.

Will advances ever closer, outstretched arm holding the phone.

I snatch the phone and dropkick it across the room.

No, I don't. But I want to. Or I could cover it in Nutella and toss it to the dogs.

"Mom," I say into the phone, the same way one might invoke the name of their mortal enemy as they meet for one final showdown.

"Jenna!" She's thrilled to hear my voice, totally unaware of anything else. Then, "Jenna, oh no, Jenna," and in an instant she's tragic mom. "Everyone is so upset with me, and I don't know why, because I did what they told me, and how was I to know it wasn't the exact way they wanted it done?"

I look at Will, searching for some hint of what's happened, but he studiously looks in the other direction.

Okay then.

"Mom, what happened?" Of all the words in the English language, these three strung together in this order are my least favorite. But when my mother is in the midst of a crisis—and they arise semiregularly, spaced roughly six months or so apart—she is all sorrow and no reason. It's always, "How was I to know?" Or, "Who could have seen that coming?" Her favorite, though, is, "I don't understand why these sorts of things always happen to me."

"Jenna, I'm afraid you're going to be very mad at me too," Mom says now.

And that's new. Because Mom's schemes have not actually touched my life in a very long time. But they're not only touching me. Mom is on Will's phone. Which suddenly strikes me as odd.

Huh?

I look at the phone screen. It says *Mom*. His, of course. Which means that his mother called Will, and then somehow the phone was passed to my own mother.

Will's mother and my mother are in the same room.

Horror-movie violins screech in my head as the dots finish connecting and I realize the worst of it. Danny must be close—I can't imagine Mrs. O'Leary being far from her newly awoken son. Which means my mom is near Danny.

Oh God, what did she do?

I sit down. "Tell me, Mom."

"You sound upset. Like you've got a headache. Did I catch you at a bad time? Because, I can—"

I glance at Will, painfully aware he's listening. So instead of pounding the phone against the table while pretending it's Mom's head, I take a deep breath. Then calmly, "Mom, remember that time we didn't talk for almost three months? This time it will be six."

The three-month freeze came after Mom decided I absolutely had to attend my ten-year high school reunion. She even went so far as to give the main coordinator (some chipper Kerry) my phone number. After that I boycotted Mom's calls. To say it upset my mother is an understatement on par with declaring that Stephen Sondheim has written some pretty good songs. She wept when I finally answered, begged my forgiveness, and swore she'd never overstep like that again.

But I've always known it was only a matter of time, and her next words confirm it.

"Okay, okay, at least let me start at the beginning. When I found out about Danny, I sent over a little gift. Nothing big, of course. Just a card, though I had a hard time finding one. *Congratulations* didn't seem quite right, and obviously he didn't need to get well soon, not anymore, now did he? I finally found one that said, 'You're moving on up in the world.' I think it might've been meant for a work promotion. Though, are you meant to give someone a card for that? It wouldn't occur to me, but I suppose it's a nice thought."

"So you sent him a card," I nudge, not wanting to remain lost in the minutiae of greeting card etiquette.

"A card, yes. And well, some of our bathing blocks. An assortment really, because people can be very touchy about scents, you know. Can you believe some people don't like florals? Isn't that strange? I mean, it takes all types, I guess—"

"Mom!"

"Jenna, stop pushing me. Do you need to use the bathroom or something? Because if you do, I don't mind waiting."

"No, I don't need to use the bathroom. I want to know what happened after you sent the card and soap."

"*Bathing blocks*, sweetheart. I told Allie to send you some, but she refused. Said you wouldn't appreciate the gesture. And well, you know I don't like to take sides, but she might have a point—"

"Mom, please." I nearly sob the words. She's broken me. She always does.

"Oh, all right. I'll send you some bathing blocks, baby. You shoulda told me before you were interested. I'll even put them in a nice little gift bag like I did for Danny. Men never appreciate those things, but you can't leave a gift just wrapped in a plastic shopping bag. Anyway, I left the gift at the house yesterday, or was it two days ago?"

"I couldn't say."

"Well, the day after I left the gift, Danny's brother, Will—you remember, Will, don't you?"

"Mom, he's at this moment standing here in my apartment. I'm talking to you on his phone." The man in question has wandered slightly farther from me, now staring out the windows.

"Jenna, I didn't ask if you can see him. I asked if you *remembered* him. Anyway, Danny's brother, Will, called me. He wanted to thank me for the kind gift and mentioned how very much Danny enjoyed the soap. "

"And he asked for my contact information," I guess.

"Well, yes," she admits. "But I told him I couldn't give out your phone number. I remembered how much you didn't like that. But your address...I figured he'd send you a note. I mean, how could I have

73

known that he would get on an airplane that very same day? You can't be mad at me for that, Jenna."

I press my forehead to the table, the place where my head has slowly sunk. "Mom, let's get to the point, okay?"

"Well, since Danny liked the soap so much, I figured I'd drop a few more off. I couldn't remember if I'd put one of the lavenders into the gift I'd left. I thought he might like to give it a sniff. Now I was simply going to drop it at the house, but when I got there, this very nice girl opened the door. I guess she's one of his caretakers. Very pretty girl. Sweet as pie too. Dimples when she smiled. If I were a man, I'd fall at the feet of every girl with dimples who smiled at me. There's something about those little cheek dents—"

"Oh for God's sake!" I hear this in the background in a tone I remember so well it sends an actual chill down my spine that snaps me up into perfect posture. A scuffling sound follows, interspersed with:

"I was talking!"

"Give it to me, you idiot woman. It's my phone."

"I was in the middle of a sentence. And now I don't even remember what it was, but interrupting is very rude—"

"Don't talk to me about rude! You barged into my son's room."

"I was invited!"

There's a grunt, a thump, and a long pause before I hear someone delicately clear her throat. Then, "Hello, Jenna. I was going to let your mother sort this out, but time is of the essence, and I simply cannot stand here another moment while she makes incredibly stupid remarks and utterly fails to reach the point of her story."

I say nothing. The phone is in my hand, held away from my ear, but I can still hear her clearly. Mrs. O'Leary has one of those piercing voices. Each and every word comes out crisper than a newly printed dollar bill.

"Jenna? Hello? Are you there?"

Still I say nothing.

I am eighteen and powerless again.

I am so filled with angry words that they clump up together and not one of them can get through.

I am sweaty and short of breath, as if the monster who lives under my bed climbed beneath the covers with me and demanded a cuddle.

A hand connects with mine. Warm where my own is icy.

It's Will. Of course it's Will. And for a moment it's almost like he's offering comfort as his hand settles over my own. But then he peels my fingers away from the phone until it's back in his own hand. His warmth and the phone are gone. He doesn't retreat to the hallway. Instead, he sits down at the table, places the phone face up between us, and presses the Speaker button.

"This is ridiculous. I can see the call hasn't disconnected. Can you simply say hello, Jenna? It won't kill you." Mrs. O'Leary's voice comes out in angry staccato bursts. "I really hoped you'd changed. Grown. I prefer to believe the best of everyone, but you are as silly and selfish as ever."

"How dare you! That's my daughter!" my mother squawks in the background.

"Oh, I give you full credit for her character. I'm sure you taught her everything you—"

"Mom, that's enough," Will cuts in.

"Will." Amazing the way her voice softens with that one word. "I didn't realize you had your phone back."

He folds his hands, again weaving his fingers together. Watching him I wonder if this is part of his process, just like I press two fingers to the hollow at the base of my throat before stepping onto stage. It centers me, focusing all my thoughts on the performance.

"I put you on speakerphone, Mom. If you could do the same with your phone, then we can all be on the same page together. I know you're eager to get this all cleared up."

"That's true," Mrs. O'Leary admits somewhat begrudgingly, but cannot resist adding, "Although there wouldn't be a problem if she'd stayed away from Danny."

"How was I to know you were telling him a pack of lies?" Mom jumps in again, even though I am sending her silent brain waves, asking her to just this once hold her fucking tongue. "You're lucky I was quick enough to catch on. I coulda corrected him, and then you'd really be in trouble, having to explain why you weren't telling him the truth."

"How dare you!" Mrs. O'Leary shoots back. "We *are* telling him the truth. Selectively. Bit by bit instead of all at once. Not that it's any of your business, but we have a mental health professional working with us as we carefully bring Danny up to date. He doesn't even remember the accident. For us to tell him that over twelve years of his life are gone—"

Her voice breaks. Mrs. O'Leary goes suddenly and disconcertingly silent.

I stare at the phone, not wanting to see Will or for him to notice the tears in my eyes.

It's not Mrs. O'Leary being upset—it's the thought of Danny. I can see so clearly the look on his face when he was confused. Eyebrows drawn together, mouth pursed. Like a little boy trying not to cry.

"Here, sweetheart," I hear my mom say softly, and I know with 100 percent certainty that this whole time she's been digging in her purse until she unearthed some tattered old tissue from the bottom of it.

"Thank you," Mrs. O'Leary answers with a sniff. After a slight pause, she adds, "This doesn't look clean."

"It's a little smooshed from being in my purse."

"It has a piece of what appears to be..." There's a sound of revulsion. Not a gag. Mrs. O'Leary's too refined to lose her lunch like us commoners do. It's more like an audible shiver. "There's chewed peppermint gum wrapped up in it."

Will's eyes meet mine from across the table. I expect him to look disgusted. Or tragic, that his mother is being forced to suffer such fools. Instead his shoulders shake with suppressed laughter. And suddenly the whole thing seems so absurd. A little hiccup of laughter escapes me as Mrs. O'Leary and my mother bicker about the cleanliness of the tissue.

"Well, here, let me take that part out."

"I'd rather you—"

"Look, here's another tissue. No, I insist you take it. Go on now."

Stop it, I mouth to Will, pointing a finger at him.

He blinks. Swallows. And with obvious effort, pushes his face back into a neutral expression.

"This one also has gum in it!" Mrs. O'Leary exclaims.

And that's it. We die. Any control we had is gone. Tears stream down my face, while Will clutches his side, nearly falling out of his chair. The dogs, unsure what's happening, bark madly.

"What is going on?" Mrs. O'Leary demands, becoming increasingly shrill until finally Will chokes something out while I shush the dogs.

There's something about laughing like that with somebody. In some ways it's almost more intimate than sex.

I'm watching Will as that last word flashes through my mind. He glances at me.

Our gazes catch and hold, but this time it isn't shared laughter.

It's almost like the charged moment before lightning strikes.

10

"Mama Will Provide" – Once on This Island

Or maybe I'm misreading it.

Will sniffs the air, frowns, sniffs again, and then leans back to look under the table. I do the same, and together we discover Pippin horking up what appears to be large chunks of toaster waffles. Stupidly, I'd left the box on the counter, close enough to the edge for Pippin to jump up and grab it.

Now the remains of the waffles are on the floor, along with lots of slimy doggie digestive juices. As I watch, Pippin gives it a sniff and then, apparently liking what he smells, takes a nibble. Clapping a hand over my mouth, I fight not to gag.

"Enough of this nonsense," Mrs. O'Leary declares, unaware of the horrors being enacted on this end of the conversation. "In a nutshell, your mother told Danny that Jenna's performing in a local production of *Annie*."

"She *is* performing in a local production of Annie," my mom interrupts.

I shake my head. I can't tell if Mom is purposely baiting Mrs. O'Leary or if she's merely oblivious. Oh, who am I kidding? She's oblivious.

"Which is true. They say stick to the truth as much as possible when lying, and that's what I did."

Yep. Oblivious. And pleased with herself as well.

Meanwhile, I watch as Will picks Pippin up and tucks him beneath one arm like a football. With Pippin secured, he grabs some paper towels and dish soap off my counter and with a few efficient swipes has the whole mess beneath the table cleaned away.

I am so grateful for him taking care of it that I do not stare at the strip of skin above the waistband of his jeans that's exposed when he leans over. I glance *briefly* and then heroically look away.

Mrs. O'Leary's hits back at Mom again. "Danny is now determined to see Jenna's show. How perfect. Especially since his doctor told him earlier today he should start taking small excursions out into the world. That it would, in fact, be good for him! How am I supposed to tell him he cannot go to this show without admitting he'd have to travel all the way to California for the pleasure, since this is where your daughter currently resides?"

"Seems simple enough to tell him another lie," my mom answers. "You already told him Jenna was out selling bathing blocks—"

"I'm doing what?" I interrupt, shocked into speaking.

"Oh, you are there," Mrs. O'Leary says with her snide levels cranked to their max. "How nice of you to join the conversation. Yes, the soap salesperson was my idea. Danny wanted to know where you were, and we said you were out of town on business. Then he wished to know what sort of business, and, well, as your mother said, it's best to keep lies as close to the truth as possible. I was going to make you a flight attendant. That would certainly fit your skill set. But I didn't know how long we could keep such a story afloat when you failed to reappear. Then I spotted that horrible soap. Danny already knew it was connected to your family, so it was the obvious answer. We told him you were out, desperately trying to convince various stores and boutiques to carry your soap."

"Bathing blocks," I interject. I refuse to be a make-believe soap salesperson.

Mrs. O'Leary sniffs. "I don't really care. Danny believes it, and that is all that interests me. To explain why you haven't called, we told him your business is failing. Again very believable. Your current trip is do or die, and because we are very sensitive to that, we have not yet told you about Danny so that you can fully focus on making those sales."

Will shakes his head. Clearly he did not cosign this little tale. For some reason this comforts me, and it's the only reason I don't tell Mrs. O'Leary to fuck off.

Well, I don't tell her using those exact words. Instead, I do it the polite way. "Look, eventually he's gonna realize I'm not showing up and you'll have to tell him there was no business trip and there is no show. Pull the Band-Aid off fast. That's my advice."

"Oh, is that your advice? That's very helpful. Thank you for that." This isn't said sarcastically. I'm sure Mrs. O'Leary considers sarcasm a rhetorical device for lesser people. Instead her delivery is so clipped and snotty she almost sounds a little bit British. Like she's doing an impression of Maggie Smith as the countess on Downton Abbey, demanding to know, "What's a weekend?"

"And I have some advice for you: grow up. You are able bodied and healthy. Two things my son cannot claim. He's had too much time stolen from him, and I will not allow him to be set back any further by your selfishness." She takes a deep breath, and I wait for her to rip into me again, but instead she abruptly changes gears. "Now, Will is going to make you a generous financial offer."

Will frowns. "Mom—"

"No." She cuts him off. "I don't want to hear it, Will. We agreed. If Jenna won't do the decent thing on her own, we dangle a cash reward. Clearly we have reached that point."

"Okay, wait a minute." It's unbelievable how quickly this is spiraling out of control. I open my mouth to tell Mrs. O'Leary that I can't be bribed and have every intention of this phone conversation being our last. Or alternately that, of course I'm going to come see Danny, although on my own terms. But instead I hear myself say, "How much money are we talking about here?"

"I was wondering that too," Mom helpfully chirps.

"Ha!" That one staccato huff of victory and disgust from Mrs. O'Leary. "I told you, Will. It was always money she wanted. Right from the very beginning."

I look up at Will to find that we are no longer on the same team. He is glaring at me, and his jaw has hardened to granite. The iceman returneth.

It's surprising how much that stings. I bite my lip to keep from blurting out that I'm sorry.

And I am sorry. Of course I don't want to be the type of person who says things like, "What's in it for me?" I want to be good and kind and altruistic. Well, as long as it doesn't get in the way of my nap time.

But Mrs. O'Leary thinking the worst of me, makes me want to take her expectations and lower them even further. And if I can walk away with a hundred or so extra dollars in hand while doing so, well then, all the better.

"You and Will can hash out the numbers once we finish this call." Clearly she is above the dirty work of haggling. "We're almost done. All I need to know is how many people are in the cast and what it will cost to transport them here."

"Mom, no." Will raises his voice for the first time. "That is absolutely out of the question."

"You are totally bonkers, lady," I add.

Mrs. O'Leary ignores us both. "Your mother said the show was Annie. I assume that means children will have to travel with their parents, which will unfortunately increase costs, but there's nothing we can do about that. And the director must be in attendance as well, I suppose. I'd prefer to limit any other backstage personnel. We can find people locally to move sets. I've already spoken with Heather earlier today. She says—"

"You don't mean Heather Bennett, do you?" I ask.

I don't want to ask. I don't even want to remember her name. But the fact that she's still in Danny's life makes me a little sick.

"I do mean Heather Bennett," Mrs. O'Leary answers, sounding

smug, because she knows it got under my skin and that's a victory for her side. "Although it's not Bennett anymore. It's—"

"Mom," Will interrupts. "I thought you wanted to stop going off on tangents. So let's focus. You called Heather. I assume about using the new auditorium at Niven?"

There's a sniff in response. Mrs. O'Leary is clearly not happy with being reprimanded by her son.

"Yes," she says at last. "Heather, as you know, owes me a favor, and she agreed to get us the space regardless of how many arms need twisting. Of course, the principal and school board will have the final say, but you know she has sway with them, and after all we've donated to the school, it would be shocking for them to say no. She did think it might be a nice gesture if a few Niven children might be allowed to participate as orphan extras, and I don't see any reason why that would be a problem on your end."

"Actually, it would be a huge problem. Our Annie doesn't have any kids," I say.

I don't know why I offer this information, when our version of Annie is not going on the road. Nor will it be performed at one of the snootiest private schools in western New York. If people here were shocked, then having it performed at a school that starts grooming kids for Ivy League colleges in kindergarten...Heads would explode. Mrs. O'Leary's included.

Ooooohhh. Suddenly there's a devil sitting on my shoulder. It whispers in my ear, "How much would you pay to see that?"

That same devil takes control of mouth. "Adults play all the roles, and certain changes were made to make it more relevant to a modern audience."

"Hmph," Mrs. O'Leary says, obviously annoyed that she can no longer criticize it for being pedestrian. "And I suppose you're Annie?"

"I am."

Again, "Hmph." Not impressed. Then, as if it's all decided, "Fine. Talk to your cast. See how many people want to go. Again, we'll pay for travel and one night's stay as well, I suppose. I'll host a dinner. Everything else will have to be their own responsibility. If you lose a few people, I'm sure we can easily replace them. We'll schedule it for this Saturday. That's four days. I'll need a final head count by Thursday at the very latest."

Will reaches for his phone, as if he can put his hand through it and keep her from steamrolling us all. "Mom, hold up."

"Yeah," I add in, suddenly panicked, as if Mrs. O'Leary has the power to snap her fingers and instantly transport me back home. "I didn't agree to this."

"You will." She says it with the confidence of someone who can see into the future. "Will, talk to her. Figure it out. With a red-eye flight, I should see you both bright and early tomorrow morning."

And she hangs up. As if it's a done deal.

11

"Hey Big Spender" –Sweet Charity

"Ten thousand dollars," Will says out of the blue.

This is after we've sat for a while saying nothing, catching our breath and replaying that phone conversation in our heads.

"Ten thousand is how much I'm supposed to offer you."

"Holy shit," I say, because *holy shit*. That's a lot of money. I can't help but imagine it in my bank account. I could pay off my truck. I could take a several-months-long vacation from my customer service job. Ten Gs would buy a whole lot of napping time.

But it's ridiculous. Ten grand is so much money. It's insane.

Something else occurs to me.

They keep saying, "Danny wants to see you." Like that's it. Like he simply needs to see my face. Hear my voice. And then I'm free to go. The end.

But you don't give someone ten grand to stop by, say hi, reminisce a little, and then pull out with an "Oh, look at the time. It's been real. Let's do this again real soon." For all those zeroes, it's gonna be more than a one-night show. For that kind of cash, you better like your part because you're gonna be playing it for a long time.

"Ten thousand in exchange for what exactly?" I ask now, because that amount suddenly seems less like a windfall and more like I'd earn every penny.

Will frowns, and his eyes slide away from mine. He looks distinctly uncomfortable. "Well," he says, and that's it. Nothing else follows.

"Well, does Danny think I've spent the past decade and change sitting by his bedside—that is, when I'm not crisscrossing the country desperately trying to sell soap—just holding his hand and hoping he'll wake up?"

"Not exactly," Will hedges. He focuses on his own hands curled into fists in front of him, as he admits softly, "Danny thinks it's been only a year."

"A year that I've been selling soap?"

"No." And at last Will looks up at me, his face haughty and frozen like his mother's. "A year since his accident."

Damn. That's what Mrs. O'Leary meant about easing Danny back into the world. It's totally nuts. No wonder Will looks so uncomfortable. It's difficult to take the moral high ground on this one.

Oh, but he's still clinging to it anyway.

"It sounds odd," Will starts.

"Odd? Yeah, okay, we'll go with odd. That's not an understatement or anything."

Will abruptly stands. Scrubs his hands through his hair. "You weren't there when Danny woke up. He was confused. He had no memory of the accident. Or even the days before it. For him it was January thirteenth. He was planning on driving up to Niagara Falls with you."

My hand comes up to my mouth, unbidden. The way my heart jumped, it could've popped right out between my teeth.

January 13 was the day we got married. But Will doesn't know that. No one knew about it except me and Danny. We were gonna tell our parents that weekend. But then he had the accident. And now if Danny thinks it's January 13, even he doesn't remember we got married.

With a shake of my head, I force myself to focus on Will. He's pacing, his long legs turning my galley kitchen into a runway.

"We had to explain the accident. And that he'd been asleep. Danny thought it was a few days. A week at the most. 'No, it was longer than that,' we said. 'How much longer?' he asked. And none of us could answer. My parents were there. I was beside them. But not one of us said a word. How could we tell him he wasn't twenty anymore? That he had missed an entire decade of his life?"

I close my eyes, imagining myself into that room. Trying to find words to tell someone that while he slept, the world kept going on without him. I don't know if I could do it.

"Okay, I get it. But can't he see that everyone looks older?"

Will shrugs, looking uncomfortable. "He only mentioned me."

"You?" I ask. I know exactly what Danny must've mentioned, but I want to hear Will say it.

A barely there yet unmistakable blush warms Will's face. "He wanted to know when I..." His eyes practically beg me to put him out of his misery and finish the statement.

But instead of admitting that Will has become a deliciously marbled piece of prime USDA beef, I blink innocently. "Cut your hair so short? You did used to wear it longer, right?"

Like someone is cranking the heat, his blush gets another shade darker. "He wanted to know if I'd been using his weight bench," Will finally blurts out.

"Ooooooh. Okay." I squint at him, like I'm struggling to notice these changes that Danny referred to. "I guess you're more buff. But it's not like that would be the first thing I'd notice when coming out of a coma."

Liar. I don't even know why I'm lying. What would be the harm in saying, "I've also noticed how amazingly stacked you've become. If possible, could I lightly run the tips of my fingers over your ab muscles? Just once? It probably sounds weirder than it actually will be."

Yeah, that's why I'm lying.

I steer our conversation away from Will's new swole status.

"He's gonna notice more than that. Like phones. Phones have changed in the last ten years! And the president has changed. And slang. There's all new slang. And dance moves. He missed twerking, and now it's pretty much done. And Gangnam style. There are so many pop culture jokes that are gonna go right over his head."

"Yeah, jokes going over his head. That's pretty much same for Danny."

Oh, right. That's true. Danny was that guy who would laugh with everyone else and then wait two beats before admitting, "I don't get it."

"You have to tell him the truth," I say, certain of this.

"*We* have to tell him the truth, Jenna. Slowly, we have to help him understand how things have changed, but that we're still here for him."

"Why do I have to lie? You and your parents. You're family. Of course you're gonna be there, but I'm not gonna stick around and pretend we'll go back to the way things were."

Will's jaw hardens. "You'll need to stay for however long it takes. Until Danny is mentally and physically able to handle the truth."

And there it is. Ten grand to give them my life for an indeterminate amount of time. When you look at it that way, they must think I'll come pretty cheap. I stand. It's impossible to be properly indignant while sitting down.

"Stick around and pretend I'm eighteen again. Is that right? And in love with Danny. Of course. And what about the baby? Is your mother going to borrow one and pretend it's mine? Or maybe she already has? OH!" I clutch my head and reel around with the jolt of a new revelation. "What about sex? Does that money include making sure Danny can still perform? Or is there some sort of bonus structure for extras?"

Will folds his arms over his chest. Once again the calm one, watching as I fly off the handle. "Don't try and turn this around. You need a payout to do the decent thing. Admit it."

"Do the decent thing? I'm sorry. I don't speak your coded language.

Does that mean I'm only on the hook for hand jobs?"

Will's jaw clenches. "Jenna," he says, a warning in his voice.

But I'm not stopping. "You said you'd fly to Antarctica to get him ice. You wouldn't come to the California desert to get him laid?"

That does it. Will's fist finds the table and gives it a resounding thump. "No one said anything about sex. You're the one bringing that into this."

"Hello. The last time I saw Danny, we were boning pretty regularly. What reason could I give for not going at it again after I've supposedly been waiting a whole year for him to wake up?"

"Tell him you're worried it'll be too much for him. He's still weak. He may not even want to—" Will's eyes sweep up and then back down my body. He swallows. Takes a breath. And regroups. "If it's that much of a concern for you, we'll make sure you aren't ever alone together for too long. Unless..."

"Unless what?"

He sighs. A full-on, real-person sigh. "Unless you decide to pick things back up with him—"

"WOAH! What? Are you..." I sputter before finding words again. "Pick things back up? I don't think I'm still eighteen! And...and you know better than anyone where Danny and I left things. If the accident hadn't happened—"

"But it did," Will helpfully inserts.

As if I'm confused on the details. As if I don't wake up every day remembering that I'm currently living on the timeline where I goaded my boyfriend into a coma.

"I know it did!" I yell, my voice cracking. The dogs bark again, but I merely yell louder to be heard over them. "But if it hadn't happened, we would've been broken up by the end of the week."

"Yeah, and what about the wedding vows you exchanged with him? You wanna pretend they never happened either?" Will shouts.

I stare at him, unable to believe he knows. That he must have always known. The dogs settle down while the room spins around me. All this time, Will knew Danny and I were married. He could've used it and he didn't.

"How?" I finally ask.

Will shoves his hands into his pockets. "Danny told me the night before. He couldn't hold it in anymore. You gave him permission to tell the dog, he said. So if he told the dog while I was in the room, and if I just happened to overhear..."

I roll my eyes. Danny had been dying to announce our upcoming nuptials. I was less sure and begged him to keep it quiet, to let me get used to the idea. But knowing he wasn't great at keeping secrets, I'd said he could tell his dog. Figured it would act as a sort of pressure release. Seeing as how the dog was twelve years old, I'd been fairly certain Bruno would take that secret to his grave.

"I told him not to go through with it," Will adds softly. "You were both too young."

"We didn't," I say. It comes out of my mouth like truth. "We chickened out at the last minute. Danny tore up the license, and we threw the pieces over the falls." It didn't happen that way, but it could've. But why lie to Will about it all these years later? Why lie at all? I guess because it's all complicated enough, I'd rather not add a marriage that was nothing more than Danny and me playing pretend.

Or I lie because of the way Will's looking at me now. Like he's recalculating the complicated equations that bind Danny and me together.

"Does that change things?" I ask, wanting him to admit it. "Am I a slightly less awful person for having walked out on my boyfriend instead of my husband?"

Will shakes his head. "I don't know. Maybe. Yeah." He scrubs his hands over his face, and when he looks at me again, he's slightly chagrined. "I've spent all these years thinking of you as Danny's wife."

I bite my lip before I can ask how often he's thought of me.

Suddenly the door bangs open, the dogs lose it once more, and

Stella—staggering beneath the weight of three black garbage bags—makes her entrance.

Dropping the bags, she falls to her knees and throws her arms out. The dogs surround her, licking, jumping, and in Pippin's case actually shivering with delight. Once every dog's ears and/or belly has been rubbed, Stella pops back up.

"Guess who brought lunch!" Her gaze sweeps the room and lands on Will. "Hello. Who are you? Are you single? I am. You look single. Want to stay for lunch? Better yet, why not join us for a Florida road trip? Me, Jenna, nine dogs, and hopefully...you."

Will blinks. Frowns. Looks to me as if I should answer for him.

"Actually, he was just leaving," I tell Stella, fully expecting Will to insist on staying.

But instead he nods, grabs his sweatshirt, and heads toward the door.

"Wait," I call out.

"I'll be here waiting for all the juicy details," Stella chirps as I rush past.

I catch Will in the hallway. "Will, this isn't settled. So don't think...I mean, I'm not..." I stop, uncertain of what I'm trying to say. Or even what I'm going to do.

"Why don't we take a few hours to think things over. Okay?" He digs in his back pocket and pulls out his wallet.

For a moment I'm convinced he's about to hand me a crisp twenty-dollar bill as a down payment on that cool ten grand.

But he holds out a business card instead. "My cell's listed. Call me."

I take the card and shove it into my pocket. "And if I don't call?"

This earns a wry smile. "My mother would say not to take no for an answer. But if you call and say no..." He shrugs. "I'll assume that's your final answer."

And with that Will walks away.

I stand there unable to believe this is it. I am certain he'll turn around. He has to. There's no way he's leaving without playing his trump card.

But he does. I watch him go down the hall, then down the stairs, and presumably into his car and away. I stand there and wait. And wait. And wait. But Will doesn't return.

He's just...gone. Gone without once mentioning the day of the accident.

Will was there that day. He saw the whole thing. He knows it's my fault.

Even worse, he heard the promise I made to Danny all those years ago.

The sun has been up for hours. It's another hot desert day. And yet I can't help but shiver.

I wrap my arms around myself as time folds in on itself.

I was so miserable back then. And trapped. It seemed like something drastic would have to happen to set me free.

And then it did.

12

"Tell Me It's Not True" – Blood Brothers

"WHOOOOO!"

I hate-watched as the three girls, clad in nothing but UGGs and string bikinis, clung to the top of an air mattress as it wobbled down the snow-covered hill. Their *whooos* crescendoed and then shrilly peaked as the air mattress, half-deflated and patched with duct tape, finally buckled, tossing them into the snow. Instead of rushing over to help the girls, the boys, in a lower bass-baritone register, *whooooo'd* right back at them.

Whooo was the rallying cry for those at the peak of their youth. It was a more mature and, let's admit it, drunker version of childhood's innocent *wheeeeee*.

But not for me. I'd been brought down mid-whooo. Two pink lines on a Dollar Tree pregnancy test ended my fun before it had barely begun.

"Jenna, c'mon. What are you doing?" Danny plucked a can of Labatt Blue from my hand and tipped it upside down, pouring the beer into the snow.

"Alcohol abuse!" yelled one of Danny's idiot friends.

Danny chucked the can at him, then looked back at me. I watched as he struggled to focus. He was all gung ho on me being the perfect little baby maker, while he was getting blasted per usual.

I shoved Danny, mad at him for putting me in this position. He'd promised it'd be okay. That we'd be in this together. That was a week ago. One week and already returned to his regular fun life, while I was left on the sidelines watching.

"You suck," I told the guy I loved, and then I exited stage right. Of course, I couldn't really exit because we were in the middle of nowhere. Still I committed, wading through the snow toward a destination only known as away from Danny. At least moving warmed me up.

"*You* suck," Danny yelled at my back.

I turned to give him the finger, but he was already stomping in the other direction, heading toward the bikini girls. All three shivered and squealed about the cold, but not one of them rushed to find her coat.

I hated them. I wanted to be them. Two weeks ago I was.

It didn't help that one was Danny's ex. Fucking Heather.

Whatever.

I didn't have a bikini, but even this early in the pregnancy my already generous boobs had started to get plumper. I unzipped the front of my jacket and tugged the V-neck fleece beneath it until the top edge of my bra appeared. Va-va-voom. Cleavage.

I glanced back once more to see Heather hanging on Danny's arm. Swinging my hips (not easy while hiking through three feet of snow), I headed straight toward Danny's friends and laughed loudly, flirted outrageously, and sneaked sips of their beer. They were happy to let me get away with it. Eventually those sips added up. I got warmer and warmer even as the sun sank lower and lower.

Somehow I ended up supervising the guys as they piled a bunch of snow in the middle of the hill, building a ramp.

"If you hit it just so, you could get some major air," one guy said, totally talking out of his ass.

"Oh wow." I gave him my best wide-eyed look of awe. "That would be so amazing."

We were about done with the ramp and ready to try it out, when the killjoy arrived.

"Drunk bus is here," Will announced from the bottom of the hill.

"Who's getting on?"

Actually, it was the delivery van for the family carpet store. Three hours ago all eight of us had piled into it, along with three coolers full of booze. As Will opened the back doors to let us out, Danny offered a half-hearted, "Hey, bro, you should stick around, take a few rides down."

"I have a big test tomorrow," Will answered, climbing into the driver's seat. Will clearly didn't mind missing out on his prime *whoooing* years.

Now that most of the booze was gone and no one could feel their toes anymore, Will's arrival was greeted with some obligatory groans, even as everyone moved swiftly toward the warm van.

"Hey, guys, wait," I called to their backs. "What about our snow ramp? Nobody got to try it!"

"Next time," one of them yelled over his shoulder.

Next time. Right.

This was a yearly ritual. It had started when Danny was in high school, years before I was in the picture, during this one Martin Luther King Jr. weekend when three feet of snow fell overnight. Danny and his friends wanted to go sledding, but every store was sold out. So someone suggested an air mattress, and another person mentioned this hill out in the middle of nowhere. Just like that, a tradition was born.

The previous year was my first time being included. After a rainy week, there was no snow, only mud. It only made the day better. I wore a bikini, slugged down five beers, and went down the hill twenty times or more.

"Look at my girl. She gets it," Danny bragged, a huge grin on his face.

And when I'd ended the day puking, he'd held my hair and rubbed my back and told me I'd been a champ. The back rubbing turned into boob rubbing, and we had sex on his bath mat so we could stay close to the toilet in case I needed to vomit again. My guy, always thinking of my needs.

Now, only one year later, and oh how things had changed.

That was nothing, though, to what another year would bring. Despite what Danny said about being "all in," I already knew that when it came to things like his annual sledding outing, he'd still go, and I'd be stuck with the baby.

A baby. Jesus. I wished he'd given me chlamydia instead. You know what no one says about chlamydia? "Well, maybe you'll feel differently once it's yours." And there was never any protestors when you went to get rid of chlamydia, was there? If I'd told Danny to expect chlamydia instead of a baby, he wouldn't have called it, "A cool adventure. Kinda like backpacking through Europe together."

This last desperate thought turned me toward the air mattress left forgotten halfway down the hill. It was in my hand as I charged up, nearly to the top, when I heard Danny call, "Jenna? Hey! What are you doing?"

I didn't bother answering.

"Jenna!" he yelled again, louder and obviously annoyed. "Come on. We're leaving."

I reached the top of hill and positioned the mattress, aiming straight at the ramp. Then without wasting any more time, I flopped onto it belly first and—

Got nowhere. It was a fucking metaphor. Danny blocked the way, his shins ending my forward momentum before I went more than a foot.

"Move." I glared up at him, awkwardly craning my neck.

"We're leaving."

Unable to argue while facedown on an air mattress, I rolled off and pushed myself to my feet.

"Great." Danny grabbed the air mattress. "Can we go now?"

He took a step, somehow thinking this was over. Like he got to call the shots and I'd trot along behind him. Like I had no other choices or options. Rage, in the form of a scream, built inside me, starting way down at my toes and boiling up until it came burning out my throat and across my tongue.

"Fuck you. Fuck you, Danny!" I shoved him, and it felt so good. No, not good, but right, like I needed to either push him or tear my own face off. I did it again. "I spent the whole day out here freezing my ass off."

Danny whirled back around, his face red. No way was he apologizing. Instead, he made it my fault. Classic Danny move. "I told you, you didn't have to come!"

"No, you told me *not* to come. 'Oh, Jenna, it won't be any fun for you.' That's what you said. Then when I spend hours making that snow ramp, you wanna leave without even trying it."

He rolled his eyes. Then he tried to play the sensible adult card. "Jenna, c'mon. It's late." But he ruined it by adding, "So stop being a bitch and let's go."

"Because you say so, right? Because you don't care about what I care about."

"You don't care about that snow ramp!" There was nothing to punch, so he kicked the air mattress for emphasis. This I knew from many many, *many* past arguments was a good sign. It meant I was winning. I pressed my advantage.

"I do care. I care deeply." I didn't. Except I did now. "Is that why you won't even try it? Because you can't ever let me have anything?"

I started crying. Usually I didn't cry this early into an argument. It was probably the pregnancy hormones. Or the cold combined with the constant misery of knowing I was pregnant and this was my life now. Crying meant I was losing, so I tried to stop. But I couldn't. Instead I cried harder. As snot rolled down my chin, I wiped it away with the back of my mitten.

Danny looked down at where Will and the rest of his friends were waiting and listening to our argument.

"Get in the van, Jenna."

He was embarrassed, and I was glad. Glad in a still sobbing sort of way. "I don't want this baby. I don't want to play mommy and daddy with some loser who dropped out of college and got a pity job from his father."

Danny reeled backward as if I'd punched him.

You spend enough time with a person, you learn their tender parts. If you love them, your job is to help guard those spots from the rest of the world. But if you love and hate them at the same time, well, then you know exactly where to stick the knife in.

We'd had bitter arguments. I'd told him he was a shitty boyfriend and that I didn't orgasm for the first three months we were together. He'd told me I was a nasty bitch when PMSing and that he hated going to my shows.

We were pulling our punches.

But not anymore.

"Don't talk to me about losers, Jenna. I've been to your house. I've met your mom and your sister and your sister's kid. My mom was right about you and your whole family—"

My head exploded. I screeched at him, a string of vowels pouring out while my fists rained upon his chest.

For him to bring HIS MOTHER into this.

I couldn't. It was too much.

Someone pulled me back, arms wrapped around me in a bear hug.

"Jenna. Danny. Let's take a breath." Will's voice in my ear. I sagged against him, suddenly drained.

"I want to go home," I cried softly.

"Yeah, okay. You can sit up front with me," Will said. He moved his arms so he wasn't holding me back but holding me up instead.

We were halfway down when Danny yelled, "Gonna make one more trip down the hill, Will. I thought Jenna was flirting with my friends, but it turns out she was making this super-special ramp for me. So I gotta try it out."

Oh, I knew this move too. It was the spiteful being the bigger person game. We'd spend an hour arguing over what movie to watch, and

97

finally I'd say, "Fine, let's watch your dumb action movie." And he'd respond, "No, I want to watch that boring indie movie you're so excited about."

"Danny, it's dark," Will said. He was right. The sun had sunk below the horizon while we were fighting.

"It's all good, bro. I'll be quick."

Will swung us both around in time to see Danny kneeling on the mattress, lurching down the hill. In the dark of East Bumfuck, only the van's headlights kept us from utter blackness. Danny was a dark blob against the white snow, streaking downward with increasing speed.

As it turned out, Danny's friend wasn't talking out his ass after all. You could indeed get some major air if you hit our snow mound the right way.

"Wh—" Danny hollered. It sounded like the beginning of a *whoo*, but it cut off abruptly as he flew up up UP. Into the air. He lifted so high. Impossibly so. The mattress rising with him. Both airborne and then they separated. For a moment there was only Danny hanging above the horizon, his form a dark shadow against the last few streaks of pink in the sky. He seemed to float there forever, like he'd gained wings and learned to fly.

Except, of course, he didn't.

I didn't see him fall. One second he was up, and the next he disappeared. A thud. A crack. A grunt. Then Will tore away from me, rushing toward that awful trio of sounds, and I stumbled behind him. The hill had gotten slippery—the top layer of snow had melted and refrozen, leaving everything slick. My feet slid out from under me. I landed hard and sat there, staring up, surprised to see a small sliver of moon shining down.

For a moment, I was certain I'd been the one who went down the hill. That I flew into the sky and that was why I was lying there.

I wanted it to be true. I wanted this to be the way it happened.

But then I heard someone yelling, "Call 911!" And girls crying and calling Danny's name.

Pushing myself to my feet, my legs somehow both stiff and trembling, I stumbled toward the clump of people.

"Nobody touch him," Will ordered, his arms spread out, physically holding everyone back.

"Danny!" Heather lurched forward, and Will grabbed her.

I moved around them and looked down at Danny. He lay half on his side, one of his legs bent back at an odd angle. But otherwise, he looked fine, almost like he was sleeping. Except his breathing was wrong. Loud and labored. Like he was scared. Or hurt.

"Danny." I sank into the snow beside him.

"Don't touch him!" Will said again, like he was in charge. Like he knew anything about what Danny needed.

"He'll think he's alone," I said. "I'm just gonna hold his hand."

I took it gently, making sure not to move his arm or any other part of him. He wasn't wearing gloves. He must've taken them off already. I ripped off my own mittens. The second one stuck. My fingers were stiff with cold. My body shook with exhaustion and anger and the shock of Danny lying here in the snow. I ripped the mitten off with my teeth. Then gently, carefully, I grasped his hand and sandwiched it between both of mine.

I choked back a sob. I couldn't fall apart. Not yet.

"Danny, I'm here." I leaned in closer. "I'm here with you, and I am not going anywhere."

13

"Chiquitita" -Mamma Mia!

"Wow," Stella says after I catch her up. "So *Annie* lives on after all."

"No, it doesn't," I snap back at her. "Have you listened to nothing I've said? I'm not going home."

We're in my living room, surrounded by plastic moving boxes. I graduated from the cardboard kind years ago. Even though I've told Stella multiple times that I don't need help, that I have a system, she keeps shoving stuff into those boxes. Finally, after the third time watching me empty out a box she'd declared "ready to roll," Stella grumbled something about "getting it" and collapsed onto the couch.

Now she adds, "But then why are you packing?"

I roll my eyes. "Because I was evicted."

"Oh right. I forgot that part. Although I'm sure I could talk to Uncle Frank—"

I wave a hand at Stella. "Nope. It's time to move on."

"Okay then. And where are you moving to? I sorta got the feeling you weren't really feeling the Florida plan."

I pause in the middle of taping up a box and send Stella a weak smile.

"Don't say a word. I get it. And honestly, I had a moment of clarity the other day. I think your talent is what messed up my vision of *Annie*. It's supposed to be so bad, it's good. But you're just too good, you know?"

"Oh, okay, I guess," I say, surprised.

"Yeah." Stella nods like it's settled. "So what are you going to do with the ten grand?"

Carefully packing my stack of books into the bottom of a box and then covering them with my couch blanket, I glance over at Stella. "Um, nothing. Did you also miss the part where I said I'm not going?"

"Jenna, c'mon. You've got no other plans. Why not head home for a few months and collect the cash?"

"I *do* have other plans."

"Really. Wow. Tell me more."

I grab a new box with a bit more force than necessary. "I'm going...somewhere else."

Stella snickers.

Trying to recover my dignity, I add, "Anyway, the whole financial bribe is a little icky, isn't it?"

"No, it's not!" Stella replies without hesitation. "It's a lovely gesture. Like a thank you note with a little gift card inside. Now let's pretend spend your money."

"You mean the money that I'm not getting, wouldn't take anyway, and absolutely, positively will be unable to spend anywhere that doesn't accept imaginary currency?"

"You're a real downer sometimes."

"Okay, fine." I relent. "If I suddenly had an extra ten grand in my checking account I'd..." Chewing my lower lip, I ponder the question. "I'd leave it there. Or open a savings account. It'd be a nice rainy-day fund. In case the truck got smashed up or—"

"JENNA!" Stella's screech startles the dogs who, to my relief, have settled down since her arrival. "You're supposed to use a sudden cash flux to change your life, not continue on with the same crappy one you've already got."

"My life isn't crappy. My life is fine. Why are you so upset about this?"

Stella, still agitated, takes several deep breaths. "You know when

101

we did that workshop for those high school students? I was really struck by how good you were with the kids. They all rolled their eyes at me, and I wanted to smack their heads together."

"They rolled their eyes at me too," I interject before Stella can get too carried away.

"Yeah, but you didn't care, and somehow you won them over and they were hanging on your every word. I was amazed. Like what? Is this Jenna? My Jenna, working with these nasty teenagers like she's some kind of pro? Now I don't want to say you're not a people person, but...you're always holding something back. Except when you're on stage, of course. But in real life, you have this sort of tourist mentality. Like you know you're not gonna be around that long."

"Um, hello? I do have feelings."

"Shush. I'm getting to the good part. You have a gift on the stage, but also maybe sharing your love of theater with the next generation. I could really see you getting a degree to teach or something. You know, instead of your work from home, helping people on the phone purchase expensive furniture and vases gig. A job, I might add, that you couldn't care less about."

"Stella, I like not caring. It's a benefit, not a bug." I seal a box and carry it to the front door, where it joins the stack.

Stella follows me. "I don't believe you. You do theater because you love it, but it's the only thing you love. Life isn't supposed to be that way. You're allowed to love lots of things. And people too. That's how you have a nice life. And Jenna, you deserve a nice life. Go ahead. Find a mirror and say it to yourself. 'I deserve a life. A nice one.'"

I snort. "Maybe you should get a degree in psychology. Since you so enjoy digging in my head."

Stella stands up a little straighter. "I've actually taken some online courses. I think I have a gift for it." She darts a glance at me. "Just like you had a gift with those kids."

Shit. She's like a dog with a bone. Or like Pippin, eating and regurgitating the same shit over and over again. "You're reading too much into an afternoon. I didn't connect with them. I don't even remember their names."

"You don't remember anyone's name. That doesn't mean you didn't connect."

"Okay, fine," I say, hoping she'll let it go. And also because, Stella's right. I did connect with those kids. And the rest of the day I had this stupid sort of high. Like a bubble of hope in my chest.

I wouldn't call my life crappy, but there are times when it seems slightly inadequate. That feeling has been growing lately, and even though I never mentioned it to Stella, I have been flirting with the idea of other opportunities.

A few months back I received a long letter written by an older woman who began by apologizing in advance for any typos, because her eyes weren't what they once had been. She'd lived in the same small Texas town her whole life, and after her husband died (God bless his soul) ten years ago, she'd made it her mission to spend the money he'd made (in oil, of course) on building up the arts in her town. Especially the theater arts.

The theater company she'd started had grown, and she'd recently found an old Methodist church (which had been deconsecrated, she assured me—she wasn't the type to step on God's toes) that they were working on transforming into a theater space. She'd presumed to attach some pictures in case I was interested.

Once I clicked on the photos, I was hooked. The little white church out in the middle of nowhere was so charming, my breath caught.

But here was the part that really got me. Mrs. Ethel Penelum didn't simply want me to come and star in one show.

A friend of mine saw you in Hello, Dolly! *a few years back and couldn't stop raving about how talented you were. For this reason you came to mind as I began looking for talented people to be part of my new theater project. I Googled you (yes, even us old ladies know how to Google now) and found some YouTube videos. Dear, I'm sure I'm not the first to say it, but my goodness, you are an amazing talent! What a voice! What presence!*

Silly old woman that I am, I found myself clapping at my computer screen.

Now this may seem odd, but I want you to come to Texas. I can offer you the apartment at the back of the church for your living accommodations. In exchange, you would be the director of our fledgling theater, choosing shows, directors, and whatever else needs doing. I am aware you haven't experience in these areas, but I never had experience in doing anything until after my husband (God rest his soul) died, and sometimes I find that works best. Besides, I'd imagine with all your travels that you might have picked up some ideas about how things ought to be done. Perhaps you'd like to put some of them into action.

The email continued on after that. It was probably the longest email I'd ever received. And the most convincing. I wanted to say yes.

No. I wanted to be the type of person who'd say yes.

But I couldn't. I'd let Ethel down. I'd let them all down. I wasn't ready for that type of commitment. I only needed to look at the mess I'd made of *Annie* for the evidence.

I wrote Ethel and turned her down. "This was so tempting," I wrote. "If I was ever going to settle down, this is the exact job I'd want. But I'm not ready for that level of responsibility and commitment."

She replied ten minutes later with, "Sit on it awhile longer. Give me your final answer after your current show closes."

I've been dreading the moment when I had to say no to her again. Dreading, but not second-guessing. She's wrong about me. I am not at all ready for new challenges.

"So you're really gonna turn that hot guy down? And his ten grand?" Stella asks, breaking into my thoughts.

For a second I think she's talking about Ethel, who I'm fairly certain is not a hot guy. Realizing I've been folding the same dish towel all this time, I quickly drop it into the box.

"I am not turning down a hot guy. Or ten grand. I am saying no to emotional manipulation."

Stella nods. "Sure, sure. Makes sense."

I swallow, or try to, but my mouth is dry. "You think I'm a terrible person now, don't you? I mean, I am a terrible person. But you know I can't get on a plane. And even if I did, what about all my stuff? And my truck? I can't just leave it here."

"Do not have a panic attack on me. Breathe, Jenna. Breathe." Stella comes over and pats my back like I'm a baby. Slowly the panic recedes.

She steps away and claps her hands. "Okay, I was gonna try and make this seem like your idea, but we don't have time for that. So here's the plan. I take your truck and your stuff and meet you in Buffalo."

I gasp, horrified. "You are not taking my truck. The HMS Pinafore only likes to be driven by me. And no offense, but you're a terrible driver."

Ignoring me, Stella scoops Pippin up off the floor and coos at him while he licks her face. "This sweet baby will go with you. He's a wreck when we travel by car. I think he'll do a lot better on an airplane. Besides, you two have bonded. I can tell. The way he looks at you, it's love."

Stella holds Pippin out to me, and after a moment of hesitation, I take him. His warm little body and wagging tail are comforting in a weird way. And he does look at me in this almost cross-eyed sort of way, worshipful and confused all at once. Still, I do not let the little shiteater lick my face. There are limits.

"He's kinda sweet," I concede.

"The sweetest," Stella agrees. "And his carrier fits perfectly under the airplane seat. He'll be such a comfort to you, flying again after all this time."

I put Pippin back down. "Stella, I appreciate you trying to help. I do. But I am not getting on that airplane. With or without Pippin. And I am not going home."

"Okay, real-talk time," Stella says with a deep sigh. "Let's put ourselves on the line here, all right? We've got nothing in common. Honestly, we should've even be friends."

"I wouldn't say *nothing* in common." I blink, strangely hurt.

Stella shakes her head. "Oh, sweetie. You were such a mess when we met. I felt sorry for you. But I also thought, 'I can help this ragged scrap of humanity.'"

I stare at Stella as if I've never seen her before. "So...are we even friends?"

"Of course we are!" As if to prove this, she throws herself toward me with both arms outstretched, but then—before the embracing can begin—abruptly freezes. "You don't like hugs. I know that because I'm your friend. And I struggle with it because I like to hug my friends. Which you are." She eyes me, her arms still reaching, begging me to lean in. "You're sure you don't need a hug right now?"

"I don't."

Stella's arms slowly lower to her sides, but in a twitchy sort of way, like they may spring back out with the slightest provocation. "Jenna, friends care about each other. They meddle in each other's lives. They share their problems. And if they don't share their problems, friends wait, patiently, until the day those problems are ready to come pouring out. And then a friend is there, with tequila. And hugs." Her arms rise again.

I shake my head. "No hugs."

She grins. "I knew you were gonna say that. Because I'm your friend, and I know you. When you told me all that stuff last night about Danny and his family wanting you to come home, I knew you would do it."

"Except I'm not home," I can't help but point out. "I'm here. And once again, I cannot get onto an airplane."

"Yes, you can," Stella counters immediately. "You don't like flying, but you do love Danny. Or you did, and well, love is like that Einstein theory about matter not being created or destroyed. So if you loved him, it's still there. Which means you gotta get on that plane. Because that's part of the deal."

"That's kinda poetic."

"It sure as shit is. Now answer me this—why, after all these years, did you finally tell me about Danny?"

"I got the call telling me he'd woken up and..."

"And it changed everything," Stella finishes for me.

"It changed nothing. I still don't want to go home—"

"Liar, liar, pants on fire," Stella breaks in. "You act like someone in exile. Like you were forced to leave and can never return. Like someone said you weren't deserving of happiness and you believed them."

I scoff. "I don't."

"You do. When you talk about your family, especially your niece, or the wonderful spaghetti parmesan in Buffalo or how no one else can make chicken wings the same way—"

"You can't put some random hot sauce on a wing and call it Buffalo-style!"

Stella nods, like I've proven her point. Which, maybe I have. The truth is, sometimes I do feel a little homesick.

Realizing I'm losing this argument, I try again. "But..." I search for something to fill in the rest of the sentence. Nothing comes to me. I don't have a *but*.

Suddenly, I remember the moment when I realized I loved Danny. It was months after the first rush of being together had passed.

I'd convinced Danny to go see Shakespeare in the Park with me, and he'd dozed off about thirty minutes into *King Lear*. I waited until most of the people had cleared out before gently shaking him awake. He was like a teddy bear when first waking up, a bit growly but in a soft and fuzzy sort of way.

"It's over?" he'd asked, both relieved and embarrassed. "Why didn't you wake me?"

I leaned over to kiss his nose. "Because you're so cute when you're sleeping."

He frowned. "You think I'm an idiot."

"What? No. Danny. I know Shakespeare isn't your thing."

Stubborn, he shook his head, then rubbed at his eyes with hands balled into fists. As he looked back up at me, his bottom lip pouted out. "I never meant to date a girl like you."

"What's that supposed to mean?"

"I mean, like you're smart. Not nerdy like Will. But you say funny things all the time, funny things I never coulda thought of. And you like stuff, like this Shakespeare thing." He gestured to the now empty stage. "You always know the words to every song that comes on the radio, and obviously you sound good singing along." He stops and frowns, and I can see him thinking. "You're just all these things I never expected but are pretty cool now that I have them. I mean, have you."

My heart swelled. My eyes filled. "I love you." I threw myself at him. And then said it again. "I love you."

He rolled so I was underneath him. "Well, yeah, of course. I love you too."

Now Danny is asking for me. He was once mine, and some part of him always will be.

I don't want to go, is a lousy excuse.

When someone wakes up after being in a coma for over ten years and when they specifically ask for you, well then, you go.

So *of course* I'm going to see Danny. It was always gonna happen that way.

Shit.

I try to glare at Stella, but instead feel my lower lip trembling.

"Okay, I think I need that hug now."

14

"I'm Flying" –Peter Pan

"If Pippin doesn't fly, I don't fly." It's a bold declaration and one I couldn't have predicted coming out of my mouth only twenty-four hours earlier. And yet here we are.

In a strange way, there's comfort in traveling with someone whose anxiety level matches my own. Pippin began trembling the moment we left my apartment. My own shakes had started the moment I dialed Will's number into my cell. Despite Pippin having pissed on my couch, I feel like perhaps the two of us were meant to make this journey together. Kindred souls united in our suffering.

So if he isn't going, I'm not going either.

And according to the lady at the counter, Pippin and I are not getting on that plane.

Except Will steps in, using an elbow to nudge me out of the way. Tall and poised and confident, he speaks softly but with authority, mentioning reward points and frequent flyer miles.

The woman is apologetic, not in that fake way, but as if she really hates disappointing Will. Her eyes dart to his hands and then to me.

"Sir, I wish I could be of more help to you and your wife."

I rolled my eyes at this weak bait, certain Will won't bite.

"Oh no," he says with a swift shake of his head. A little too swift if you ask me. "No," he repeats, 'cause I guess once wasn't enough. "Actually, this is my brother's fiancé. Or she was until she got cold feet and ran away. I've convinced her to give him a second shot. We're on our way home now."

The woman claps both hands over her mouth. "Ohmigosh, that is sooo sweet." She eyes Will with a flirtatious look in her eye. "What a wonderful brother, playing cupid."

Will shrugs, all false modesty. "It's the least I can do."

And that's all it takes. Suddenly, Pippin is fine to fly, and the woman even gives Will her number—along with a wink—just in case we have any further problems.

"That was a lie," I inform Will as we walk away. "A big one. They're gonna revoke your Boy Scout card when I report this."

"I'm not a Boy Scout, nor have I ever wanted to be one."

I throw Will a skeptical glance. He is *such* a Boy Scout, whether he has the uniform or not. But he doesn't notice my raised eyebrows—he's too busying studying the woman's number.

I'd thought Will wasn't aware of his new hotness. Maybe I was wrong. Maybe he's turned into a total player. The type who gets off on having ladies fall at his feet.

"Committing it to memory for the next time you're in town? But who knows when that will be? Why don't we just take a later flight? I'm happy to wait a day or week or longer even so you don't miss out on hooking up with Little Miss Thing."

"Little Miss Thing?" Will slants a semi-amused glance my way. "I thought you were pro women who make the first move?"

"I am. One hundred percent. But *that* woman was making the first move while on the job. As someone in the customer service field, I find that very unprofessional."

"*You* work in customer service?"

"Why do you sound so surprised? You think I can't be pleasant? Or at least pretend to be? Let me tell you, I've been employee of the month four different times. That's spread out over several years of working for the same company, but still four times is a record for one person. No one services customers like me." I frown. "Wait. Let me rephrase that."

But Will is already laughing. "No, I think that was perfect."

As we push through the crowds, Will asks me more about my job, and I tell him how I was doing temp gigs as I moved from town to town, but sometimes it was hard to find a new placement. That's when a theater friend told me about work-from-home jobs. I applied to a few, got hired by a furniture and homewares company, and have been with them ever since. They're flexible with my hours, and when I need to take a week or two off for a show, it's never a problem.

I'm explaining how the staff discount is also a great perk, when I suddenly realize we've reached the front of the security line. My stomach churns at this unavoidable reminder: we are IN AN AIRPORT. Slowly, I load my stuff on the belt and then pass through the body scan machine.

Behind me, it's Will's turn to be scanned. I watch as his hands go over his head. My eyes follow the long length of his arms back to those wide shoulders, still unable to get over how big he is. He fills the machine.

Finished, he turns. Our eyes meet.

"Good form," I blurt and then turn to the conveyor belt.

My bag still isn't out. Instead several TSA people have gathered round the x-ray screen. My belly clenches as I watch them confer. Finally, my bag is pulled to the side, and a nice security lady beckons me over so I can watch while she digs through my personal belongings.

Although, honestly it's not that personal. Stella packed it for me. Called it my emergency kit. I meant to check and make sure she didn't put anything illegal inside. It would be just like Stella to include a baggie of bud in case I need to mellow out.

With this horrifying thought in mind, I put what I hope is an innocent expression on my face while the woman takes things out one by one, laying everything out in a neat little line.

Three pouches of gummy bears. A tub filled with chocolate-covered raisins. Red Vines shoved into a gallon-sized Ziploc bag. Potato chips crushed into confetti. A variety of suckers. A whole box of Twinkies.

This is what Stella had been doing when she ran into that convenience store at the car wash. It looks like a six-year-old packed a bag to run away from home.

I debate whether to explain myself to the expressionless TSA woman and Will, who of course is waiting and watching off to the side, when the woman pulls out a long, thick object wrapped in aluminum foil. I frown, wondering what kind of candy fits into that shape. Then I remember the sandwich shop next door to the theater.

Stella knows I'm obsessed with their super-veggie sub. It has roasted peppers, eggplant, and tomatoes. But the deep-fried goat cheese is the kicker. If I'm feeling naughty, I sometimes add bacon. It's basically heaven on bread.

I smile at the woman. It's probably a no-no to admit I didn't pack my own bag and had no idea any of this stuff was in there. So I shrug and say, "You know how it is on long flights. Sometimes you get a little h—"

I choke and stutter to a stop as the woman peels back the foil, revealing not my beloved sandwich but my beloved vibrator.

Now there are some vibrators out there that the casual observer might mistake for an especially robust type of electric toothbrush or an MP3 player. But not mine. It's pink, has sixteen functions, and a little extra appendage that looks like two bunny ears, and yet the main bit of it is undeniably phallic. Like if the Eiffel Tower was ribbed for her pleasure.

The woman looks at me in this "I've seen it all, but you're still an asshole" sort of way.

I gulp. "I heard it still counts for the mile-high club."

"Uh-huh." Shoving it into my bag, she pushes the whole sweet mess across the table toward me. "You're good to go."

Will says nothing as I zip the backpack closed and then gather my shoes and purse and what is left of my dignity. He still says nothing as we walk toward the gate. Nothing as we sit and wait to board.

Mortification holds my fear at bay.

Then they begin boarding the plane, and it all comes rushing back to me. Certain my stomach is going to revolt, I run for the bathroom. Nothing comes up. But I stand in my stall for a long time. Okay, I'm stalling. Hoping the plane will leave without me.

Will's voice echoes through the bathroom. "Jenna, they want to search your bag again? That's okay, right?"

I run out, ready to throw my body over that bag like it's a live grenade. They can arrest me before I go through that again.

But it's all a clever ruse. I sputter at Will while he slowly but surely propels me through the bridge and down the aisle and into our seats.

Such high-handed, conniving, managing, and completely aggravating behavior. I'm tempted to march right back off the plane. The only thing stopping me is Will stretching up to store my backpack in the overhead compartment. As he reaches upward, his shirt climbs as well, exposing what I immediately dub *unicorn abs*.

Never in my life did I ever expect to view—at close range no less—such a rare and wondrous site.

Having stashed my bag away, Will's arms—and shirt—lower. I hurriedly jerk off my jacket, ball it up, and thrust it at him. "Would you mind putting this up too?"

He does not mind, and I get to see the whole show again.

Then he has to ruin it all by sitting beside me and droning on about airplane engineering and how planes are designed to stay aloft and how actually crashing one is an anomaly. It's both boring and terrifying. Every time he uses the word *crash*, my whole stomach clenches. I'm ready to spring out of my chair and run right off the plane, when we lurch into motion.

"Be quiet," I snap. "I need to keep this plane in the air."

I hold my breath, squinch my eyes closed, and concentrate every particle of my being into helping the plane lift itself off the ground. I don't care what Will says about aerodynamics. Planes are huge and full of people and all our assorted stuff. Each time one lifts off the ground and then safely lands again is a minor miracle.

Eventually I realize we are in the air. Flying high above the ground. My jaw hurts from clenching it. Slowly I peel my fingers from the armrests.

Will glances over at me. "You okay?"

My throat is still too tight for words, but I manage to jerk my head up and down.

"Let me know if you need anything," he says and then returns to the papers on his lap.

"What's that all about?" I rasp, looking over with interest.

Will glances at me and then shifts the papers so that they're not quite as easy for me to read. "A list. I use graph paper because..."

"It's neat and orderly," I finish. Even though Will and I are pretty much exact opposites in every way, I totally get the graph paper thing. All those little boxes stacked one upon another remind me of my own moving boxes. There is something satisfying about making order out of chaos.

I watch as Will numbers one to ten, his handwriting neat and careful.

1. Gym
2. Gym
3. Gym
4. Gym

I snort. Clearly those unicorn abs require some serious maintenance.

Will clears his throat. "I've missed several gym days with all the travel."

"And your trainer is a real hard-ass?"

This almost gets a smile. "No, it's just my way of...releasing stress. Staying balanced. Clearing my head." He shrugs. "However you want to say it. If I go too many days without, I feel less in control."

"Yeah, you looked way out of control making your little list there."

"Right." Will nods. "Maybe we should try to get some sleep."

Immediately I regret my snarky reply. Before I can apologize, Will reclines his seat, closes his eyes, and recommends that I try to sleep too. As if that's going to happen. Will is apparently one of those people who falls asleep instantly, which leaves me alone in the dark plane with nothing to do but watch the drink cart's slow but steady progress up the aisle.

Very slow progress. Impossibly slow.

Suddenly the only thing I want in all the world is a drink. Not even an alcoholic one. Just a ginger ale. Something to sip and settle my tummy, which hasn't been having the greatest day.

And a quiet flight to go with that drink would be nice too. Isn't that the usual on a red-eye? Everyone sleeps until the plane lands? Someone forgot to inform the kid behind me how this works. The seat-kicking kid. As if there's any other kind. Imagine my intense delight.

The kid kicks. The drink cart inches ever closer. Five more rows. Four more. Three. I can hear the soft fizz of the pop can opening, the gurgle as it flows into a little plastic cup full of ice. My mouth, dry with terror and a lingering hangover, begs me to end the drought. Two more. I'm nearly bouncing in my seat. The kid behind me is excited too. His thumps grow in intensity.

Then the announcement comes. "I'm sorry, but due to turbulence, we are momentarily suspending beverage service. Please make sure your seat belts remain fastened."

The flight attendant who moments ago had been leaning into the row directly in front of me, taking drink orders, is now moving in reverse, pulling the beverage cart farther and farther away until she disappears from view entirely.

THUMP!

I bounce up out of my seat, actually getting air as the boy kicks my chair once more. It is the final straw. Those people need to control their child. They—

My brain catches up with the rest of me.

Turbulence. That's the word the pilot so calmly used on the loud-

115

speaker.

The plane thumps again, and I realize it is not a child.

And it isn't just fucking turbulence either.

This is the end. We're going down.

All at once I am shivering and sweating. My heart hurts, radiating pain outward. And my stomach too. I gasp for air, sucking for it like I'm trying to get an extra-thick milkshake through a tiny straw.

I'm going to die. I knew if I got on a plane I'd die. And now it's happening.

"You're not going to die. Breathe." Will's hand lands on my shoulder and then slides across my back, finally landing in the spot between my shoulder blades. Normally that would be comforting. Except right now my back is a canyon in the midst of a flash flood. Sweat pours down my spine, and I'm almost certain there's going to be a big damp spot on my ass when I stand up.

I shrug Will off and wrap my arms around myself. Not wanting to explain the whole sweat situation, I go on the offensive instead. "You made me get on this plane, and I didn't even get a complimentary beverage before I die."

The plane shudders and jerks, reminding me that ginger ale is not coming. That I will, in fact, never again enjoy the sweet gingery taste of that beverage or any other one. As if to reinforce this thought, the plane thumps once more, this time with enough force that one of the overhead bins flies open and someone's bag tumbles out.

A woman cries out. A man nearby curses, a big ole "Goddamn it!" You know it's bad, because he doesn't even follow it up with an apology for his language.

We've officially entered the part of our disaster where everyone wakes up and realizes the *Titanic* is sinking.

Well, maybe not *everyone* realizes it.

"It's turbulence," Will says in a low voice. "We're gonna be fine."

Something touches my feet, and I squeal.

"It's just the dog," Will assures me. He looks up and around, sorta poking his head up above the seats. "She's okay. Nervous flyer. That's all."

It occurs to me then that my squeal might've been louder than I'd thought.

"Sorry," I mutter.

Although, I'm not. I've never really seen the point of dying with dignity. I prefer an old-fashioned theatrical death, complete with choking, coughing, and chest clutching, all while sobbing my heart out. In between the sobs and coughs, I'd have a speech. The type where I'd make those left behind promise to remember the love we had, or some bullshit like that. Then at the end, I'd sort of smile, not at the people around me, but at the ones I'm seeing in the great beyond. "Mama, Mama. I'm coming," I'd whisper. And those are my last words.

Now, that's the type of death that'll get a standing ovation.

Pippin's carrier bumps against my feet again. His high, pathetic whine is audible over the engines' hum. He probably realized this plane was going down before anyone, the same way animals sense when an earthquake is coming. Even though no less than three different airline employees reminded me not to remove the animal from his enclosure, I'm fairly sure none of that applies in an emergency situation.

Unzipping the bag, I pluck Pippin out. He's a shivering, quaking mess. Curling both hands around him, I bring him up to my chest, placing his body against my heart. It seems to calm him. I wish it did the same for me. Instead it's almost like I'm absorbing his anxiety.

The speaker crackles, and we're treated to yet another announcement. "This is your captain speaking."

I moan softy, certain this is the part where he tells us to say our prayers.

"We're almost through this storm system. The last little bit here might be bumpier than the rest, so hold tight and know we'll be past it soon."

No sooner does he finish speaking than we get hit so hard, the plane groans in protest. I have a violent image of myself, still clutching Pippin, being sucked out into the sky. Teeth chattering, I squeeze Pippin tighter.

Will peels the fingers of my left hand from the armrest and folds them into the palm of his hand. Then leaning in so that his arm presses against the full length of mine, he puts his mouth so close to my ear I can feel the warmth of his breath.

"Why don't you swat flies anymore?"

"Huh?" I blink at Will. This is the conversation he wants to have right before we die? Shouldn't we be agonizing over all the wrong turns we took in life?

"There was a strip of fly paper outside your apartment door," Will explains, although I'm not really sure what this has to do with anything.

Before I can ask, the plane thumps harder than all the other thumps put together. Hugging Pippin tighter, I moan and curl into myself. Will presses in closer, his leg now molding to my own. Funny, every little point of contact does seem to help. His lips brush against my hair. "I'm only asking about the fly trap because you're Jenna the fly killer. One in every generation is born..."

The shock of his words cuts through the panic, twisting my stomach in knots. I snap straight up in my seat and stare at Will.

He gives me a half smile, like I'm supposed to find this amusing. But it's been so long since I've heard that or even thought about it.

"How do you know about that?"

"Don't you remember? You told us. It was family dinner, and we had that fly buzzing around the table. Mom was going crazy."

Oh no. I do remember. It was awful. Just thinking about it makes me feel humiliated all over again.

15

"Don't Rain on My Parade" –Funny Girl

When I was fifteen, our air conditioner crapped out in mid-August.

Mom bought a window unit for her bedroom. At night she'd blast it, and all three of us would camp out on her queen bed, with me and Allie fighting over the blankets. Mom would make jokes about how she'd always wanted a threesome, but not like this. We'd groan.

Usually when I think about Mom and Allie, I remember how annoying they were. But that memory, that's a good one. All these years later and those hot summer nights in that freezing-cold bedroom do something I hadn't thought was possible. They make me miss my family. It comes swift and hard, squeezing my chest. For a moment, I'm glad to be going home. To hear Mom's god-awful shriek when she sees me walking in the door. For Allie to roll her eyes before hugging me too.

I give myself a shake. The flyswatter. I am remembering the flyswatter.

During the day we flung open the windows. Most of which didn't have screens. The ones we did have were ripped and tattered. Flies poured in.

Besides singing and theater stuff, I didn't have that many skills. Or any really. At school, I was a solid B minus on the verge of slipping to

THE SHOW MUST GO ON

a C student. Anything involving sports almost always ended with me taking a ball in the face.

But when those flies invaded, I discovered a latent talent. I was the fly killer. With nothing but a dishcloth, I'd strike. Once I got three flies with one swing.

Mom and Allie loved it. They treated me like a conquering hero returned from battle.

"My gawd, it's a gift," Mom would say. "That one guy, he thought he was gonna get away. But not with Jenna in the house. No way."

Allie was the one who came up with this whole bit about "The chosen one. The fly killer. Into every generation there is one born." We were both super into *Buffy the Vampire Slayer* at the time, and she meant it as the ultimate compliment.

And I was proud too. I mean, I knew it was dumb, and they weren't giving college scholarships for fly killing or anything, but still, I was so damn good at it. I wasn't an idiot, though. I didn't go around bragging about it outside of our family.

Until I did.

Fast-forward two years later. It was that same summer when Danny and I hula'd in front of *The Price Is Right*. But this was later in the summer. Once again another hot and sticky August.

It was a plain old Wednesday, nothing special, but his dad was grilling up these gigantic steaks for dinner. He went in and out of the house a million times. First for a lighter, then a spatula, then the steaks.

You could tell it was driving Mrs. O'Leary crazy. She snapped at him a few times, "Oh for heaven's sake, what do you need now?"

He'd smiled, probably because we were all sitting there munching on the fancy olives and cheese that Mrs. O'Leary put out most nights as predinner snacks. In my house we'd rip open a bag of potato chips, but she put everything in these fancy little dishes. Even then you couldn't grab an olive and pop it into your mouth. You had to stab it with a little fork and transfer it to a bitty plate before, finally, filling your piehole.

Anyway, Mr. O'Leary smiled in that tight sort of way, like he was grinding his teeth. "Cook's rules."

"That's not even a thing," Mrs. O'Leary grumbled, but she'd waited until he'd gone back outside to say it.

We finally sat down to the steaks. Gigantic ones, and we each got our own. There were grilled potatoes and salad too, because the O'Learys always did things right. Except that night one thing was off. A fly had gotten in and buzzed around our heads. Danny sort of waved his hand at it, and Mrs. O'Leary told him to ignore it.

So we ignored it, or pretended to, until the fly had the temerity to land on Mrs. O'Leary's steak. That was all it took. She exploded. Standing at the head of the table, shouting down its length to Mr. O'Leary, who sat at the opposite end.

She started with the fly and how that was so like him. He couldn't focus. He did things half-assed. And by the way, she'd wanted her steak medium rare and it was practically a charcoal brick. He never listened. He was thoughtless and careless. And lazy. Why couldn't he ever pick up his own dry cleaning? It was on his way home from work. And she was sick of red meat. She'd told him that. They needed to eat more fish. She'd pointed out that article the other week. Hadn't he read it? She told him to read it. How hard was it to read an article?

It went on and on and on.

And no one yelled back. We just froze.

I finally darted a glance sideways. Danny was sitting beside me. I expected him to wink or something, but even after I nudged him with my elbow, he kept staring down at his plate, fork and knife clutched tight in each hand. Somehow my gaze strayed to Will across the table. He didn't look any happier than Danny, but at least his silverware lay safely on his plate. Our eyes met. He shrugged and gave me a half smile, as if to say, "What can you do?"

All the while the fly kept buzzing. In fact, Mrs. O'Leary would begin settling down, and then the fly would buzz by and it'd set her off all over again.

It occurred to me that the fly was the problem here. I could get rid of the fly and save dinner. Maybe then Mrs. O'Leary wouldn't say things like, "You're here so often, Jenna, your own mother must miss you."

So I took the cloth napkin (yes, cloth! Perfect snowy-white too) lying on my lap and dampened it in my water goblet (always the crystal water goblets for dinner) to give it some weight. I twirled both ends between my hands until it was taut. And then stood.

The fly shot past.

I flicked my wrist. The trick to hitting flies is all in the wrist.

The napkin cracked.

The fly fell...

Landing directly in Mrs. O'Leary's glass of chardonnay.

Still, it stopped her rant. She stared at me, then down at her wine, then back at me. Silent.

My face burned. I knew it was bright red. Mrs. O'Leary's shouting had been painful, but the silence that followed felt even worse.

I gulped and then started talking, pretending at a confidence that was long gone. "Oh, by the way, you should know, if you ever have any fly problems in the future, I'm the chosen one."

Danny blinked, like he wasn't sure it was me standing beside him. Everyone else stared. I held the napkin tight in my hand. And for some reason I could not make myself shut up.

"Jenna the fly killer. One born in every generation. That's what my mom and sister say. No fly can evade me. I always get them with one shot." I snapped the napkin, demonstrating, as if they hadn't seen it the first time. "My mom calls it my gift," I finished lamely.

"Well." Mrs. O'Leary picked up her wineglass, calm and in control. "And here I thought you were only good at singing. My, my, my. What other secrets might you reveal?" This was delivered with a smile, but the words were acid, meant to burn. And they did. Mrs. O'Leary plucked the napkin from my hand. "Let me get you a fresh one. I doubt we'll need a repeat performance."

"Thank you," I mumbled, humiliated. I stared at Danny, trying to communicate the word *help* with my eyes.

Shaking his head, he leaned toward me so only I could hear him. I expected a joke. A comment about how his mom was...

Well, Danny never actually said anything bad about his mom. He couldn't. He became incoherent in the face of her lectures on how he needed to shape up and take hold of his life. "She makes me so...Why does she have to be such a..." He'd rage, never finishing the sentence.

I expected something along those lines. Instead I got, "What were you *thinking*, babe?"

"Beautiful night tonight, isn't it?" Mr. O'Leary's voice boomed, overly hearty. "If the weekend's this nice, we'll have to take the boat out. What do you say, boys? And Jenna too, of course. You're invited as well."

Tears filled my eyes. The whole thing was too awful.

It wasn't over though. One final bit of mortification remained.

Will's chair screeched. Low-key, no-drama Will stormed out of the room.

"Will, where are you going?" I heard his mother call.

"I lost my appetite," he yelled back.

He was so sickened by my display, he had to leave.

I hated him more than ever after that.

16

"Spread a Little Sunshine" -Pippin

I want to be the one who gets up and walks away this time. But obviously that's not an option on an airplane that's barely holding itself together. I settle for twisting my body away from Will. It's uncomfortable, and the woman across the aisle is staring at me in a squinty sort of way.

"Can I help you?" I ask.

"That's not a real dog, is it?" She stretches an arm across the space separating us.

I do not like the way she reaches with a single finger extended, like she intends to poke Pippin in the eye.

"Of course not," I say and spin away from her while tucking Pippin deeper into the crook of my arm.

Staring straight ahead, I can still feel Will's eyes on me. But I refuse to look at him.

"Jenna, I've never seen anyone stop my mother mid-rant. It was amazing. *You* were amazing."

This gets to me. I turn to him. "You didn't think so then."

There's a flash of surprise on his face, before I look away.

"That's *exactly* what I thought then. Yes, I was embarrassed. It was bad enough when Mom did that in front of me and Danny, but to have you there witnessing it..."

I don't want to go over ancient history point by point, and yet I find myself doing just that. "You walked away. You said you'd lost your appetite. Clearly you were disgusted."

"Yeah, I was." Will shakes his head. "With Danny. He didn't stick up for you. It pissed me off the way he would let Mom constantly take swings at you—"

I wait, wanting him to say more. But as he abruptly goes silent, I can tell he's already said more than he meant to.

Probably he's realizing that he shouldn't help me recall Danny's worst moments. As if I'd forgotten Danny was a less-than-perfect boyfriend. I still remember the exact excuse Danny used to give me when I asked why he let his mother tear me to shreds. "I'm with you, aren't I? And, babe, you know, sometimes she does kinda have a point."

It was shitty. But I never thought Will saw it too. Maybe I'd misjudged him right from the beginning. And since he's currently feeling chatty about things past, why not ask him? I take a deep breath and give Pippin a squeeze for courage.

"What happened that first time you invited me over to your house? After you turned down my fake girlfriend bit?"

Frowning, Will glances my way and then forward again. I can actually see him playing that night back in his head.

"You mean the time you came for dinner and then disappeared? Only to have us discover you hours later, drunk and half-naked with Danny."

"No. Damn it. You don't get to remember it like that." I shake my head, furious with myself for even starting this.

"You mean, remember the way it happened?"

"No," I counter. "That's cherry picking, and yes, when you put it that way, it sounds bad. But I heard you."

Will frowns. "What do you mean, 'you heard me'?"

"I left to find the bathroom but then couldn't remember which door it was. I could already tell your mom was uptight and didn't like me, so I didn't want her to find me poking around, thinking I was snooping.

125

I went back to the dining room. All your floors were covered in thick plush carpeting, so I guess you didn't hear me. I was about to walk in, when I heard you talking."

"Oh." Will blinks at me. "What exactly did you hear? Sometimes things taken out of context can be easily misunderstood."

"Seriously?" I throw my hands up, and Pippin startles out of his sleep. I stroke his back a few times until with a shudder, he closes his eyes once more.

"I saw that thing move! It is a real dog!" the woman across the aisle cries.

Placing a protective hand over Pippin's soft little belly, I turn to see the woman jabbing at her Call button. Of course, no one's going to come because all the flight attendants are buckled in like the rest of us.

I smile at her. A small embarrassed smile. And then lie to her face. "It's fake. I have anxiety, and animals are supposed to help, but I'm allergic to them, so I got this instead. It's meant to look realistic and feel realistic. That's how it helps me."

The woman frowns and blinks in this confused way. I can see she's torn between calling me a liar and apologizing. The plane thumps, and a moan escapes me. My very real reaction seems to convince her, because she sorta mumbles something about being mistaken and sinks back into her seat.

Ha. Good. With that taken care of, I turn to Will. "Where were we?"

"I was saying that things can be taken out of context, and you were, I believe, preparing your counterargument."

"Right." I nod. "So context. Let me tell you what I heard, and then you can let me know what I might've missed. The first words I heard were your mom's. She said something like, she knew you were just a boy, but she didn't think you were the type to be tempted by a girl who wore her shirt so tight it looked as if it were painted on. Stupid me. I actually waited for you to defend me. To say I looked nice and was in fact a nice girl. But instead you said, 'Of course she's not my type.

Jenna's future plan is to be an actress. I don't think she's even heard of college. Her sister got pregnant and dropped out of school. There's also a persistent rumor that during middle school Jenna's mom dated her school bus driver. The bus would be parked in front of their house after school.'"

"Okay, if you'll let me explain," Will interjects.

I ignore him. "I especially loved how you found out about Mom's school bus afternoon delight. If there was one good thing about my sister getting knocked up, it was that most people let the bus thing go. But you had to bring it up. So at that point I was feeling pretty shitty, but then you added that I was the exact type of girl your mom would *least* like for you to bring home and that's *exactly* why you'd invited me. You then threatened to invite me to your grandparents' fortieth wedding anniversary party if she didn't cease and desist in her efforts to set you up with her friends' daughters."

Will has the good sense to look sheepish. "Okay, you definitely understood everything."

"Yeah, I know." I close my eyes, fighting back the old hurt.

A part of me is still that girl, stunned at Will's betrayal. The thing that really got me was that he could've told me he wanted to make his mom crazy. I would've been on board. And then some. I'd have chewed gum the entire time—except during dinner, when I would've placed it on the edge of my plate for later. I would've been an asshole for the ages, and if Will's mom looked down on me, I wouldn't have cared because I'd have been in on the joke.

Instead, I thought Will was holding out the promise of friendship, and I'd agonized over what to wear before finally settling on a turtleneck, hoping it might disguise my gigantic boobs and make me look like the buttoned-up type I figured Will's parents would like.

I lift Pippin and hold him against my cheek. He sighs softly and then licks me right on the mouth, and for a moment I don't even care about the poop-eating thing.

"Jenna," Will says softly. "I'm sorry. It's not an excuse, but I was pissed at you."

This surprises me into looking back up at him. He's got that laser-beam focus again.

"*You* were pissed at *me*? What? Why?"

"My pride was insulted. I thought Danny had set it up. You coming on to me. Sitting on my lap. It's the type of thing he would've done thinking he was being a good big brother."

Oh, I can see that.

Danny wasn't the typical big brother as bully/tormentor. Instead he treated Will like he was delicate. In need of protection. But more than that. In need of help being...normal. Several times I saw Danny hand Will the phone number of a girl that he described as a "sure thing." And once I overheard him giving Will this long lecture about how he needed to pop his cherry already and that would probably solve, like, 110 percent of his problems. Which was really sweet in a way, but anyone with the slightest bit of sensitivity could see that it made Will crazy.

So I get it now. Will hated the plan. Hated the idea he couldn't get a girl for real. Hated me. Which yeah, okay.

"All I wanted was to approach you like a professional, with a quid pro quo type arrangement. I didn't mean to insult you. The part where I sat on your lap was too much. I can see that now. I wanted to close the deal. Give you an offer you couldn't refuse."

Running out of words, I smile wryly, then mime zipping my lips so Will knows I'm done.

Whirr. Whirr. Whirr. I can almost feel Will's eyes drilling into my head. I want to turn away again, occupy myself with Pippin, but instead I'm caught, staring at him, wishing I could drill right back into his and figure out what's going on in there.

"You know we'd had classes together. Not that year, but in previous years. You acted like we were perfect strangers..." Will trails off.

I lean farther into him, feeling like I'm missing something important here. "Yeah, but we also weren't friends. Or even like sorta acquaintances."

"Right. I know. The thing is..."

I hold my breath. It feels like Will is about to say something that might just change everything.

"Excuse me. Can I get you something to drink?" The flight attendant leans into my space, a napkin ready in her hand, breaking the spell.

I jerk to attention, staring at the girl, unable to believe the plane is still in the air. My sudden movement wakes Pippin, and his head pops up.

Now it's the flight attendant's turn to be surprised. She clutches her chest. "Oh my, that's a real dog."

"I knew it!" The voice of the lady from across the aisle soars over the drink cart.

"He really needs to be in a carrier. Immediately," the flight attendant adds.

Just as I open my mouth to say of course and I'm sorry, Pippin ruins everything by wriggling from my arms. He hits the floor, dashes between my feet, and disappears.

Forcing myself to unclench my teeth, I give the horrified flight attendant my best ingénue smile.

It's dewy, fresh, and innocent as fuck.

"You know, I'd really love a ginger ale if you've got it."

17

"Any Dream Will Do" –Joseph and the Amazing Technicolor Dreamcoat

Pippin is banned from all future flights.

The flight attendant who finally captured him—and then was promptly peed on for her trouble—actually screeched, "THIS DOG WILL *NEVER* FLY AGAIN!"

And apparently she has the power to make that happen.

Honestly, it's for the best, because after that thumping, bumping flight, I'm certainly not getting on another plane. I actually fall on my knees after reaching the safety of the O'Hare airport terminal. I've survived. With that realization, whatever had been holding me together evaporates.

Strong arms reach around and pull me off the floor before I can start kissing it. It's Will, of course. He then settles me into a chair and keeps his arm around me as the tension releases in a flood of salty tears.

Sometime later, after I've cried myself out, Will hands me a Starbucks napkin.

"Rental car?"

I nearly fall to the floor again—this time to kiss his feet. I can't believe he's not going to force me onto another airplane. He's not even going to try. Instead he buys me a gigantic strawberry smoothie, parks me and Pippin at a table near the door, and promises he'll call when the car is ready.

It is beyond decent of him. Which is why I'm ashamed that when he pulls the car up to the curb, the first thing I say is, "What? They didn't have a golf cart available or a tandem bicycle available, so you took the next smallest thing?"

In my defense, the Mitsubishi Mirage—a type of car I didn't even know existed—is absurdly small. It's the type of ultra-compact vehicle that screams DEATH TRAP! Having already cheated death once today, it sorta feels like getting in this sardine mobile might be pushing my luck.

Because, here's the thing. The world is random. And cruel. And remorseless. Bad things happen when and where you least expect them to.

Over the years I've developed a sick sort of hobby out of collecting stories about people who have died in horrible ways. Like the woman crushed to death by a Taco Bell sign. Or the stripper who suffocated inside a surprise cake she was meant to jump out of. Or the kid whose neck was broken by a ride at the state fair. I always read these hoping somewhere in the article it will say something along the lines of, "Turns out this person was very bad, not quite Hitler levels of bad, but close. They totally deserved it." That never happens though. Instead these people are just normal guys and gals blundering through life the best they know how, when suddenly, BAM. It's over.

I don't explain any of this to Will though. Instead I quickly backtrack.

"Sorry, sorry. I'm overtired. This car is great. Perfect, actually." I open the door, throw my carry-on into the backseat, and then jam myself and Pippin into the tiny bit of room up front. "Oh yeah," I lie through my teeth as my knees battle the glovebox. "This is so great."

Will does one of his non-sighs before pulling away from the curb. "I'm going to need some coffee."

Ten minutes later we're parked in front of a minimart. Will glances over at me. The car is so tight that we're practically nose to nose.

131

"Since neither of us got much sleep last night, why don't we take turns driving? You look exhausted, so I'm happy to take the first shift."

"Wow, thanks for letting me know I look terrible." I don't know why I'm giving Will such a hard time. Maybe it's because I cried all over him and now the power balance feels all wrong.

"Jenna, you look beautiful. You always look beautiful," Will tells me in a tone I can't quite interpret.

"Skip the false flattery. I get it. You gotta convince Danny I'm still twenty. And in my current state, there's no way he's gonna buy it. We'd have to invent some sort of industrial soap accident to explain how awful I look."

"Okay." Will opens his door. "I am getting coffee. You can..." Instead of ending that sentence, he slams his door shut and walks away.

I jerk down the mirror on the back of my visor. And oh wow, Will was right. I look exhausted. Basically, lack of sleep + hangover + crying = OH HELL NO.

Unfortunately, despite my very real exhaustion, I am way too knotted up for sleep. Hoping some sugar will temper my cranky mood, I stretch an arm into the seat behind me, feeling for my backpack full o' candy. When all else fails, at least junk food never lets you down. Grabbing the bag, I pull it over the seat and onto my lap. Except it's not my bag. It's Wills.

As I attempt to toss it, the top flap yawns open and a pile of graph paper whooshes out. Frantic, I shovel the papers back into place, but they stick to my sweaty palms. It was an accident, and yet I have this horrible vision of Will returning and finding me in the midst of all his papers. It would look like I was pawing through his stuff. And I'm not. As if I even care about his lists. Or his...

I pause while smoothing an extra-crumpled paper. Not snooping exactly. Simply making sure it's still legible despite the wrinkles.

DAILY, WEEKLY, MONTHLY, AND YEARLY GOALS—DANNY

These words march across the top of the page in exceedingly neat handwriting. A lump forms in my throat. Will drew little calendars too. Perfectly formed with nine squares making up each day. Just enough room for him to write in all those daily, weekly, monthly, and yearly goals. Funny how in this one piece of paper I can see how much Will cares. How the entirety of his big, gigantic brain is being used for his brother. I can't decide if that's tragic or inspiring. Maybe it's both.

Tenderly, I find the folder and place the papers inside. Right as I'm closing it, I spot my name. On the first little calendar. November. It's today actually. The eleventh.

JENNA ARRIVES

That's it. Just those two words.

Slapping the folder closed, I shove it back into the bag and then heave-ho the whole thing over my shoulder, not caring where it lands.

I put my hand over my chest. My heart is beating. Too fast. Panicked. Is this car getting smaller? I try to put my head between my knees, but hit the dashboard instead.

Why is *my name* on Danny's daily, weekly, monthly, and yearly goal calendar? Will can't just write me into Danny's life.

Making plans for Danny, okay, fine.

But making plans that include me? No way. I didn't agree to that.

I didn't agree to any of this. Somehow I got swept along, and now here I am sitting in this car waiting for Will to return and drive me home.

No, not home. Not my home.

This is why I didn't want any of this. Give an inch and suddenly I'll be chained to Danny's bedside again.

No no no no no nooooooo—

The door opens, and Will neatly slides in. Neat. That's Will. Nice and neat and tidy. Everything charted out on graph paper.

Including me.

"Still awake?" he asks mildly as he turns the key in the ignition. The engine whirrs softly. I've had blenders with more power.

"I'm not tired," I snarl as we jerk into motion.

Will nods, unshaken by my outburst. "All right. Let me know when you want to switch places."

It is so reasonable. So fair.

I was bracing myself to be scolded and told to sleep because he wasn't bringing the crypt keeper home to his brother. Instead I don't even get an "It's your funeral."

Clearly he's not looking for a fight.

But I am.

"Just so you know. I'm not staying." My fingers drum the middle console. "I'll check in with Danny. Catch up with him and tell him whatever lies you want. But after *Annie*, that's it. I'm out."

"Okay." There's a slight edge to his voice.

"And don't bring up the money thing again, because that's not changing my mind. The ten grand's off the table."

"I always assumed you'd turn it down."

"You did? I mean, yeah I would've. Probably. No matter what your mother thinks, I'm not financially motivated."

"I know," Will cuts in. To agree with me.

It's disconcerting.

"Right. So good. We're on the same page. I'd stay longer, but I gotta get settled before the holidays. Unless you want me spending Christmas on the streets. Hard to have a happy new year when you're homeless. So to recap. After *Annie*'s done—I'm out. Gotta find a place. Get a job. Be ready for spring auditions. Just, you know, lots to do."

Will nods tightly. "Anywhere specific in mind?"

"Oregon," I say, for no reason other than it's the first state my mind grabs. "Never been there. Heard it's nice. I've been thinking I oughta head that way. Maybe Portland. Well, outside of Portland. The outskirts of the outskirts. I prefer the quiet of the non-city."

"Aren't there more theater opportunities in the actual city though?"

"I'm fine with less options."

This doesn't get a response for so long I wonder if Will's giving me the silent treatment. But then he finally speaks in his horribly reasonable adult tone. The one I hate. "You want to tell me where this is coming from?"

"Where *my life* is coming from? My plans? Sorry I can't pause my existence for you. Also, I never agreed to anything except this trip and the show. Whatever else you thought might've been promised. It's not—"

Will interrupts again. "I get it. This is a limited-engagement performance."

I'm momentarily diverted by his choice of words. They're so incredibly perfect. Gathering myself, I manage, "Yeah. One night only."

"Fine." He sounds all calm and diffident. "I understand travel is difficult for you, and I appreciate you making the journey. Especially when you'll have to do it again to reach Portland. I'm sure by the time you leave, we'll figure out what to tell Danny."

And that's it. The big blow-up I'd wanted is over before it even began. And I'm left feeling silly for making such a stink.

How did Will do that? I'm almost impressed.

Slumping in my seat, I stare out the window and replay the conversation. By the end of it, I realize that of course Will isn't going to argue about how long I'm staying. He's counting on the shock of seeing Danny guilting me into it instead.

Which could totally happen.

I can't let that happen.

My one slight edge is having seen Will's goal sheet. He's thinking ahead, trying to put everything back the way it was. Including me. Will probably blames himself for letting me get away. Now he wants to make things right.

Which means he's gonna use all his not insubstantial smarts to try and box me back into Danny's life for good.

If I want to outsmart him, I gotta get a lot smarter. Fast.

18

"Helpless" -Hamilton

Exhaustion eventually catches me, and I sink into thirty minutes of slumped-over sleep in the front seat.

I wake up groggy and stiff. As I wriggle up from my slouched position, Pippin, who'd been keeping my left thigh warm, leaps to the floor, resettling on my left foot.

"Water?" Will asks, a fresh bottle in his hand. His tone is light. No residual stiffness lingers.

Taking the water, I match his tone. "Yes please, and thank you."

After glugging half of it down, I'm awake enough to realize that music is playing. Not just any music. *Hamilton*. For any musical theater lover, it's a top playlist choice.

"You're a fan?" I gesture to the stereo.

Will nods. "The history. The music. Cabinet rap battles. Especially the cabinet rap battles. How did I live so much of my life without cabinet rap battles?"

"You do seem to enjoy the combination of those three words."

"I do! The thing about *Hamilton* is that it feels like something I wanted forever but didn't know I wanted. Or needed."

He's unabashed in his enthusiasm. Which is how I remember him. Whether it was some sci-fi show or a book he was reading or...whatever. He never pretended to be too cool. Or even a little bit cool. I always loved when he dorked out over something.

No, not loved. Admired. Appreciated.

Now to see Will loving *Hamilton*. Well, he's definitely speaking my language.

"I heard it's amazing live."

"Oh it is," Will quickly replies. "I saw it in previews. And then again a few months ago, and it was stellar both times."

"Shut. Up. You've seen it twice?"

He shrugs. "With my mom. Years ago she suggested a trip to New York City for the two of us to see some shows together." A slight pause as Will darts a glance my way. I'm not sure why, until he adds, "It was after she noticed I was listening to cast recordings as a way to pass the time while sitting with Danny. I'd play *Ragtime* or *Rent* or *Sunday in the Park with George*."

Oh. Those are all musicals I'd introduced Will to. That we listened to together. Does he remember that? He must. But why bring up those memories from when we were almost friends?

No, we were friends. We were *almost* something more.

Cutting me off before I can head down memory lane, Will adds, "On the first trip, at a matinee performance of *Les Miserable*, my mom attempted to set me up with her friend's son."

"She didn't!" I laugh. "Your mother." I shake my head. "She doesn't care which way you swing, so long as you end up with one of her friend's children."

Will laughs too. "It's true. She was unreasonably disappointed when I told her I wasn't interested. She said, 'Are you sure? He's such a wonderful boy. And next year he starts at Harvard Law School.' Like she thought I'd say, 'Oh, well, that changes everything.'"

I crack up, and there it is again, that shimmering feeling between us as we share a joke. For a moment I try to look at Will as he is, without the screen of the past between us. Try to see him as I would if I met him today without any preconceptions.

The first thing I'd notice would be the muscles. So many muscles. And he dresses nicely. Not too on trend, but not ten years behind either. For travel he has jeans and a hoodie. Both look pretty well lived in, but not in a sloppy way. Just comfortable. Definitely the clothes a girlfriend would steal out of his closet. Or pick up off the floor and throw on after...

No need to go there.

Okay, one minute of wondering what Will's like in bed. If he was someone I'd met without any previous ties to him or his comatose brother, it's something I'd probably wonder about. I mean, that intense way he has of studying everything around him, you can't help but consider how that would translate to the bedroom.

Is it getting hot in this car? The heat is blasting. Will cranked it when I got in. I was shivering in my long-sleeved T-shirt that had been perfect for the California desert, but less so for Chicago. I can't change because our suitcases are on the way to Buffalo. Even worse, in my hurry to get off the plane, I'd forgotten to pull my jacket out of the overhead bin. And it only went up there because I'd been drooling over Will's abs...

There's probably a lesson in there somewhere. Like possibly I should stop thinking about getting naked with Will. Because obviously he's more than just a super-hot package. No, I am not thinking of his package.

Well, now I am, damn it.

If I met him today, I'd think he was nice. The way he distracted me with that fly story. And comforted me in the airport. Then all the chivalrous stuff with the rental car. Nice in a way that isn't blah or a code for boring. Because he's not.

He's just, quiet. No drama. Solid, not merely in the packed-with-muscles way, but like it would take a lot to shake him.

But he's not perfect.

There's that cold, reasonable tone of his. Then there's the folder full of graph paper and lists. Including the one with my name on it. I can't forget that.

Also he got a little snippy with the flight attendant after she finally

138

caught Pippin. The lady was blowing off some steam, lecturing me. "This is why animals must be contained."

It didn't bother me. I was only half listening and mostly relieved Pippin didn't have a number two accident (or if he had, no one realized it yet). Then Will said, "That's enough. We've got it. Thanks." It wasn't the words, but the way he said. Like he was channeling his mother. Even if I hadn't known his mother, I would've been like, "Oh wow, what was that?"

"Hey." Will, perhaps sensing I'm adding up his worst traits, interrupts. "You control the radio, okay? That was always the rule, right?"

It was the rule.

And that's his biggest negative of all.

Will insists on bringing up the past. Constantly. In fact, he is literally at this moment driving me back to it. Which means there's no separating him or me from everything that came before.

Like the radio rule.

19

"There's a Fine, Fine Line" –Avenue Q

In the months before Danny's accident, we went from constantly fucking to constantly fighting. We broke up and got back together at least twice a week. Why we didn't just break up for good, I don't really know.

I fell in love with Danny so hard and so fast, even when it was obviously broken I kept holding on. I couldn't admit that what we'd had was over.

It's also possible a tiny bit of our inability to let go was that we both wanted to stick it to Mrs. O'Leary. We'd said it was true love so many times while she rolled her eyes. Breaking up would mean admitting she'd been right the whole time.

So we stuck, but in the meantime the fights were awful.

We were almost always at Danny's house because at mine there was nowhere to go. I shared a room with Allie and Maxi, who was a toddler then.

Also, Danny was a dick about my family, so I tried to keep him away.

If Allie went out with friends, he'd get all judgmental and insinuate she was a terrible mom. If she brought a guy home, he'd make jokes about how Maxi would soon have a little baby brother or sister. And I was supposed to laugh and sneer with him. When I didn't, he'd say that I couldn't take a joke.

He also made fun of Mom, asking if she thought she was my sister with the way she dressed and that she wasn't fooling anybody. After we'd leave, he'd make a big show of enjoying the silence and rub at his ears like they were hurting. Which, okay, yes, my mom has a booming voice. Maxi had a scream that threatened to shatter the windows. And Allie, well, Allie, when she brought a guy home, would sometimes ask us to keep an eye on Maxi and then have very loud sex. Very. Loud. Like headboard pounding while she screamed, "Yes. Yes. Baby. Harder. Harder. Oh. Yes. YEEEEESSSS!"

I'd try to distract Maxi with *Sesame Street*, while she smiled and pointed up at the ceiling saying, "Mama. That Mama. Mama having fun. Maxi go have fun with Mama."

Meanwhile, Danny did his best impression of his mother, crossing his arms over his chest and pressing his lips into a thin disapproving line.

It's not like my family didn't embarrass me. They did. Or that I thought it was a great idea for Allie to be loudly banging some guy she'd been dating a week. Or for my Mom to squeeze into my T-shirts and say, "It's so great we're all the same size."

I hated those things. But Danny did *not* get to hate those things. What the fuck did it matter to him anyway? Where did he get off acting so superior? His mother might wear pearls instead of rhinestones and skirts that didn't show her underwear when she bent over, and when she had one too many it was wine instead of wine coolers. But she wasn't perfect. Far from it.

In my family, when you said you loved someone, everyone else automatically loved them too. When I walked into Danny's house, his mother sighed. She did it every time. Meanwhile, my mother squealed when Danny came home with me. She stocked the specific beer and spicy snack mix he liked. No one else was allowed to touch it.

But it was like Danny couldn't see any of that.

So I'd defend Allie, reminding Danny she was only a year older than him and deserved to have a little fun too. For Mom, well, mostly I'd just tell him to leave it, but once I said, "At least she's not a mean drunk, which is more than I can say for *your* mother." That didn't go over well.

Over time it got so I didn't mention hanging out at my house, and it was assumed we'd be at Danny's. Which was fine.

His house was huge with plenty of space. When we wanted privacy (a.k.a. sex), he had his own room with a door that locked. I was not allowed to "sleep over." Mrs. O'Leary's rule that essentially meant Danny had to drive me home sometime before the sun came up.

Toward the end, Danny and I would fight, and then instead of driving me home, he'd leave. Leave his house without me. Essentially stranding me there since I had no vehicle. If it was early enough, I'd call Mom or Allie, but any time after 9:00 p.m., I risked waking Maxi, which meant I'd be responsible for getting her back to sleep. Which meant I might as well stay up all night.

The first time Will offered to drive me home, I was sitting in Danny's room after he'd just stormed out. I knew he wasn't returning anytime soon since he'd pulled the same stunt only three days earlier. Despite promising he'd never do that again, at that stage our promises didn't mean much.

I'd finally decided to call a cab and make Danny pay me back for it later, when Will came looking for him, saw me alone, and realized Danny had left. After a long somewhat bewildered pause, Will asked, "Want me to drive you home?"

I did.

After that it sorta became a routine thing. He'd find me or I'd hunt him down. Usually he was doing homework on the downstairs couch, so he wasn't hard to find.

The first drive was awkward and silent, with pop radio in the background. Then one night I insisted on plugging my new iPod in and playing some show tunes. Unlike Danny, who hated musical theater, Will was interested.

Although, as we talked, I soon learned that Will was interested in everything. He was always reading some article. When we listened to

Rent, he talked about this book *And the Band Played On* about the AIDS epidemic. *Ragtime* got him all excited about WWI and the turn of the century.

His interest in the world made me want to know more. When he said things like, "Did you know that a ten-gallon hat will only hold three quarters of a gallon?" or "Actually, a *jiffy* is the scientific name for one one thousandth of a second," it became a goal to respond with, "Yes, I have heard that" instead of, "Oh wow, no. That's crazy."

I got a library card just so I could get the book about AIDS. It was the first time I read a whole book that wasn't assigned by a teacher.

Eventually it seemed natural to extend our rides, hitting the McDonald's drive-thru for shakes and then sitting in the back of the parking lot talking about books and movies and music and anything else that occurred to us.

Sometimes we'd get out of the car and Will would name the stars for me. He knew them all and would talk about working for NASA someday. Not as an astronaut—Will confessed somewhat sheepishly that after suffering motion sickness on a carousel, he knew he'd never cut it on a spaceship. Luckily, he'd been born with the kind of brain that could design spaceships or come up with the calculations needed to figure out how to bridge the distance between us and Mars.

Eyes shining, he told me, "If I designed even a single panel on a ship that might eventually find another viable planet...Can you imagine? In a small way, I'd change the world."

"You will. I know you will," I'd tell him.

It wasn't flattery. Will was so smart and so passionate, I could see the future as he imagined it. And I could see his important place in it.

It got so bad Will even convinced me to borrow a bunch of his favorite sci-fi DVDs. I wasn't a huge fan of *Star Trek*, but found myself hooked by *Battlestar Galactica*. And then that was one more thing for us to talk about.

It was funny. We started out having nothing to say to one another, and by the end it felt like we'd never run out of conversation. He'd pull up in front of my house, and I'd open the door but then have to say one more thing. Then he'd have one more thing. Sometimes I'd be half hanging out the door for over an hour as we tried to wrap it up. And failed.

Danny knew Will was driving me home. But he had an idea that we couldn't stand each other. Probably from the many times I insinuated Will had a stick up his ass. And who knows what Will said to him about me. It's not like we'd deliberately set out to deceive him. We didn't like each other...until we kind of did.

Or until I did.

I really really liked him. A lot.

Then came the night I kissed him.

I liked to think of it as planets colliding. It was bigger than us. Inevitable.

But that's a lie.

The truth is, I'd started shrugging Danny away when he put his arm around me. He'd lean in to kiss me, and I'd turn my head, claiming a bad case of Dorito breath. I didn't exactly pick fights with him, but I'd lightly blow on the embers.

Meanwhile, I was touching up my makeup before searching out Will. Running a brush through my hair and loosely tying it back so it didn't look like I was making an extra effort.

I'm not sure if I was trying to fool him or me.

The night of the kiss, my fight with Danny was quiet. I'd bailed the night before on our casual plans to see a movie with his friends, to babysit Maxi instead. Allie was depressed, staying in her pajamas all day, responding to all inquiries with, "What's the point anyway?" I figured she needed a night out more than me.

Danny accused me of putting him last. As always. Like it was a pattern.

As supporting evidence he cited my job stocking shelves at the local grocery store. It was a late-night job, usually starting around 8:00 p.m. and going until eleven. Danny didn't see the point of the job, didn't seem to understand the necessity of money for people whose parents couldn't afford a generous weekly allowance. Then even though I wasn't in a show at that time, he mentioned all the times I'd ditched him for rehearsals and performances.

I called him a spoiled little shit. Told him when he was ready for the real world, I'd be happy to give him a tour.

We went on from there, hitting all the major themes and progressions. He was stuck up. He was a college dropout. A dumb jock. And a mama's boy who'd never had to work for anything in his whole life. I was white trash. My whole family was garbage. I was obsessed with musical theater, which was weird and boring and dumb.

We were gearing up for the big finish, which was kind of like the finale at a fireworks show. We'd basically repeat all the stuff we'd already done, except this time louder and faster and all at once.

Boom. Flash. Crash.

Except on that day, I didn't join in when Danny raised his voice for the final volley. Instead, using my best back-of-the-house voice, I asked, "Why are we even together anymore? Why do we keep doing this?"

It stopped Danny cold. To be honest, it surprised me too.

Then he got his wounded-bear look. All grumpy and fluffy and wounded. "Fuck, Jenna," he finally said. "Because I love you. Don't you love me?"

That hit me hard.

Love was a word we hadn't been using much lately, unless we were discussing pizza. If I'd been a betting girl, I'd have put money on him saying, "Maybe we should break up."

We'd had a few breaks over the last few months, though none had gone longer than half a week.

Danny stood there clearly expecting me to say, "*Of course* I love you too."

But I didn't say anything.

Usually at the moment when I was most certain it was over, I'd experience a fresh charge of feeling, manic and desperate, almost like it had been in the beginning. Memories of all the times he'd been sweet and kind would fill me with longing.

And then I'd remember all the things we'd talked about doing together. Him coming to New York City with me. Or us taking a cross-country road trip after I graduated. There'd even been that time we babysat Maxi together when he's said, "Maybe someday we'll have some kids together."

Regret for everything that might've been would make my heart ache and send me back into Danny's arms.

But not this time. This time I thought of Will.

How he listened to me. And challenged me. And respected me.

And never, not once, talked shit about my family.

"Jenna." My name in Danny's mouth was both a warning and a plea.

"I'm tired of fighting," I told him. Because I wanted to be honest. And also because it sounded better than "I might be falling in love with your brother."

He swallowed. Hard. Like a little kid taking his medicine. And resenting it.

Standing there, watching him, I *was* tired. The constant combat was taking it out of me. Part of me wanted Danny to take me into his arms and say he didn't want to fight anymore either.

But another part wanted him to call it. Say we're done and we'd been done for a long time.

But he did neither.

Instead he threw his arms up, like he couldn't take it anymore. "It's not my fault we fight all the time," he declared, sulky and hurt. "You say all these mean things to me and make like it's my fault. As if I want to be fighting. I just—" He spun away, but not before I caught the wetness in his eyes and realized he was choking up.

"Danny—" I called out even as the sound of his feet pounding down the stairs told me he was already gone.

I sat in his room for a long time, thinking he might come back. When

146

the door pushed open and it was Will instead of Danny, I felt guilty for the way my heart leapt. For how happy I was.

Which, of course, made me feel even worse.

But not bad enough to turn down Will's ride home.

Or to skip our usual milkshake stop.

It was sort of an unspoken rule between us that we didn't discuss Danny. And we definitely didn't discuss my fights with Danny. In fact, I'd noticed that Will wore headphones while studying or doing his homework. I couldn't ask, but I figured it was so he wouldn't hear me and Danny shouting.

Maybe he hadn't been wearing the headphones that night or maybe something in my mood gave it away, like I was trying too hard to pretend everything was fine.

Whatever the reason, Will broke the rules.

"It was a bad one?" he asked.

I frowned, not sure what he was talking about.

"The fight. You and Danny. It was a bad one?"

I sucked at my milkshake, hoping Will would realize his mistake and change the subject. But that wasn't Will. He didn't say anything without first thinking it through. Having decided to bring up Danny after all this time, he wasn't gonna let it go.

As the silence stretched on, I looked over at him. He stared straight back at me. Steady. Without judgment. Tears filled my eyes.

"Oh, you know," I said with a shrug, trying to pretend it didn't matter even as my eyes overflowed and I cried in earnest. "The usual."

And then I was sobbing. Will's arms come around me, and it felt natural to put my head on his shoulder. To collapse into him. And when I was all cried out, it seemed right to tip my head up, meeting his eyes once more.

Mere centimeters separated our lips.

I waited for him to kiss me, the anticipation part of the pleasure, like lying in bed Christmas morning before rushing down to see what Santa had left under the tree.

147

But he didn't kiss me.

We stayed together yet separate for what seemed an eternity, and then finally, he blinked.

In that moment the air changed. The tension left. All the bubbles and fizz evaporated. I could actually see him making the decision to pull away.

So I kissed him.

I shoved my hands into his hair, because I'd been wanting to do it forever.

Will had a habit of running his hands through his hair when he got excited about something, and I'd wanted so long to follow their path.

I pressed my lips to his.

And I sighed his name, like a declaration.

This is me, kissing you. This is not a mistake.

He groaned. I took the opportunity to slip my tongue into his mouth. His hands gripped my arms. Tight.

I mmm'd my approval of his take-charge attitude.

And then he shoved me back into my own seat. "I can't do this." His heavy breathing filled the car, while I sat stunned, not making a sound. "I can't. You know why. I don't have to tell you."

He didn't. We almost never mentioned Danny, but he'd been there all the while.

Will started the car. Drove me home. Neither of us said another word.

The next day I told Danny I was sorry, that I loved him, and that I didn't know why I was such a bitch sometimes. It was all true.

I wouldn't have said a word of it if Will had kissed me back, but that didn't make it any less true.

A week later, Allie's car broke down. It needed a new radiator. I had nine hundred in savings, which went into the car. In return I gained equal ownership rights.

For three months the car ran great, during which time I never had to ask Will for a ride. When it finally broke down again (the transmission this time, which was the final bell toll for the Chevy), I was coming out of the dollar store with a pregnancy test.

While I waited for the tow truck to come and take it away, I used the bathroom of the Subway next door and discovered my suspicions were correct.

I was knocked up.

Danny came to pick me up, and when he asked why I was at the dollar store, I lied and said something about needing a birthday card for a friend.

Eventually, I told Danny I was pregnant. I wasn't there when he passed that news along to the rest of his family. By my own request. But I imagined that Will must've sighed with relief. Like a man who'd dodged a bullet.

It wasn't fair or based on anything I knew to be true, except my very real need to pretend that I hated him with all my heart.

20

"The Word of Your Body" –Spring Awakening

"Y ou don't have to control the radio," Will says, pulling me back into the present. "You just always had such strong opinions about what we should listen to." He pauses before adding, "But that was a long time ago."

I blink at him. It was a long time ago, and yet I can't help wondering if I should apologize. For whatever that's worth. With the distance given by time, it's now blindingly clear.

I was the asshole all those years ago.

I built up in my head this romance with Will that wasn't happening at all. He was being a nice guy. A friend. I misinterpreted and went in for a kiss he didn't want.

I've had guys do the same to me. Make a move and then when I reject them, get all butt-hurt, like they're the wounded party.

I shoot a quick glance at Will. Our eyes meet and he raises his eyebrows before turning back to the road.

No apology, I decide. The past is done. Our futures will only be entangled for a short time. Why make it more difficult than it needs to be?

"Actually," I say, "if you don't mind, let's go back to the beginning of *Hamilton*."

"Sure. As long as you don't mind me occasionally rapping along."

"Oh wow." I laugh. "I have got to hear that."

And boy do I hear it. Will is a true *Hamilton* fanboy, and he seems to have catalogued every single word in his gigantic brain. Knowing the lyrics is half the battle, especially in *Hamilton*, where they come fast and hard. But Will has some decent flow. Not like Eminem needs to be worried or anything, but he's definitely decent. It's only when he ventures into the actual singing parts that it gets dicey.

He's pitchy.

That's the kindest way to put it. But at least Will knows it. He winces and then says, "How do you make it look so easy?"

Obviously, I'm not immune to that type of flattery. I join Will, and suddenly we've got a full-on karaoke happening. The whole time, I can't get enough of watching Will as he listens to the music. I've always loved his way of becoming so still and focused. You can tell his mind isn't drifting, that he's taking every last bit of it in.

Two hours later, *Hamilton* has played through twice and we've made great time getting through Indiana. Eventually we stop to let Pippin have a potty break and refresh our snacks. Walking back to the car, Will mentions Ron Chernow's *Hamilton* biography.

"It's interesting," he says. "How the real-life facts where changed for the musical."

"Yeah, like Angelica's line about having no brothers, when in reality she had several." It's delightful to see the surprise on his face, but he quickly recovers.

"And she was already married when Alexander met Eliza."

We grin at each other, and it's like old times. It's not just the conversation. Or how he's so easy to be with. It's also that old feeling, like there's a string between us.

No, not a string. A rope, wrapped tight around my chest. Almost painful, but not so much that I want it to stop.

The last time I had this feeling...I can't even remember. It's possible I've spent the last decade avoiding men who make me feel this way.

Because it's dangerous. Like being a little bit drunk. Or a lot drunk. I'm not totally in control of myself as the rope connecting me to Will pulls taut, urging me closer and closer.

The worst part is, I've got no fucking clue if he feels it too.

Pippin barks like crazy as we approach the car, where he's been alone for less than five minutes. As I get in, he plants both front paws on my chest so he can lick my face while wagging his tail like a maniac. In short, he is more thrilled to see me than any person has ever been in my entire life.

Over the years I've gotten used to my solitary road trips. If asked, I would've said sharing a small enclosed space with another human being for hours on end was my idea of torture. And adding a small dog to the mix? Forget it. Except now it feels natural to have Pippin's soft fur beneath my fingertips. I especially love the way he rolls onto his back, then throws his legs out, as if to say, "If you're looking for something to pet, here's my belly."

Once we get back on the road, I give Pippin all the belly rubs he wants as Hamilton plays once more.

But now I am distracted. Twitchy even. I glance over at Will, but the musical has him fully in its hold. Meanwhile, the past casts a shadow over the present.

Me then watching Will, looking for an excuse to touch him, to get closer, to maybe even kiss.

Me now watching Will, looking for an excuse to touch him, to get closer, to maybe even kiss.

I know personal growth hasn't been a huge goal of mine these past years, or even on my radar at all. But this is ridiculous.

I force myself to focus on the music, except it's impossible to do that without paying attention to Will as well.

Right now "Cabinet Battle #2" is playing. This is where Thomas Jefferson and Hamilton debate whether to send troops to France to aid in their own revolution. It's a song I sometimes skip, but Will is super into it, rapping along with every word.

Suddenly I'm not merely remembering how much I used to like Will. I'm refeeling it. Being around him made the world better. Brighter. Lighting up bits I'd never seen before. He made me better too. It got so I hated the negative space between us. And time too. When I wasn't with Will, I plotted ways to see him again.

Now I don't have any fantasies of Will + Jenna 4eva. Will isn't my soul mate. Obviously. It's just attraction. Pheromones combined with warm memories.

But they are some potent pheromones.

With every breath I get more wound up. But also sorta melty too.

Like butter left on the counter. Easily spreadable.

Oh. I swallow. That's a slippery metaphor.

Now I'm thinking about butter and sex and being slippery and easily spreadable...

No, don't go there. That's pornographic.

And intriguing.

I give my head a hard shake. Something must come loose. Or fall into place because all at once I see a solution.

It's an awful idea. And possibly a brilliant one as well.

There's something between me and Will.

Despite his rejection, I'm pretty sure it was there thirteen years ago too. And it's still simmering away.

Right now. Right here.

We need to get it out of our systems. Finally. At last.

Except we can't. Because of Danny.

Or maybe we should, because of Danny.

That's where the awful and brilliant part comes in.

If Will and I bang it out, I bet he won't be so eager to plan the rest of mine and Danny's life together. He'd have to lie to Danny or else tell him the truth, and that would upset everything. It's an awful conundrum for him, until I solve it by removing myself from the equation. "I don't want to come between you two. I think it's best if I go." That's my line. Then I'm off and away into the sunset. Not a heel leaving behind the guy who just woke from a baker's-dozen coma, but the heroine, nobly sacrificing her own happiness.

My throat is suddenly dry. Because not only do I have my grand plan, I also know how to set it in motion.

Uncertain whether to go through with it or not, I twitch in my seat, earning the stink-eye from Pippin each time he resettles himself. As *Hamilton* comes to an end, Will glances over at me.

"What should we listen to next?"

"Let me see what's on my phone." I scroll through my music library, pretending to deliberate. Really, though, I'm gathering my courage. This is it. My opening.

"You know," I say casually, like I'm musing aloud. "I should have gone with my original plan."

"What original plan?" He has a slight smile on his face.

Poor boy. He has no idea. "When I first approached you. In the library. In high school. That was plan B. Plan A was the one I decided *not* to go with."

Yep, it's another trip in the time machine. I can see Will's face registering this. Though not in a resistant way. But what he doesn't realize is we're not once again replaying old, tired memories.

This time I aim to do a bit of rewriting.

"What *was* the A plan?" Will asks, feeding me the exact line I wanted.

"We-ell," I say, drawing it out. "My original plan was to ask you to tutor me in algebra or, I don't know, chemistry or something."

"Tutor you in...chemistry?" Will squints at me, suspicions clearly raised.

"Yep." I smile at him, bright and guileless. Open as a convertible on a sunny day. "We'd be sitting side by side. Kinda like this. But closer, so we could look at the same book together."

The car is so tiny, there's only the smallest space between the two seats as it is, just enough room for them to stick an emergency brake there. After gently lowering Pippin to the floor, I shift over, the brake neatly—if not comfortably—fitting between my ass cheeks.

Now I am so close to Will that my shoulder presses against his, and the smell of him fills my nose. For a second I lose track of the script as I breathe him in. Meanwhile, Will doesn't say a word, and I am not brave enough to look over and see how he's taking this.

I forge ahead.

"And I'd say, 'Can you explain that thing about the periodic table again?'" I dart a hand out, tapping the tips of my fingers to the knuckles of his hand wrapped tightly around the steering wall.

It's the barest touch. A moment of pressure and then release. But there is something electric in it. I'm left tingling, and not just in my fingertips.

Still staring straight ahead, it's impossible to see what Will's face is doing, but he did twitch slightly as our skin connected.

Maybe it was surprise.

Or revulsion.

That thought so thoroughly chills me, I momentarily freeze. If Will reminds me in his best grown-up voice that I really oughta stay on my own side of the car, the humiliation will be brutal.

He clears his throat. I brace myself.

"Right. The periodic table can seem overwhelming at first. But remember, it's simply a classification system. Sort of like how librarians use the Dewey Decimal System."

"Oh no," I say, even though it's the opposite of how I'm feeling.

Really, it's all I can do not to jump up and start singing.

More times than I can count, people have said to me, "Oh, musicals? I don't like them. It's so unnatural. Who just breaks into song?"

I pity those people.

Clearly they've never had a moment in their lives—a moment like this one—where happiness bubbles inside like champagne, where you feel so goddamn good, giddy even, that standing up and spontaneously launching into song seems like the only way to express it.

Right now if I were to do exactly that, the song would be, "He's Playing Along (Holy Shit What Does It Mean?)."

Of course, I don't stand up and burst into song (with what would no doubt be a showstopper of a number), because I'm in a car. Even if I wasn't, I'm sitting next to Will. And if I'm moving, it'll only be so that I can get closer to him. Also, an impromptu song and dance might change the mood that's currently brewing, and that is the last thing I want to do.

Especially when he's been good enough to play along, it would be ill-mannered—loutish even—to leave him hanging.

"Oh no," I say again, my voice low and sweet. "Will the Dewey Decimal System be on the test too?" I am nervous and looking for reassurance, or my character is, so it seems natural to let my hand fall to Will's thigh.

It lands slightly farther north of the knee then I'd intended. In fact, I'd say I'm much closer to where the thigh bone's connected to the hip bone, than to where it's connected to the knee bone. I slide to safer territory, the tips of my fingers running along the inside seam of his jeans.

He shudders, and his voice is rough. "No, that won't be on the test. But if there's an essay question—"

"An essay question in chemistry?" I snort, forgetting this is make-believe and wondering what kind of sadist my imaginary teacher is.

Will laughs, which is lovely but not quite so compelling as that sandpapery sound he had earlier.

"Multiple choice then," Will corrects, laughter *and* tension still lurking beneath every word. "I forgot this is an intro course. So we'll focus on the basics—"

"Right." I cut him off before he actually lectures me on the various elements. "I'm gonna take notes—oops!" I throw both hands up, which means giving up the contact with Will's thigh.

But I've got bigger fish to fry.

"I dropped my pencil," I announce as I lean forward, reaching between Will's legs, my hair spreading across his lap as my fingers touch the floor, searching for my imaginary pencil.

Suddenly, Will's hands close over my shoulders, lifting me. No. Pushing me. Away. Except—

Fuck!

My hair stays behind, nearly taking a piece of my scalp with it.

"Owwwww," I squeal.

"Your hair's tangled in the keychain," Will says tersely. "Hold on."

All right. Do I have another choice here?

The wheels screech. Above my head the steering wheel spins. Clearly we are headed somewhere in a hurry.

I bite down on my lip, refusing to cry. Will has clearly rejected me once more. Because he thinks I belong to Danny? Or maybe he's simply not interested. Really, though, does the why even matter? Sometimes two people don't click, and there's no reason for me to have this hollow ache in my chest. No reason at all.

After what feels like a long time, our speed slows and we bump bump bump along, my head thumping against the steering wheel. Finally, the car jerks to a stop. Will carefully twists the keys out of the ignition, and immediately the pressure on my scalp decreases.

Mortified I scoot back over to my side of the car.

We're no longer on the thruway, but instead have discovered a barren stretch of Ohio. There's nothing but a truck stop—an extra-seedy looking one at that. It's littered with potholes big enough to swallow our entire car. It's almost postapocalyptic looking, which fits my mood perfectly. Carefully, I extract the keys from my hair.

At last free, the culprit is obvious. A little cartoon man with gold horns.

Will clears his throat. "It's Loki. From the Marvel universe."

"Right." I pass the keys back to him.

"Rather appropriate actually. In Norse mythology he's known as a trickster god."

Oh wow, this is uncomfortable. We were having so much fun, and then Will pushed me away, and now he's getting ready to lecture me on Norse mythology. Or the Marvel universe. I don't know which is worse. Nor do I intend to find out.

Time to pretend his rejection was no big deal. I don't even care. It was all just for a laugh anyway.

Forcing one of those laughs, I say, "So obviously the seduce-Will plan would've been a bust. Thanks for helping me work through that scene. How it—thankfully—didn't happen. Yikes. Right? Clearly I should've done everyone a great big favor and gone with plan Z instead. That's the one where I never went near you at all."

Suddenly Will's arm comes around me. He drags me toward him, then twists and lifts so that I land squarely on his lap. Stunned, my eyes meet his, difficult to avoid when I'm straddling him with a steering wheel at my back.

"No," he says.

"No...what?"

"No to plan Z. Also, we didn't finish the scene."

That's when I realize the look in his eyes. Lust. I don't know any other way to describe it. Hot and intense too. I can almost see the pornographic movie starring the two of us that's playing in his head. I want to crawl in there and watch it with him.

No. I want to stay right here on his lap and act it out.

I gulp.

Will smiles in a wolfish sort of way that I would've said didn't fit him. But it does. Oh, it does.

"I believe we left off with you dropping your pencil," he says.

I blink. "It was an imaginary pencil." My brain is short-circuiting, so even though this is an incredibly stupid response, I'm proud I actually formed a complete sentence.

"Right," he says as if his brain's short-circuiting too. We stare at one another for what feels like a long time. Finally Will asks, "What made you decide to go with plan B instead?"

"I don't know. It seemed shady, pretending to like you just to manipulate you into liking me." I hesitate and then decide to be honest. "But I also wasn't sure I could pull off the role of seductress. You might not have been interested."

Will snorts. It's nerdy. It's delicious. "Trust me. I would've been interested."

He leans in, and then his mouth is on mine and we are making out like our very lives depend on it.

21

"I Could Write a Book" –Pal Joey

This is my second time kissing Will. But it's his first time kissing me back.

And oh what a difference that makes.

As an adult, no one talks much about kissing unless someone is egregiously bad at it, like too slurpy or one of those people who get stabby with the tongue action. "Oooh, how was he in bed?" is the question a friend asks the morning after. Not, "Did he kiss you so good it felt like the final scene and the credits were about to roll?"

First kisses are worth talking about, but every one after that is just another kiss. Or that's how it seems.

And yet we treat kisses like the bowl of free snacks on the bar. Stale popcorn or snack mix that has a chewy quality because someone sloshed their beer into the bowl. You don't really want it, but you have a few because hey, why not?

A true kiss should be an appetizer. The best appetizer ever. The kind that's so delicious and filling you could eat it as an entrée.

I've had too many bar snacks and not enough appetizers. I actually forgot kisses could be more than just a salty snack to make you thirstier. It's been almost two years since I've had sex, but how long has it been since I was kissed?

Really, truly kissed? Like this?

This is the question Will asks. Not with words, though he does use his tongue.

He's lecturing. Giving a seminar on how to suck face.

He kisses like the nerdy kid he was, the one who studied up, wanting to do more than ace the test. The curve breaker. He's gonna need an extra blue book because his essay answer is more like a final thesis.

He kisses like he does everything, with his full concentration. Every ounce of him focused on the task at hand. And I am right there with him. It's impossible not to be, with his hands in my hair, gently coaxing my head to tip one way, then the other, like he's using the scientific method, trying out all possibilities, systematically calculating the best angle for our lips to meet.

So far, they *all* work for me.

This type of kissing is a revelation. I feel like I've been converted. A new member to the cult of kissing.

Then Will's lips disconnect from mine. I gasp. Surely the ride can't be over already?

"You okay?" he asks, and I realize this is only intermission. A chance to catch our breath, maybe gulp some water.

"Huh" is all I get out, my lips as useless as my legs after that one time I tried a spinning class.

As Will's brows lower in concern, I clarify, "Uh-huh. Good. Good good."

A smile on his face, Will leans in again. His forehead connects with mine, and we silently pant, his warm breath mingling with my own.

"That," I finally manage to say.

"Yeah," he answers, totally getting it.

I smile. "Let's do it again."

As his lips find mine, I can feel the curve of his smile. Then his tongue flicks the seam of my lips and—

I pull back. "Wait," I gasp.

Ever the gentleman, Will freezes. His eyes, gentle and concerned and gorgeously honey brown stare into mine.

"You should make this into a TED talk. The rest of the world deserves to know."

He laughs, eyes crinkling at the corners. This doesn't sound like a sexy detail, but trust me, it is. It's not just the crinkles that have my heart pinching in that achy, yearning sort of way. It's that he gets the joke. He gets me.

"You would have to put it into words," I clarify. "You can't kiss the entire audience."

Will's fingertips trace the line of my jaw. "That's a tricky translation. I'd need to go over everything multiple times to make sure I'm getting it right."

I sigh softly. "I could help."

Our mouths meet once more.

And now our hands join in too.

Tentatively. Teasing. Testing.

Both of mine curl around his biceps, squeezing. He traces the curl of my ear. I slide my hand down the back of his shirt, mapping the area between his shoulder blades. We shudder and moan and by mutual unspoken accord keep it all above the waist.

Well, the car helps with that. Our mechanical chaperone. It squeezes us together but also makes sure we can't move far enough apart to unzip or unbutton anything that leads anywhere too interesting.

Still I test the boundaries of the space. Leaning back so the base of the steering wheel acts as a rather painful lumbar support, I run my hands down Will's front. It's not enough. I want skin. I reach down to where the edge of his sweatshirt is stuck between our overlapping legs. Will vibrates beneath me.

That would be quite the compliment, except he's not vibrating in a horny human kind of way.

"Your phone?" I pant.

"Ignore it," he says at the same time as his hands brush the sides of my breasts.

Every thought goes out of my head. *Ignore what?* I wriggle against Will, and we both whimper, wanting more. Time to return to the problem of his shirt.

But there it is again. Someone persistently vibrating his phone. Which means it's someone annoying. Or with bad news.

Danny did just wake up from a coma.

Even when I was giving my mom the silent treatment, I still answered the phone. I'd ask, "Is anyone sick or dead or dying?" She'd say no, and I'd hang up.

"Will." I press my hands to his chest not to map out his musculature but to push myself back. "What if..."

"No." He shakes his head but then frowns, his brain making the same connections mine did.

And now my phone rings too.

Will groans. "It's my mother. I know it's my mother."

"How can that be? She doesn't even have my number."

Will gives me a disbelieving look.

"Okay," I concede. "That's an easily overcome obstacle."

"Exactly. And if there were some sort of emergency, every cop between Chicago and Buffalo would have a description of us and this car."

"But we're in a rental..."

Will shoots me the look again.

"Right. Easily overcome obstacle."

"Child's play," he confirms.

I smile. "So no emergency means we can return to what we were doing?"

My phone stops ringing. Only the sound of our heavy breathing fills the car, and then my phone ring once more.

"Maybe I should silence that first."

Will's eyes close, and when he opens them again, I can see defeat written there. "I have to call her back."

It's the right thing to do, yet disappointment fills me. "Yeah. Of course."

"She'll be a level-ten disaster area. And once she gets to a certain point—"

"I get it," I cut him off. "You don't have to explain."

We sit for a moment. Silent, facing each other. Not kissing.

Suddenly it feels incredibly awkward to be wrapped around Will. I move sideways, aiming for a graceful dismount. Failure comes quickly. I elbow Will in the eye. The back of my jeans catch on the underside of the steering wheel, and I partially depants myself. And just to make sure I am fully humiliated, I conk my head on the ceiling.

Will takes hold of me, and the same way you'd turn a key in a sticky lock, he jiggles me one way, then the other, twists, and I'm back in my own seat. I grab my pants and haul them up so they are fully covering my ass once more.

"I'm gonna step out to call my mother," Will says, his hand already on the door.

"Wait." Will turns, eyebrows raised in inquiry as I blurt out, "You're not gonna tell her, are you?"

The steam that had been on the windows crackles into ice. That's how quickly the temperature changes.

"Despite the jokes I made earlier about my mother's omniscience, she doesn't actually have eyes everywhere. Nor do I make a habit of reporting back to her every time I enjoy a woman's company."

Enjoy a woman's company. Yikes. Never has something so fun been described so...dispassionately.

I want to correct him. We weren't having a tea party. We were pre-fucking.

Then I remember.

This chill in the air. This awkwardness. This is all part of the "Make Will beg me to leave" plan.

Well, it's going great so far, that's for sure. Really super great.

Yay. For. Me.

With a shake of his head, Will climbs out of the car. I catch hold of his door before he can swing it closed.

He's standing. I'm stretched across the front seat looking up at him.

"Why did you kiss me?"

I ask as part of the plan. Not because I am desperate to know.

Will stares down, making me feel small. And exposed. Because I have just given him an opening to say something cruel. Which would be perfect for the plan. But less so for me and my ego, which could give a flying fuck about the stupid plan and only wants to rewind time back to when Will's mouth was on mine.

"Never mind." I retreat, pulling the door closed.

Will nods and then turning on his heel, walks away.

My throat is tight. Staring down at my knees, I silently curse myself. Pippin jumps onto my lap and makes this little doggy noise like there's no other place he'd rather be.

Suddenly my door opens. Will stands there.

"Because it was time," he says.

Before I can react, before I even realize he's answering my question, the door closes again and Will walks away once more.

The tips of my fingers find my lips.

I pull them away, putting myself to work stroking Pippin's back instead.

"Did you hear that, Pippin?" I muse aloud. "He said it was time."

I stare out the window where Will stands tall and solid in the middle of the empty parking lot. And sigh.

"That really wasn't part of the plan."

22

"Anthem" -Chess

Desperate for a distraction, I dig my phone out. I've missed approximately five thousand text messages from Stella. At least fifty are pics of the HMS Pinafore. Interior and exterior shots from several different angles taken every few hours: visual reassurance that my beloved Pinny is in good hands.

Her latest series of texts (which always come across like bad beat poetry) read:

Nearing Kansas!
Whoo!
Making Great
Time.
Made calls–
All in for
Annie!
Except Frankie
Jr.
His Mommy said
NO!
HA. LOL.
Sounded like he
Was trying not to
Cry

When he called me.
Told him it was for
Best. You're not the
Sticking type.

I frown at this last bit. Not sure why it bothers me. It's true. I'm not the sticking type. And even if I was, I have zero interest in getting stuck to Frankie Jr.

I text back: *Why are you texting me so much? You better not be texting and driving.*

No response.

I also have voicemails from Maxi.

"Shit," I mutter, worried that something has happened. Maxi and I only text. She says talking on the phone is weird. "People should only call someone if they're really pissed off and need to scream or if it's an emergency."

As I press Play on the hour-old message, I can only hope it's the former.

"Hey, Jenna." Her voice is reassuringly breezy as the message begins, and I relax. "So Grandma and Mom are freaking out. Apparently this lady told them you're coming home today, or something? They were angry, like grab-the-pitchforks-and-torches kinda angry. Just so you know, I had your back. I tried to be all, 'Hey, maybe she's going to surprise us or something.' They shut me down so hard. It was all, 'Jenna does not do surprises. Not good ones anyway.'"

Ouch.

Maxi agrees. "Harsh, right? So anyway, now they're trying to convince the frat boys from the duplex across the street to pretend they live at our house. So when you knock on the door, they'll be all, 'Yeah, no, your family doesn't live here anymore. They left years ago. Last I heard they were living out of a van.' At this very moment the frat bros are in our living room. Drunk. Grandma is flirting with them, and Mom kinda was too, but then Nadine showed up, and now they're screaming at each other. And the guys are gross and smell like they bathe in their cologne and they keep telling me I should be dating college guys instead of my current boyfriend, and one of them keeps touching me and telling me I'm uptight and saying I should drink more. Which I'm totally not going to do. These assholes. I'm afraid to drink a glass of water in my own house 'cause they might roofie me. So hey, could you do me a solid and call Grams and tell her you're on your way home and can't wait to see her? Cause then we could ditch these douche bros, and that would be super helpful. Mm-kay? That's it. Bye."

Oh crap. I scrub my hands across my face. This year the daughter of the year award goes to...not me. Sister of the year, aunt of the year...also not me. I want to give myself some credit for not simply forgetting, for making a conscious decision to *not* tell them I was coming home. But maybe that's worse.

The awful truth is, I wanted to give myself room to make a full three-point turn and head back in the opposite direction. Once I told my family, there's no way I could bolt. It would be beyond shitty, and I try to draw the line at being just plain old shitty.

But now thanks to Mrs. O'Leary (wow, it's gonna be so great to see her again after all this time), the beans have been spilled and consumed, and the air is ripe with their aftermath.

Before I can find an excuse not to do it, I call Mom.

"Well, Jenna, hello. How's California today?" she asks in this uber-chipper sort of way.

"Mom, I'm not in California. I'm in Ohio. I got kicked off a plane in Chicago. I have a dog with me, and Danny's brother, Will. We're all on our way home."

"Well," she says, clearly at a loss from this barrage of truth. She recovers though. "And after so long away, do you even know the way?"

"Nah, but Will does, so we should be okay. He says we're about five or six hours out now, depending on how often we stop. The little dog's got a small bladder."

Finally, Mom cracks. I'm surprised she held out this long. "Jenna! You're finally coming home. Oh, baby, my baby, I can't wait to see your face. Allie! Allie! Your sister's coming home!"

"Yeah, Mom, I'm coming home, but only for a week. It's not a long stay. Okay?"

It's like she doesn't even hear me. "Oh, this is such perfect timing! We just got a big order of bathing blocks, so if you wouldn't mind pitching in—"

"Mom, look, I gotta go. It's my turn to drive, and I don't want to hold us up."

"Oh, sure sure, I know. I gotta go too actually. We had a...Well, we had some people over. These boys from across the street seemed like nice boys, except for the parties they throw every weekend, but well, they're young. Anyway, Maxi put a knife in one of them."

"Jesus! Mom!"

"Oh well, that sounds worse than it was. It was a cheap steak knife from the Dollar Tree. Barely even broke the skin and wouldn't have done that if he'd been wearing pants instead of shorts. That's really his own fault. Who wears shorts in November? And flip-flops too, though at least he wears socks with those. So he must have a little sense. I wanted to tell him to use the money they must spend on beer—judging from the empties all over their lawn come Sunday morning—and buy himself a—"

"Mom!" I interrupt before she can get too far down this path. "What happened with Maxi and the knife?"

"Oh that. Like I said, it was nothing. I mean, he was bleeding and screaming like she tried to take out his liver. He called her a little bitch, which I strongly objected to. I mean, coming into my house and calling my granddaughter names, it's uncalled for. Then Maxi made it worse saying she was going for his balls but couldn't find them." Mom laughs. "She reminds me of myself when I was that age. A little spitfire. I'm not sure if I ever told you about the time—"

I reel her in again. "Maxi, Mom. What happened to Maxi?"

169

"Nothing happened to her. Jenna, what do you think? I'd let them carry her away? Oh sure, they were making threats. Luckily, Nadine came in and did her lawyer thing. I honestly couldn't follow all of what she said, but it shut that boy up pretty quick. And I thought that was the end of that, but then one of the other boys started up, saying his dad was a lawyer and two could play that game. Jenna, can you imagine? The whole thing was giving me a headache and, to be perfectly honest, ruining my buzz. So I dragged the garden hose in, and sure enough the moment I began spraying them down, they ran. You'd think they were made of sugar. Which reminds me—if you're planning to sleep on the purple couch tonight, that's out. It usually takes at least a week to dry out. But I'm sure Allie will be happy to stay at Nadine's so you can have her bed."

In the background I hear Allie loudly objecting to Mom giving her room away. Nadine says something in response, but her voice doesn't carry quite like Allie's, so I can't make it out. Then Maxi joins in, and there's this whole babble of voices talking and shouting and laughing.

Suddenly, I miss them so bad it hurts. I mean, sure it's crazy. That story is all the things that had me wanting to run away from home long before I ever did. And I love having my own space where no one would dare hose down guests who overstayed their welcome. Not that I have many guests. I rarely invite anyone over. Which means it's quiet. Peaceful even. My own personal retreat...that is sometimes so damn lonely I talk to George of the Jungle as he's paused on my big-screen TV.

After Mom and I say our goodbyes, I flip through my email, which is mostly just sales notices.

Then imagining Maxi with that steak knife, I laugh. That's so like her. At least I think it is. You can only know someone so well through text messages.

That earlier ache of homesickness increases.

I don't want to go home. I wish we were there already.

One week, I remind myself. One week and then I'm out. It's the

170

way it has to be. If I stay, then I'm trapped. And I don't deserve to be trapped. Which means I don't deserve to be home.

The car door swings open, and Will drops back into his seat. I turn to him, not sure what to expect. It's not good. There's a funereal air about him.

"I have a favor to ask," he says.

"Uh-huh," I answer, careful. Not wanting to be the jerk who immediately says no.

"Danny's upset. Suspicious. He knows something's going on."

"Okay." I nod. "It was gonna happen eventually."

"It was," Will agrees. "Yet my mother's still attached to this idea of Danny's slow, natural discovery. Which means she wants you to FaceTime with him, say a few nice things, tell him how excited you are to see him again..." He trails off and then shrugs. "Danny's unmoored right now. He needs familiar faces."

Unmoored. Yeah, I get that. Except unlike Danny, it's a state I've purposely sought out.

"Okay, I'll do it," I say, not because I want to do it. Hell no.

But I'm gonna have to see Danny eventually. It'll be easier to video call first. A sort of rehearsal. If it gets bad, I'll cut the call and blame the cell service.

Better that than running out of the room when we go face to face for real.

"Great. I appreciate it." Will looks relieved. Like he was prepared to do some serious arm twisting. "I know this isn't easy for you. For any of us. And video calls are always a little awkward."

"It's fine. Let's get it over with."

With a nod, Will opens the FaceTime app, but he hesitates before making the call. "You should be prepared. Danny's not..." Will stops to clear his throat, and I realize with horror he's choking up. "He's not the way you remember him."

I force a smile, trying to reassure him. "I was there for the first year, remember? I saw him..."

171

What word can I use that doesn't feel cruel? The way he shrunk? Shriveled?

By the time I'd left, his legs and arms—once robust and muscled—were thin bones covered in sagging skin. I could hardly look at his face. The way his eyes had sunk into his head.

In the early days he looked like he was peacefully sleeping. But toward the end, he was a corpse.

Suddenly, I'm choked up too. "I remember."

Will's hand finds mine. In mutual accord our fingers lace together. Amazing how comforting such a small thing can be.

"It's not only the way he looks. Danny has trouble speaking. He'll lose words or stutter. If we try to help, he gets upset. But if we don't and let him fumble too long, he gets frustrated. Angry."

"Will, if you're trying to talk me out of this, you're doing a terrific job."

"Maybe I am. Maybe—" Will cuts off whatever he was going to say with a sharp shake of his head. Then pulling his hand from mine, he opens the FaceTime app.

We wait as it rings, and then Mrs. O'Leary's face is on the screen.

"Well hello," she says, faking a smile. Her eyes dart between me and Will, narrowing suspiciously.

I resist the urge to grab Will's hand, or even a corner of his shirt, for a little added security.

But this is Mrs. O'Leary on her best behavior as she chirps out, "Danny, look who's calling! It's Jenna and Will!"

We get a view of the floor (carpeted, of course) as Mrs. O'Leary moves toward Danny. Then our view switches to the ceiling. It goes back and forth as Danny and Mrs. O'Leary struggle over the phone. "Danny, let me hold it for you. You'll wear yourself out!"

Finally, Danny's face appears on the screen. Even after Will's speech and my assurance that I was prepared—I wasn't.

Danny looks both young and old all at once. Like he was mummified at age twenty. In a way, I guess he was. All the fleshy parts of his face are gone. The bones stick out. And his eyes, those bright, flashing blue eyes, are enormous. He's almost beautiful. Like those emaciated supermodels strutting the catwalk during fashion week. Exotic and also a little bit ugly. Slightly alien in their intense beauty.

I can't cry. Will didn't say so. He didn't have to. What right do I have to cry? The girl who ran away does not get to cry.

Will's hand is holding mine again. I squeeze tight as I can. Then I clench my back teeth and force myself to smile.

"Danny! My God! You're awake! I can't believe it!"

He smiles back. Though it takes him a minute to do it, like he's still trying to remember how his face works. It hurts to watch. My hand spasms, gripping so hard the bones in Will's hand crack in protest.

And finally Danny speaks. "J-J-J-J-J-J-" The smile disappears as his face scrunches into a frustrated scowl. "ENNA!" he finishes in a sudden burst.

My throat seizes up, and I tighten every muscle in my face, refusing to let even a single tear work its way out. It's actually a relief when the phone swivels once more and Mrs. O'Leary is on the screen.

"His speech is always a little worse when he's emotional. Or tired. And he didn't get his nap today because he was so worked up about seeing you and Will and then disappointed when we found out about your flight problems." All of this is related lightly, with a smile, but there's no mistaking the twist of the knife.

In the background Danny protests, "M-M-M-M-OM."

"All right, Danny, we'll turn it to you," Mrs. O'Leary says, but the phone stays firmly on her own face. "But why don't you rest and let Jenna talk. She can tell you about her and Will's travel problems. And perhaps she'll let us know how she got on with her soap sales. Or she could even—"

"No." This one word from Danny is solid. Unmistakable. "No b-b-b-b-boring t-t-t-t-talk. J-J-J-J-J-enna sing." Finally the phone swivels to Danny. His forehead is furrowed in concentration. "Sing D-D-D-D-D-Danny song."

That's the last thing I expected him to say. Danny mostly asked me to please *stop* singing. Maybe I'm misunderstanding him.

"You want me to sing?"

He nods vehemently. "D–D–D–Danny."

"'Danny Boy,'" I say, understanding. This earns another nod.

Of all the things for him to remember after all this time. But then I remind myself, he's still stuck in the past—for him it was only a few weeks ago that I sang it for him.

I gave it to him as a birthday gift on the same night he knocked me up.

23

"Heart and Music" –A New Brain

Danny's birthday came about a month after the almost kiss with Will.

I'd been planning on buying him something nice, a watch maybe.

For my last birthday he got me a necklace with a little diamond chip in it. I knew it was expensive from the fancy box stamped with the name of the jewelry store. Afterward we had dinner out at this pricey restaurant where it cost fifty bucks for a steak that didn't even come with french fries—you had to pay for those separately. What a rip-off!

Meanwhile, for Danny's previous birthday, I'd bought him a couple used DVDs from the local video store that was going out of business and tagged along to the birthday dinner his parents paid for.

This year I was gonna make it up to him, but instead I'd ended up spending every last penny I'd been saving on Allie's car.

Desperate, I decided to get creative and prepare a special birthday song especially for Danny. Somehow, despite all evidence to the contrary, I convinced myself he'd love it.

Danny was not into my "theater thing," as he called it. When we were first dating, I'd sometimes ask him to listen to an audition piece I was working on, and he would visibly zone out. His comments would be along the lines of, "Yeah, that was great. You sing good, babe. You always sing good."

Still, I didn't have any other idea for a gift, so I went for it. I practiced under my breath while stocking cans of dog food and as loud as I wanted while driving to practice. Instead of doing homework or memorizing lines, I practiced Danny's song. I wanted it to be perfect. I wanted him to be blown away.

Spoiler alert—he wasn't.

It was the middle of winter, so I'd had to get creative with my concert spot. I snuck Danny into the theater at the community college where I was rehearsing. I'd jammed the lock on my way out earlier and hoped no one would notice.

Danny definitely appreciated the sneaking in aspect. But as soon as I stood on stage and opened my mouth, his eyes glazed. He wasn't mean about it. He tried to look interested. I watched as he fought a yawn and finally let it out between clenched teeth. When I finished, he clapped.

Then he said, "That was great, babe. Loved it. Great warm up. So, do I get my gift now?"

I stood there fighting a mixture of anger, shame, and embarrassment. How could I tell him "That was your gift, you dope? It was a fucking love song!" without it causing a huge fight?

I couldn't.

So I sang happy birthday in a sexy Marilyn Monroe voice, all while stripping my clothes off piece by piece. My grand finale was a happy birthday blow job. Or it was meant to be, but Danny wanted to get horizontal on the stage. I was already pretty uncomfortable and worried about getting caught. But it was his fucking birthday. So I went along with it. Right up until he said, "Oh shit, baby, I don't have a condom."

I began taking the pill soon after Danny and I started dating. At first I'd insisted on using condoms too, but eventually let him go without. But in the last month I hadn't been able to afford the co-pay for my pills. I told Danny, and he offered to give me the money, but by then I'd already missed a week.

With a sister who'd had a baby at sixteen, I did not mess around with that stuff. I told Danny he needed a condom every time. No excuses. Ever. At least until my birth control was current again.

Yet there we were. On stage. Trespassing. I was naked. His pants were around his ankles. And all the while he was giving me the pleading puppy dog eyes.

"I'll pull out, baby. I promise."

I wanted to get it over with and get out of there. I didn't want to make my crappy gift any crappier.

Quickly, I did some back-of-the-envelope calculations. It should be fine. I was still weeks away from my period.

"Okay, just this once," I said.

But once is all it takes.

Happy happy birthday, baby.

24

"One Song Glory" -Rent

At eighteen "Danny Boy" had seemed a little bit sad and a lot romantic. I'd mostly focused on the part where it said, "Oh, Danny Boy, oh, Danny Boy, I love you so!"

But at thirty-one, singing it to a boy who has spent nearly all the intervening years asleep, the lyrics aren't simply sad. They seem specifically made to provoke weeping, and the type of tears best measured in buckets filled.

For a short song, it packs a powerful punch.

On any other day, I'd tell you that the thing I love about singing is the way that words and music combine to create something that slips right through your barriers to find your soft and squishy parts. And man oh man, "Danny Boy" works exactly that way. The lyrics pair perfectly with the doleful melody, so there's no avoiding the aching sorrow.

But I try.

First, I close my eyes to remember the words, to get the music running in my head. As bad as my memory is for faces and names, once learned, a song is with me forever. So even though I haven't sung "Danny Boy" since I did it for Danny all those years ago, it comes to me immediately.

I attempt a more upbeat rendition. Make it the love song I once believed it was. But it gets away from me on the first line with "the pipes are calling." My throat thickens, and the only way to keep from crying is to forget Danny and slip into the song, losing myself inside it.

It's not that I'm unaware of what's happening around me, but my focus is internal. The feel of the song, the sadness and grief and longing are all flowing through me, but more distant, while I also track my breathing and make sure the words are clear.

In short, I'm performing.

When I finish, Danny has this look on his face. It's not the bored, uninterested one. He almost seems mad. Or like he's thinking through some complicated problem. Brows furrowed. Lips compressed. Jaw clenched tight. But then he blinks, and I notice his eyes are wet.

He clears his throat, nods, says softly, "Yeah, th-th-that's the s-s-s-s-song."

Mrs. O'Leary takes control of the phone. "That was lovely, thank you," she says, her voice thick with emotion and not a shred of disdain to be found. "That's enough for today. Danny gets tired quickly, so..." She shakes her head and dabs at her eyes with a tissue. "We'll see you tomorrow."

And that's it. The call is over.

I turn to Will. He's wiping at his eyes too.

"Here," I say, shoving the phone back at him. My hands are shaking. My whole body is shaking. "Happy now?"

"Jenna, that was—"

But I don't get to hear Will's review, because I can't hold it in anymore. I bury my face in my hands while sobs burst out of me, racking my whole body.

I had food poisoning a few years back. Had my head in the toilet for over five hours as my body ejected the bad sushi and everything else inside me. Emptied me out entirely.

This feels similar.

Like there is something hard lodged inside my chest and I need to choke it out. I haven't cried this hard since...since the last time I saw

Danny. Since the day I ran away.

Will puts his arms around me, and I crumple against him. He doesn't say "shush" or "it's okay." He simply—for the second time today—holds me and lets me cry.

Like a fast-moving storm, it's over as quickly as it began. The tears dry. The shuddery little gasps for air cease. I still feel broken, but it's no longer bubbling up for everyone to see. Which means it's time to pull away.

Instead, I inhale, using Will's good, fresh smell as aromatherapy. Wanting more, I press my nose to his neck, breathe him in, and then pull back so his eyes meet mine. We stay like that, staring at each other.

Time slows.

We've fallen into a hushed and languid dimension. A place where you could discern roses unfurling petal by petal.

But I'd rather watch Will. He swallows, and his throat moves, Adam's apple lifting and then falling back into place. Licking my lips, I observe the way his eyes focus on my mouth. He swallows again. I lean forward. Press my lips to his throat, wanting to taste that motion.

Wanting. More.

Will's hands tangle into my hair, grasp my skull, and tilt my face up. I leave a trail of kisses along his neck and chin before our lips finally meet.

The slow-mo ends abruptly.

Suddenly we are frantic. Herky-jerky and desperate for each other.

It's the opposite of an out-of-body experience. Instead I am totally *in* my body and completely out of my mind. There are no thoughts, except, want want want more more more.

Ten minutes later it's over.

180

25

"Contact" -Rent

Slowly...slowly, I return to myself.

I am straddling Will in the backseat. My jeans and underwear remain caught on my right ankle. Will's pants didn't make it any further than midthigh. The rest of our clothing is fully in place.

We are panting, I notice next. And my throat is raw from screaming. I'm not usually a screamer. It feels showy and isn't great for the vocal cords either. This scream, though, just came out, like it had been trapped and finally saw an opening. I think Will screamed too. Both of us fucking our brains out and screaming in each other's faces.

Yeah, shit. That happened.

Also, Twinkies.

They rained down on us.

No, I rained them down on us after Will had the presence of mind to gasp, "Condom."

"Got 'em," I'd replied, remembering Stella shoving a long strip of them into my carry-on.

Grabbing the bag, I shook shook shook.

The snack contents went flying. Including the Twinkies. And condoms.

Will and I grabbed for them at the same time. A little tug of war ensued before I ceded the battle to him, focusing instead on wiggling my jeans off.

Then bang bang bang. Screaming. Orgasms all around. And end scene.

Except Will is still here beneath me. Looking as shell shocked as I feel.

Somehow that makes it a little better.

I extract myself, lifting up and then scuttling backward until my bare ass connects with the cold window. Quickly I get my underwear and jeans into place. Shifting to give me more space, Will adjusts his own clothing. Then we sit side by side in the tight confines of the backseat, both facing forward, only our knees touching.

I notice then that the driver's seat is reclined almost flat. Not sure if it's supposed to do that or if we broke it in our mad scramble to get back here.

We really, truly lost our minds for a while there.

"So that was..." My brain is still rebooting. That's all I got.

Luckily, Will's brain is already fully powered up. "Cathartic. From the Latin *catharticus*, or the Greek *katharsis*, with a *k*. It's a word used for Aristotelean drama, or in a more medical sense—"

I press my hand over Will's mouth. "Stop. Please stop."

"Done," he mumbles against my fingertips.

"You promise?"

He nods solemnly.

I take my hand back.

"Sorry. I get a little pedantic when in unconventional situations."

I laugh. "Really? You consider *this* unconventional? Which part?" Realizing I'm sitting on a Twinkie, I shift to grab it. It's flattened, but still good. Removing the cellophane, I take a bite. Hold the rest out to Will. "Want some? Postcoital Twinkies. What's unconventional about that, right?"

Pippin, smelling food, pops up from between the front seats. My vibrator dangles from the side of his mouth. Clearly, Pippin found a new chew toy.

"A boner!" I yell, shaking with laughter.

Confused, Will half smiles, not getting the joke. How can he not? It's hysterical. I'm laughing so hard, I'm crying. No, I'm just crying now. And shuddering as the tears flow once more.

Suddenly there's Danny's face. Or it's been there all this time, and I was pretending not to see it. The way he looked...So delicate. Broken. I don't want to see him like that. Not again. Certainly not in person. Face to face. I can't. I can't—

Breathe. My chest squeezes. My throat too.

"Jenna? Are you okay?" Will's hand lands on my back. "Put your head between your knees. You're having a panic attack."

Of course I'm having a fucking panic attack. This ain't my first rodeo. I don't say that. I can't say anything. I can barely get enough air in my body to stay alive.

Will presses me forward, my head banging against the back of the seat. "Deep breath in through your nose, then out through your mouth."

Ignoring him, I continue huffing away, certain I'm going to die here in this miserable little car. They might as well forget the casket—just go ahead and bury me in the Mitsubishi.

"Jenna." Will's voice is stern, cutting through my thoughts. "Come on. Breathe in for a count of five. One. Two. Three. Four. Five."

I do it.

"Good, good. Now out for five. No, no, not like that. Slow. Come on. In again for five."

We continue like this for I don't know how long, until finally the panic attack passes and I'm able to slowly sit up. Even then Will's hand remains on my back, rotating in a small circle.

I look at Will then and know he'll understand. Like he did with the airplane. I couldn't do it. He saw that. He'll understand. He will.

"Will, I can't see Danny again. I want to. I really do, but I can't. I'm sorry you spent all this time and came so far. Please drop me wherever. Leave me *here*. I'll figure it out. I'm just...I'm so so sorry, but I *can't*."

Somehow during this speech, my hands grabbed on to the front of his shirt.

Meanwhile Will's hand on my back has gone still. "Jenna." He pauses, frowns. "You *can* do this. It feels too big right now, but when the time comes, you'll get through it. I'll help you get through it. Okay?"

I shake my head wildly and chew on my trembling lips. Truly, I'm losing it. I'm barely holding on here.

"Please don't make me." I whisper the words.

Will sighs. His hand comes off my back. "I think you're overtired. Why don't you—"

It's the reasonable adult voice again! More superior and knowing than ever. I can't fucking believe it!

"I am not a hysterical child." I hear my voice, and it sounds hysterical. Okay fine. "Maybe I am hysterical, but I'm not a child. A little nap won't make everything better. Don't tell me it will when I just saw Danny and he's..."

My lips purse around the words, holding them in for a moment before I finally spit them out. "He's *fucked*. Don't tell me he's not. Don't pretend he's gonna get better or be normal again. He won't. And I'm not gonna sit by his side and pretend. Lie to make you feel better. Not lie for him. It's for you. And your mother. Because trust me, I saw Danny's face. And he knows. Maybe he doesn't *know* know, but deep down Danny hears that voice in himself. And that voice is telling him the truth. It's saying, 'Danny. You. Are. Fucked.'"

"Shut up." The words are harsh and soft all at once. Whisper shouted from between clenched teeth.

I shut up, my mouth collapsing into a flat line.

Will and I stare at one another. His face is hard with disgust and dislike. After a long shaky exhale, he opens his door and steps out. Crying, I watch as he walks around the car to the driver's-side door. Without a word he gets in, puts the key in the ignition, and then drives across the pitted parking lot and back onto the thruway.

That's when I remember my plan. My brilliant evil scheme to sleep with Will and make things so super awkward that he can't wait to get rid of me. Somehow my plan worked exactly as I'd wanted. And also, not at all.

Well, I went this far. I might as well finish it.

Wiping my tears away, I pitch my voice just loud enough to reach Will's ears. "You planning on telling Danny we slept together? That we fucked ourselves silly moments after I sang him his little song?"

The engine revs. "Jenna." The one word full of both hurt and anger.

I wait for him to say the rest. That I'm awful. That he wishes he'd never met me. I want his words to tear me apart.

But he doesn't say anything else. Miles go by, and he remains silent. Finally, I realize that one word was his answer. And it's the only one I'm gonna get.

26

"Lost in the Darkness" –Jekyll and Hyde

I wake with a start, disorientated.

It's dark, and for several long moments I struggle to remember where I am. Finally, it comes back to me.

Mitsubishi. Will. Pippin.

Hell.

I sit up, my whole body groaning in protest. I'm groggy in a way that only comes after a long, deep sleep. Long enough that the sun's skimming the horizon. Long enough that I'm alone in the car. Long enough that someone got a blanket to cover me up.

Easing the door open, I swing my legs out and look around. We're parked near the dumpster at the back of a Burger King. The air's cold. Bitter even, where you can feel it in your teeth. Even as I shiver, it feels good on my face. Fresh. Even that greasy french fry smell is better than the stale fake lemon scent inside the car. After a minute though, the cold hurts. Reaching into the car, I grab the blanket and wrap it around myself.

I turn in a little circle, searching for Will, and finally spot him at the other end of the parking lot. He's crouched in front of Pippin, and they appear to be having an earnest conversation. Curious, I approach quietly, not sneaking exactly, but not announcing my presence either.

"C'mon, little man," I hear when I get close enough. "We both know defecation is inevitable. You ate all those Twinkies and I don't even

186

know how much candy. Yes, you regurgitated some of it, but a little must've stayed inside."

Pippin looks up at Will and wags his tail.

"No, don't give me that look. That's the same look you gave me at the last stop, and not five minutes later you had a really messy number two. This is a rental car. We cannot have another messy number two."

"Sounds like I missed a lot," I say.

Will stiffens, then slowly stands and turns to face me. I guess he has not yet forgiven me for the truly heinous things I said about his brother. Can't say I blame him.

At least Pippin still likes me. He yips like a madman, feverishly straining at his leash, desperate to get to me. I crouch down and rub his belly.

"How far from Buffalo are we?" I ask, trying to figure out how mad Will is. If my overdue apology will even get through to him.

"Just under three hours. I would've made better time, but your dog and I had some issues. I've spent the last hour attempting to return the car to the state it was in when we first received it."

"Oh. Sorry about that. Thanks for cleaning." I pull the blanket tighter around my shoulders as the wind comes whipping past. "And the blanket too."

"I was trying to air the car out, and you don't have a coat." Will explains away this small kindness, somehow making it seem like my fault for not being properly dressed for the weather.

With a sigh, I reach down, scoop Pippin into my arms, and hold him close. I don't even care about the messy number two. Pippin's warm and he likes me. Right now that's enough.

"Well, I can take driving and dog duties for the rest of the way while you sleep."

"I'd rather continue driving."

I stare at Will. Obviously, he doesn't trust me to keep going in the right direction.

"Okay fine." I snatch the leash from Will's hand. "I'll take dog duties then."

Spinning on my heel, I march back toward the car. I'm about to slide in, when I remember Will's conversation with Pippin.

"Did I overhear something about an accident occurring on this seat? Is that the reason you want to drive? So you don't have to sit here?"

"I cleaned it," Will says in this sniffy sort of way. Like how dare I question his motives. "It's damp still, which is why a towel's covering it."

It's too cold to stand outside arguing, especially when I don't have a coat. So with a shrug I get in.

The next hour crawls by without another word exchanged. The radio is off, and this time Will doesn't remind me that I'm in charge of music. Okay then. Time to check my phone. There are twenty-four new texts from Stella.

Apparently, an old friend who drives a truck for a living (Stella, of course, has friends everywhere in all occupations), was having a hard time after an ugly divorce. She met up with him in Nevada and asked him to come along with her to Buffalo, selling it as a fun chance for them to catch up. Amazingly, he agreed.

Relieved to know Stella isn't texting and driving, I simply ask her to pass along the truck rules (You dirty it, you clean it. No feet on the dashboard) and remind her to be safe.

After that's taken care of, I take refuge in the mindlessness of Candy Crush Saga. I've just used up all my lives when Pippin squirms on my lap. He jumps down to the floor, turns a few times, then leaps onto my chair. I reach for him, thinking to calm him with some belly rubs, but he wriggles away and makes a break for the opening between the two front seats. Snagging his collar, I grab him before he can make it into the back.

"What's going on, mister?" I ask him.

"That's exactly how he was acting right before the blowout," Will says.

I'm so relieved to hear Will's voice I don't even care that we're discussing the dog's bowel movements.

"I think he's gotta go again," I say as Pippin whines softly. "I think he's gotta go bad."

The engine revs as Will floors it. Of course, that only gets us moving marginally faster than before. "Hold on. It's about five miles to the next exit."

I look down at Pippin, who's thrashing around, fighting my hold on him. "Hold on, Pips. Okay? Let's not make another car mess."

He trembles in response. Poor guy. He's trying to hold it in, but it's a losing battle. Fairly certain he won't make it, I search for something to contain the mess. Plopping Pippin in the middle of my blanket, I bunch the rest around him so that only his head sticks out.

"What did he eat?" I ask. "Just Twinkies and candy?"

"Well no..." Will scrubs a hand through his hair. "I had a turkey sub. I set it aside when I stopped for gas, and when I got back in the car, it was gone. Even the wrapper was gone. He ate it all."

I groan. "Stella said to treat him like a bear crossed with a gremlin. Keep all food up high and out of reach. And if he does eat, prepare for monsters."

"Pippin would actually be a mogwai. The gremlins are what spawn from it," Will corrects me.

At the same moment a noise comes from beneath the blanket covering Pippin.

We all freeze. Even Pippin. Like he's more shocked than anyone. Then a terrible smell fills the car and a warm dampness spreads through the blanket where it rests against my legs.

"The gremlins are coming out now," I announce grimly.

"Exit." Will points and then stomps the gas pedal even harder.

TTHHHBBBTTTT. Pippin releases another bomb.

Gagging a little, I unroll my window, desperate for fresh air, not caring about the cold blasting me.

At last the exit appears before us. Will zooms off the freeway and screeches to a halt on the side of a deserted road.

"Hold on," he orders, jumping out of the car.

"Do I have another option?" I clutch the blanket closed, even as Pippin's secret treasure starts seeping through. After what seems like an eternity, my door swings open and Will reaches in, his hands covering my own.

I fall a little bit in love with Will at that moment. His nearness. His touch. The fact that he says, "Okay, I got it," and then takes the whole bundle of dog and excrement out of my lap.

It makes me feel a bit like Lois Lane, doomed, falling from a great height to certain death. Then suddenly the hero arrives. Superman, grabbing Lois close, carrying her up and away. Meanwhile she relaxes against his solid chest and enjoys the view, knowing she's safe and cared for.

Except presumably Lois Lane wouldn't look down and realize, yeah, the two wet round spots on the thighs of her jeans...that's definitely not doggie drool.

It's terrible, and then it's more terrible, and then it's so terrible that it's almost a little bit funny. Somewhere in there Will and I become friends again. We have no choice. In these situations, it's either bond like superglue or kill each other.

Perhaps it also helps that we're careful not to mention any of the following things: the kiss, the sex, my panic attack, the horrible, awful things I said, Will telling me to shut up, and finally and most of all, DANNY. His name does not cross our lips. Not once.

Now it's nearly midnight as Will turns onto the street where I grew up, where my mother and sister and niece still live. It has taken us over five hours to get through the last three hours of our journey. And yet instead of leaping from the vehicle, I sit for a moment more.

I'm no longer bothered by the smell of the car, a terrible mixture of doggie dysentery and bleach. Similarly, I long ago ceased to notice or care that I'm not wearing pants. I can't say the same for Will's shirt-free situation, which is a bit more distracting.

Being a gentleman, he gave me his fleece sweatshirt to cover my ass after I removed what had once been my favorite pair of jeans. As he peeled it off, his T-shirt crept up too. After our backseat shenanigans, it shouldn't have affected me. But it did. My mouth went dry. Then Will tugged the T-shirt back down, and I was left wishing the show had gone on longer.

It turns out sometimes you can get what you want, because on Pippin's third—or was it his fourth? Well whatever. While cleaning up after one of Pippin's many gastric episodes, the little shitter unexpectedly swung around and left a smear of poo across Will's midsection. His T-shirt joined the other items drip drying in the backseat, and Will had no choice but to slide behind the steering wheel bare chested.

All that skin on display. His rippling muscles flexing just below the surface. It was difficult to keep my eyes away, so I didn't even try. Every time we passed beneath a streetlight, I'd memorize a new patch of skin.

In between rubbernecking Will's body, the never-ending feces explosions, and subsequent cleanups, we talked. It wasn't like the kiss and sex and crying hadn't happened. We simply put it aside, too focused on surviving the rest of this drive to deal with that mess too.

I trotted out all my most amusing "the show must go on" stories. Like the time I had the stomach flu. Buckets were positioned on each side in the wings so I could rush off and vomit if necessary. Which I did. Or when the whole orchestra pit took a day trip to a Renaissance festival and got caught in a twenty-car pile-up on the way home. Only the drummer had stayed behind, so that night we did the show acapella with drums.

I admit, I hammed the stories up, acting out different bits, encouraged by Will's laughter.

Somehow I ended up telling him about Ethel's offer too. Almost immediately I regretted it. Will said it sounded amazing and asked what was holding me back. I didn't want to explain how the idea of settling down made me sick. So I mumbled something about hating Texas and quickly switched the subject.

"What have *you* been up to these past years?" I asked in an unnaturally perky voice, like I was head chair of the reunion committee.

I couldn't help gasping and stuttering in disbelief when Will said he worked for his dad's carpet store. Somewhat sheepishly, Will admitted to being lost after dropping out of college. School had always been his thing. Without it he wasn't sure what to do. He ended up at the carpet store, found he was a good fit for watching the books and that the previous person had been a bad fit, in that he'd stolen nearly ten thousand dollars.

Working the back room still seemed like a loss, so I felt better when Will said he eventually returned to school. But when I asked what he majored in, he got a little squirrelly again. "Well, I'm near to finishing degrees in a few different areas."

"Like what?"

"Uh, a doctor of physical therapy degree. And I just recently started an architecture program with an emphasis on accessible design, and I've taken a half-dozen classes working toward an MBA."

"Oh, is that all?"

This earned a wry grin from Will. "Actually, no. I forgot to mention that for a few years I've been taking online classes wherever I can fit them in to earn a master's degree in mental health counseling."

"That's totally bananas!" I laughed. "What are you going to do with all those degrees when you finally finish them?"

"Help people who've suffered traumatic injuries."

There was a long, uncomfortable silence, before realizing I needed to say something. I finally got out an "Oh."

He didn't mention Danny's name, but he might as well have been sitting between us.

"Primarily, my focus will be on people with serious brain injuries," Will continues.

I can hear the intensity in his voice. This is something he's obviously put a lot of thought into.

"Families who come to me will receive a full plan. I'll address all the patient's physical and mental problems going forward. We'll even discuss ways they can rehab their homes to better fit the patient's needs."

Getting it, I chimed in. "And this'll be your business, so you'll need the MBA to know how to run it."

"Exactly!"

I was blown away. And more than a little embarrassed. Will had this grand plan he was working toward. Meanwhile, I had...what exactly? An idea to sorta head toward Portland.

Better not to dwell on that. "So which degree will you finish first? Sounds like you're close on a bunch of them."

"I'm not sure..." Will hedged. "Maybe physical therapy, but I was also considering a nursing degree, which would set me back. Possibly a law degree too. Sometimes there are legal issues involved with these things. I want to have all the bases covered."

Oh no. Suddenly the picture became clearer. Will wasn't working toward some grand plan, no matter what he said. He'll end up staying in school, collecting degrees like they're stamps until...I don't know. Maybe his mother will smack some sense into him. I wonder why she hasn't already?

There was no comfort in knowing I wasn't the only screwup. I didn't want Will stuck at my level. It was awful and tragic and pissed me off. It wasn't my business, and yet I couldn't help but ask, "Why wait? Why not jump in with what you have now?"

"Why not move to Portland proper instead of way out in the exurbs?"

Shit. He had me there.

Using my brightest voice, I pivoted. "Well, it's great to hear the carpet store is doing well!"

Will paused, sent an "I see you" look in my direction, and then obligingly launched into a story about King Carpets' top salesperson:

his mother.

Before she'd had kids, Mrs. O'Leary had worked the sales floor. She'd been one of their top sellers. A few years ago, she decided to go back to work. She was worried about money and continuing to make sure that Danny had everything he needed. Not surprisingly, many of the qualities that made her a pain in the ass also made her a great salesperson. Six months into the job she was landing national accounts, and after two years, profits at the store had doubled.

Just as Will finishes up with the story of his mom convincing a national movie theater chain to give them all their business, the lights from his car land on the mermaid mural painted on our garage door.

There's *my* mom in all her glory. Parts of her tail have flaked away, but her gigantic tits covered with two teensy seashells still bounce above the waves. No wonder I remember the artist spending the most time there. Mom insisted on posing for him multiple times so he could get the shadowing right.

I sigh, a mix of emotions filling me. They say you can never go home again, but here I am and it looks...pretty much the same. More run down than I remember, but still, it's home. So familiar it almost hurts. Even Mom's mermaid mural brings more nostalgia than embarrassment.

Across the street the frat boys seem to be in the midst of some sort of Thursday night bacchanalia. The temperature is in the low twenties, but a large handful of people stand in the driveway loudly talking and laughing while smoking cigarettes. Annoying college kids have always lived in this neighborhood—lots of upper/lowers and duplexes leads to lots of rentals. The bass thump of music paired with the shouts of drunken youths were the sounds of my childhood.

"You okay?" Will asks softly.

"Yeah." I nod. "Just mentally preparing to deal with my family."

But that's not true. The house is dark, which means everyone is probably asleep.

Oddly, I'm disappointed. I wanted to step into the full chaos. Allie giving me hell for taking so long and not visiting sooner and who the hell said I could bring a dog. Mom asking a million questions about the ride and Will and Danny while also offering to make me a drink or a sandwich. "You know what's good?" she'd say. "PB and J with a screwdriver. Two classics. You can't go wrong." Meanwhile Maxi would...My imagination stutters to a stop. I don't know Maxi well enough to guess how she'd greet me. A pang of loss vibrates through me.

"Okay," I say, grabbing my backpack of goodies in one hand and Pippin's limp body in the other.

About two hours ago Pippin finally powered down the poop machine. Afterward he sat at my feet chewing his new favorite dog toy—my vibrator. But apparently, all those bowel movements took it out of the poor guy in more ways than one. He soon fell asleep and has barely moved since. Now he lifts his head, licks my hand, and closes his eyes once more.

I turn to Will. "Thanks for the ride."

It's the same thing I always said to him after he drove me home. Now it pops out. The past shimmers between us again. Both an obstacle and an unbreakable connection.

"Anytime," Will answers.

He waits in the car as I walk up the driveway to the back door. I give the doorknob a jiggle and it opens right up. Leaning out the door, I wave to Will and stay that way, watching as the car reverses and drives away.

"Whoooo!" someone calls from across the street.

"Whoooo!" I yell back.

Then there's no putting it off any longer. At last I step inside the house I'd half expected to never see again.

27

"The Merry Old Land of Oz" –Wizard of Oz

"Auntie Jenna. Ohhh Auntie, wake up."

I squint one eye open.

Maxi is beside me, bouncing on the bed with Pippin cradled in her arms like a baby. His tongue lolls out the side of his mouth. Clearly, he's in heaven.

While I feel slightly hellish. Stretching my arm out, I pat the bedside table until I connect with my phone. I bring it close. Squint at the time. With a groan, I fling the phone away and clamp my eyes closed once more.

"Too early."

"Well, sorry," Maxi says in a way that indicates she is not at all sorry and that she has, either through nature or nurture, absorbed her mother's love of sarcasm. "I wouldn't be up this early, except I have school. And I wouldn't be in your room if I had anything to wear. Which I don't. Also, I didn't know you were here when I came in, so it's not like I was *purposely* trying to bother you. Umm, I hate to mention it, but you might want to know there's a wet spot at the end of the bed. I think it's dog pee."

"It definitely is." I sigh as Maxi gives the bedsprings another jolt. "Could you please stop bouncing?"

"No. If I stop bouncing, you'll fall back asleep." She gives an extra little jolt to emphasize this.

I groan. "You know, years ago I could've smothered you in your sleep. I didn't, but I could've. So maybe you could return the favor."

"That doesn't make sense. To return the favor, I'd have to not smother you in your sleep, which obviously I didn't. And I won't. Unless you snore like Grandma after she's had a few too many, which is most nights. Then I might be tempted. But I probably won't act on it. So there. Favor returned. Probably. Also, it's not really a favor to not suffocate a helpless infant. Is it?"

"Well argued. You should be a lawyer. Quick go study for the lawyer test now. I hear it's hard."

"Actually, I might." This is so surprising that my eyes fly open as Maxi clarifies. "I might be a lawyer. I'm not going to study for the bar right now. Or did you mean the LSAT? That would make more sense, but not really since I have to get through undergrad before I can even think about law school."

I scrub at my eyes and then scooch up to a half-sitting position. There's no falling back to sleep anyway. "You're really considering being a lawyer?" No one in our family has ever aspired to anything requiring an advanced degree.

Maxi shrugs. "Maybe. Nadine, that's Mom's girlfr—"

Annoyed, I interrupt. "I know who Nadine is."

"All right, all right. Calm down. You're terrible with names, and you've never actually met her, so I wasn't sure you'd remember."

She has a point there. "Fine," I grumble. "Continue."

"Well, Nadine's a lawyer, and she always has really nice clothes, and she lives in this cute little house that's all hers. She has central air and pays someone to mow her lawn during the summer and shovel her driveway in the winter. Plus she's never, not once, had any of her utilities turned off. I asked her once if it's because she's a lesbian. Like not having men on the brain makes you better at life, but she said she knows loads of straight people who pay their bills on time, so she doesn't think it's a gay thing."

I frown, not quite sure what to deal with there. Or if I should say anything at all. As the drop-in aunt, am I allowed anything beyond, "Hey, cool. Good luck!" I'd be okay sticking with that limited script, except seeing Maxi after all this time is breaking my heart a little bit.

She's so sleek and confident and grown-up. The way she keeps flipping her long hair over her shoulder is so Allie, but the bubbling energy is all her own. I've missed so much. And when I leave again, I'll miss so much more. The least I can do is be fully here for the short time I am here. And that means giving advice, even if I'm not quite sure how to do it. It seems like Nadine's got things covered educating Maxi on queer experiences, so I focus on the career stuff.

I approach it cautiously. "So you want to be a lawyer to make money? Not that there's anything wrong with that, but..."

Maxi rolls her eyes. "No, I also think it'd be an okay job. Nadine says it's not as sexy as they make it seem on TV. But it's not as boring as people say it is either. Plus, there's a lot of different specialties, so you can sorta figure out what interests you. So yeah." Maxi stands and drops Pippin into my lap. "Good talk. I gotta get to school, and I only came in to raid mom's closet, but she's pretty much transferred everything worth stealing to Nadine's." She cocks her head slightly and gives me her sweetest smile. "Where's your luggage, by the way?"

"You can't have my clothes. And why do you think they'd even fit you?"

"I'm not a child anymore. Look at me." Maxi holds out her arms and then to emphasize the point, thrusts out her chest. Or to be more precise, her boobs. The ones she didn't have seven years ago. "You know what's amazing about the women in this family? We all have nearly the exact same body. It's like we came out of some Play-Doh mold. Big boobs, small waists, flat asses, curvy calves, ugly knees and elbows, small stubby fingers, and narrow shoulders that cause our bra straps to constantly slip off."

I blink at Maxi, stupefied by this spot-on recitation. She holds out a hand, and I place mine over hers. She's right. Stubby fingers. Gently I curl my short little fingers around hers. "I have two good bras that I got at a specialty shop after a personal fitting, and they never slip off my shoulders. I paid out the ass for them, and it was totally worth it. My suitcase is at the airport, but I'll be getting it later today. If you take either one of those bras, your fingers won't be stubby, they'll be stumps. You get me?" I give her hand a little squeeze.

Maxi's eyes widen, and then she grins. "So everything else is fair game?"

"As long as I'm not wearing it."

"Great!" She turns and practically skips out of the room. Right before shutting the door behind her, she turns to add, "I'd never wear someone else's underwear anyway. Gross. I don't know where that's been."

I slump back into bed. *Now* I can imagine how Maxi would've greeted me last night. A smile stretches across my face as Pippin burrows beneath the covers beside me.

It's strange how good it feels to be home.

Something weird is happening.

I slept.

Last night, after finding a note on the kitchen table saying Allie was at Nadine's and I could have her bed, I climbed into it, pressed my face into a pillow that smelled strongly of her brand of hairspray, and almost immediately fell asleep.

This could be chalked up to exhaustion. A body can only be deprived of sleep for so long. But this morning after Maxi woke me, I lay in bed listening to her move around the house, and then finally the front door thumped shut behind her. Again I noted the scent of Allie's hairspray. Also the smells of the house itself. A combination of mildew, because the place is old and rotting away, and burnt Pop-Tarts. It doesn't smell good exactly, but it's familiar.

I breathed the house in and out. Somewhere in there, sleep grabbed hold of me.

And now, unbelievably, I've slept till almost noon.

Groggy, I stumble out of bed and into the bathroom for a quick shower. Back in the bedroom, my phone has several text messages. One from Will simply says, *Pick you up at 1?*

It's a basic text, but seeing Will's name on the screen scrambles my insides. That kiss comes to mind first. I think I was dreaming about it.

I give myself a mental slap. Will is setting up a time to take me to Danny.

DANNY.

My stomach clenches with dread. Yet my breathing remains steady. While I still feel sick at the idea of seeing Danny, it's not in the same desperate panic from yesterday. I still don't feel up to it, but I'm not freaking out. Maybe getting some decent shut-eye made the difference. Not that I'd ever admit it to Will.

Ignoring his text, I shoot one to Stella instead. I haven't gotten any new messages from her since yesterday.

Made it to Buffalo late last night. Where you at?

I stare at the phone a few moments, willing a response, but after several minutes of nothing, I toss it aside. First coffee, then I'll deal with Stella. And maybe I'll text Will back too.

Actually, first clothes.

Everything I was wearing yesterday needs to be burned, so I turn to Allie's closet and discover Maxi was right: Allie has taken everything good. Still, I need clothes, so I keep digging until I find a sweater with a few moth holes in it, a T-shirt to wear under it, and a pair of faux black leather pants with the tags still on. A size six instead of Allie's usual eight, they were obviously bought during an optimistic moment.

Maxi was right about another thing. We do all have similar bodies. Allie, however, is hippier than me, so I'm able to squeeze into the pants, though buttoning them is slightly painful. I solve this by looping a hairband through the buttonhole and then around the button itself. This extra inch of space means I'll be able to sit without wincing. And according to the full-length mirror on the back of the door, the extra-tight fit gives me a Sandy-at-the-end-of-*Grease* look.

Pippin is curled on top of my pillow, gnawing away on my vibrator and overall looking content. Leaving him there, I head downstairs.

I find Allie in the kitchen, where she has a mini photo studio set up on the table. Bathing blocks artfully arranged in two pastel-colored towers sit at the center of a miniature white tent. Allie stands behind a pricey-looking camera set up on a tripod. Two lights on stands glow from opposite corners of the room.

I watch, fascinated and more than a little impressed as she snaps away. This actually looks professional.

Allie glances up at me, then back to the camera. "Don't expect me to drop everything because you finally showed up."

I refuse to take the bait. "I'm just watching. And looking for something to eat."

Allie sighs, refusing to be appeased. "Mom was waiting for hours this morning. Wanting to say hi. Welcome you home. She had to go out, but she left breakfast for you. Your favorite." She jerks a thumb at the box of donuts sitting on the counter.

I shouldn't. Especially not with these pants on, but I find myself drawn to the box anyway. Paula's Donuts. Flipping it open, I discover that Paula makes some generously sized donuts. I slice one in half. It's filled with strawberry jelly *and* fluffy white cream. What is this beautiful madness?

Standing over the sink, I make happy food noises while I eat the donut and watch Allie work. She moves the soap around, or interchanges one bar with another. I surrender to the inevitable and eat the other half of the donut. Even if these pants split open the first time I bend over, this donut is worth it.

"Where'd Mom go?" I ask.

"Brunch meeting for small-business owners. She's networking."

"Wow." The realization hits that Allie and Mom are serious about this soap thing. Maybe it's not a scam after all.

As Allie shuts off the lights and carefully puts her camera to the side, I reach for one of the bathing blocks and bring it to my nose. It smells amazing. Floral and fresh. I could easily imagine it being sold in some expensive boutique.

I'm feeling like an asshole for every nasty thing I ever said or thought about the bathing blocks...until I spot some words printed into the side. Squinting, I bring it closer. It's smudged, but still readable if you look close enough.

"Allie." I hold the block of soap out to her. "Why does this say 'Made in China'?"

Allie snatches the soap from my hand. "Ugh, are you kidding? They stamp some of the soaps. Maxi's supposed to check for it when she rewraps, but she doesn't always catch them."

"Wait." I hold up a hand. "So the soap you claim to make yourself from all natural and organic ingredients is actually made in China?"

"We make it ourselves in old-fashioned marble basins actually."

I gape. "You don't even know how to make soap, do you?"

Allie rolls her eyes. "Oh please, don't be naïve. *Everything* is made in China. No one really cares. They just want good stuff, cheap. And our bathing blocks are better than good. And because they're made in China, we've been able to seriously undercut the competition. Anyway, I came up with all the scents by myself. That's the important part. I told them how much of this and that to put in. Then I'd smell it and tweak. It turns out I've got one of those super noses. If I'd known earlier in life, I could've been some sort of professional smeller person by now."

"A professional smeller?" I cannot stop the smirk that takes over my face. "Don't they usually use dogs for that type of things?"

Allie's face goes red, which is always a sign that she's about to lose her shit. And she does. Because some things never change. She slams the bar onto the table.

"Fuck you and your fucking high horse, Jenna. You think you're so much smarter and better than everyone else. After all this time you finally bother to come home, and this is how you act? God, I was gonna have this talk about how you need to stay and help take care of Mom, but fuck it. Go. Okay? Go back to your glamorous jet-setting life."

Here's the thing about Allie. She seems confident and bossy and assertive. Most of the time she is all these things and also annoying as hell. But then she'll get upset, and suddenly it all slides away, revealing this person who's totally insecure. Vulnerable even. I always end up feeling terrible for blowing her cover. For making her expose all the maggoty doubts eating her up inside.

So I show her some of my own.

"Allie, I am not a glamorous jet-setter. I can't even get on a plane without having a panic attack. That's why we drove most of the way here from California. And I have a crappy customer service job, and I do shows at little community theaters in towns no one has heard of. I spend most of my time alone. And a lot of the time, it's lonely."

I am surprised to hear this last bit come out of my mouth. Not because it's untrue. But because it's something I've never admitted to anyone before.

Allie sniffs. "If it's so bad, how come you never come home?"

"Because I can't. Or...I couldn't. I was in self-imposed exile. I ran away from the whole Danny situation, and I was afraid to come back, and then when I wasn't afraid anymore, I felt like, I don't know, like I didn't deserve to."

I watch Allie as she thinks this over. Finally she shakes her head. "That doesn't even make sense. You're such an idiot. And by the way, next time you want to wear my clothes, ask first, okay?"

Just like that, Allie is herself again. It's a mixed blessing. "And like I was saying before, now that you're back, it's your turn to take care of Mom. I'm moving in with Nadine, and Mom refuses to sell the house and go into one of those active adult communities. Nae and I were

203

gonna let her live with us, but I'm thirty-three years old, and I deserve to have a short time in my life where I'm not living with mother."

"No, no, no. I didn't say I was *staying*. I have—"

"Nothing," Allie interjects. "You just said so. Your life sucks. You wanted to come home, and now you have. You can do theater and your crappy customer service job here."

"I want *more* than that!" The words burst out of me. "I have a job offer in Texas to run a small theater company, and I'm seriously considering it." Again I'm surprised by the statements coming off my own lips. But not unhappy. They feel right.

Allie plants her hands on her hips. "So that's it? You're gonna leave again? Let me deal with Mom?"

"I don't know. Nothing's certain yet. I probably won't take it, but I can't stay here. I've actually got plans to go to the Portland area, but maybe in a few years—"

"Maybe," Allie repeats, her voice dripping with scorn. "Well, that's just fucking great. Let me mark that on my calendar so I can look forward to it. In a few years. Thanks a lot."

Oh yeah, the sarcasm is on full blast.

This is normally when I'd make an excuse to get off the phone. Probably won't help if I mention to Allie that a perk of being away is hanging up on her.

The back door slams, and I expect Mom to come in and take both of our sides and make everything worse, but instead it's an incredibly tall woman in a parka and ski mask.

Pulling the mask off with one hand, she sticks the other out toward me. "Hello, I'm Nadine. You must be Jenna."

I take her hand, and she shakes it firmly, sizing me up while I do the same. She's different than I expected. First off, none of Allie's pictures made it clear how incredibly tall she is. Second, her hair is a curly short mop that flips this way and that in a manner that's almost mesmerizing. But mostly I gawk because she's gorgeous. Allie says Nadine doesn't like having her image online, so I've only seen her as

204

a blurry person in the background where all I could really tell was that she seemed to be human shaped.

"I was outside chipping away at the ice on the driveway so we are not all slipping and sliding," Nadine says after finally releasing my hand and then moving to Allie's side, where she loops one of her long arms around my sister's shoulders. "I hired a neighborhood boy to shovel. Very nice boy, excited to make a little money."

She speaks with a slight accent, and I remember Allie saying her parents are Russian and they immigrated here when Nadine was a teen.

"But your mother, she decides last week it is too cold for boy to be outside shoveling. So she tells him to come in. She makes him a hot cocoa. Okay, fine. Maybe her heart is too generous, but I appreciate the impulse. But then she puts liquor into it. Bailey's." Nadine makes a face. "She tells me later that this is not liquor. Well, I agree with her there. It is certainly nothing I would ever drink. But that boy, huh, it was liquor to him. Did he finish the driveway? No, he did not."

Nadine sighs in this epic way, and Allie joins in, so they are sighing in tandem. It's pretty adorable actually.

"And so we are slipping and sliding again." Nadine stops to shake her head. "Do not get me wrong. I love your mother. She is an original person. But she should not intoxicate young men who are meant to be shoveling the driveway. Or she should at least wait until they are finished."

"And," Allie jumps in, "the boy's mother called and said he wouldn't be coming over anymore. She said it was inappropriate for Mom to give him booze and to ask him personal questions. Can you believe that? I asked Mom what the hell she'd said. I find out she was interrogating him on his sex life. The kid's only fifteen. I think she was trying to pick him up!"

"Oh, c'mon," I interject, before Allie gets Mom classified as a pedophile. "She was being friendly. *Maybe* a little flirty."

Allie tilts her head back to look up at Nadine. "I was trying to tell

Jenna, when you came in, that she's got to help. Mom's getting out of hand."

"She's always been like that," I protest.

Nadine shrugs in this way that comes across as elegant and international. "I believe this."

"Nae." Allie elbows her. "I haven't told Jenna about our news. I was waiting for you to come in. *News*, which you agreed, changes everything."

"Ah yes." Nadine smiles beatifically. "Our news. You tell her now." In an unmistakable gesture, Nadine puts her hand on Allie's belly.

"Holy shit, you're knocked up!" I exclaim.

"I'm not knocked up! Only idiots get knocked up. I've been invitro'd at this fancy clinic. When you walk in, they ask if you want a cappuccino. And if you ask for water, it's got cucumbers and lemons in it."

Nadine rubs Allie's stomach. "She was very uncertain about IVF. She tells me it is 'weird and unnatural.' She says, 'Why not call Maxi's dad?' She will bone him a few times—"

"I didn't say *bone*. I said *bang*," Allie interrupts.

Nadine waves this away with a flutter of fingers. "Then we arrive at clinic, and she discovers the beverage situation. After that, it was all enthusiasm. Now, when I want something—"

"I take her to the Starbucks." This last bit Allie and Nadine say together, perfectly in sync.

"Clearly you've told this story before," I observe.

"It's part of her set," Allie says in her *duh* voice. "I've told you, we met at a class on how to do stand-up comedy. Nae became the star pupil—"

Nadine blushes. "I don't know about that."

"You were," Allie insists. "And now—"

Remembering, I cut in. "—she does open mic gigs on the weekends. I remember. I just wasn't expecting to hear stand-up in the middle of the kitchen. But that's a good bit, about the Starbucks. Does it play well?"

"It got some laughs last weekend," Nadine says with a shrug.

"It got *good* laughs," Allie corrects. "I'm telling her to expand the bit. They would sometimes have a harpist playing in a corner of the reception area. Just, you know, hanging and playing the harp for our entertainment. That's funny shit."

Nadine nods, obviously considering Allie's advice. "It is funny. But where is the punch line?"

"I don't know. Say I tried to tip her. Or that I clapped."

"No." Nadine shakes her head. "That did not happen. And besides, I do not make joke of you like you are clown or dancing monkey. You are not my punch line. Not ever." She takes Allie's face in her hands, and suddenly I'm not there. I've disappeared.

I watch as they kiss, a little embarrassed, but also weirdly touched. They love each other. It's in the way they stand together, touching. And how they talk and share stories and work together on Nadine's stand-up act.

Honestly, I'd been skeptical of the whole relationship. Allie was boy crazy from birth. Even after she had Maxi, there was always a guy. Usually a loser, even though Allie would act like he'd invented daylight. Then suddenly there was Nadine. We never had an official "So hey, I guess you're gay now" conversation. Instead I pretended like Nadine was just another guy. I'd figured she'd be gone in a few months. When those months passed, I decided it was a phase. An early midlife crisis or something.

But that's not what this is at all. This is love. The kind where two people make each other better when they're together.

Okay, the sweet kiss is turning into a make-out session, and I'm getting uncomfortable. Loudly, I clear my throat and start talking as if they don't have their tongues in each other's mouths. "That story about Mom getting the kid drunk might be good for your act. I mean, it's kind of a funny story, right?"

They turn to look at me with twin looks of disdain.

"Mmmm," Nadine says at last. "I will consider that."

Right. Time to change the topic. "So it took? You're really having a kid?"

"Two of them," Allie tells me with a proud smile.

"Twins? No fucking way! Congratulations! And congratulations again!"

They both nod and grin, happiness pouring out of them.

"Does Maxi know? And Mom?"

"Of course they know." Allie rolls her eyes. "They were there when I peed on the stick, and we were all screaming and dancing around."

"We popped champagne," Nadine says with a grin.

"And then didn't let me drink it," Allie adds.

I can see it. The celebration. Allie pouting because she can't drink. And I have no right to feel hurt because I wasn't there. No right to even wish she'd told me sooner. But I am.

I swallow that down, refusing to let it show. This is not about me. "Well congrats, you guys. That's amazing. I'm so happy for both of you." Cupping my hands around my mouth, I crouch so I'm at stomach height. "Did you hear that, little babies? Your aunt Jenna can't wait to meet you."

Allie suddenly sniffs, and I look back up to see tears glittering in her eyes. "It's the hormones," she says as they spill down her cheeks. "I just...I don't only want you home to deal with Mom. I mean, that's a big part of it, don't get me wrong. But you were so good with Maxi. So close with her. Almost like her second mom sometimes. After you left, there were so many nights when she cried for Wenna."

Wenna. Maxi's baby name for me. I'd almost forgotten. Now my throat tightens at the memory of it. "You never told me that."

"Well, you had a lot of shit going on, so I didn't want to pile on."

I stare at Allie. I hadn't known she was capable of being sensitive to feelings other than her own.

Then she adds, "Also, you probably didn't notice, but I was so pissed after you left that I didn't talk to you at all for six months."

Oh. Actually, I hadn't noticed. I know better than to admit this aloud.

"Anyway, I want Aunt Wenna to be there for these babies too. I want you to be part of their lives. And not just the beginning, but their whole lives."

Like the Grinch, it feels like my heart's attempting to grow three sizes. "I'll be there for them," I promise, and I know it's true. Even if I go to Portland or wherever, this time I won't stay away. This time I won't be in exile.

I am swept into the middle of a three-way hug, and it isn't until I'm released that I remember how I usually hate being hugged.

I guess, like many things, it's different with family.

28

"How Could I Ever Know" –The Secret Garden

"Wow, those are pants," Will says when I get into his SUV, which is really one of the nicer compliments I've ever received. It's the delivery that sells it. And the way he looks at me, his gaze hot enough to melt a hole in the borrowed pleather.

I forget that I am in distress. Forget that Will texted me sixteen times and then leaned on the doorbell until Allie ("For fuck sake, you do *too* hear that") answered, all part of his quest to lay me at the feet of his brother's bed.

But I don't forget how another part of me wanted to run to the door and throw it open, ready to jump into Will's arms. Like after a day in his company, having him beside me started to feel essential. And after only half a day away—I missed him.

Now with him looking at me like that, I again recall that kiss. Not the crazy sex. That still plays in my mind like something that happened while I was high. But that kiss...I don't know that I'll ever shake it.

For one moment, I let all the other crap fade away. Will is just a boy admiring my ass and I am just a girl admiring him back.

Intending to fully enjoy the moment, I reach over and tousle Will's wet hair. "I thought I'd slept late, but it looks like you just crawled out of bed and into the shower."

He gives his head a shake, sending a few droplets of water my way. "Actually, I did sleep late. Usually, I'm at the gym by eight. I've been told that certain employees set their watches by me. Imagine their shock when I strolled in at half past eleven." He grins in this dorky way that for some reason makes my heart skip half a beat.

"Wow, so you've been, what? Lifting weights for the last hour and a half?" This is absolutely a fishing expedition. I want to hear about his workout routine. I want to imagine it and replay it on a loop in my head. Like a physical fitness porno.

"Actually, weights are Monday, Wednesday, and Friday. Tuesday, Thursday, and Saturday I swim. I've heard from so many physical therapists while working with..." He trails off here. He almost mentioned Danny, and it looks like last night's rules are still in effect. Will recovers nicely though, making the pause seem like it was only him checking his blind spot before pulling onto the street.

Once in forward motion, he picks things up as if the quick edit never occurred. "Running can be really hard on your body over time. So I began swimming, and I love it. It's peaceful and lets me turn my brain off. The only problem is that sometimes I lose track of time. Like today. I looked up at the clock and realized I was going to be late. I pretty much ran through the shower and then jumped into my car and headed straight here." Will holds a hand out to me. "Look. My fingers are still wrinkled."

I take his hand in mine and trace the tip of my finger over his, which is indeed wrinkled. Cool to the touch too. And despite that shower, I do catch a faint whiff of chlorine. It's nice though. Without thinking, I cup his hand between mine, and bringing my mouth close, I blow warm air over him. The car jerks slightly, and Will abruptly reclaims his hand.

"Sorry," Will says. "Safest to drive with both hands at ten and two."

"Absolutely."

Actually, it's a relief he took that hand back when he did. I was *this* close to licking him. And friends do not lick friends. Which is what Will and I are. Friends. You can tell we're friends, because I didn't ask if he wears tiny tight-fitting swim shorts. That's not an appropriate question for a friend to ask another friend.

We sit in awkward silence long enough for me to remember our destination. The dread returns. I'm not ready. Not yet. I need to stall.

"I'm starving," I say, even though that gigantic donut is still sitting in my stomach. "Is that all-you-can-eat buffet still up the street? China something. They had the best orange chicken. Maybe we could stop there?"

Will frowns, and I can see him searching for a polite way to refuse. Before he can, my phone rings.

"I need to take this." I grab the phone like it's a lifeline.

Stella skips the more traditional greeting. "Don't worry. Your truck—what's her name?—the HMS Pinnacle, is fine."

"HMS Pinafore," I correct. "And it's a he."

"Really? Huh. I've gotten more of a feminine vibe. Almost like an Olympic gymnast, you know? Muscular but still obviously girlish. Or—"

"Stella," I interrupt. "Debating the gender of my truck cannot be why you called."

"Oh." There's a pause, then she admits, "No. No, it's not. I..."

She hesitates, and I remember—Stella is a travel disaster. I mean, yes, I am a travel disaster with my flying phobia. But once on the road, I get where I'm going with a minimum of drama (yesterday being an obvious exception).

Not so for Stella. Her flights are always delayed. Her rental cars get a flat tire twenty minutes after she's left the parking lot and ten minutes after she is good and lost. When we met in Vegas for a four-day vacation, Stella didn't get there until the end of the second day. When she came to see *A Funny Thing Happened on the Way to the Forum* in Wyoming, she missed opening night. Then she missed the next night as well. Returning home, she got lost going to the airport even though I'd put her in a cab. Apparently, she'd convinced the driver she knew a shortcut and ended up missing her flight.

Which is all to say—I know. Some sort of Stella disaster has struck. "You're not going to be here on time, are you? Will you even make it before the show tomorrow?"

"I swear, hand to God, it's not my fault."

"So that's a no?"

"Jenna, you have no idea what I've gone through. It's been crazy. Totally insane." If she were any other person, this is when she'd cry. Instead Stella barks out one of her crazy laughs. "Oh, Jenna, they took my babies." Another growl of a laugh erupts, except this one splinters at the end.

"What? You mean your dogs?"

"Yes my dogs! Because of that asshole Zeke. Remember I texted about the trucker friend I brought along for the trip? Well Bam Bam wanted to kill him."

"Bam Bam?" I'm surprised. He's one of the two elderly black labs. "But he's so sleepy." There's really no other word to describe him. Besides his gray muzzle, sleep is his main distinguishing characteristic.

"I know, but he's always had this weird thing about men with beards, and Zeke has this gigantic bushy one. I think Bam Bam might've been abused or mishandled at some point in his life by someone with a beard, because I've never seen him this way. He growled at Zeke constantly. Would even sorta bristle. All of us being together in a small contained space didn't help things. Then Zeke started taking it personally. So I said to Zeke, 'Look, it's your beard. Why don't you shave it, and the rest of the trip will go so much nicer.' Well, he acted like I'd suggested he cut off his own dick. 'Do you know how long it took me to grow this beard?' he asked me. Um, it's hair. It grows back. Get over it. But no, he wouldn't budge. It was a real turnoff, I'll tell you that. If I hadn't been drunk, I never would've slept with him."

"You slept with him?" I repeat, just to make sure I heard right.

"Well, yeah. We stopped in Ohio for the night and went to the bar for some celebratory drinks. After three drinks the beard situation didn't matter as much. After five drinks I forgot about the beard entirely. By the sixth drink all I could think about was how he drove that truck. So confident and manly. Like it was an extension of himself. And I thought to myself—"

"I'm gonna stop you right there," I cut in.

But Stella talks right over me. "Let's see how he does taking me for a ride."

"Please tell me you didn't have sex in my truck."

"Oh, no no. Never. Zeke has back problems. We returned to the room and, well, I don't want to give you play by play, but the beard was surprisingly—"

"Nope, nope, nope," I reply loudly, drowning out her next words, though I still make out the words "lady parts." "Can we skip to the part where Bam Bam takes the stage?"

"Bam Bam, right. Well, to be honest, he's always been a voyeur. I can't tell you how many times Bam Bam sat and watched me and Brian go at it—from foreplay to finish. It creeped Brian out. He felt like he was being silently judged. I tried to tell him, 'What do you care if he thinks you're a lousy lay?' Then Brian would say I was projecting, and I'd say, '*You* think the dog's judging you. And you really believe you're earning perfect tens every time? Wow, man, you nailed the dismount!'" Stella pauses for a moment. "What were we talking about?"

Honestly, I'm not sure anymore. "You and Zeke and Bam Bam."

"Oh right. Well, long story short, Bam Bam bit Zeke's balls."

I burst out laughing, and a moment later Stella's loud bray follows.

"I know, I know, it's funny. And it was only a puncture wound. No lasting damage to Zeke's boys. That's what he called them. He was cupping them with both hands, screaming, 'My boys, my boys.' I might've giggled. I shouldn't have. It was nervous laughter. Zeke was not amused. Even after the doctor told him everything was fine down there, he was still threatening to sue. The big baby even called animal control. Said I was hoarding dangerous animals." And now Stella finally sounds upset. "Why would he do that? It's mean. Cruel even. Makes me wish Bam Bam had gone ahead and bitten his balls right off. Would've served him right."

I sort of agree with Stella and tell her so. Then I add she should focus on getting her babies back and not worry about *Annie*. I have it all under control, and anyway it's only one night, and never mind that tech week never happened and that we'll be in an unfamiliar space. I'm sure it'll all go great.

"Oh good. I was hoping you'd say that." And then she rattles off a list of things I need to do. Contacting everyone about rehearsal times, printing programs, making sure we have all the necessary props, getting sets in place...It goes on and on.

Desperately I gesture to Will with little scribbling motions. He, of course, hands me a bunch of graph paper. I have barely gotten it all down, when Stella adds, "Oh, and you have a meeting with the art director of Niven Academy at noon today."

"Noon?" I sputter. "That was an hour and a half ago."

"Yeah," Stella agrees. "You're running late."

After that I grit my teeth and get the last few to-do items down. By the time we finally say goodbye, I sag in my seat, pre-exhausted by all that needs to be done. Stella may be a shit co-director, but she's an amazing organizer. I'd been vaguely aware of how much she was doing for the show, but now seeing it written down in front of me, it seems like more than one person could possibly accomplish.

"Will, could we possibly take a short detour to Niven Academy?"

"I'm already headed that way," he answers immediately. "I assume you don't want the Chinese buffet anymore?"

"Chinese buffet?" It takes a moment to recall my procrastination attempt. "Uh, no, sorry. Maybe afterward?"

"Right." Will nods. "Um, I should apologize. I overheard some, well, actually *all* of your conversation. Your friend's a loud talker. I was going to turn the radio on, but I wasn't sure if it would distract you, so..."

"It's fine," I assure him. "Actually it's great. Now I don't have to do a recap. And we're already on our way to Niven, so I'll be slightly less late than I already am."

"Yeah." Will frowns. "Eli Wallace can be prickly when you first meet him, but—"

"Eli Wallace?" I interrupt, horrified. "I did shows with him. Prickly? He was a fucking diva. Oh fuck. He's the art director of Niven? Shit."

"So he's your theatrical nemesis or something?" Will asks, slightly amused but doing his best to keep it under wraps.

I give him a little side-eye so he knows I'm on to him, and then I spill. "It's worse than that. We were friends."

"You've lost me."

"We went to different schools, but we did tons of community theater shows together. Like basically from when I began doing shows in third grade, he was there too. Around sophomore year we made a pact that whenever we weren't in a show together, we'd meet every Wednesday at this little store that sells sheet music. We'd trade gossip and talk about upcoming auditions. Eventually we made plans to move to New York City together after graduation."

I don't add how after I ended up in Florida, I thought about Eli. Wondered if he was in NYC. Even thought about going there and tracking him down. But I couldn't. It felt too much like picking my life up as if Danny had never happened. Like I wasn't just leaving him behind, but forgetting him too. One was bad enough, but the other...I couldn't. You gotta live with yourself. I never went near New York or any other city like it.

The closest I ever came to reconnecting with Eli was a few years back when I read *Mean Girls* was being made into a musical. Remembering mine and Eli's own aborted attempt to give *Mean Girls* the Broadway treatment, I attempted to friend him on Facebook. The request was denied. I was a little hurt, but not surprised. Our friendship had ended badly, and Eli was not the type to let bygones be bygones.

"He was upset you didn't follow up on plans to move to New York?" Will asks, perceptive as always.

"No, he was upset that after...after, well, *after*." I pause, and Will nods his understanding of what I'm not saying, both of us still working to keep Danny's name out of the conversation. "I ghosted him. I missed the Wednesday meetings. I mean, going didn't even occur to me. My whole life just stopped. Eli called. Emailed. My mom filled him in, but he wanted to talk to me and...I didn't want to talk to him. To anyone. I ran into him once. I was at the grocery store picking up milk and cereal. Our eyes met, and I panicked. I turned and walked in the other direction. Stuck the milk and cereal on some random shelf and left the store."

Will doesn't say anything at all, and I find that I'm afraid to look at him. Finally he sighs. "Jenna, I'm sorry. It was bad for all of us, but I think you took the brunt—"

"No, no, no, no. NO!" I bark out the last one and punctuate it with a double foot stomp. "We're not talking about that. I know I brought it up, but I didn't mean to, and that wasn't the point. The point is, going head to head with Eli is not something I need today. And there's also this list." Pinching it between two fingers, I wave it in the air. "This fucking list of phone calls and supplies and endless to-dos that I am not equipped to deal with."

"Okay, take it easy. My mom is great at that type of stuff. And this whole show was her idea. We'll give her the list—"

"Nooooo-ooooh. Your mom already hates me."

"She doesn't *hate* you."

I roll my eyes. "Oh please, that's what Danny always used to say." Crap! I used the D word! It just slipped out. I clap a hand over my stupid loose lips. But it's too late. I've let the ex-boyfriend out of the bag.

Will's rueful gaze meets my own.

"Pretend I didn't say that."

217

"Jenna, you're going to see him today. We can't keep pretending—"

"We *can* keep pretending. It was one slip. I'll unsay it. You unhear it. Besides which, we might not even have time today. And tomorrow is looking pretty packed too."

Will pulls over to the side of the road. We're on a residential street crowded with cars, but he parallel parks, neatly slotting his SUV between two smaller cars.

"We don't need to stop and hash this out," I protest.

"Actually we're stopping because Niven is at the end of this street. The parking lot always fills up when school's in session, which is why we're parking down here."

"Oh. Great! I should go then..." I grab my purse and am reaching for the door handle, when Will grips my shoulders and firmly turns me back toward him.

"My mother does not hate you. I know she was hard on you when you were dating Danny and after the accident she really leaned on you—"

"*Leaned* on me?" I repeat incredulously.

"I know. She shouldn't have, but we were all reeling, and you were there for her. And for Danny too. She still talks about how you showed up day after day. Never complaining. Never making excuses. She said if she hadn't driven you home, she was afraid you would've stayed there all night."

I blink. This does not line up with how I remember things. Will's sugarcoating it because it's his mother and he doesn't want to think badly of her. Right?

"Toward the end she was worried about you. She wanted you to take some time off, but didn't think you'd go for it. She told me she nudged you to try out for different shows, and you'd shown no interest at all."

She was worried? About me? The whole world is tilting sideways. I do remember her reading auditions notices from the local paper a few times, but I always thought she was taunting me.

"After you left," Will continues. "She fell apart a little. Partially she

218

was mad at me for dropping out of school and worried about where you'd gone and if you were okay. For a week there, even your own mother didn't know where you were. She said you'd packed a bag, so we hoped you were safe. Mom had just hired a private investigator when—"

"She was that worried?" I can't imagine it.

In my version of events, she was raging, furious that I'd gotten away. For months after leaving, I kept expecting to see her outside the motel, waiting to drive me home. Funny, the mixture of relief and disappointment I felt after realizing she wasn't there. I can't quite remember when I stopped expecting it. When the hope and fear evaporated, leaving me free of entanglements, alone in my new life.

"We were all worried." Will tugs a hand through his hair. "It was my fault. The way I handled things. I wanted to get you out of that room, but I shouldn't have done it like that. Mom was furious. That I'd gone over her head. That I'd upset you. Finally Dad and I strong-armed her into going on a cruise. She needed the time away as well."

Will isn't holding me in place anymore. I'm free to go. But I sit frozen.

"She really doesn't hate me?" I finally say, not quite able to make it a statement.

"No," Will affirms, but then he hesitates. "She is though, I think, hurt. I'm not sure any of us expected you to disappear so thoroughly. When months and then years passed without any sign of you—not a call to check in, not a letter or postcard, nothing—it..." Will trails off.

He'd been so gentle, so apologetic, but now I glimpse one of those flashes of anger that occasionally get away from him. Turning away, he starts the car up. "I can get you closer and drop you off."

I should try and explain. Though I've never been able to fully rationalize it even to myself.

I just couldn't go back. I was afraid I'd be trapped in that room for the rest of my life. And later, after enough time passed and those fears seemed ridiculous, like a nightmare reassessed in the clear light of morning, I was embarrassed. Ashamed even. Several times I'd had my phone in hand, ready to call Danny's house, wanting to know how he was, if there was any change, if there was any hope. But I couldn't. Too much time had gone by. I'd revoked my rights to him.

Now looking at Will, I see the one who had stayed. He dropped out of college. Took a job at his father's store. Dedicated his life to Danny. How could he feel anything but contempt for my choices?

I throw my door open as Will maneuvers away from the curb. "It's okay. I'll walk," I call, already jumping out.

I don't wait to hear his reply. I do what I am best at.

I run.

29

"I Can Do Better Than That" – The Last Five Years

I run all the way to Niven...and then am left to sit and wait for over thirty minutes on a bench in the front office.

Finally he comes striding in. "Jenna, hello, so glad you were able to make it." His words are sincere. He shakes my hand warmly. And yet when his eyes meet mine, there's no doubt I've entered the coldest place on earth. Eli turns to the secretary watching us. "This is a reunion you're witnessing. Jenna and I did theater together when we were kids."

She makes some polite noises about what a small world and how nice for us to see one another again. Uncomfortable, I smile and nod and play along. Our previous connection recognized and dealt with, Eli sweeps me along on a tour of the theater space. It's gorgeous, of course. Only the best for Niven Academy. Brand spanking new and state of the art.

With the same professional detachment he might use with a prospective parent or donor, Eli explains how for years—dating all the way back to when he himself was a student here—Niven Academy has been known for its performing arts programs.

"Yeah, I remember coming here to see *Singing in the Rain*," I say, trying to remind him that I was once a pretty good friend. "You were robbed out of the lead. The guy they picked was a great dancer but couldn't carry a tune to save his life."

That's when Eli abruptly turns to face me, like we're dueling with pistols at dawn.

"That's right. You have *opinions* now about how shows should be produced. How interesting. I gathered from my conversation with your producer that you've taken *Annie* in a more experimental direction. Why don't you tell me more about that?"

I gape and stutter before blurting out, "Well, it's basically *Dirty Annie.*"

"*Dirty Annie?*" Eli repeats these two words back at me, highlighting their inadequacy. Highlighting *my* inadequacy.

My mind spins with a mountain's worth of bullshit. I could tell him it's a feminist statement about the way women are viewed, or about how we have increasingly sexualized children, or the way capitalism corrupts.

But you know what? Fuck it.

And fuck Eli Wallace.

"Yeah, we basically took *Annie*, added sexual innuendo, and then removed all the things people actually like about the show. It's crap, to be totally honest. Also the rights to perform it were pulled. We were shut down this past Tuesday, which was supposed to be our tech week, so we haven't even had a full dress rehearsal."

Tears well up. I quickly scrub them away with the back of my fist. "The only reason we're doing it here is because my mother told a man who just woke up from a coma about it. And I guess he's trying to be a supportive boyfriend, because he thinks he's still my boyfriend." Even as I say this, another explanation for Danny's sudden interest in musical theater occurs to me. "Oh God. Actually my mother probably told him it's *Dirty Annie*. That's why he wants to come. He's been unconscious for over a decade, but he still knows how things work. His mom won't be okay with him going to Peppermints men's club, but a night at the theater sounds sedate enough that she'll allow it."

A few more tears escape, and I smack them like mosquitoes. Shoo, shoo. "So he gets to see some ladies shaking their asses, and honestly some of the girls ordered tops that weren't much more than tassels and sequins, and we didn't have a dress rehearsal, so who knows how those will work out, but I wouldn't be surprised if a boob or two popped out. In the end it might be even better than Peppermints."

The last word comes out on a sob. After which the floodgates open. Apparently I am now one of those people who cry over everything. I sink to the floor. You'd think I'd be self-conscious sitting in the middle of a stage sobbing, but I've spent so much of my life standing up here looking out over seats—empty or full—that it feels no stranger than having a good cry on my own couch (which is currently plastic wrapped and sitting in the back of my truck somewhere in Ohio).

Swiping at my tears, I dig through my purse for a tissue. No luck. There's not even a scrap of paper. Anything with any absorptive qualities was used on Pippin's ass last night. Pulling my shirt sleeve down over my hand, I scrub it across my nose.

Eli sighs. The kick-ass acoustics make it sound like an ill wind a coming. "You're pathetic, you know that?"

I nod.

"I hope you don't expect me to whip out my magic wand and fairy godmother this mess of yours."

I sniff and then dig deep. And then a little deeper still, until—there it is. A tiny speck of spirit. "You wouldn't even accept my friend request on Facebook, Eli. So no, I don't expect anything of you."

"No." Eli shakes his head. "We will not autopsy our past friendship to discover where it went wrong, who trespassed first, and what finally finished it. Sorry, but these days I keep my drama on the stage."

"Well, we are on stage," I can't help but point out.

Apparently having no response for that, Eli exits stage left. But then he pivots, and I realize he's just pacing. Finally he stops and faces me. It's clear from his face that he's come to a decision. "This show is on my stage. My students are being enlisted to help run the house and

223

pitch in backstage. While I'm sure they'd find endless amusement in being part of your shit show, it's not really the type of educational experience our brochures promise."

"You're cancelling us?" I ask, equal parts hopeful and defeated.

Eli stands over me.

"Get up," he demands. I stand. "Your show is terrible. Fine, it happens. Now fix it. You know how to pull a show together."

"I'm not a director," I protest. "I'm just—"

With a sneer, Eli cuts in, "A poor little piece of driftwood lost on the great ocean of life."

I gulp. Ouch. "Maybe that's true, but some of the waves have been killers. Like tsunami-type waves."

"Oh, your life's been rough? Try this. Two years ago I was a month away from marrying one of the best men the world's ever produced. Then he notices a pee-sized lump on his ballsack. Turns out it's cancer. Suddenly, we're discussing chemo and life with one testicle and if we want to preserve some of his sperm. Did that mean we cancelled the wedding? No, we did not. Did we ignore our friends and drop out of life? No, we did not. You know what we did? We pretended like we were the fucking queens of England, kept a stiff upper lip, and carried the fuck on."

In my shoes, Stella wouldn't hesitate to reach out and hug the shit out of Eli. I wrap my arms around myself instead. "Is he okay now?"

"No, he's dead."

I gasp.

"I'm fucking with you. He's fine. That's not the point. We went through hell and survived it. And I know it's not the same as your boyfriend-in-a-coma tragedy. I know you were eighteen and pregnant and ill-equipped to handle all of it. But—newsflash—you are not eighteen anymore. You're an adult. Pull your shit together. If the show's an irredeemable train wreck, at least make it an entertaining one."

I stare at him. Oh God, Eli is right. He's right about everything.

224

I can't fix the mess I've made of my life. But I can fix this show. Or make it suck less.

Hard on the heels of this revelation comes another one. I can't fix Danny. I can't go back in time and change what happened. But I can suck it up and go see him. I'm not a kid anymore. I need to do what I should've done years ago. No Chinese buffet. No more crying. No more procrastinating of any kind—the show must go on.

I give Eli a watery smile. "I think you just fairy godmothered me."

Horror flicks across Eli's face, and for a small moment the power balance shifts. But he recovers before I can fully savor my small victory. "Tomorrow at noon you have the student talk."

"I w-w-w-what?"

"Didn't your director tell you? She said you'd done something like it before. Or was that all bullshit?"

"No, I have, but—"

Eli cuts me off. "Let's walk and talk." As he leads me backstage and then into the dressing rooms, I'm given my marching orders. "The students are coming in on a Saturday. Your talk is extra credit for those who attend, based on the supposition that you have experiences worth sharing. You will take some time between now and then to make sure you have experiences worth sharing. Understood?"

I salute, and Eli gives me a raised eyebrow in warning. Years ago I helped him master that trick. I held the compact mirror from my purse in one hand and with the other pinned his left eyebrow in place while he practiced shifting his right one up and down.

"The talk shouldn't take more than an hour," Eli continues. "After which the theater is yours. That should give you more than enough time to run a full dress and tech rehearsal, and work out enough of the kinks so the wheels don't fall off halfway through the show."

"Really?" I turn to him, buoyed by his generosity. "That's amazing. I thought we were gonna wing it—"

Eli interrupts me once more. "I imagine you'll be tired after such a full day, so we'll wait to go car shopping until after Sunday brunch.

225

You're not invited to brunch. We'll pick you up after."

I stare at Eli. "Did you just have a stroke or something?"

He spins on his heel and stops in front of me. I stumble to keep from slamming into him. It's a masterful move. As is the way he manages to look down his nose at me despite being a good six inches shorter. "I am not some magical gay here to flit into your life and point out where you've gone wrong so you can continue toward your happily ever after."

"I understand that. I also know you're not an accessory." Long ago we had a huge argument about whether Stanford in *Sex and the City* was Carrie's gay best friend or just another one of her high-fashion accessories. Eli argued, compellingly, for the latter. "I get it. You don't bibidi bobidi boo. Especially not for me. Honestly, I assumed you were doing this out of pity and maybe a shred of residual affection."

"Hmm..." Eli eyes me up and down, as if assessing my sincerity. I must pass, because he shrugs. "Pity. Yes. Affection...let's not get ahead of ourselves. Either way, I refuse to be a bit player in someone else's story. Which means that you will accompany my husband and myself as we go car shopping this weekend. To be clear, we're not merely looking for a vehicle, but a symbol of our future together. He'd prefer a family friendly vehicle for when we start one. I, however, see us in something small, sleek, and environmentally friendly. Perhaps a car seat could eventually be squeezed into the back, but I'm not set on it."

"And where do I come in?" I ask, already scared of the answer. "I'm a mole secretly working to make sure you get what you want?"

"No, dear. You're supposed to ensure we both get what we want. You'll be mediator, go-between, and referee. Most of all, *you* will be the fairy godmother ensuring that as we drive our new car off into the sunset, we both feel certain of our happy ending. And you will do it all with a smile. If my husband asks, you will say that you are happy to help, that there is no place you'd rather be, and really there's no need to thank you—you're only trying to be a good friend."

226

I shoot Eli a hard look. "Trying, huh? If the car shopping ends successfully, will you accept my friend request?"

Before he can answer (almost certainly with a devastating put-down) a thin blond woman comes out of nowhere and winds her bony arms around me. It's a hug, I think. Pulling back, she graces both of my cheeks with air kisses, at which point I finally recognize her as Danny's ex-girlfriend, Heather.

She looks good. Grown up. Very professional mommy with nice jeans and smooth perfectly highlighted hair.

"Jenna! My gosh! It's amazing to see you after all this time!"

Her greeting is so enthusiastic I feel bad for remembering her as being the worst.

"You look..." She takes a step back and looks me up and down. Then she clucks her tongue and gives a dismissive wave. "Well, never mind that. It's been a rough week with the news about Danny, huh?"

Okay, now I remember why she was the worst. Heather is fake nice. All smiles and snide remarks. I didn't see her often, only when Danny's larger group of high school friends would get together. She'd pretend like we shared some sort of secret code because we'd both been with Danny. Then with a broad wink she'd say, "When it's all over between you two, we'll be able to *really* talk." Because, of course, Danny and I were only temporary.

"Heather, hello, so glad we ran into you." Eli steps between us. "Jenna, Heather wanted to send out an email blast to the Niven Academy families, letting them know about the show. Is there anything specific you'd like her to say?"

"Ugh." I stare at Eli and then Heather, my mind blank. "Well, it's sorta..." I stop as Eli gives a swift head shake, letting me know the whole *Dirty Annie* bit won't work here. He's basically forcing me to come up with a whole new concept for the show right here on the spot. And sell it to Heather too!

Finally, after what feels like hours of sweating and staring at Heather's perfectly raised eyebrows, I say, "It's a modern, edgy take on Annie. Slightly naughty, but with a knowing wink. Part cabaret, part burlesque, and a little bit rock and roll!"

Eli slices his hand across his throat. Cut. Thank God. I was just about to add Stella's "Annie meets *Fifty Shades of Grey*" bit.

Amazingly, Heather looks intrigued. "Really? Would it be possible for me to sit in on a rehearsal? That way I could give my own personal recommendation. Not that I have all that much influence..." She trails off with this faux modesty, looking up at us beneath her lashes, obviously waiting to be corrected.

Eli obliges. "You have tons of influence. Our very own Niven Academy trendsetter."

Heather nods, a queen accepting her rightful due.

I jump in, not wanting Heather anywhere near this show until the curtains officially open. "Unfortunately, the last rehearsal was earlier today. Such a shame you missed it. We would've loved hearing your thoughts. You always had such an amazing sense for what's current and new."

"Well, that's true," Heather says.

Eli jumps in. "I don't want to put words in your mouth, but you could say something like, it's the Annie you'd always imagined but never believed could be fully realized."

Heather's eyes light up. "Ooh, I like that." Her lips move as she silently repeats it back, clearly committing it to memory. "I'm going to send that email now, while it's in my mind."

I get treated to another round of air kisses—thankfully missing the hug this time—and then she's gone as abruptly as she arrived.

I turn to Eli. "And what do I owe for that intervention?"

"You see, that's the problem right there. You think that was about you, when it was strictly for my own pleasure." He smiles. "I personally cannot stand Heather O'Leary."

"O'Leary?" I ask. "Heather O'Leary?"

My eyes widen as my brain fires away with the implications. Heather married Danny while he was comatose. Or Heather married Will. Will married Heather. Will kissed me. So Will cheated on Heather? Will divorced Heather?

Somehow I manage to say goodbye to Eli and promise to return tomorrow at noon, while all these thoughts continue to swirl. I am so lost in my head that as I leave the school, I walk straight past a tall guy in a puffer coat as he lightly runs up and then back down a small flight of stairs leading to an empty soccer field. It isn't until he calls my name that I realize it's Will.

What I intend to say is, "Take me to your brother. Right now. Quick as you can. Before I change my mind." But instead, somehow, these are the words that come shooting out of my mouth, "Did you marry Danny's ex-girlfriend?"

30

"She Used to Be Mine" -Waitress

"No," Will says calmly. "My father did."

While my mouth is hanging open, he adds, "I just got off the phone with my mother. We're in agreement. We've been unfair to you, and we're sorry. This whole episode has been misguided. I'm driving you to your mother's house. Or all the way back to California if you prefer. You don't have to see Danny. We'll come up with some sort of excuse—don't worry about it."

I'm hallucinating. I must be. This is the way I imagined it happening, not the way it's really supposed to go.

"Huh?" I say.

Will nods. "I know. We drag you all the way here and then change our minds. Honestly, I've been thinking about it since yesterday, but it wasn't until our talk on the way here that it really hit home. You came all this way. You even sang to Danny. That was amazing. I didn't say it at the time, but it was. You've already gone above and beyond. You don't have to do anymore. It's enough."

I've won. I got what I wanted. Now I can hide out at Mom's until Stella arrives with Pinny. Then it's off to Portland.

Fucking Portland.

I hate it and all of Oregon too.

Will stares at me expectantly. I clear my throat.

"Okay, thanks for that. Although, 'above and beyond' is overly generous. To be honest, I've been plotting ways to blow this pop stand from the beginning."

"I figured as much."

"Right. Well. Let's go then."

"Okay." Will pauses. Frowns. "Um. Where exactly? If we're going to California, I'll need to pack a few things first."

I hesitate, realizing this isn't a test. Will is really and truly letting me off the hook. I'm free. But not really. If I leave now, I'll never return. That's the ugly truth, and I know it. It'll be too difficult to attempt it again. I'll have a panic attack at the state line, and that'll be it. I'll turn around and go back in the other direction.

The thing is, I need to be here. No, I want to be here. Not full time. I'm not quite ready for that level of commitment. But for occasional visits. Two, maybe even three times a year. For Mom and Maxi. For Allie's twins. And apparently to take Eli and his husband car shopping.

"No," I tell Will at last. "I've had enough of California. I want you to take me to Danny. He still wants to see me, right?"

I can't quite decipher Will's expression as he registers what I'm saying. He definitely wasn't expecting this.

"Very much so," he finally says.

"Great. Let's go before I lose my nerve."

Taking me at my word, Will rushes me there as if he were delivering ice cream in a heat wave. I squirm in my seat, my borrowed pants feeling too tight and itchy. Or maybe that's my skin. Will glances over at me several times, and once it seems like he's about to say something, but whatever it is, he swallows it back down.

Then we pull into the O'Leary's driveway. It's weird to be here after all this time. Inside, the house looks totally different. There used to be steps up and down, but those are all gone now. It seems like some walls have been removed too. Will leads me through to the back of the house. Where there used to a den and office, there's now one solid wall with two French doors leading into what must be Danny's room.

And I'm not ready. I need another minute. Or a week. A year. A lifetime.

I grab hold of Will's sleeve.

"I need you to wait out here first," he says. "Danny will want to prepare himself."

Oh, of course. Danny needs a minute. Probably more than me.

Shit. Eli's right. I'm a self-centered asshole. He didn't say it in so many words, but the subtext was in three-inch bold print. Yeah, this sucks for me. But it sucks *way* worse for Danny. Why is it so hard to remember that?

A young girl with a fresh-scrubbed face, high ponytail, and one of those nurse-type tops slips out of Danny's room.

"Oh." She startles as she notices me standing there.

"Sorry," I say. "I was just waiting to go in."

"You're Jenna!" she exclaims as a kaleidoscope of expressions cross her face, starting with happy, then confused, and finally upset but trying to hide it. "He's been waiting to see you. For days. Well, for years, but he doesn't know that." She's sweet, so even her censure comes across gentle.

"I'm sorry. Who are you?"

She gets as wide eyed and confused as Bambi discovering his dead mother. "Oh, I'm Danny's nurse. Well..." She hesitates and blushes so prettily it's like watching roses bloom. "I'm only a CNA right now, but I'm going to school and..." Again she trails off, uncertain.

I get the feeling this is the way she communicates, all stop and stutter.

"I'm sorry. You're not interested in my life story."

I'm not, but it's rude to say so. I change the subject instead. "Can I go in?" I jerk my head in the direction of the door, and she leaps in front of it.

"No!" She startles at the volume of her own voice. "I mean, no, please don't. Not yet. Will's changing his sheets. Danny demanded the catheter come out, even though Jeremy—that's his physical therapist—said it was too soon. He can't make it to the bathroom without help, so sometimes..."

I can't help but note, with fascination, how her hands flutter as she talks.

"Oh, I shouldn't be telling you this. Danny doesn't even like me to change his sheets. And he wouldn't let me empty the pee bag when he still had it, even though it's my job. He asked Will if he'd take care of it. He's so sweet like that."

Again she blushes, and this time I finally get it.

Will walked into the room, and then she came out of it all twitter-pated. And yeah, I can't really say anything, because Will has the same effect on me. So why do I want to pin her down and pluck out her long fluttering eyelashes one by one? 'Cause Will empties Danny's pee bag so she doesn't have to sully her precious hands? Or because I'm jealous?

Oh God, I'm jealous.

First I thought Will was with Heather, and I was ready to sit down and cry for the rest of my life. Now he's flirting with this wannabe nurse, and I have a sudden desire to punch something. Or someone.

"Yeah, Will is sweet," I finally agree from between gritted teeth.

She cocks her head, looking more fawnlike than ever. "Will? Oh yes, he's so sweet. Such a good brother. Everyone says if it wasn't for him and all the experimental treatments he researched, well, who knows if Danny would've woken up." Her eyes grow wide and glisten wetly as she brings a fisted hand to her mouth. A long moment passes before she's able to speak again.

"Sorry. I just...it's so wonderful. I imagined Danny waking up so many times, and now it's happened..." Gently she dabs her tears away. "I'm terrible. Mrs. O'Leary says I have to be strong for Danny. He's having a hard time adjusting. I can't imagine. All those old pictures, you can see he was so big and strong." She smiles tremulously. "I keep telling him, he's more handsome now...at least, I think so." Another flush of pink dots her cheeks. "But he wants to be who he was. Who wouldn't, right?"

233

She looks to me. I take my cue and nod.

Appeased, she continues, "Mrs. O'Leary says he simply needs to envision a new future for himself. Not worse, just different than the one he'd imagined before. And I promised Danny"—she pauses, her eyes shining and fixed on some distant spot—"I'll be here for him as long as he needs me."

OH. Oh shit. She doesn't like Will. She likes *Danny*. Really likes him to the point of believing she's in love with him, if I'm (finally) reading this right.

It sort of makes sense. Danny's always been at his most charming when he showed off his wounded boyish side. And this girl, she must be all of twenty, if even that. Of course, she'd fall for a guy who's been out of a coma for less than a week. Hell, it sounds like she was half in love with him while he was still comatose. She definitely seems like the dreamy sort who would find it romantic, like Sleeping Beauty in reverse.

Before I can ask a few probing questions to test my theory, the door opens and Will steps out.

"You can go in now," he says, as clinical and distant as a doctor.

"Aren't you coming?" I ask, because walking in there alone feels too much like opening night before I've had time to read my lines, much less memorize them.

"He wants to see *you*," Will answers.

Which okay, yes, right. I remind myself of my pep talk about doing this for Danny. About not making it about me. I'll be fine. I'll improvise.

Will's hand lands on my back, warm and reassuring. "It'll be okay," he says.

I lean into him. Only a little bit. For a moment. Then I notice the cute little CNA watching me.

No. Watching me. With Will.

Watching us. Together.

His touch. My lean.

Her brow furrows, and I can see her connecting the dots. Suspicion fills her face as our eyes meet.

And I blush. Probably less prettily than her. But the effect is the same. It's an accidental confession. A sin I hadn't even let myself acknowledge.

I love Will. I loved him a long time ago, and somehow it never quite went away.

Immediately, I shake that thought away.

I *like* Will. I like his body. Okay, I might actually love his body. And I loved kissing him. I really love the idea of doing more than kissing, preferably not within the confines of a compact car. Except I won't be doing any of that with Will because I'm leaving and Danny—

Danny. Right. Come on. Focus.

I step toward the door, grab the handle, and the little CNA lays her hand over mine. "Be gentle with him, okay?"

I wonder how much she knows about my part in Danny's accident and if this is a subtle dig. But then she sniffles, and I realize she's in a totally different story. One where she nobly gives her true love to the cold, undeserving woman who ran away. I don't deserve him, but if Danny wants me, she'll stand aside and let us ride off into the sunset together.

I don't know what makes me do it, maybe some evil imp living inside me. Whatever it is, I take her hand off mine and give it a squeeze.

Then in the same throaty, slightly hammy voice I'd used in *Annie Get Your Gun*, I say, "If he wanted gentle, he wouldn't be asking for me."

Spinning on my heel, I exit stage left, letting the door swing shut behind me with a soft *ba-dump*.

31

"What I Did for Love" –A Chorus Line

It turns out that seeing your previously comatose ex-boyfriend on an iPhone screen is not adequate preparation for seeing him in person. It's sorta the equivalent of using a night of drunken karaoke to prepare for opening on Broadway.

I knew this, but still...

I stumble, tripping over my own feet, the shock of seeing his body shrunken and small shudders through me. It's amazing I manage to stay standing at all. My face is a candle left in the sun. My smile slides off no matter how many times I attempt it.

Needing some recovery time, I cut Danny out of the picture and focus on the rest of the room. Always when I'd imagined him, it was in that same room where I'd left him. Surrounded by a sea of beige. Even knowing he was home, I'd waited outside his door expecting to experience the color monotony once more.

But this room is the opposite of that. Windows everywhere let the light flood in. A fresh bright-white wallpaper covered in a colorful mix of birds and butterflies takes the place of those old beige hospital walls. The overall effect is bright and whimsical and...hopeful. This is the wallpaper I'd have picked if I was trying to banish the beige.

"G-g-g-girly walls," Danny says from behind me, where I've managed to shut him out as if he were still comatose.

I spin, facing him once more. No more prepared the second time around.

I attempt to concentrate on Danny's face instead of his wasted body, which makes me want to sob.

"They're gorgeous walls," I say, because I have to say something and "How are you?" feels ridiculously inadequate.

Danny rolls his eyes. "M-M-M-Mom." He wants to say more, but is clearly frustrated. Stopping with that one word, he jerks a thumb in the direction of the closest wall.

"Oh, she picked the wallpaper? It's really nice."

That seems to finish our decorating discussion. I stand in the middle of the room desperately searching for some other topic.

Danny finds one first. "K-k-kiss?"

His eyes, so huge in his hollowed-out face, meet mine. There's no begging or pleading. It's a demand. No, simpler than that. An expectation. Because I'm his girlfriend. How long does he think it's been since that awful sledding day? I can't remember what they told him. It doesn't matter though. For him it probably feels like no time has passed.

Slowly, I walk toward his hospital-style bed. The only part of this warm and homey room with that old beige feeling. It's tilted, sitting him up. Finally, in front of Danny, I hesitate. "I don't want to hurt you."

He scowls. "W-w-won't h-hurt."

The expression paired with the words makes me feel like I'm with a little boy. I'm tempted to steal a scene from *Peter Pan* and hand him a thimble like Wendy gives Peter, telling him it's a kiss. But that won't cut it. Nor will some peck on the cheek like you'd give your grandma. It has to be a kiss on the lips. Deep enough to appear meaningful, but not lingering till we end up in tongue territory.

Danny's hand slides into mine. "S-s-sit," he orders.

I do, perching on the edge of the bed. I take his hand and then lean in to kiss him. My lips meet his briefly, and then it's done.

"N-no." He stares at me, his face working, jaw clenching, teeth

237

grinding. He's trying to get his words together and can't. Finally, he blurts out, "S-s-sex me."

I rear back. "No way, man."

His eyebrows slam down. "S-s-sex." He repeats. Louder this time.

"Okay, I get what you're saying. You want more of a tongue-wrestling-type kiss and then all the stuff that follows it, but no. Sorry. That's not happening right now."

The straining stops. He looks at me sadly. No, it's more than sad. He looks lost. And broken. More broken than when he lay silent in the snow and it seemed possible he might die.

"M-m-missed y-y-you," he says.

I grimace, fighting back tears. I grab both his hands and hold them. "I missed you too." It's the truth. Suddenly, the hole he left in my life gapes open, wide and empty. It's been there all the time. I just somehow got used to it.

"T-t-t-twelve years," Danny adds.

I stare at him, not sure if I heard correctly. Or if it means what I think. Because twelve is how many years it's been. Almost been. Which means he knows. Someone told him, and he knows how much he's lost.

The severity of it hits me fully for the first time. All those years I was moving around and doing shows and finding office jobs and falling in love with my truck and dating different guys—*all those years* Danny was lying here, switched to the Off position. Now he's awake in this shriveled body and with a brain that can barely find the words to express how much that sucks.

My eyes fill with tears, and finally I say it. The one thing I've wanted to say from the beginning. It won't help, and it won't change anything, but at least it's sincere. At least it's true. "I'm sorry, Danny. I didn't mean for this to happen. I didn't, and I am so, so sorry."

I am once again crying, and then Danny's eyes overflow and he is too. We end up holding one another. When we finally pull away, I do not feel absolved. Or like a weight's been lifted, which is a stupid thing people say. But I do feel like I've faced something terrible and survived it.

I am still the person who ran away. But now, at least I am also the person who came back.

And maybe there's a silver lining here too. The distance of all those years makes it possible for me to see how desperately Danny needs someone to level with him. I scooch over farther so I'm more comfortably situated on the bed. "So you know how long it's been since the accident, huh?"

Danny nods.

I bet his little assistant nurse squealed. Or else he read it on her open face. She seems like the type who couldn't tell a lie even if she wanted to.

"What else do you know?" I want to get it all out there.

"M-m-married?"

I debate telling him the same lie I told Will. Say we chickened out and didn't go through with it. But it was a dumb lie, and I'm pretty sure Will saw right through it anyway.

I spill. "Yeah, technically we were. I mean, I guess we still are. I never told anyone. Not my family. Not yours. It'd probably be easy to get a divorce because of everything that's happened."

"You," he says, the one word clear, without a stutter. And then, "L-l-l-left."

My stomach clenches. There's that old self-loathing. But this isn't about me. Swallowing, I nod. "Yeah, I did. I'm sorry. That's why you can divorce me pretty easily for abandonment or whatever." I hesitate. Should I say more? Try to explain? Tell him how I stayed for over a year, spending every day at his bedside?

But Danny renders all that moot with a shrug and three words. "T-t-t-twelve l-l-long t-t-t-t-time."

And that's it. He never expected me to stay at his side. Not for twelve years anyway.

Abruptly Danny jabs a finger in my direction. "H-h-how old?"

Surprised by this sudden change of subject, I check to make sure I'm understanding correctly. "How old am I?"

This gets a nod.

"I'm thirty. I'll be thirty-one this coming May."

Danny's eyes widen in what can only be interpreted as horror. "Th-th-thirty?"

I don't remind Danny that he's two years older than me, making him already a member of the third-decade club. I guess you can know twelve years have passed, but not think of it in terms of aging—for yourself or others.

And for Danny it's especially weird. After years in stasis, his life on pause, Danny looks closer to thirteen than thirty.

He really is Peter Pan. And I'm Wendy from when Peter returns years later, not realizing that's she's grown up. Peter doesn't understand until finally she explains, "I am old, Peter. I am ever so much more than twenty. I grew up long ago." I always thought it one of the more touching scenes I've ever played (and also a major missed opportunity to give Wendy a good heartbreaking ballad).

I'd always been more of the adult in my relationship with Danny. Thanks to Maxi, I knew the true responsibility of having a child. I had a job and savings and a car that broke down and had to be fixed without running to mommy and daddy. I'd done my own laundry since I was ten and been left to figure out my own dinner for nearly as long as I could remember.

I *did* grow up long ago. And since then I've grown up even more. Maybe not with the same milestones of marriage and kids and promotions as most, but even so without even meaning to, I've grown up. And here I am. Ever so much more than twenty. And there's Danny, able to understand my leaving, but not how I could've let myself get so old. For him this is the worse betrayal.

No, not just that I've let myself get old, but that he has too. Gotten old before he'd gotten even the barest sip of his twenties. His best whooing years. Gone.

I've gone silent. Remembering Danny is in the bed beside me, I try to give it a positive spin. "Thirty isn't so bad! All my older friends say it's much more fun than their twenties. They're more settled. Not, you know, going in circles trying to figure out where they fit."

It's the wrong thing to say. That last bit especially. I can see it immediately.

Danny's brow furrows. "Where d-d-d-do I f-f-fit n-n-now?"

I hear my own voice telling Will, "Danny is fucked." It seems even crueler now.

I paste on a big, stupid smile. The kind used to sell a particular type of lie. The sort no one actually believes. "Well, you'll fit wherever you want. I mean, once you get back up on your feet. I heard you're getting physical therapy, so that shouldn't take long. Soon you'll hit the ground running and be right with everyone else."

Danny's hands curl into fists. "W-w-with ever-r-ryone else?" He reaches behind me, where a water bottle is resting on a tray. Picking it up, he holds it for a moment and then throws it across the room. Actually, it barely clears the edge of the bed before tumbling to the floor. This only increases his frustration. He kicks his heels beneath the blankets. Slams his hands against the bedrails. "I—" BAM "c-c-c-c-can't—" BAM "t-t-t-t-t-talk" BAM. His anger only increases his stutter, which in turn upsets him even more.

I grab hold of his hands, not wanting him to hurt himself. It's hideously easy to overpower him. We used to wrestle as foreplay. I'd loved how strong he was. Joking, he once made a big show of holding me down with one hand while eating a sandwich with another.

He sags now, going limp. I release him, and he turns away from me, his face pointedly staring in the opposite direction.

This is the Danny I could never stand. The one who couldn't take any criticism. He'd complain about working at the carpet store, and I'd tell him to get another job.

"Oh yeah, I'll stock shelves with you," he'd sneer.

We both knew the real problem was he didn't want to work at all. So next time I'd say, "Why not go back to school?"

He'd roll his eyes like this was the dumbest idea ever and then bitch how they expected him to do all this reading and write all these papers and he just couldn't get it all done, that only a semi-genius like Will can get through college without totally losing his mind.

That's how it was with Danny. He had a million excuses, and all he wanted was for me to agree with him. Yes, school was too hard. How dare they ask him to write papers and read? And yes, work was impossible. Unreasonable how they expected him to show up on time and wait his turn to take a lunch break so the sales floor wasn't left unstaffed.

But I could never bring myself to play that game for him. I'd roll my eyes. Tell him to try living in my world a few weeks and then he might not bitch so much.

This time, though, I can't do the whole world's tiniest violin routine. This time everything *is* going to be hard for Danny. Really, waking up was the easy part. I think he already knows that.

A pack of cards on his tray table catches my eye. On the day we met (which I once called "the day we fell in love"), we got drunk and played cards until we were half-naked, and that's how his mom found us. Even with that ignominious ending, I still rank it as one of the better days of my life.

Gambling that Danny retains the same warm memories, casually I toss out, "How about some strip poker?"

He turns back to me, interested but wary.

Pulling up a corner of his blanket, I peek beneath. "You got pants on under there, right? Otherwise, it's not gonna take me long to get you naked."

Danny laughs. It's his old laugh. Without any stutter or weakness. And his eyes light up, the blue in them taking on a nearly incandescent glow.

My heart squeezes painfully, and suddenly there it is. Love.

What did Stella say about love not being created or destroyed? She might've been right. You'd think time would've worn away whatever was left of what I felt for Danny, but maybe something always remains.

It feels natural then and not at all forced to lean forward, cup his face between my hands, and kiss him. Firmly I plant my lips on his. No tongue. No teeth. No crazy I-want-every-inch-of-your-skin-on-mine thing like I had with Will yesterday. This is tender. And a little bit sad. A kiss goodbye instead of hello.

And I'm pretty sure Danny gets all that. Or some of it. Enough that he doesn't try to turn it into something more.

He grabs my hand and just holds it. I give his hand a squeeze. He squeezes back. The moment is so incredibly bittersweet, I can already feel a permanent bruise forming inside.

Gently, slowly, Danny places my hand over his crotch.

"Damn it, no!" I jerk my hand away. "Dude! We were having a moment. That is not cool."

Instead of pouting, he gives me the puppy dog eyes, laced with the frustration that seems to constantly simmer beneath the surface. "M-m-make s-s-sure it w-w-w-works."

Right. I can see that being a concern, and Danny's so weak he probably can't handle the jackhammer himself. But I am not letting this particular hand job get passed to me. Instead I offer an alternate solution. "You know, your little CNA out there might be a better candidate. She's medical, which means she's trained to handle your equipment. Plus, she likes you."

He doesn't puff out his chest and accept it as his due, like he once would've. He colors slightly and looks down. Down at the very small lump his body makes beneath the blankets.

Trying to distract him, I add, "Only you could have a girl swooning when you're not even conscious." This gets a small smile as his attention turns back to me. "Trust me. She really likes you."

Danny smiles slightly, hopefully. "She d-d-does?"

"She does," I confirm.

He sits up taller at this and then thinks about it for a minute. After several long beats, the smile grows into a shit-eating grin. "D-d-does g-give g-g-good s-s-sp-sponge b-baths."

"Sponge baths?!" I pretend mock outrage. "C'mon. You don't need me. You're already halfway to getting a good old-fashioned two-hander from Bambi. Who knows? It could be the start of something special."

Danny says nothing in reply, but he looks thoughtful.

I feel like I'm pimping out the CNA, but let's be generous and say it's more of a matchmaking thing.

Maybe there really is something there between him and Bambi, because the grim curve of Danny's mouth has softened. Maybe a new love is just the thing he needs. Which means now's a good time for me to leave. Bambi is probably still hovering outside the door, and I don't want to stand in her way.

I stand. "Well, I should go and—"

Danny catches my hand as I'm backing away. "S-s-strip p-p-p-oker?"

Oh right. Despite the walls getting closer, I force myself to take a deep breath and smile. "Okay, but to be fair, I should tell you ahead of time, these pants are tight. The only way they're coming off is with scissors." I do a full turn, giving Danny an eyeful of my pleather-clad ass.

"D-d-d-deal," he says, and follows it with a laugh that again sounds perfect. Like he's the same Danny as before.

I decide then and there to squeeze as many of those laughs out of him as I can.

I lose the first hand and my shoes. Danny insists with his one word rebuttal of "b-b-both" that I treat two as a single item. On the next hand I roll up the bottom of Danny's blanket and peel both his socks off. I make a big show of flinging both of them over my shoulders, and as we laugh, I stop pretending to have fun and discover that despite all my expectations to the contrary, I'm really and truly enjoying myself.

Three hands later when Will, Mrs. O'Leary, and the CNA walk in, my bra is hanging like a tie around Danny's neck, his shirt is on the floor, and I am beside it, rolling around with my pants half off, trying to peel them from my lower legs. Danny and I are both laughing so hard we don't even notice we've got company.

"Oh hello," I say, catching sight of them. I smile up at them as if my pants are not hanging off my ass. "We were just playing some strip poker. Anybody else want to be dealt in?"

32

"Only Us" –Dear Evan Hansen

Mrs. O'Leary wastes no time pulling the plug on the poker game. "Danny," she scolds, "the doctor warned you not to overdo it."

This apparently is Will's cue. He pulls me up and out of the room so fast I barely have time to tell Danny goodbye and that I'll see him later. I definitely don't have time to straighten my clothing. As Will drags me, I hop along, attempting to yank my pants upward. Without much luck. We keep going, heading into the basement, which I can only hope isn't now being used as a dungeon. At the bottom of the stairs, Will comes to an abrupt stop and releases my hand like it's radioactive.

"What the hell?" I ask, stung. "I thought we were friends again. Sort of. Maybe."

Will says nothing. Obviously he's upset with me. Even though I did an amazing job of completing the mission. I saw Danny. I made him laugh. We both gained a bit of closure. What the fuck else does he want from me?

I glare at Will as I resume the battle of little pants, big bum. Unable to take his lack of response, I can't help but goad him a little bit. "Little help here?"

It's a dare. One I expect him to refuse. But I guess he's in a daring mood, because with a shake of his head, Will steps forward and slides his hands into the top of my pants. As he pulls upward, his knuckles scrape my thighs and then catch on the bottom edge of my underwear.

He freezes. I freeze.

There is no further movement on the pants.

Up. Or down.

There's nothing at all except heavy breathing.

Mine. And his.

Our eyes lock.

"I do not like you getting undressed with my brother," Will says at last, his voice rough.

Will is jealous! My brain sends out this information like it's a crucial breaking-news alert. In response my heart beats faster.

"I was trying to cheer him up. I didn't hurt him. I was very careful."

Will's hand clenches. I feel it against my skin. And can't help the shudder that runs through me. His eyes darken in response.

"I'm not worried about Danny."

"Okay. What's the problem then?"

Will stares at me like I'm being deliberately obtuse. Which I am. Still, I glare right back. I want him to say it. I want to hear it.

Of course he doesn't.

Instead, he leans in and his mouth captures mine.

It's possible I wanted that too.

They say the first bite of something is the best. It's a diet-tip thing. If you're dying for chocolate cake, have one bite. Like most diet tips, it's total and complete bullshit. First of all, where do you even get one bite of cake? Second, even if the first bite is best, everyone keeps eating regardless, hoping to recapture the perfection of that first bite. Sometimes I feel like this explains my entire relationship with Danny and how we lasted for so long. Well, that and we were young and stupid.

With Will, though, each bite is better.

He pulls away panting, and when I reach for him, he scrubs at his face and turns away.

I'm sick of Will pushing me away. Frustrated, I jerk my pants into place and button them. I stalk farther into what appears to be Will's own personal living space. There's a bed, desk, clothes, flat-screen on the far wall, and even a mini fridge.

Wow. Will lives at home. In his mom's basement.

It's a nice basement, nicer than anywhere I've lived. But still, it's the same basement he moved into a few months after Danny and I started dating. Which is to say, a few months after Danny and I began having incredibly loud sex in the room directly next to his.

I look back at Will. "You live here? Still?"

He turns to me, arms crossed over his chest. "I like to be close for Danny. My mom too." His tone is stiff and angry. There's no indication that we were just kissing and his hands had sorta been in my pants.

"Are you mad at me?" I ask, at the same time that Will announces, "Don't worry. I'm not going to tell him."

I frown. "Tell who what?" But then, a beat later, I get it. This is Will answering my awful question from yesterday, when I asked if he was going to tell Danny. Was it really only yesterday?

Seems like an entirely different lifetime, back when I was an unenlightened asshole. I mean, I'm still an asshole, just one with way more clarity.

"I won't come between you two. I never wanted that," Will adds.

And now I really get it. Will has it in his head that Danny and I are back together. Which okay, Danny and I did break up and make up on a regular basis. But the breaks were usually forty-eight hours, not twelve fucking years long.

Also, "I'm into *you*, you idiot. Danny's into his nurse. CNA. Bambi or whatever her name is. We were playing strip poker because he needs to feel normal, not like some sick baby man who lost over a decade of his life."

Will digests this information. Finished processing, he doesn't fall into my arms or reciprocate with a romantic declaration of his own.

Instead, *this* is what he got out of my speech. "You *told* Danny how long it's been?"

"Jesus. No! I didn't have to. He knew. Okay? He knew. Do you think Danny's such an idiot he wouldn't figure it out? Give him a little credit. And maybe instead of spinning all these stupid lies with your mom, you could help him deal with the truth and, you know, prepare him for what his life is gonna be like from now on."

Will stares at me for a long ugly second. Then a hand covers his face. "You're right." With stumbling steps, he moves to the couch and sinks down into it.

Hesitantly, I follow. It feels weird to hover, so I sit beside him. Then gently, not sure if I'm crossing a line, I place my hand on Will's back.

"Danny will be okay. I mean, he's trying to figure it out. He was really working on convincing me to give him a five-fingered hug—"

"A *what?*" Will turns toward me so abruptly I nearly fall off the couch. "Is a five-fingered hug what I think it is?"

I ball my fingers into a fist and jerk it up and down. Will's face goes red, like angry red.

"I didn't do it," I add. "I told him his little CNA—you know, Bambi with the eyes and the blushes—might be willing to help him out."

Will takes a deep breath. "You didn't do it," he repeats.

"I did not."

He nods. Then almost smiles. "You call Emma, Bambi? Mom and I refer to her as Snow White."

"Mine's better." Feeling brave, I add, "You're jealous, right? The dragging me out of Danny's room and getting all upset about the rub and tug—it's turning you green, isn't it?" Do I sound slightly hopeful? Perhaps.

Will looks at me straight on, those eyes of his boring into my head. "You want me to be jealous?"

I shrug. "Maybe. It's only fair. I wasn't happy at the idea of you marrying Heather. She's awful, and I already shared one guy with her."

Will sorta winces at that.

"What?" I ask.

His hand lands on my knee, immediately sending tingles throughout my entire body. "Heather and I did once..."

"Noooo."

Will nods. "Mom was on her cruise. Heather was on summer break. We were drunk and started talking about our guilt over Danny."

"*Your* guilt? And *hers?*" I don't bother to hide my surprise.

"Yeah, sorry. You don't have a monopoly on guilt," Will replies dryly. "I was there with you at the top of the hill. Do you know how many times I've replayed that moment? I could've stopped him."

The couch seems to tilt sideways, or maybe it's the earth itself. Amazingly, in all my imaginings of how it didn't happen, this was not one of them.

"And Heather," Will continues. "She knew she was stirring shit up between you two. Even after finding out you were pregnant, she couldn't let him go. She felt terrible. Said that her little voice of reason was telling her to wait, because no way would you and Danny survive co-parenting a baby—"

"That bitch," I interrupt. "I mean, it's true. But still. What a bitch. And after that you slept with her?"

"One drunken time." Will shrugs. "Then a year later she was engaged to my father. And with child."

I slap my hand over my mouth, shocked to the point where I'm a little giddy. "That's some Jerry Springer shit right there. 'I slept with my comatose brother's ex, and she married my dad.' Or, you could've gone on Maury and done a paternity test to see who was the true baby daddy."

"Okay, that's my little sister you're talking about," Will says, but he's laughing. "Everest is amazing, even if she does love to change the ringtone on my phone."

"And Heather and your dad, they're happy?"

This earns another shrug from Will. "I guess. They seem to be."

"Huh." I think about it for a moment. All the times Danny and his mother implied my family was trashy...Well, look who's trashy now. "So holidays are super awkward now, right?"

"Well..." Will hesitates.

I know he's withholding something juicy. "Spill."

"I probably shouldn't tell you this..."

"Oooh, you know that makes me want it more."

Will's eyes darken, like sexy storm clouds are rolling in. I smile back at him innocently, pretending I'm totally unaware my words had any innuendo. "It was the first Thanksgiving after Dad and Heather married. She was seven months pregnant. Mom invited them over, said they needed to be adults about this."

"Uh-oh. Let me guess. Food fight?"

"I wish." Will closes his eyes and shudders. "At first it was fine. Mom was subtle with her digs."

I snort, because yeah right, subtle my ass.

"But two bottles of Cabernet later, right as we were cutting into the pumpkin pie, Mom says, 'Aaron, does it bother you that both of your sons slept with your wife before you? Is it something you try not to think about? Or perhaps it's a turn-on knowing she settled for you, after sampling both of the newer, flashier models?'"

"Oh no." I giggle and gasp. "So terrible. And hilarious. Funawful."

"Oh, it gets better," Will promises, and I clap my hands with glee. "First there was dead silence. I tried to fill it with a, 'Does anyone want a scoop of ice cream with their pie?' Then Heather got up." Will stands, doing a good imitation of Heather. One hand is at the base of his back. The other flips his hair and then gently cups the front of his imaginarily rounded belly. "She says, 'Will doesn't count. It was only the one time, and we were drunk, and I pretended he was Danny.'"

"That bitch!"

"After he and Heather left, my mom cried." Will shakes his head, and the smile that had been lingering around his lips fades. He sinks back onto the couch beside me. "Finally, when I thought the worst was over, Mom said, 'Will, please tell me she wasn't your first. I simply cannot go on knowing that bitch took your virginity.'"

I'm not sure if I'm supposed to laugh, but I can't help myself. A titter escapes me. And then another. "Your family might actually be worse than mine."

"Might?" Will asks, and though his expression is stern, his eyes crinkle with amusement.

"Fine. Your mother is superior in all things, especially in being the worst."

"She is *very* competitive."

"How, though, did she even know you'd slept with Heather?"

"Oh, didn't I mention that part?"

I press my hands into prayer formation. "I have to know."

"The next morning after we...Well, actually, morning is generous. The sun might've just been coming up over the horizon. Anyway, Mom stood over us. Apparently, she took an earlier flight home than expected. She said, 'Will, I see you've stayed occupied while I've been away.'"

"Is she never at a loss for words! It's unbelievable. And her ability to walk in on her sons. She's a fucking bloodhound! A sex hound!"

Will frowns, pretending at seriousness. "This is my dear mother you're talking about."

"Right, right. Sorry." Somehow I choke back all my laughter. "She's a wonderful person and a loving mother. I'm sure after she made that scene at Thanksgiving, she felt incredibly sorry and begged your forgiveness."

Will frowns even harder, but his shoulders shake, giving him away. "Actually no, there was no begging of forgiveness. In fact, she was really hung up on the idea that Heather might've deflowered me, as she so delicately put it. So while helping her wash up, I had to explain to my mother that no, Heather did not take my virginity. And then she didn't even believe me! According to her, I was only saying it to make her feel better..." Will sighs. "So I had to provide details."

252

"You didn't."

"I told her with the driest recitation possible that I had relations with my college roommate's girlfriend, who I'm pretty sure felt sorry for me after hearing my tragic brother-in-a-coma story."

"Will, you idiot! She didn't feel sorry for you! You're hot, and she wanted to bone you."

Will frowns. I get the feeling he's about to say something important. Momentous even. "I shouldn't have done it. She was my roommate's girlfriend, and he was out of town for his grandma's funeral. But...she was a theater major. She sang to herself when she was studying, although not in her sleep, which...you know you do that, right? She wasn't actually that much like you, but still..."

My chest tightens. Is Will saying what I think? I test it. "You pretended she was...someone else?"

"Not *pretended* exactly. It just felt like, if things had been different, it could've been you..."

You. He said it straight out. He wanted her to be me.

I smile at Will. It feels tremulous. "You know, I was never planning on college."

"If *lots* of things had been different."

Hope mixed with a horrible grief rushes through me. *If lots of things had been different.* What I wouldn't give for a time machine, to go back and do it all again—but better.

Somehow Will's hand is holding mine. I grip it hard, not wanting him to get away.

I was half in love with Will, and amazingly it seems like he felt the same way about me.

It's wonderful.

And messy. Because Danny will always be there too. A piece of shrapnel embedded in the bone.

But even that wasn't enough to keep me from kissing Will. Or climbing into that backseat with him. As much as I told myself it was like crazy funeral sex, it wasn't. We weren't reaffirming life. We were reaffirming each other.

Oh, hey, you. I remember you. I remember all the things I hated and loved about you. Now you're the same but also different, and somehow I like you even more.

This isn't casual. Especially not if we keep going, following this thing between us to wherever it leads. It feels like sliding down a hill toward a mound of snow. If we catch it at the right angle, we might fly.

Or wreck ourselves beyond repair.

Will's hand squeezes mine. "You okay?"

I hesitate. Right now I can walk away. Not quite guilt-free, but close. I've done my duty to Danny. My final obligation is to get *Annie* on stage. I should be figuring out ways to make it work, not playing how it didn't happen with Will. Especially now, when I'm realizing the game might have real stakes.

I'm not ready for that.

Or maybe I am. The show must go on. Not just *Annie*, but the Jenna show as well. I've had a few dress rehearsals, several undressed ones (ha!), but no opening night. Obviously, it can't be a forever thing, not with Danny in the middle, but a short run while I'm in town might be nice. And possibly, in the future, some cross-country booty calls wouldn't be out of the question.

"I'm good," I say at last. "I was just thinking about something." Leaning into Will, I flip so I am straddling him. "The theater major. Heather. All this pretending, it's practically role-playing. And here I am thinking you're so straightlaced."

Will pulls me in closer so my legs spread wide, and I connect with him where he's hard and upright beneath his jeans. "You thought I was some innocent choirboy?"

"No." I gasp and groan as he thrusts his hips. "More of an innocent..." My brain struggles to find the word, because sexy banter is my new favorite kind of foreplay. But the neurons fail, and all I got is, "Library worker."

Will laughs, his mouth against mine. "Librarian."

"That's it," I mumble between kisses.

And then sexy-banter time is over. Our mouths are too busy with other more important things. My hands are busy as well. I tug at Will's shirt, determined to get it off this time. Getting the idea, he removes my shirt with one fluid movement. And whoops, there's no bra because it's still around Danny's neck. I don't mind though, as Will's large hands quickly cover me. My eyes drift closed. I briefly lose sight of my goal to remove Will's shirt as every part of me sings the hallelujah chorus.

This is going to be the best sex of my life. I am almost certain of it. As long as we can get my pants off.

A throat clears. Loudly. Once. Twice.

Somehow we both realize at the same time that we are not alone. As one, we turn to find Mrs. O'Leary standing at the bottom of the stairs.

"I knocked," she says.

I grab my shirt and clutch it to my chest.

Mrs. O'Leary smiles. "Let me guess. Strip poker again?"

33

"We Go Together" -Grease

After straightening our clothing, Will and I head upstairs to meet Mrs. O'Leary in the kitchen. It's like walking into the Colosseum—who knows if I'll make it out alive. It doesn't help when Mrs. O'Leary comes at me with both arms outstretched.

But instead of choking the life out of me, I'm wrapped in a hug. Not the uncomfortable pinching type that Heather gave me earlier. This is more like a Stella hug. Full bodied and sincere.

I can't help but hear Will's words again, telling me how his mother leaned on me. I'd gotten so used to remembering her as the monster. My jailor. But she wasn't sitting in that room to torture me. She was sitting there for the same reason I was. We were both waiting for Danny to wake up.

And for the first time ever, I wonder what might've been if I'd stayed.

If instead of taking Will's money, what if I'd returned to the hospital the next day? Would they have sent me and Mrs. O'Leary on that cruise together? Is it possible the two of us could have become...not friends. That's a bridge too far. But allies maybe? The way she kicks ass at the carpet store and the powerful tactics she uses everywhere else to make shit happen...I wasted time being terrified when I should've just been in awe. And taking notes. Asking for lessons if I caught her in the right mood.

In retrospect it seems like an easy choice. But back then, nothing would've convinced me it was possible.

"Thank you," she says after pulling away. "I know how difficult this has been for you. I want you to know I truly appreciate it."

I stare, stunned stupid. "Okay," I say.

Luckily, Will steps in. Pulling his mother aside, he calmly explains that Danny is self-aware. I'm grateful he immediately states I was not the one who told him. Mrs. O'Leary noticeably sags as she receives the news.

"Deceiving him was a mistake," she says at last. "And dragging you and the entire cast of your show here. My God, what was I thinking?"

"Mrs. O'Leary." Stepping forward, I put a hand on her arm.

Immediately, her other hand closes over mine. "Please, call me Lynette."

"Okay...Lynette." It feels wrong using her first name, but somehow I get it out. "For what it's worth, I'm sorta glad you brought me here. And that you sent Will to get me, because I wouldn't have made it here on my own. It was good to see Danny too. He's better than I thought he'd be."

Tears fill Lynette's eyes. "That's so good to hear. Every passing day he seems more like himself." Pulling what looks to be a freshly pressed handkerchief from her pocket, she dabs at her eyes. Finished, she waves the bit of linen. "I invested in these after that used-tissue debacle with your mother. I sent her a package as well. You're lucky to have her. She's a sweet woman, and she was very patient with me."

Stunned at this glowing review, I nod and lie, "Oh, she'll like that a lot."

Waving this away, she launches into the next bit of business. "Now, what's to be done with *Annie*?"

I hesitate. Once again, I'm off the hook. I could walk away from *Annie* guilt-free. Except..."The show might be good for Danny, if you want it to go on. We took out so many songs, the running time's nearly halved. Also, it's quite...bouncy. I think Danny will like it."

Mrs. O—Lynette—frowns. Not mean, but thinking. Why have I

never seen that before? Will does the same thing. "He has been oddly enthusiastic about it. Apparently, your mother showed him some pictures you'd sent her of the cast in their costumes."

Ha! I knew it.

Lynette gives my hand a squeeze. "Are you sure? It's not too much for you? Will said you lost your co-director."

I shrug. "She wasn't much of a director."

"Oh." Still appearing lost and uncertain and not at all the woman I remembered, she finally throws her hands up helplessly. "All right then. We have the auditorium, so we might as well go forward. And if there's any way I can help. Will mentioned a rather daunting list..."

"I've got it under control. Or I want to have it under control. I'm trying to adult."

"Adult?" Lynette raises her eyebrows, amused. "I see. Well..." She leans in, and at this point she's been so nice, I'm expecting something heartwarming. A "you go girl" type thing. Instead she says, "In that case, you may want to consider keeping your clothes on more often."

Direct hit. I didn't even see it coming. That right there, that's the sign of a master. Still, I smile at Lynette. "I think you're really gonna like the show too."

Deciding this is a good place to leave things, I turn to Will. "I should be getting home soon. My family's having a special welcome home dinner."

It's a lie, but they don't know that. Lynette hugs me goodbye and again insists she'd be happy to help with *Annie*. "Really anything," she says. "Even an extra chorus girl. You know I did some theater in my college days and always quite enjoyed it."

Even though it's tempting to picture Lynette in one of the orphan outfits, I assure her we should be covered.

Back home, I find out my special-dinner lie isn't a lie after all. Mom went way overboard with the Chinese takeout. I find her in the kitchen unpacking three overflowing bags. Unable to remember what I liked, she ordered one of everything.

She wraps me in a tight hug as Maxi comes charging up from the basement, where she was "making soap" with her boyfriend. Nadine and Allie might've been making some soap of their own, because they look a little disheveled as they come downstairs.

And Pippin. Amazingly, I missed him too. Picking him up, I listen as Allie bitches about the number of accidents he had in the house. With a straight face, I swear that it must be the unfamiliar environment, because usually he's so good.

Even though I tell everyone people food upsets Pippin's stomach, I see Mom slip him an eggroll and nearly half a container of beef and broccoli, so it's fairly certain my "such a good, easy dog" lie will be blown wide open before the night is over.

Still, I don't let that bother me as we eat and laugh and finish off a whole box of wine. My cup literally overfloweth. And then Will texts me.

I'm really sorry about my mom walking in.

Yeah, I reply, *I told you. She's a fucking bloodhound.*

You may be right. She usually doesn't come into the basement. She doesn't like to invade my space.

Yep. She sniffed us out. Her whole "I knocked" thing was suspicious too.

Agreed. I watch the little pulsing ellipsis telling me he's typing something else.

If she hadn't come in...

I wait for the rest of the text. Nothing. Unable to take the suspense, I text, *Is this a fill in the blank question?*

Trying to recall exactly where we left off.

That's when I abruptly excuse myself from the table and hustle upstairs. Several minutes later, I send Will a very nice (gently filtered) shirtless selfie.

This help?

He texts me a blushing smiling emoji. Adorable and very on brand. Since turnaround is fair play, I ask for the thing I want most.

Please send me a pic of you in your swimsuit.

It's in my gym bag, he texts back.

I'll wait.

So I wait. Getting bored, I cue up *George of the Jungle*, but it doesn't hold my attention. In fact, it doesn't do anything for me. It seems I might be over George. George and I have been seeing each other steadily for over four years now. It's my longest relationship ever. I am taking a moment to process my grief, when my phone chimes.

Come outside.

Okay, mourning over.

I fly down the stairs, and there's Will, wearing nothing but his puffer coat, blue swim shorts (sadly, not the tight-fitting kind), and a beat-up pair of Nikes. Like he was delivered straight out of my dreams, Will leans against his SUV while a soft flurry of snow flutters around him.

Obviously, he needs help keeping warm. Being a helpful person, I wrap myself around him.

We kiss until the frat boys across the street catch sight of us and start whooping and hollering. Then I drag Will toward the house.

"Wait," he protests. "There's several cars in your driveway. Who's here? I'd really like to put some pants on..."

"Don't worry about it. We're very informal." I tighten my grip and keeping pulling him along behind me.

Most guys would pretend not to notice the large group of people gathered around the kitchen table watching us pass through with undisguised curiosity (and some lewd catcalls because this is my family, after all). But Will's polite.

"Mrs. Batton, hello again. And Allie." I can see him taking in the other faces as he zips his jacket up to his chin

"Aw, don't do that," my mother protests. "We're not formal here."

"See? I told you." I smile at Will. Then I handle the introductions. "You remember my mom and Allie. This is Allie's daughter, Maxi. And

WE GO TOGETHER" -GREASE

my sister's girlfriend, Nadine. And this is Maxi's boyfriend, whose name I don't know."

Maxi rolls her eyes. "I've told you like six times. Tonight."

Will shakes everyone's hand while I nearly shake with desire. My mom mentions dessert, and I just know Will is about to say yes, because again with the polite thing.

"No thanks. I'm having him for dessert," I say, and then I pull Will up the stairs, and he yells over his shoulder, "Thank you. Maybe later."

And finally, I get the answer to my question. It turns out that, yes, Will does have the strength and determination to get Allie's pleather pants off me. In fact, he has the strength and determination to do many, many things that go way beyond pants removal.

34

"Some Enchanted Evening" –South Pacific

Sometime later, panting, lying against Will, using his amazing sculpted chest as a pillow, I sigh happily.

"You falling asleep?" Will asks.

"No," I say, even though my eyes are threatening to close. "I can't sleep. I have to figure out how to fix the show, and it opens tomorrow night."

"Fix it?"

And that's when I finally tell him everything about *Dirty Annie*.

"Okay," he says when I finish. "So how are you fixing it?"

It's his calmness, or the way he takes it as a given that I'm capable, that instead of whining "I dooooooon't knooooooooow," I start throwing out ideas. Ideas that have been in my head for a while now as I've watched the show drag on like a pathetic flesh-seeking zombie that's lost most of its limbs.

Will mostly listens, but he chimes in here and there, offering his own two cents. Or adding to my thoughts. A few times we get off track and end up talking about something else. It feels like old times, when we could talk forever about everything without ever running out of conversation.

Eventually I'm bouncing on the bed, excited as the ideas come together. Which in turn gets Will excited. Not sexually, unfortunately.

Instead, he insists on running out to his car for his beloved graph paper. Cruelly, he retrieves his pants as well. Maybe that's for the best. I'm better able to concentrate as Will makes not one but two lists. The first with all the ideas we've just brainstormed and the second with everything that needs to be done tomorrow. I'm not gonna lie—list number two is daunting. Luckily, Will makes a third list, splitting up all the tasks from list two between his mother, himself, and me.

Suddenly, it seems doable.

"You're one of those people who gets off on making lists, aren't you?" I say to Will, not sure how I feel about that.

"No," he assures me as he begins on yet another new list. "I'm actually one of those people who gets off on checking finished items off a list." Helpfully, he points down to the list where he's written and checked off *Make Jenna come.*

"Is that the correct spelling?" I ask.

"Should we get a dictionary? Or..." Will moves his thumb, which had been hiding the next item on the list: *Make Jenna come again.* "Should we work on checking off item number two?"

"Wow. I really like this list." I toss it aside. "Let's not get it wrinkled or stained."

Amazing how lists can help focus the mind. When we're done, I mumble to Will as we're falling asleep that he's earned not just his checkmark but a gold star too.

I wake up not long after, freezing. Mom always turns the heat down at night, and the blankets are in a heap on the floor. Will wakes as I work to fix them, and then remembering dessert, we creep downstairs to see what's left. Turns out fortune cookies and three cartons of ice cream, including my favorite, cookie dough.

I also find a note from Allie. "Your dog shat everywhere. Mom said not to bother you. We cleaned it up. You owe me. PS. Nadine thinks it's hilarious the dog has an old vibrator as a chew toy and wants to add it to her act. You don't mind, right?"

A soaking-wet and sorry-looking Pippin appears. It's clear Allie gave him a good scolding. I gather him into my arms and tell him he's a good, good boy. In return he gazes at me like I'm the best person on the planet.

It's a good feeling, and I'm savoring it, when Will asks, "I've been meaning to ask, what's the story with your fear of flying?"

My spoon freezes halfway to my mouth. Normally, I'd make jokes about being a basket case and skirt around the real issue. But this is Will. He saw how bad it was, and also he is already scooping more ice cream into my bowl because somehow he knows this will help.

"Actually, fear of flying is my second phobia. And it doesn't bother me that much—"

Will pokes his elbow into my ribs, a gentle admonishment to skip the bullshit. It's so ingrained at this point, I hadn't even realized.

Recalibrating, I try again. "Well, it doesn't bother me so long as I don't have to get on an airplane."

"What's your first phobia then?"

"Fear of sleep," I admit with a sheepish grin. "I guess you'd call it insomnia, but that sounds so serious, and it's not that big of a deal. It began after Danny's accident. And it's gotten sorta worse over the years."

Will nods, like this all makes sense and isn't totally crazy-pants stuff. "To die, to sleep. To sleep, perchance to dream. Ay, there's the rub. For in that sleep what dreams may come."

My mouth falls open. Will scoops a spoonful of ice cream into it, and I mumble around it. "You quoting Shakespeare at me?"

"Hamlet. I did a course a few years back for my English credit where we did nothing but dig into the Danish Prince."

"And you can still quote it from memory, because of course you can." I shake my head, wondering how it was that I ever found his know-it-all tendencies anything other than endearing. "That is so hot."

This earns a wry grin. "That was my goal. Well that, and to point out that sleep is often compared to a small death. It's not hard to draw the line between Danny's coma and your sudden sleep phobia."

I crinkle my nose. "The psychoanalysis is kinda less hot."

"I know. I've been in therapy for over almost two decades now. It sucks."

Shocked, I sit up straight in my chair. "What?"

Will gives his ice cream, which has melted into a sad puddle, a stir. "It's not a secret. But it's also something I'm never quite sure how to casually work into a conversation. I can't introduce myself with, 'Hi, I'm Will. Just so you know, if you want to chat about mental illness, I'm your guy.'"

"Whoa!" I hold out both hands. "Mental illness? That's..."

"Serious? It can be." Will shrugs. "My first episode was in seventh grade. I took a bunch of pills. My parents flipped, and I didn't know what to say, so I told them it was triggered by that dumb commercial being rediscovered."

I gasp. "The pee-pee commercial?"

"Yeah, that one." A rueful smile crosses his face. "It wasn't the reason, but Mom and Dad wanted one. Something they could solve. Really, the commercial was one of many things. After we did family therapy, my parents started to get it. But Danny, he continued threatening anyone who even thought about it in my presence."

Totally disgusted with myself, I push my ice cream away. "I'm so sorry, Will. I didn't know. I mean, of course I didn't, but still, I'm cringing remembering how I told you everyone was still laughing about it."

Will waves a hand. "I didn't care. Maybe I did a little. I would've preferred if everyone had forgotten all about it. Danny's dumb threats didn't help." He shakes his head. "But it was fine. I was in an okay place."

I lean in and kiss him, unable to resist the urge any longer.

"Let's put a bookmark in this conversation. Come back to it later," I suggest.

He plants his hands on my shoulders, and no matter how I try, his lips are kept tantalizingly out of reach. "That sounds like avoidance."

I pout. "Okay, fine. I had a sleep problem, but I took care of it. I now make room in my schedule for daytime naps."

"You didn't take care of it. You worked around it," Will corrects in this intractable sort of way. "Same thing with flying. Instead of dealing, you drove."

I can't help but feel defensive. "What about *you* dropping out of college to take care of Danny? What happened to NASA and changing the world?"

Will frowns. "That's not the same. I grew up. I made different decisions. And hopefully, I've found a different way to change the world."

"But you still don't have a degree. Or a major. So what decision did you make? You've basically majored in taking care of Danny." I grab for his hand to take the bite out of this criticism. "Which is amazing, don't get me wrong. Bambi told me you're basically the reason he's awake—"

This earns a sharp shake of Will's head. "She exaggerates. I researched some different therapies, we gave them a try, but..." Will stops. "We're not talking about Danny."

"No. We're talking about you."

"No. We're talking about *you*." Will leans in, trapping my knees between his. "Insomnia is a bigger problem than not settling on a major. What happens when you get an important job and can't take afternoon naps? Or when you need to get on an airplane and have a panic attack?"

Hating this conversation, I shrug.

Will pulls me in closer. "I'm not trying to beat you up here. I'm simply suggesting you consider professional help."

"I don't think it's that bad."

He jerks his chin up and eyes me hard, challenging me. "You can't sleep. You can't fly. You have panic attacks. Am I wrong about any of this?"

I roll my eyes. "No, but...it's not all related. The insomnia is a getting older thing. The flying is because I was in a plane that almost crashed. It wasn't just turbulence like our flight to Chicago. That was nothing."

"Really? That was nothing? It's funny, from the way you kept insisting we were all going to die—"

I smoosh my hand over his mouth. "In retrospect it was nothing. Okay? But I promise you, this flight was truly bad. We lost air pressure, and the oxygen masks dropped down. Have you ever had to put one of those things on?"

Will shakes his head.

"It's awful. They smell like when you leave a burnt french fry at the bottom of your oven. I could barely get the stupid thing on...I was shaking."

Just talking about it, I feel like I'm there again. Will's hands close over mine, and I squeeze them tightly, holding on.

"I didn't expect to survive. I knew, I just knew, deep in my bones, this was it for me. Me dying made more sense than anything had in a long time. Not like I was happy about it. I didn't want to die. I didn't. But I'd taken the chance of getting on that plane, and well, there it was."

I am crying. Again, goddamn it. Will gathers me close, like he did in the airport and in the car, except this time he doesn't have a shirt to absorb my tears. With my face pressed against his warm skin, I admit the worst of it. The thing I've never admitted to anyone ever. "Randomly bad things happen all the time. To people who don't even deserve it. Stuff way worse than Danny's accident."

Will's hand strokes my hair. It's so amazingly reassuring. "Like what?"

"I'll show you." Pulling away from Will, I run upstairs to retrieve my phone and find the list of bookmarked links (subheading: *DEATH*). I hand it to Will.

"It's all there. This kid who died from carbon monoxide poisoning. He got into the car to warm up, and his dad didn't realize snow was blocking the tail pipe. It's something most people around here would know, but they didn't and..." My throat tightens.

Will squeezes me. "You don't have to recap each—"

"I know. It's just...no one is safe." I sag into him. "The universe is cruel, and there's no real way to protect yourself."

"I know." Will sighs the words into my hair. "But the universe is also random and generous. Sometimes giving you exactly what you need when you least expect it."

My heart thumps hard, and tears fill my eyes as I acknowledge the truth in this. Will coming to my door. Will driving me here. Having him hold me right now. Yes, the universe has been incredibly generous lately.

"We need to go back upstairs. Now," I tell him.

Will gives me one more squeeze. "Maybe think about talking to someone, a professional someone, okay?"

Before I can respond he stands and takes our dirty bowls. I watch as he rinses and then places them in the dishwasher. He follows this up by wiping the table and counter clean. I half expect him to ask where we keep the vacuum, just to get any lingering crumbs. Because taking care of things, that's what Will does.

But instead of the floors, it's my turn. Will helps me up, and with our arms slung round one another, we make our way upstairs. Gently he lays me down in bed and then fusses around me, plumping pillows and straightening blankets.

Impatient, I pull him down beside me.

"I should go," he says.

"Stay."

I kiss him, and it must be convincing, because he lands on the bed beside me.

We go slow, and it's different this time. Sweeter and less urgent as we draw each moment out. Not dawdling, but savoring.

I hate the term "making love." It conjures images of candles burning and Kenny G on the stereo. So moony. Prudish too. Like c'mon—you fucked yourself silly. It's okay to admit it.

Earlier Will and I fucked ourselves silly. We did, and it was awesome. But this time...This go-round we might've accidentally made love instead. Or also. Can you do both simultaneously?

It's a good question, but before I can find the answer, I'm asleep.

35

"Find Your Grail" –Spamalot

Fifteen high schoolers stare at me, waiting for me to share my wisdom. Or waiting for me to say something so dumb, they can openly mock me.

Stalling, I gulp the coffee Eli brought me from the teachers' lounge. Eli himself stands at the back of the classroom, arms crossed over his chest and a "don't fuck this up" expression.

Okay then. The silence is awkward, and that's on me.

"I've done more than fifty shows in my thirty years of life. I'm not sure of the exact count. I used to save programs, but I move a lot, and eventually I threw that stuff away. It wasn't worth it to pack up and haul around yet another box of programs I wasn't gonna look at again. Again? What am I saying? Actually, I never looked at them. Not even to check if they spelled my name right. I don't care about that. Did they put my bio in? Eh, whatever. No one cares about your bio except your mom and grandma." This gets a laugh. I give an exaggerated shrug, and coffee slops over the rim of my cup. The teens titter again, but not cruelly. They're not sure where I'm going with this, but they're interested.

Well, I know how they feel. So where am I going with this?

I guzzled the rest of the coffee and set the mug on the teacher's desk. Hope whoever's desk this is doesn't mind me sitting on it. My legs are bit wobbly after I convinced Will to shower with me this morning.

"You need a hot shower," I'd told him, "So when you go out into the freezing-cold morning with nothing but your tiny swimsuit, which not to get off topic here, but speaking of your swimsuit, don't you have a smaller, tighter one? I mean, that can't be very aerodynamic, can it?"

Ignoring my question, Will stepped into the shower. He was heading to the gym straight from my house, but agreed to share the shower to "keep me company." Generous. Not just the sharing of his company, but more importantly his incredible effort in convincing me he could outperform my stolen vibrator's bunny ears. And I have to say, it's heartening to know there are still some things a man can do better than a machine.

The teens stare at me, probably wondering if I'm losing it since I've gone quiet while reliving the best shower of my life.

I clear my throat.

"You know what does matter? What you *do* remember? The songs. Oh sure, the lyrics in a few sections get fuzzy, but overall it's amazing how much sticks. But what I especially remember are the great shows. Maybe you know what I'm talking about. Those nights when all the actors are on, the audience is fully engaged, and the feeling is electric. It's rare. It doesn't happen for every show. And it doesn't happen for every performance of a show. In fact, it's almost terrible when it happens early in the run, because you spend every show after that magical one, chasing it, wanting to feel the magic again. It is a sort of magic, right? When you bow at the end, it feels like you did something big. Something amazing. People are gonna go home talking about this show. They're gonna remember it. Years later, they'll hear the music or see someone else putting that same show on, and they'll sigh and think, 'Wow, that was good, but not quite like that one extraordinary night.'"

Some nods from the kids, some way too enthusiastic, like they want to make sure I see it. Others are still, watching me, their eyes lit up. But the best is Eli at the back of the room, his arms uncrossed.

There might even be something like respect on his face. Or no, wait. That's indigestion. He chewed up a handful of antacids before we came in, while muttering something about how working with high school students will give you ulcers.

Right now I don't need Eli's approval. Because lucky me, even though I am 100 percent talking out of my ass, it turns out my ass is a secret genius.

So yeah, I got this.

Like a dork I call Will as soon as I exit the school. Eli's begrudging "The kids really enjoyed that—you're good with them" still ringing in my ears. (Though he added, "Rather screwed my plan. I assumed it'd be a disaster and I could present you as a cautionary tale of wasted promise.")

Forgetting that bit, I ask Will how he's doing with his jobs from list number three. Of course, everything is on track. Will even sends me a screenshot of the checked-off to-do list.

After that it's my turn to frantically run errands and then rush back to the school where the cast is waiting, along with a few new cast members. I update everyone on the changes, and it's met with a collective shrug. To be fair, they're disappointed to discover that New York City is not "around the corner," as Stella led them to believe, but rather a seven-hour drive away.

It gets worse once we run the show.

It's been less than a week since our last rehearsal, but it might as well have been years. A girl who has only one line forgets it. Halfway through the opening number, we realize one of the guys who should be on stage is sleeping in the dressing room.

Under my breath, I continuously remind myself of the old theatrical superstition that a bad final dress rehearsal means a successful opening night.

At last we get through it. Then I sit everyone down and give notes. Instead of cursing them all out like I want to, I attempt a "clear eyes, full hearts can't lose" inspirational speech. It doesn't go over well, and my earlier victory with the Niven theater students feels like a fluke. Or maybe I used up all my mojo.

I remember Stella telling me that I hold myself apart. I don't want to be that person anymore. So I try something crazy—I open up and tell them the truth.

"Over ten years ago, my boyfriend went into a coma due to an accident that was in large part my fault. A little over a week ago, he woke up from that coma and asked me to come home and perform this show for him. That's why you're all here. And I would consider it a personal favor if you'd all give it your best tonight."

All eyes are on me, so it's easy to see they are wide and shocked.

"Jenna, my gosh, we had no idea," says one of the Boylan sisters, a hand over her heart. Around her, heads bob in agreement.

"What exactly was the accident?" asks one of the orphan girls, her eyes wide. "Did you break his penis? I've heard of that happening."

I laugh. "No, I didn't break his penis." And then amazingly, like it's story time, I relay the whole tale of me and Danny. When I finish, they sit silently. One girl wipes away tears.

After all this time, I've finally got them. But just to make sure, I add, "And of course, I'll be covering the first round of drinks at the bar tonight."

A round of cheers go up, and then to my surprise, Roosevelt announces that my money is no good and that he will buy the first round. In quick succession, Mrs. Hannigan and several of the orphans chime in offering to buy rounds as well.

I'm not quite sure how or why, but my little confession seems to have changed the whole dynamic of our group. For the first time, we're all in this together and working toward something more than a good time.

Head reeling, I tell everyone to break for ten, then stumble offstage. Will squeezes my hand and whispers, "Well done."

I grin a big goofy smile, but then remembering how much still needs to be done, get us back on track. "I noticed my newest cast member nailed his part. Of course, I expected no less from someone who dropped out of college with a four-point-O GPA."

It's Will's turn to smile. "I can't believe you talked me into doing this."

"You'll be great," I promise and then seal it with a kiss.

After that time speeds up. Dinner. Touch up makeup. One last check to make sure everything is in place. The traditional opening-night text from my mom arrives telling me to BREAK A LEG BUT NOT REALLY, and then...it's showtime.

I am taking my place on stage for the opening number, when Stella tackles me.

"You made it!" I say after disentangling myself. "That's so great! The student stagehands could really use the extra help."

"Oh no." Stella shakes her head. "I'm not staying. Honestly, I can't stand to sit through this again, and anyway my babies are in the car. I just wanted to wish you good luck and let you know I am in for the after-party."

There's no more time to argue, and really, I don't care that much. In a way, having Stella gone simply makes the show more mine. For better or worse.

And at first, it does seem for worse.

The opening number, "Maybe," despite my best efforts, is sluggish. I'd played with the idea of cutting it, but couldn't. I love the song. The range is also perfect for my voice. But keeping it was the wrong choice. "Maybe" doesn't fit with the tone of everything else we're doing.

I whisper this to Eli, who's stationed himself backstage, and instead of scolding me, he actually smiles. "Now you're thinking like a director."

I don't have time to figure out how I feel about that, before I race back onstage for "Hard Knock Life." The orphans come up through the audience, and even though fake money was pressed into every person's hand along with their programs, only a few people throw it at the girls like they were encouraged to do.

Honestly, the audience seems confused. I hear them murmuring as the orphans gyrate around in their skimpy costumes. As the girls finish on mini trampolines (Will borrowed from his gym in exchange for a shout-out at the top of the show), one lone "wh-wh-whoooo" comes from the first row.

I'm almost positive it's Danny, who's in his wheelchair, parked beside Bambi in her aisle seat.

The rest of the audience, though, is hesitant.

The curtain closes as we frantically work to clear the orphanage set (bunk beds that also double as stripper poles are heavy to haul. Amazingly, Stella somehow convinced her ex to pay for the shipping, saying he owed it to the show) and put the New York City street in its place. Along with a group of at least ten, I strain to lift my bit of the bunk while hissing a reminder to the others not to let it scrape the floor. Eli promised me a date with the floor buffer later tonight if even a single board was scratched.

There's a murmur from the crowd, and I see that Will has taken the stage.

"Woof!" he says.

My heart leaps into my throat. He'd been shaky as the audience had taken their seats, realizing people would really see the show this time.

"This is crazy," he'd said, pacing the length of backstage. "I don't do crazy things."

"You did me," I offered.

Will shot me a look letting me know that was unhelpful. So I told him to hide inside his character. What does Sandy the dog want? Why is he rapping? What are the deep wounds of his life that he's trying to overcome? Basically, I gave Will a homework assignment, and like a good nerd, he sat down and set his brain to work.

Now, listening, I'm pretty sure I'm gonna give him an A on his assignment. Taking over for our previous Sandy, Dentist Dave, was no small task. Dentist Dave (so called because he introduces himself as Dentist Dave, and if you try to call him just plain Dave, he will correct you by saying, "Actually, it's *Dentist* Dave.") really made the part his own.

Back in California I'd come up with the idea of having Dentist Dave go on stage while we were moving the set, to keep the audience from getting restless. I'd told him to prance around the front of the stage, but Dentist Dave took it a step further, composing his own rap, and then adding more to it with each rehearsal. The first time I heard it, I'd begged Stella to veto the rap. I couldn't watch it without feeling embarrassed for him. But Stella, who didn't have strong feelings about anything else in the show, said it had to stay. "It's so bad, it's good," she'd insisted.

"So bad, it's good," with a dash of *Rocky Horror Picture Show*, is the concept Will and I came up with last night. I even had the programs printed up calling this the *Annie Horror Picture Show*. It seems like the audience isn't quite understanding the reference. Although, from the laughter building out there, maybe they're starting to get it.

We clear the second bunk bed, and I can't resist peeking around the edge of the curtain to catch the rest of Will's performance. Will Skyped with Dentist Dave this afternoon for over an hour so he could learn the rap. His delivery is definitely different than Dentist Dave's, who—bless his heart—sometimes stumbled over the words that he himself had written. In contrast, Will's delivery is smooth and delivered with a large wink. It's this that begins to win the audience over.

Or it could be the costuming. We went in another direction with that too. Dentist Dave had volunteered to rent a full dog costume from a local shop, but being budget conscious, I borrowed a fur vest from Allie's closet and sewed some socks onto a winter hat. The small vest nicely displays Will's arms and some of his abs too.

Now as Will begins the final verse of the rap, I can feel the audience having a collective epiphany. This is *meant* to be ridiculous. And bad. And hopefully, fun too.

"Hey, I'm just a son of a bitch, though I call her Mom. I ain't got a name, but when you call, I come running. This is my town, and I ain't beggin', but you might before we're through. Hot diggity diggity diggity diggity dog," Will finishes, and then he lopes off the stage and into the audience. They cheer and clap as he runs up the aisle and out the back doors.

At this point, we take a pretty stark departure from the source material. Oh, the songs are the same (though I cut a bunch of them), and not a single line of spoken dialogue has been altered. But like a glass of lemonade spiked with a full bottle of vodka, it's got quite a kick.

In short, it becomes less the story of how Annie and Warbucks find one another, but instead about the forbidden love between a girl and her dog. Yeah, we go there. Amazingly, the audience loves it. After Will comes running to me, convincing the dog catcher that he is my dog, he licks my face, and then I lick him back.

Groans and "oooohs" are the predominate response, and I worry I've pushed it too far, that we've lost the audience again. But then Will licks me once more, and someone with a boisterous *HA HA HA* cuts through the rest of the noise. As if they've been given permission, more people join in.

I'm still tense though. The audience hasn't fully bought into this experiment and might turn on us yet. It all hinges on this next part, as Daddy Warbucks takes the stage.

Wearing a tailored suit in a rich cream color and with her hair freshly blown out, Mrs. O'Leary strides onto the stage. She is powerful, authoritative, formidable, and absolutely, undeniably feminine. It doesn't matter that she doesn't have Will's ability to memorize quickly—she has something better. A gift for improvisation that catches me so by surprise that I have trouble not laughing out loud every time she goes off script.

After that, I relax. No, I do more than relax. I have fun with it. We all do. The cast. The audience. We're united in this wacky experiment.

There's no intermission. I axed so many songs that the running time was nearly cut in half. It's better this way. If the doors had opened and everyone flooded out and lined up for the bathrooms, they would've talked and started questioning what we had going here. I don't think we could've withstood such scrutiny. Right now it's an inside joke among the hundred or so people here tonight. Attempting to explain it to anyone outside this theater would only end with a, "Well, I guess you had to be there."

But it still felt like there needed to be some sort of break between the first and second acts. So I brought Nadine in to do a quick set of stand-up. She was thrilled to accept the gig. The audience is a little confused when she first gets up there, and well, Nadine's delivery needs work. There's a hesitancy to some of the jokes that the audience picks up on. She's not quite bombing, but it's not great either.

Then Allie stands up from her seat in the front row. "Hey, that was good stuff. Why are you people not laughing? You go crazy over a lady in drag, but can't even giggle for some legitimate humor?"

Thinking Allie is part of the act, this gets a laugh. Allie turns pink with pleasure and sits down again. But when Nadine's next joke again fails to land, Allie's up once more, admonishing the audience. Nadine, recognizing what's going on, calls Allie up. After that it feels like they planned it this way. By the time they finish, the audience claps so long and loudly that I'm tempted to let the show end right there.

Of course, I don't. The show must go on and into the second act, even if I am pushing our luck.

I knew the whole naughty-Annie shtick would get less funny with repetition, so I aggressively trimmed most of the second act. Heart in my throat, I keep my own performance moving along at a fast clip and hope the others follow. They do, and the audience holds on, and before I know it, we're at the end of the show with Will—er,

278

Sandy—and I humping each other's legs, while Mrs. Warbucks and Mrs. Hannigan try to pull us apart, the two of them united in their disgust of interspecies dating.

To my amazement, the audience surges to their feet, treating us to a hooting, hollering standing ovation. I grin and bow and then bow again, my hands held tight with Will on one side and Mrs. O'Leary on the other. This moment feels too perfect to be real, and then it gets even better as the audience finally lets go of the fake money we'd given them, throwing it up into the air like confetti.

And with that, it's official.

We've made magic here tonight.

36

"Good Thing Going" –Merrily We Roll Along

The after-party is epic.

By which, I mean that I do shots with Mrs. O—I mean, Lynette. Along with a few members of the cast, we order tequila shots. Neat, per Lynette's instructions.

"The lime and salt is unnecessary foreplay," she announces.

We order another round and are ready for one more, when Lynette stands. "That's enough. We will not have any drunken spectacles tonight."

Chastened, I order a beer and nurse it as people I used to know come over to say hello and admit with some confusion how much they'd enjoyed the show. Eventually, Will asks if my cheeks are hurting from all the smiling. I'm stunned to realize they are.

As the crowd thins, Danny rolls our way in his state-of-the-art wheelchair. As the unofficial guest of honor, he's been surrounded by everyone wishing him well and congratulating him on his recovery. From what I can see, he seems happy. And Bambi's at his side the whole time, smiling down at him in her gentle way.

"G-g-g-g-good sh-sh-show," Danny says.

"Oh, it was wonderful," Bambi gushes. She takes Danny's hand in her own. "I've never heard him laugh so loud."

My chest tight, I say a quick prayer they stay this way. That Bambi will be there for the long haul. If I could, I'd give Danny twenty of her, just to make sure he's taken care of. And I'd make it so the more she gets to know Danny, the more she gets to love him. Because there is so much that's lovable. It was the wrong balance for him and me, but maybe for them it'll be different. Especially if he continues looking at her in that way. Like he knows what he's got. Like he won the lottery.

But also like, he doesn't know what she would see in him. Which breaks my heart a little. He'd been so confident once. Overly so. When we first met, he assumed I'd be interested. There was no doubt in him. Maybe this new uncertainty will make the difference for them. Maybe both people need to feel like they got lucky.

And I hope they do.

In fact, I whisper this to Bambi as we say our goodbyes (Lynette having ordered Danny home after noticing his fatigue).

"Make a move. My money says you'll get lucky."

She blushes a beautiful pink and becomes flustered in a way that I will grudgingly admit is adorable. Finally Bambi mumbles something about not understanding what I mean. Behind her back, Danny grins at me and winks before being wheeled away.

I'm still watching him, feeling equal parts protective and hopeful, when a sharp elbow digs into my side. Turning, I discover Allie wearing her confrontational face.

"Hey, great show. Thanks for giving Nae the gig. We're gonna go home and celebrate, if you know what I mean. Can you grab Mom when you leave? And make sure she doesn't get into any trouble until then?"

"You're kidding, right?" I search the bar. I see Mom at the back, hanging with a bunch of the orphan girls. They seemed to be comparing moves, using the pool cues as improvised stripper poles. As I watch, Mom loses her balance and topples into the dart board.

With a sigh, I turn back to Allie. "Why can't you drop her home now? It looks like she's had enough."

This earns me the mother of all eye rolls. "You're going to the same place as Mom. I'm not. Also, for one fucking night, I don't want to worry about her. Can you just once think about someone other than yourself?"

"Fine." I throw my hands up. "Will's my ride, but I'm sure he'll be happy to take Mom too. Happy?"

"Yeah, I am," Allie answers, already turning away. Over her shoulder, she calls, "Keep an eye on her or else she'll wander off with the first horny old guy to give her a compliment."

Sometime later, when the bar is nearly empty, Mom sways near the jukebox with some guy she briefly introduced me to, saying, "He's a pretend Santa Claus." Which explains the long white beard. I can hear Mom bantering with him, asking if he's going to put her on the naughty list. He keeps replying with hearty ho ho hos. It's kinda creepy, but so long as he keeps her out of my hair, those crazy kids have my blessing.

Meanwhile, Will and I snuggle in one of those old-fashioned narrow wooden booths at the back of the bar. Which is when the question slips out of me.

"Move to Texas with me."

"What?" He sits up straight and pulls away from me.

"I'm moving to Texas. I probably should've started with that. Remember the theater director position I told you about? Well, I accepted it. Right after the curtain call, I emailed Ethel and told her, 'I'm in.' And..." I take a deep breath for courage. "I want you to be in too. Not working at the theater. You don't have to move in with me either. Or you could. I don't know. Is that too soon? It's too soon, right? At first I was gonna suggest a long-distance thing. I drive here and stay for a week. You fly to Texas whenever possible. But it wouldn't be enough. Would it? It wouldn't be enough for me. So...come to Texas with me. I know you're going to school, but there are schools in Texas, and it could be great. *We* could be great."

I'm trembling by the end of this speech. I've never put myself on the line like this. Never had the opportunity or desire. But Will is worth taking a chance on. And I am Jenna the fly slayer. Or I was once. And I want to be that brave stupid girl again. Even if he rejects me. Which, with the expression on his face, he might.

Will is silent for too long, folding his long fingers together. Carefully, he asks, "I thought you weren't interested in that Texas offer?"

"No, I was interested. I was always interested, I just...I was stuck, I guess. I felt like I wasn't grown-up or experienced enough for that type of job. But now..."

"Now you are?" Will sounds skeptical.

It pokes a hole in the confidence that's been growing in me all day. It silences that excited little voice saying, "Holy shit, I can do this!"

I gulp. "You don't think so?"

Will sighs. "No, I think you're still selling yourself short." He hesitates, but then his eyes lock on to mine, and I know something rough is coming. And it does. "You're still running away."

I slide sideways so no part of me is touching Will. This is what I feared. Will wants to tie me down. Hold me here. "Accepting a job offer is not running away."

"What about your family?" Will counters. "I never understood why you never came home to see them. The way you used to talk about Maxi, like she was your own kid. Then there's your mom—"

"People have fled the country and changed their names to avoid my mother."

"Your mother is an original," Will concedes. "But you were tight with her too. And she was supportive in her own way. You said she'd come to your shows every night. That Allie would scream at you to stop singing, and your mom would tell you it was okay, she wouldn't mind hearing it a few more times. Or the time she dated the manager of that music store, hoping to get his discount on sheet music."

I can't remember telling Will all this. It must've been during those nights when he drove me home. What's even more amazing is that he's remembered. Every bit of it.

"I won't stay away forever," I say, my voice small. "I just want to build on tonight."

"Build on tonight? In another city? In another state? How exactly does that work, Jenna?"

I grab one of Will's hands in both of mine. "With you and me together, making it work. We're a great team."

He doesn't pull his hand away, but instead lets it lie in mine like a dead fish. "What about Danny?"

"He can come if he wants. Might get crowded in my little one-room apartment, but hell, why not? Bambi's invited as well." I attempt a joke. A bad joke. It worked onstage tonight.

But it doesn't work now, and Will's hand slips free. "Danny asked earlier how we didn't kill each other. He thinks you still can't stand me."

I blink. "I guess you didn't tell him how we're sleeping together."

"No, I didn't tell him. I don't think..." Will drags a hand over his face. "He wouldn't be okay with it. It's one thing for you to have moved on. It's another for you to have moved on with me."

I attempt a smile, though my heart is rapidly sinking. "That's why we test things out in Texas. Danny doesn't have to know we're in the same city or even the same state. We can wait until he's ready and then—"

Bam! The table shakes as both of Will's hand slap it hard. "Wait until he's ready? Ready for what? It'll be years, if even that, before he can live a normal life. Meanwhile, where am I? Hiding out with you in Texas or wherever else the wind blows? Not going home until someone arrives to drag us back?"

My own hands clench. "That's not fair."

It's like Will doesn't even hear me. "I can't walk away without a backward glance."

"Like me, right?" Tears fill my eyes, but not for pleading.

Fuck that. Fuck him.

Giving the table a push, I stand. "I looked back, Will. Yes, it's true.

I didn't actually physically come back, and I regret that. Trust me, I get it now. All the moments, all the people, all the *everything* I missed and will never recover. I will never stop being sorry for all I lost. Lost because of stubbornness. Stupidity. Whatever you want to call it. But don't you dare say I didn't look back or that I didn't care. I thought about Danny every damn day. And I'll still think about him. Except I'll also be moving forward in my life. Because I can't hold myself back for Danny anymore. And I won't hold myself back for you either, Will. That's why I thought...this would be a chance for both of us to sorta move forward together. This could be our shot."

I sniffle hot snot and tears, and then despite the look in Will's eyes telling me not to, I keep going. "You sure like to criticize me. You tell me how you see a therapist and act like you've got it all figured out, but come on—who are you kidding? You live in your mom's basement. Think about that for a moment. And after graduating at the top of our class, you now work in your father's carpet store. Yeah, yeah, I know you're going to school, and you're working toward your master plan, and until then you can keep taking care of Danny, right? Keep being a martyr. Never mind NASA. Never mind aeronautical engineering. Never mind helping the next generation reach distant stars. Never mind—"

"Enough!" Now Will is on his feet too. My volume had steadily increased through that little rant, and now Will raises his voice as well. "I never cared about NASA. I was just talking. Trying to impress you."

"No way." I shake my head. "I don't believe that. You've never been the type to bullshit."

"Jenna, I was in *love* with you. Of course I was the type to bullshit."

In love with you. The words knock me back. He'd insinuated it yesterday when talking about his roommate's girlfriend, but to use the *L* word...An actual physical shock goes through me.

Will doesn't notice though. He's too busy telling me off. "Honestly? I didn't really know what I wanted. I only knew I was smart and everyone expected big things of me. NASA seemed big, so yes, if things had been different, I might've ended up there. But I can only go by what did happen. And yes, Danny is why I'm going to school and chasing all these different programs. Maybe I won't change the world, but if I can change one person's world, I'll be okay with that. And—"

"Okay with that?" I sneer. "Okay with emptying Danny's pee bag? And changing his dirty sheets? Stop shaping your life around him. For once, try living for yourself."

"Right. Live for me and only me. Forget everyone else," Will shoots right back.

We stare at one another, both breathing hard. This feels so much worse than any fight I ever had with Danny. Those were simply the tremors, letting us know what we built wasn't gonna last for the long haul. We knew it. We just hadn't gotten around to admitting it.

This is different though. Will and I haven't built anything yet, but it felt like there might be a good foundation there. If we wanted it.

And I really, really wanted it. I could see in my mind what we'd build and how rock solid it could be.

But that's how it didn't happen. How it won't happen.

Our eyes meet as we simultaneously realize the same thing. This show's a bust. Close it down. We're over before we even began.

Mom and her new boyfriend amble over. "Ho ho ho. Heard some shouting over here. Can Santa help?"

"Go fuck a reindeer, Santa," I snap.

"Oh, Jenna baby." Mom shakes her head at me. Then she turns to Santa. "Don't pay any attention to her. Ever since she didn't get a doll she wanted when she was three, I swear she's held a grudge. At five years old she peed on the mall Santa's lap. Said it was an accident, but I always wondered."

"Mom, go away," I growl, unable to take anymore. "And take your idiot Santa with you."

Santa draws himself up. "Now, that's no way to talk to your mother—"

Pulling at his arm, Mom draws him away. "I don't take it personally. Poor baby. She's been under a lot of pressure and has had a long..."

Will's phone rings, drowning out the rest. He doesn't reach for it, but I flap a hand at him. "Everything's already fucked. Go ahead and answer."

After a moment of hesitation, he turns away. "Mom?" he says into the phone.

I watch him, debating whether I should walk away now. But Will's remarks about me "running" ring in my ears. I don't want to be that person no one can count on.

Pushing my shoulders back, I decide right here and now, my life goes forward with or without Will. I'm taking that job in Texas. But I'm not running. I'll tell Allie that once I get to Texas and get settled in, I'll convince Mom to come stay with me for a while to give Allie a break from her. And I'll return home too. For holidays and in the summer. If Allie needs me, I'll be there. Even if it means getting on a plane, I'll figure it out somehow. Same goes for Danny. He can put me on speed dial. I'll tell him myself before I go. Maybe we'll even play another few rounds of strip poker. Ha! Will won't like that. Perhaps I'll even give Danny that hand job as a parting gift. That would really get Will. I'll show him.

Oh. I crumble as the heartbreak roars back. Or maybe I should stay. What if I pretended the whole "move to Texas with me" thing was just a joke? Except, I want the job in that adorable little theater. I've already mentally arranged my stuff in the apartment. And I have show ideas for the first season. Really great ones, like *The Light in the Piazza*, *A New Brain*, and *City of Angels*. They aren't obscure exactly, but none of them have the same name recognition as *Annie* or *Joseph and the Amazing Technicolor Dreamcoat*.

I want to take this chance. To see if I can do it. Maybe I can't. Or maybe I'll hate it. But I have to find out. I have to try.

Will abruptly whirls around to face me, the phone still near his ear. "My mom can't find Danny. The van's in the driveway, but there's no sign of him or Emma anywhere."

I can hear the worry in Will's voice. And can imagine Lynette's panic.

It transfers to me. I picture the house, the entire property, trying to imagine Danny somewhere on it, hidden.

And then, just like that, I know exactly where Danny is.

37

"Soon It's Gonna Rain" – The Fantasticks

This is how I met Danny.

On that night Will invited me for dinner, after I overheard him telling his mother terrible things about me, I ran out a side door, only to realize my mother wouldn't be back to pick me up for another hour and I had no way of calling her. Basically, I was stuck.

Also, it was cold. The in-ground pool had its cover on, and all the patio furniture was neatly stacked and covered on the porch of their poolside shed. Deciding to take shelter inside this adorable little shed/pool house, I ran across the lawn, worried about being spotted. Then I opened a pretty pair of French doors and slipped inside.

And there was Danny in gym shorts and a ratty T-shirt. He had several bags of chips, a half-empty two-liter Pepsi, and cards spread out before him in a game of solitaire.

We stared, both shocked to see the other.

Feeling like a complete idiot, I stuttered, "Oh, sorry. I didn't realize."

Before I could retreat and close the door behind me, Danny sprang to his feet. "Wait! I don't know who you are or why you're in my backyard, but please don't leave. I'm so bored, and you're so..." Eyeing me up and down, he made his admiration clear. I was young enough to be flattered as he concluded, "So totally hot. It's crazy you walking in here. You're so pretty. I probably ate too many chips and passed out and this is all a dream, but I really hope it isn't."

No one like Danny had ever paid this kind of attention to me. Looking at me like I was the only girl in the world.

"I'm Jenna," I said stupidly. "And you're Will's brother. Danny, right?" Obviously I knew his name, but I didn't want to sound like every other girl at school who had sighed when he passed them in the hallway.

He grinned. "Yeah, I'm Danny. And I am so happy, beyond happy really, to meet you. Please, Jenna, stay. You can have my chips, my pop..." He waggled his eyebrows. "My heart. Whatever you want. Just please don't go."

Of course I stayed.

I shared his chips and swigged from the same bottle of Pepsi. Then even though it was embarrassing, I felt he deserved an explanation of why I was there. I didn't go into overhearing Heather complaining about the commercials and my propositioning Will. I simply said Will and I were sort of friends.

"Only friends, right?" Danny jumped in to ask.

Later I realized it was to make sure he wasn't moving in on his brother's territory.

"Not even friends," I admitted. Then I explained how Will was using me to upset his mom.

"Yeah, Mom can be..." Looking sheepish, he said, "I dropped out of college yesterday. Drove all day, got home late last night. I didn't want to go in and wake the whole house and have everyone even more upset with me. I figured it was a warm night, so I came back here, slept on one of the chaise lounge chairs." He paused. "You wanna know a secret?"

I nodded.

"When I was a kid, I slept out here a lot. No one ever knew. I'd sneak out after everyone else was in bed. Sometimes I'd sleep under the stars, but it'd get kinda buggy, so mostly I came in here. It was nice. Like running away from home, you know? I'd pretend it was my own place."

Danny sighed, as if remembering being a kid and missing it. Then recalling he had an audience, he turned his big smile back on.

"That was always in the summer though. Turns out October nights can get pretty cold.

"It took me a while to fall asleep. So I overslept. By the time I got up, my dad was at work and Will was at school. Facing Mom without Will there as a distraction, or my dad to say, like, 'Hey, give him a break. He's still young,' would've just been..."

Danny gave his head a hard shake.

"No way, man. So I figure, new plan. Wait till Dad gets home. Come in while they're eating dinner. But Dad must be working late, 'cause I haven't seen his car yet, and then I noticed Mom cooked a 'we got company' dinner. No way was I walking into that. It'd be, like, uuggghh. Forget it. So I hit the gas station for dinner. And there ya go. I just, like, wanna do this with the least amount of drama. You know?"

I could see how hard he was working to play it cool. He didn't want to seem pathetic, hiding out in his own backyard. There was this vulnerability I'd never imagined Danny possessing when he'd walked the halls of my high school, his chest puffed out and a court of admirers orbiting around him.

If I'd met him at a school, we never would've gotten together. Even if he'd hit on me at a party (and he wouldn't have—Danny was more the type to let the girls come to him), I would've turned him down, assuming he'd heard I was easy and wanted into my pants.

If Will had invited me over one day sooner or one day later, we never would've met.

If I had managed to find the bathroom.

If I'd had a cell phone to call my mom.

If. If. If.

How many stars aligned to put Danny and me in that pool house together at exactly the right time?

Of course, I wasn't thinking about any of that then.

Danny was the only thought in my head.

I breathed in his every word. I couldn't believe he was talking to me. I couldn't believe he was so handsome. Mostly, I couldn't believe how sweet he was beneath the swagger.

Like Wendy with Peter Pan, I fell for him almost instantly.

I assured Danny I understood why he was hiding from his mother, that anyone in his situation would do the same.

"You're so nice," he said in this sweet and totally sincere way. "I feel like I could tell you anything. Like, like, I couldn't cut it at college. It was just too hard, and I hated it. I mean, you get that, right?"

I did get it. After confessing that college was definitely not in my future either, I told him about all the famous people who had never gone to college or who had dropped out because it was a waste of time.

His response? "I really want to kiss you."

"Okay," I replied, uncertain.

He hesitated. "Nah. I mean, I'm gonna, but I should wait. Like we need to know each other better first."

"Right," I said.

We sat a moment, both feeling like the awkward strangers we were. Then suddenly he lit up. "There's a few beers at the bottom of the cooler back there. Not cold, but you want one?"

I did. He did. There were more than a few. We had two each. Then we played cards, and it somehow morphed into strip poker. We were flirty, leaning into each other, exchanging playful slaps or nudges, any excuse to touch. Finally, Danny leaned in to kiss me. I placed my hand over his lips.

"I thought you wanted to wait?" I asked.

He pretended to bite down on my fingers. "I've waited too long already."

"But we should know each other first, that's what you said," I teased. "Maybe we should play twenty questions."

"Or," Danny countered, "I could tickle you."

I shrieked as he attacked. Wriggling away, I made a run for it, out the French doors with Danny chasing me. From behind me, he made an odd noise. Almost like he was choking on something. I looked over my shoulder, unsure if he was hurt or trying to trick me.

That's when I slammed into Mrs. O'Leary. We clutched each other and stumbled before regaining our balance. Quickly, I pulled away from her. Then realizing I was no longer wearing the tight turtleneck she'd objected to, I crossed my arms over my chest.

"Mom," Danny said in this horrible strangled voice.

"Jenna, baby! There you are!" My own mother's voice came out of the darkness.

"Well," Mrs. O'Leary said with a hard smile. "I feel certain there must be a story here."

I wasn't there when Danny told that story. My mom took me home after Mrs. O'Leary reminded us it was a school night. In the car, as my mom prattled on about what a handsome boy Danny was, I felt certain I'd never see him again. But the next day when I came out of school, he was standing there, waiting, a giant bouquet of bright-yellow sunflowers in his hand.

"Hey," I'd said, playing it casual, worried they might be for Heather.

"Hey," he'd answered back, equally casual, while it seemed like every single person in my high school watched. "I thought you should know, I told my mom last night..."

I can still feel the way his bright-blue gaze filled me up. I held my breath, no longer needing air as the orchestra began to play. Not a real orchestra. That would've been way over the top, and frankly, such a gesture wouldn't have occurred to Danny. The orchestra was in my head, and as Danny smiled, the music swelled.

This was it. My "Unexpected Song." "Somewhere." "Some Enchanted Evening." If I were a bell, I'd have been ringing.

Danny didn't sing the words, but in my head they'll always be set to music.

"I might be in love with you."

And that was it. By the time I wondered what we had in common be-sides one magical night in a pool house when we were both vulnerable and needing a little reassurance, well, by then I was knocked up and we were in a little chapel promising to love one another until death did us part.

38

"A Little Fall of Rain" –Les Miserable

"He's in the pool house," I tell Will.

We've left the bar, moved to the sidewalk out front, where it's quieter. Lynette is on the speaker.

"Pool house? We don't have a pool house," she answers.

"The cute little shed by the pool. Whatever you call it. He wants to get with Bambi. He wants to feel normal again. He can't do that in a hospital bed. But he also can't go far. The pool house, or whatever, it's home but not home. A way to get away without going away."

"Mom, did you hear that?" Will asks when she doesn't reply.

"Oh God, there's a light on in there," she replies. There's a scuffling noise, and I think she's running. Then the clatter of a door and finally, "Damn it, Emma. I thought you knew better than this."

A shriek follows, from Emma I presume, who's obviously surprised. In hindsight I should have warned her that Danny's mom has a gift for showing up at the exact worst moment.

"Put some clothes on," Lynette snaps, stopping Emma's hysterics.

"We didn't do anything. I know physically, he can't. He wanted to feel me, that's all. Not in a dirty way, we only wanted to hold one another. I told him we couldn't do anything more than that. Not yet." Emma's voice trembles, and by the end she can barely get the words out between her sobs.

"That's all," Lynette snaps back. "And yet he's so exhausted, he's not waking up. Danny! Danny, wake up." Something new enters Lynette's voice. A higher, more panicked note. "Why is he so cold?"

"I'm sorry. It's winter. We shouldn't have come out here, but Danny insisted." I can barely make out what Emma's saying, as she's crying. "But we've got heated blankets. I insisted on that. He's probably just chilled..."

There's a long silence. Then a huge racking sob, followed by the worst thing I've ever heard. "I can't find a pulse. That can't be right. We were talking, and then he was tired, and I told him to close his eyes for a few minutes, 'cause we'd have to go back inside soon. I closed my eyes too. Only for a minute." Emma is hysterical. "Danny, wake up. Wake up. Wake UP!"

Will sinks forward, phone still clutched in his hand. I grab him. "Easy. Sit. I'm right here." Once he's down safely, I pull out my own phone. "I'm calling 911," I announce loudly so Mrs. O'Leary will hear too.

"911. What is your emergency?"

My own voice sounds foreign as I explain the situation to the operator.

Distantly, I hear Mrs. O'Leary voice, except not her voice, because this one sounds old and broken and nothing like the woman on stage tonight. "It's too late. He's gone."

"No, no, nooooo," Emma howls. "Danny, wake up. Wake up. You don't understand. He was here a minute ago. We were talking. He wanted to marry me. And I said I would. I said, 'I do.' That's what I said. I told him, I don't care if you have to divorce Jenna first. I don't mind waiting. I don't mind being a second wife, because I'll be your best wife and I'll always be here for you. Always. Always." She keeps talking, but it becomes too garbled. Then there is a low keening coming from Will's phone.

I give the O'Learys' address to the 911 operator. Once I'm assured an ambulance is on its way and I can hear the sirens from Will's phone, I hang up.

In the cold, Will and I sit side by side on the sidewalk, listening as the EMTs work to make Danny not dead.

But Lynette was right. I guess a mother sometimes knows.

Danny's gone.

Will ends the call. He looks down at the phone in his hand, like he doesn't even understand what it is. Then he throws it as hard as he can into the street. It goes skidding along until it clatters to a stop somewhere out in the darkness.

"Let me get that for you." I jump to my feet. Wanting to do something. To help. To fix this.

"No." Will's voice is hard as he lumbers to his feet, moving like his whole body hurts. "No," he says again. Turning, he moves toward where his car is parked down the street.

I follow after him. "Will, let me drive," I say, catching hold of his arm.

He shakes me off with one hard jerk. "You're not coming with me."

The way he says it. The way he looks at me.

I back away. "Will, don't do this. I know this—" I stop and correct myself. "No, I don't know. I can only try to imagine how hard this is. My heartbreak is so small compared to what you're feeling."

"Your heartbreak is small?" Will sneers. "Really? Because usually the widow feels a bit more." Abruptly he wheels about to face me. "Did you marry him or not? You said you didn't, but Emma somehow believes otherwise. Why is that?"

Right. The whole marriage thing that I stupidly lied about and then never quite got around to correcting.

I gulp. "Technically, we're married, I guess."

Will's whole face tightens, and he spins away. I scrabble for his sleeve, desperate, wanting to find some magic words to defuse his anger. "I didn't mean to lie about it. I mean, I did mean to lie. I knew it was a lie, but I only told it because everything was already so complicated, and *married* seems like such a big deal. Like this life–changing thing. But we were only married for two days, and then there was the accident. And the whole wedding was a joke. We were playing at being grown-ups, and sorta took it too far. I never thought of Danny as my husband. I'm pretty sure he never saw me as his wife. It was like a practical joke we played on ourselves."

I am babbling, unable to stop even as Will pulls away from me.

"Will, please, stop. This is stupid. You're not really mad that Danny and I were married, are you? Danny didn't care. How can it matter that much to you?"

He stops, his hand on the car door. "He married you. I know Danny. He wouldn't have done that..." Will stops and shakes his head. "Maybe it didn't mean anything to you, but it meant something to him." He opens his car door, and then looks over the car at me once more. "He asked for you. He woke up, and he asked for you. That means something, Jenna."

"I know." My throat is so tight I can barely get the words out. "And I came, didn't I? I'm here."

Will's face crumples, and I think he's going to cry and that this time I'll be the one to hold him and this fight will be over. But it passes, leaving his face in a permanent grimace. "You're here. But where is Danny? You should be with *him* right now. You came all this way and spent less than an hour with him before pushing him into someone else's arms—"

"You asshole!" I stamp my foot against the pavement. "You fucking asshole! I did everything you asked. Everything! And I'm sorry he's dead. I am..." I place my hand over my heart, where it aches in a way I already know will never fully heal. "You're wrong though. I was not someone special to Danny. He didn't love me like that. I was just someone familiar. That's why he asked for me. Well, that and he probably remembered I knew how to deliver a damn fine rub and tug."

I choke out a laugh, which cracks down the middle. Unable to hold it in anymore, I press my hands to my face and sink to the cold sidewalk as the tears flow.

The sound of Will's car starting jerks me back to my feet.

"Will, please!" Still crying, I pound on the passenger window. Even as he maneuvers away from the curb, I follow along. "Please, Will, I'm sorry. Don't do this. Don't—"

With a squeal of tires, he's gone.

Standing in the empty street, bawling my eyes out, I realize Will was right about one thing.

My heartbreak isn't small. It's damn near big enough to swallow me whole.

39

"So Long, Farewell" – The Sound of Music

I sang "Danny Boy" at the funeral.

Will walked out. We passed one another as he strode down the middle aisle and I up it. He didn't look at me, even as I glared, daring him to meet my eyes.

The whole family—including Nadine—came to the church, surrounding me the entire time. Afterward, instead of following the procession to the cemetery, I asked them to take me home.

Showing her support the best way she knows how, Mom broke out a bottle of Jack Daniel's.

"Tequila for sex. Vodka for love. And always, always, whiskey for sorrow," my mother intoned while pouring out several fingers for each of us (though Allie's was just to sniff and swirl).

I'd slugged only half of it down when Allie started in on me. "So you're leaving tomorrow, right? And you're gonna return...when again?"

"We've already gone through this."

"Tell it to me again."

I held back a sigh. "I'm leaving tomorrow. I'll definitely be home for the birth of the twins, if not sooner."

"Sooner, right." Allie scoffed. "You know what? I don't believe you. Your word is shit."

Draining my glass, I filled it again. Stella would be making the trip with me tomorrow, so I wasn't worried about being too hungover to drive.

"You got nothing to say?" Allie demanded.

Nadine leaned into her, rubbing Allie's shoulders. "Baby, she understands."

"Yeah, Mom, you're doing that bulldog thing," Maxi chimed in. "Anyway, you said yourself, Aunt Jenna can barely keep herself alive."

"Please, don't help." My quiet request was drowned out by Allie.

"She left Mom at the bar!" Allie surged off the couch to wag a finger in my face. "You said you'd take her home, and you didn't."

"I'm sorry. How many times do I have to say it? I had some other shit going on, and I forgot."

"Girls, girls." Mom stepped in. "I was fine. Santa took me home."

"Santa took her home," Allie repeated. "This is what I'm talking about. Mom's losing it. No offense, Mom."

"It's fine, sweetheart. I'm flattered you think I had it to begin with."

"Mom, you're not losing it." I stand because everyone else is standing, and also I need another refill. "The guy had a long white beard. He plays Santa during the holidays and stuff."

"That's right." Mom nodded. "He even let me see his suit, but I couldn't touch it. Apparently, the elves get very touchy. They're in charge of the cleaning, you know."

I frown. "Mom, he was joking about the elves. You know that, right?"

"Well, I'm not sure, sweetie. He said it very seriously."

"Uh-huh," Allie said.

Okay, so maybe Mom was losing it. Or never had it to begin with. A better daughter would've stayed. But I couldn't. Not because I was running, but because I had a job offer. In Texas.

Though, to be honest, the enthusiasm for the job was gone. Even as I was telling everyone how I had to leave, that I couldn't possibly turn down such a great opportunity, I was desperate to turn it down. To call Ethel and tell her I'd changed my mind. Again.

If it wasn't for Stella, I wouldn't have made it to Texas. I would've stayed at that little town in southern Ohio or the one in Indiana or Oklahoma. Stella made me keep going. Even after I broke down at the Texas border.

"I can't go to Texas when Danny is dead!" I wailed.

My hysterics made the dogs crazy (they were all along for the ride, of course). They barked and howled (Stella had picked up a stray beagle in Kentucky), while Pippin licked up the tears as they dripped down my face.

Having the furballs there helped so much that by the time we all calmed down, I didn't even need Stella's speech (in a nutshell: "Danny's dead. You're not.") to convince me to carry on.

And now I've been here five months.

Thanks to Pippin and his travel difficulties, we ended up arriving five days later than I'd told Ethel to expect me. She didn't mind though. When I pulled the truck up outside the church, she was there, ready to let us in and take us on a full tour. Ethel was everything she'd been in her emails and phone calls: sweet, encouraging, and committed to letting me run the show.

Even the addition of Pippin (who, of course, took a dump on the stage right in front of her) didn't rattle Ethel. "I guess he's prone to accidents?" she asked.

Certain she was going to kick us both out, I cringed and nodded.

Instead she laughed. "Well, my guess is you're good at cleaning up after him. I had a cat once with a similar problem. There was one sofa we had that she wet again and again. My husband was ready to put her in a bag and take her to the creek, but I said, 'No, no, I'll take care of it.' Bless his heart, he died believing I'd broken Sprinkles of her bad habit. The truth is, I ordered a bolt of fabric that was an exact match for the couch cushions. After that, whenever Sprinkles had an oopsie, I'd get my sewing machine out and whip up a new cushion. We must've gone through at least a few dozen of them, and he never suspected."

I hugged her then.

"Your generation, my goodness. Never a handshake, always a hug. I don't mind though. Goodness, the world will be a better place when all you huggers are done with it."

For the first time, the heavy weight of Danny's death and my falling out with Will lifted. *This is gonna be good*, I thought.

It's possible I jinxed it, because as we were finishing up, Ethel said, "Now, there is one thing I need to tell you." Her sunny demeanor faded. "We have a board of directors for the theater. I like to set things up that way. My goal is to build something bigger than myself. Something to last long after I'm gone. Not that I intend on going anytime soon, but at my age one must think ahead. At any rate, the board was not entirely enthusiastic about your hiring. I wanted you to get our first season started with a bang, while they wanted to hire the English teacher from the high school to direct *Annie*."

Ethel made a face to let me know how she felt about that idea. "They relented after a small reminder that I hold the purse strings. But doing that too often makes one a bully, doesn't it? My late husband, bless his heart, liked reminding me who brought home the bacon. I can tell you, such moments did not increase my love for him. I don't want that with my board. For this reason, I didn't override their desire to open with *Annie*. I've only held them off, asking that they keep an open mind and see what our new artistic director wishes. In other words, dear, *you'll* need to be the bully. Oh, I'll back you up, but you must stand firm against those old biddies. And if possible, perhaps practice some diplomacy. Throw them a bone here and there so it doesn't devolve into full out war."

Ethel, twisting her purse strap in her hand, peeked up at me from beneath her lashes. "I should have told you all that up front, but goodness, you made it difficult enough. I was afraid to scare you away."

I forced a smile and told Ethel it was fine.

In truth, it shook me. I looked around, needing some backup. But

Stella was outside letting the dogs run around. Of course, it wasn't her hand I wanted to hold anyway.

It was Will's.

If he were there, we could've talked through strategies to deal with the board. But that was a burned bridge, and I didn't see anyone working to rebuild it anytime soon. Or ever.

After Ethel left, I thought it over more and decided to call Eli. Perhaps I knew he'd give me a good scolding. Which he did.

"Oh no, how awful," he moaned in mock sympathy. "You mean you don't get to simply come up with an artistic vision that everyone around you will be thrilled—no, honored—to support?"

I admitted that perhaps I had envisioned something like that.

"Buck up, princess," he shot back. "This is the real world. You're a grown-up. Make it work." Even worse, Eli left me with a pile of guilt too. "I can't believe I'm even talking to you after you didn't come car shopping. We've test driven twenty different vehicles, Jenna, and have yet to narrow it down. The next time you're in town, you owe me big time. Oh, what am I even saying? You're never returning."

Another person I'd let down too many times. The list seemed endless.

The next day Stella and the dogs left for Houston. All except Pippin. Stella said we deserved each other. I think she meant it as a compliment. But by that point it felt like one more person piling on.

For a week I moped. Cried. Hopeless and beaten.

Then Pippin ran out of dog food, which meant I had to leave the apartment. The pet store was next to an office supplies store. With Pippin tucked under my arm, I found myself wandering the aisles full of binders and envelope labels and every type of pen in existence. It wasn't until I held a package of graph paper in my hands that I realized that was what I'd wanted all along.

I bought it as a souvenir of sorts. A memory of what might've been. How it could've happened.

The paper sat untouched on my kitchen counter for several days, until I picked it up, intending to toss the whole thing. Instead, I took the top page out and wrote a list. Neatly numbered, I wrote out all the shows I wanted to do. Then a second list giving reasons why performing shows your audience might not be familiar with was worthwhile. And another list with my qualifications.

It turned out, list making could be addictive.

Armed with those lists, I met with the board. Nobody jumped up and down when I finished, but with Ethel on my side, they begrudgingly agreed to my plan.

Emboldened, I returned to the office supplies store to buy more graph paper. I also picked up a binder to store my lists. Then there were phone calls to secure rights to our first show and setting dates for the auditions, rehearsals, and opening night. Ethel and I talked several times a day, both of us bubbling with excitement. I added two more binders and an endless number of lists. The show went on and on and on. The only thing missing was Will.

I ached to call him. To hear his voice. To make sure he was okay and not depressed or falling apart. And also to tell him everything was going great and fuck him very much.

Mostly I tried not to think about him. And failed.

Eventually, it was time to hold auditions for our first show, *City of Angels*. I picked a cast and directed it, and the show opened. The local paper panned it, but Ethel loved it and said the board members begrudgingly enjoyed it. We had a tough time filling seats for the matinee, but every evening performance sold out.

After taking a week to recover, Ethel came to discuss which show we should tackle next, which was when I broke the news to her.

"I'm sorry, Ethel, but I'm quitting."

"Oh no. Is it because of the theater board?"

I told her it wasn't.

"It's the heat then, right? We have an air-conditioning unit in the budget for next year, if you could just hold on."

The lack of AC in the charming white clapboard church was terrible, especially since there weren't enough windows to catch a cross breeze—not that anything so refreshing seemed to exist in that part of Texas. But, as I explained to Ethel, that wasn't it either.

I told her what I'd finally figured out for myself.

"I ran away from home a long time ago, and I kept running for a long time after that. I thought coming here was my way to settle down, but it isn't. I didn't mean to, but coming here was another way of running. And now...I owe it to my family and myself to return and at least try to make a life back home, because I think, maybe, I could be really happy there."

"Oh, sweetheart." Ethel took my hand. "Sometimes we need to figure out where we're at, to decide where we truly desire to go next. And it sounds like you've done that."

"Well, I'm getting closer."

"Good for you. But not so good for me." Ethel sighed and shook her head. "You know they're going to make me do a production of that fucking orphan Annie now, don't you?"

I laughed and agreed she'd have a hard time avoiding it.

Now, as I prepare for another long road trip with Pippin, auditions for Annie go on in the church without me. A pitchy rendition of "Tomorrow" floats out the open windows as I place an economy-sized box of baby wipes into the cab of the truck. After doing one last check to make sure everything's where it should be, I shut the door and turn to see a black town car parked behind me. The windows are tinted, and as the door swings open, I wonder if it's one of the board members coming to give me one final "Good riddance."

To my shock, it's Mrs. O'Leary. I stand slack jawed as she coolly walks toward me, looking crisp and put together.

"Hey, Mrs. O'Leary," I call out with a weak wave. "Funny meeting you here."

"It's Lynette," she corrects. "And there's nothing funny about it. I came here expressly to see you." She makes a point of examining my truck bed packed with all my worldly belongings.

"Don't tell me you're moving on already?" she asks with a laugh.

I shrug, stung and embarrassed. "I'm going home. My sister's pregnant with twins, and my mom thinks she's in a relationship with the real Santa Claus."

"Oh." Her eyebrows shoot up. "I see. Well..." She seems momentarily stumped, but Mrs. O'Leary is never truly at a loss. "Let me know when you're settled in. I'd love to have your whole family over for dinner."

"Um, okay," I say, but then it feels stingy, since she's being nice and we've corresponded back and forth a few times. She found my marriage certificate while going through some of Danny's old stuff and sent it to me with a note that said, *It might not mean much now, but I thought you might like to have this.*

So I add, "I was going to write you a note, once I was settled in. Letting you know I was home and had a new job and stuff."

"A new job?"

"Eli Wallace offered me the visiting director position at Niven for next semester. Says I can offer real-world experience. It doesn't pay much." I laugh and scuff my toe in the dirt. "It pays pretty much nothing. A stipend, Eli calls it. Probably won't cover gas to get there, but it'll be good for my résumé, and it's a chance to build relationships locally, since my plan is to, you know, stick around for a while. I might go back to school eventually, but I don't know. I'm gonna take it one day at a time for now."

Lynette says nothing for a long moment, but then she nods. "Very wise."

From her it's high praise. "Thanks," I say, somewhat abashed. I'm not sure what to say next. "Um, do you want to come in for a drink? I have water, from the tap. It's pretty good though. Well water."

"No. Thank you. I left Emma waiting for me at the airport. You remember Emma, don't you? Or Bambi, I believe you called her. It fits. She is the dearest girl. I've spent hours telling her stories about Danny. Anyone else would beg me to stop, but she always wants to

307

hear more. I really should send her away, but I'm selfish, so...we're off to Paris! My treat, of course. Hopefully, it'll be good for her. She's a mess, and left to her own devices, I'm afraid she'll become..." Lynette eyes me up and down.

"A total fuck up like me?" I guess.

"Yes. Precisely. Well put. Except unlike you, I don't know if she'd be able to pull herself up again. She hasn't your spunky nature. For example, not once has she referred to me as a battleax."

Flattered and flustered by what I'm pretty sure was a significant compliment, I protest, "I never called you a battleax."

"I have excellent hearing. Your muttered invectives were always quite audible."

"Oh." I try to recall the various names I've mumbled.

"All water under the bridge," Lynette assures me, with the slight edge to her voice promising I will one day pay for every one of those whispered words. "I simply came to check in, see your new place, and tell you..." She hesitates and nearly looks uncertain, like any other human being. But it's only a flash, and I'm certain I imagined it, because she adds, "It's not my business, but I assume there's no one special you'll be leaving behind?"

"Special?" I know what she means, but it's ballsy for her to ask about my romantic life.

"Yes. I'm asking if you're currently in a relationship." Lynette levels a clear gaze at me. A dare to tell her off.

I don't. Feeling like a kid hauled before the principal, I shrug. "No. All right?"

"I didn't want to assume, but I suspected as much." She nods, satisfied. Then a smile teases at the corner of her lips. "A bloodhound senses these things."

My eyes pop wide open. "Did Will tell you I called you that?"

She lifts a single shoulder, which somehow comes off more sophisticated than a shrug. "Will mentioned it to me, as a rebuttal to my repeated encouragement for him to call you."

I'm misunderstanding something here. "You *wanted* him to call me?"

Lynette sighs. "Is it so surprising? I want my son to be happy. Candidly, he's struggling. Danny for so long was his direction. His meaning in life. Now he has to recalibrate. But it's more than that. He misses you. Will won't admit it, but..."

She sighs and looks impatient. I tense, expecting her to snap at me, but then realize it's directed at herself. "I don't believe in soul mates. It's nonsense. An excuse for why things don't work out. 'Oh, they weren't *the one.*'" The annoyance fades. Softens. "But sometimes, for some people, there is one person they get hung up on. And no matter how much time passes or how many other people they meet, they cannot let that person go."

Pausing, she appraises me, trying to gauge my reaction. My face feels numb. I doubt she can read anything there. My heart, though, gallops like it's in the Kentucky Derby, and somehow she knows it.

She nods, as if confirming something. "I think for Will, you are the one. I suspected it from that first night you came for dinner. When you got up to leave the table—and we won't discuss now how you used that time to hunt down my other son—"

I start to protest, but Lynette glares in a way that promises bodily injury to anyone who interrupts her mid-monologue. I shut my mouth.

She continues. "The moment you left the room, Will goaded me, telling me all the ways in which you were inappropriate. It wasn't until several weeks later that I realized what he'd been after. That's when I overheard him asking Aaron to give you a part in the store commercials. You see, a couple years earlier I nearly took Heather's head off when I discovered her breaking into our liquor cabinet. I should've known then what she was."

Lynette gives a hard shake of her head, clearly nurturing a grudge. "By the time I finished with her, Heather was on the floor sobbing. Aaron thought I'd been too harsh. That's when he offered her an appearance in one of his commercials. It worked. Like that, she was happy again. I suspect Will was hoping to manufacture a similar scene, except this time starring you."

My head swims, and for once it's not from the oppressive Texas heat. "He didn't tell me," I whisper.

"Why should he? His plan didn't work. I overruled Aaron. No more friends or family in the carpet commercials. Frankly, they were terrible ads, and I did you all a favor." She shudders. "At any rate, Will went to a lot of trouble for a girl he barely knew. And then there was the way he looked at you. I know you didn't see it. Your eyes were only for Danny, and that's what it should've been. But now Danny is gone..."

Her face crumples, but she quickly pulls it back together. Her chin comes up strong. "Life goes on, and we must make the most of it. If there was anyone else on the planet Will wanted, I'd be there. But it's you. It's always been you. Which, I hope I don't have to tell you, makes you one very lucky woman." She gets misty eyed again but blinks it away.

My own eyes don't tear, but a thick ball of emotion gathers in my throat. Somehow I manage to mutter around it, "But he hates me now."

Lynette snorts. "Nonsense. He's behaving very badly and more than a little stupidly. He almost certainly gets that from his father."

I choke out a laugh and nod my agreement.

"However, he's starting to come around. A few months back I couldn't stand his moping any longer and gave him two weeks to take some positive actions in his life. If he didn't, I was kicking him out of the house. I hoped this would push him in your direction, but instead he found a gorgeous loft apartment downtown."

"Gorgeous loft apartment?" I echo in disbelief. "Yeah, it sounds like he's really pining."

Lynette holds up a finger. "He's subletting it. A friend of his got an assignment in Tokyo. There were other units Will could've rented or even purchased outright, but he decided to sublet instead. What does that tell you?"

"He's lived with his parents his whole life and doesn't own any furniture?"

"Please, don't you be stupid too. We can't have that on both ends of this thing." Leaning in closer, uncomfortably close really, she asks softly, "What did you say to him?"

I stumble back, unsure whether she means to strike me. The intensity is that high. "I don't know what you mean."

Lynette sighs. "After he moved into the loft, he also gave his resignation at the store. He wants to pursue his education full time so he can graduate before he's forty."

"Before he's forty?" I can't hide my surprise. "But is that possible with all the degrees he wants?"

"No, it's not. But having thought it over, Will admitted he may need to learn some things on the job, if you will, instead of at school. He's going to finish the programs he's currently more than halfway through and let everything else go." Lynette struggles against it but is unable to fight the proud grin that takes over her face. "It's such a relief! He's no longer holding back. And he's excited! Already, he's put together a business plan. I'll ask him one little question about it, and he goes on and on."

I bite my lip. I'm happy for Will too, but somehow it feels more like sorrow. "That's great."

"It's amazing," Lynette corrects. "I can actually imagine him being happy. Almost." Pulling her exquisite Kate Spade handbag off her shoulder, she clicks it open, reaches inside, and extracts a piece of paper and pen. I marvel over her ability to find such small items in her purse with absolutely zero rummaging around. She writes something down and then holds it out to me.

It's Will's address, of course. I stare down at it.

"I was going to suggest you write him a letter. There's something romantic and old-fashioned about a letter. But, since you'll be home, you might as well stop by."

I sigh and wonder if it can really be that easy. "But it's weird, isn't it? I'm technically Danny's widow. For me and Will to—"

Impatient, Lynette interrupts with a crisp, "Don't. Be. Stupid. Didn't I say that already? I hate repeating myself. I find it very upsetting. Besides which, if my ex-husband can marry Danny's ex-girlfriend, a girl I cannot help but point out is thirty-some years his junior, then I think we can all find a way to accept a second helping of awkward around the Thanksgiving table." She holds up her hands. "There. I've said my piece. What happens next is for you and Will to decide." With that she gives my cheek a light kiss and then turns on her heel. With nothing more than a wave out the window of her town car, she's gone.

And I am left with Will's address.

I vaguely recognize the street name. Not that it matters. Right now, no matter where that gorgeous loft apartment is, it's the only place I want to be.

Since Mrs. O'Leary told me not to be stupid, I grab Pippin, get in my truck, and go.

40

"For Good" -Wicked

I'm sitting on the cheeky welcome mat outside Will's door, which reads, *Doorbell Broken. Yell "Ding Dong" Really Loud.*

I cannot decide if the mat came with the apartment or if Will placed it here. And if this was Will's choice, what does it say about his state of mind? It occurs to me that Lynette might've tipped him off. Maybe he bought the mat especially to scare me away. Or challenge me.

So after I knocked and knocked with no answer, I did, in fact, yell "Ding dong" several times. Really loudly. A neighbor yelled at me to shut up, but there was nothing from Will.

I guess this is why people call first.

My plan had been to give it an hour. It's a Saturday afternoon. He's probably running errands. Or at the gym. When the hour passes and he doesn't show, I give it ten more minutes. Then another ten. I get up, take two steps, then turn back. I'll wait ten more minutes. Again. Sitting down, I set the timer on my phone and lean against the door, closing my eyes.

I wake up to my phone alarm beeping and a warm hand shaking my shoulder. I smell him first, that wonderful Will scent, and then I open my eyes. The image doesn't match the warm hand and yummy smell. Clearly grumpy, Will frowns down at me, gym bag in one hand, pineapple in the other.

"What's with the pineapple?" I ask, which seems a better icebreaker than, "Your mom doesn't believe in soul mates but thinks I might be yours."

Removing his warm hand, he stands up straight, looming over me. "It's a housewarming gift from a friend. What are you doing here?"

"Sleeping. And waiting for you to come home."

The frown that's been on his face this whole time deepens. "Why?"

"Can I come inside first? Your neighbor's already upset with me for yelling ding dong several times, and then singing a little bit of 'Ding Dong the Witch Is Dead.' So you probably don't want to piss him off anymore."

"Why were you yelling ding dong?" Will looks mystified.

Well, guess he didn't purchase the mat. That's a relief. I stand up, revealing it beneath me. "Just following directions."

He stares at the mat and then me. The frown wobbles and compresses, like he's holding back a smile. Reaching around me, he puts his key into the lock and pushes the door open. "Go on inside."

I go and then immediately stop. Holy Patron Saint of Renters, this place is gorgeous. "Wow. When that person comes back from Tokyo, can you refuse to leave? Claim squatters' rights?"

Walking past me, Will heads toward the kitchen area. "So you talked with my mother, I assume?"

Oh shit. I probably shouldn't have said that about the subletting. It sounds like his mom and I are colluding. We kind of are, but that's not how I want this conversation to go.

Unfortunately, I haven't been able to script that conversation, despite having days to think about it while driving here. And then more days during which I went house hunting with Eli and his husband. (They finally settled the car question by each buying what he wanted, but obviously with a house a bit more compromise will be required, which means that every weekend for the rest of my life will be spent at open houses with the two of them).

After that, I thought making peace with Allie would be a good dry run for seeing Will. She's so pregnant and hormonal, she's hugging one minute and slapping the next. Nadine said once the babies come, she'll be so happy to have another set of arms that the slapping will cease. To which I replied, "But, um, that's several more months of me getting hit?"

At least Mom and Maxi were happy to see me. Maxi mostly because I hit a mall on the way up and added a few things to my wardrobe perfect for her to steal. "Oooh, you bought new shirts!" she squealed three minutes after offering to help me bring my bags inside.

Mom's joy was more pure. "Oh my baby, I always knew you'd come home. And now that you're old enough to drink, we can go clubbing together!"

There's a loud *thunk*, and I jump, but it's only Will cutting into the pineapple. "Have a seat," he says, gesturing to the tall bar chairs along the island.

I perch on the edge of a chair, watching as he takes his aggression out on that poor pineapple. It makes me nervous since I'm pretty sure he's pretending it's me.

I get up and pace.

"I moved in with my mom," I say, because I gotta start somewhere. "Funny. You move *out* of your mom's house, and I move into mine."

"Funny," Will agrees, showing no sign he understands the actual meaning of that word.

He's giving me nothing here. Absolutely nothing, and I'm not going to beg and plead and tell him I made the wrong choice. I mean yeah, some of the time I did. But it wasn't only me.

Stopping, I face him straight on. "Will, can you put the knife down and talk to me already?"

"I can cut and talk."

"I want you to look at me. Really look at me. And talk to me. Like say stuff that really means something, not 'have a seat' bullshit. Say something that matters."

Will stares at me, those eyes of his hollowing me out like they always do. Then slowly and deliberately, he sets the knife down. "All right. How about this? Whatever you think is going to happen here, it isn't happening. That's over. We're done."

I look down at my chest. Amazingly, the knife isn't sticking out of it. It's still on the cutting board. I only *feel* mortally wounded.

Turning, I stumble toward the door, because really, what else is there to say? If Lynette gets in touch again, I'll tell her, "Listen, lady, I know it's hard to believe, but even you are wrong sometimes." No, I won't say that. But I'll think it.

My hand is on the door. I wait for Will to stop me. He doesn't. I tell myself not to turn back, but my body is already doing it, nearly twisting me in two, as my feet stay planted one way, while the rest swivels toward Will.

He's still standing at the counter, staring at me.

"I began seeing someone in Texas," I tell him. "It was going well. Really well. They say it's hard to find the right person. You know, the right fit. But we hit it off right away. I hated to leave when we were just getting started, so I asked if we could try and keep going over Skype, and even though she'd never done it that way before, she said we could give it a try for a few weeks."

At last, Will cracks. "She?" The way he says it, it's almost like he's jealous.

Oh. I run my words through my head and realize how they could be misinterpreted.

I clarify. "My *therapist*. I'm talking about a therapist. Remember, you said I should talk to someone? Well, I did. And it's helped. Not like miracles or anything. I mean, I drove here. I'm definitely not getting on a plane anytime soon, but I've been sleeping better. She's got me meditating, which is probably better than watching *George of the Jungle* on an endless loop, especially since George doesn't really do it for me anymore."

"George?" Will echoes.

"Yeah, don't ask. I mean, you can ask. But I've already told you too much. And if you asked, I might also have to admit how I now sometimes watch YouTube videos of men's Olympic swimming." I jam my hands into my pockets, rock awkwardly, turn to leave again, and then remember my whole point in bringing this up. "Sorry. I really should have thought this through, but I'm trying to live in the moment. Live in the moment is a big thing my therapist—her name's Shelly. I should maybe say that instead of 'my therapist.' But anyway, live in the moment is her mantra. She says I've spent too much time looking back. Too much time, you know, trying to relitigate and reimagine the past. How it didn't happen is just how it didn't happen, and you need to let it go. Those were her words. I asked her if she could stitch that on a pillow for me, and she said no."

I laugh, hoping for Will to join in. He doesn't. Okay then.

"So anyway, I'm gonna try really hard to not think about how it could've been between us, even though it could've been good. Better than good. The best really. Everyone would've hated us because we'd be so googly eyed all the time. Then years and years would pass and we'd become that adorable old couple, shuffling along together."

I stop. Shake my head. Press my lips together and mime zipping them closed. "But that's how it didn't happen, and that's okay. It's another thing she says. Everyone has paths they didn't take. We can't keep staring down them wondering what if." I pause. My mouth is so dry, which is probably because my body's sending all moisture up to my eyes.

"That's good stuff, right? I mean, she should really have her own talk show or something. But okay, that's it. I'm leaving now. Thank you for bringing me home and recommending therapy. That was huge, and I'll never forget it. So anyway, maybe I'll see you around, because small world and all that, but if not..." I swallow hard. I will not cry. I will depart with dignity. "If not, good luck with everything and..." I throw my hands up, my throat too tight to get any more words out.

Which means it's time to leave. So I do.

Will doesn't stop me.

Not as I put my hand on the door and pull it open.

Not as I step onto that stupid mat.

Not as I close the door.

Okay, now I can cry. Quietly. I walk down the hall, tears streaming down my face. Wiping the tears with my shirtsleeve, I stab the button for the elevator again and again, urging it to get here already.

"That doesn't make it come faster," says some know-it-all. Then his arms wrap around me.

I oughta put my knee into his nuts, but I've got a weakness for know-it-alls. Especially ones who apologize.

"Jenna, I'm sorry. I'm an asshole. Please don't go. Come back inside. Let's talk for real."

"You let me go." I shake my head. "What if the stupid elevator came sooner? What if I'd taken the stairs?"

Will turns me so I'm facing him. "I'd never let you get that far."

"I was in Texas! That's pretty far! What if I hadn't returned?"

Will nods. Takes a step away. "Wait here. Okay? Please?" Turning, he runs back to his apartment. I stand there, waiting, feeling dumb, half certain this is a trick. But then he reappears with a book in hand. He strides down the hall and thrusts it into my hand.

It's a travel guide for Texas. And it's disgusting. The cover is bent and smeared with something unidentifiable. A bunch of pages look like they got wet and dried all crinkly. I stare down at it and then up at Will, mystified.

"My mom gave it to me. Subtle she's not." He grins wryly. "I threw it out. Didn't even put it in a trash bag. Just threw it into the dumpster. But that night, I couldn't sleep. Six a.m., I was up with the sun, digging in that dumpster, determined to find the *All In One Texas Fun Facts and Travel Guide*."

Again, I look down at the book. I frown. "You went back for the fun facts part of the book, right? The idea of missing out on them drove you crazy?"

"I wanted this book. All of it." Will puts his hands over mine so we're both holding the disgusting book, which I'm beginning to smell too.

"Is the book a metaphor? Am I the book you threw in the dumpster?"

"And then went back for."

"But you *didn't* come for me. You have this guide to Texas, but you didn't come." My throat tightens. Yes, I may have cherished a fantasy that Will would come knocking at my door. Yes, it may have broken my heart every day it didn't happen.

"I know," Will says. "I was fighting it. Check my internet history. Every night for the past, I don't know how long, I've been looking at plane tickets to Texas. I've come so close to pulling the trigger, and then I didn't. I should've. If you hadn't beaten me to it, I would've. It would've been me sitting on your welcome mat yelling 'ding dong.'"

"You would?" Tears again flow freely. "You'd yell 'ding dong' for me?"

Will stares at me so tenderly, so sweetly. Then he throws his head back and at the top of his lungs yells, "DING DONG DING DONG DING DONG!"

"SHUT UP!" Comes his neighbor's immediate reply.

Will and I stare at one another.

"He's really pissed," I whisper.

"I can tell," Will whispers back. "Want to come inside? Come inside and really talk this time. Figure out how we can become that old couple shuffling along, holding hands."

I sniff. "I didn't say holding hands. I kind of imagined one of us having a walker."

Will grins. "Okay, not holding hands. You're right. That's unrealistic. We'll shuffle side by side, and we'll have been shuffling together for so long that we won't need to hold hands. We'll simply know the other person's right there."

A horrible sob comes bursting out of me. "But that's how it didn't happen!"

"Will ya go inside already!" shouts Will's neighbor before slamming

319

his door again.

I clap my hand over my mouth, and Will peels it away to kiss me. Pulling back, I whisper, "I'm all snotty. It's dripping down my face."

"Would you believe that's what I love most about you?"

A giggle escapes me from between the tears. "No."

He takes both my hands and brings them up to his chest. He leans in so his forehead is lined up with mine. "Come back inside my apartment. Wipe your nose. Have some pineapple. I'll make coffee."

"A beer would be better. Or vodka."

"I have vodka, and olives too."

I wrinkle my nose.

"Or no olives. We'll sit, drink, talk, and we'll figure out exactly how to make it happen."

"Exactly?" I can't resist pressing a kiss on his lips when they're so close, but then I pull back again. "You're going to get out graph paper and make a list, aren't you?"

"Yes," he confirms, as I knew he would. "And I promise there will be such a feeling of satisfaction on the day we check 'elderly shuffling' off the list."

I fling myself at him then, unable to resist any longer. He stumbles, and we hit the wall with a loud thud.

"Shhhh!" we admonish each other.

Lurching and staggering, attached like conjoined twins, but refusing to separate, we at last make it to Will's door. He finds the door handle, pushes the door open, and we are nearly home-free, when the damn mat trips us up.

Timber! We hit the floor hard enough to make the whole building shake.

Being a gentleman, Will twists, making himself my landing pad.

"Burn that fucking mat!" I tell him.

"Are you kidding? I'm having it framed." He sort of gasps and wheezes the words out, because despite having abs like Thor, he can apparently still get the wind knocked out of him.

The upside is that I now have an excuse to kiss him and make it better. Which I do.

"Are you kidding me?" Distantly, I hear an irate voice from somewhere behind us in the hallway. "Come on, man. Do you want me to call the cops? The noise and then the banging around. At least close the damn door." He kicks at the bottom of our feet. "Come on. Scoot yourselves in."

Will shimmies us sideways. I take a quick peek over my shoulder, to see a red-faced man reach in and grab the door handle. "Now I don't wanna hear another peep," he says before slamming the door closed.

The embarrassment of it all should stop us cold. Instead, Will and I giggle in between kisses and frantic clothing removal.

That's because this time around, nothing is getting in our way.

This time, the show goes on and on and on.

Afterword

Dear Reader,

Thank you so much for reading The Show Must Go On! I loved writing this book and I hope you enjoyed reading it as well.

I would appreciate it if you would consider writing a review. Reviews help authors connect with more readers and readers connect with more books. It's a win-win!

Finally, I've written a special epilogue to The Show Must Go On that is only available to newsletter subscribers. Once you're signed up you'll also get updates on new releases, exclusive contests, and even the occasional recipe. So please make sure to look for my newsletter sign-up form at www.katekaryusquinn.com

Best,

Kate

About the Author

Kate Karyus Quinn is an avid reader and menthol chapstick addict with a BFA in theater and an MFA in film and television production. She lives in Buffalo, New York with her husband, three children, and one enormous dog.

You can connect with me on:
- http://www.katekaryusquinn.com
- https://twitter.com/KateKaryusQuinn
- https://www.facebook.com/katekaryusquinnauthor

Subscribe to my newsletter:
- https://tinyurl.com/y9zz4hp6

Also by Kate Karyus Quinn

Down With The Shine

When Lennie brings a few jars of her uncles' moonshine to Michaela Gordon's party, she has everyone who drinks it make a wish. It's tradition. So is the toast her uncles taught her: "May all your wishes come true, or at least just this one."

The thing is, those words aren't just a tradition. The next morning, every wish—no matter how crazy—comes true. And most of them turn out bad. But once granted, a wish can't be unmade . . .

(Don't You) Forget About Me

Gardnerville seems like a paradise. But every four years, a strange madness compels the town's teenagers to commit terrible crimes. Four years ago, Skylar's sister, Piper, led her classmates on a midnight death march into a watery grave. Now Piper is gone. And to get her back, Skylar must find a way to end Gardnerville's murderous cycle.

Another Little Piece

On a cool autumn night, Annaliese Rose Gordon stumbled out of the woods and into a high school party. She was screaming. Drenched in blood. Then she vanished.

A year later, Annaliese is found wandering down a road hundreds of miles away. She doesn't know who she is. She doesn't know how she got there. She only knows one thing: She is not the real Annaliese Rose Gordon.

CPSIA information can be obtained
at www.ICGtesting.com
Printed in the USA
LVHW091809180919
631478LV00004B/631/P

9 781733 666701